Re

MW01673630

The History of the Blessed Virgin Mary

Anatiposi

Rev. F. C. Husenbeth

The History of the Blessed Virgin Mary

Reprint of the original, first published in 1872.

1st Edition 2023 | ISBN: 978-3-38212-820-3

Anatiposi Verlag is an imprint of Outlook Verlagsgesellschaft mbH.

Verlag (Publisher): Outlook Verlag GmbH, Zeilweg 44, 60439 Frankfurt, Deutschland
Vertretungsberechtigt (Authorized to represent): E. Roepke, Zeilweg 44, 60439 Frankfurt, Deutschland
Druck (Print): Books on Demand GmbH, In de Tarpen 42, 22848 Norderstedt, Deutschland

THE HISTORY

OF THE

BLESSED VIRGIN MARY.

TRANSLATED FROM THE FRENCH OF THE ABBE ORSINI,

BY THE

VERY REV. F. C. HUSENBETH, D.D., V.G.,

PROVOST OF NORTHAMPTON.

TO WHICH IS APPENDED

LETTERS APOSTOLIC CONCERNING THE DOGMATIC DEFINITION OF THE IMMACULATE CONCEPTION.

LONDON:

R. WASHBOURNE, 18A, PATERNOSTER ROW.

1872.

MATER DOLOROSA.

Frontispiece.

CONTENTS.

ENTHRONEMENT OF THE VIRGIN.

THE HISTORY

OF

THE BLESSED VIRGIN,

MOTHER OF GOD.

CHAPTER I.

UNIVERSAL EXPECTATION OF THE BLESSED VIRGIN AND THE MESSIAS.

IN those ancient times which go back to the very infancy of the world, when our first parents, terrified and trembling, heard beneath the majestic shades of Eden* the thundering voice of Jehovah, who condemned them to exile, to labour, and to death, in punishment of their mad disobedience,—a mysterious prophecy, in which the goodness of the Creator was visible, even amid the vengeance of an irritated God, came to revive the dejected minds of those two frail creatures, who had sinned through pride, like Lucifer. A daughter of Eve, a woman with *masculine* courage, was to crush the head of the serpent beneath her feet, and regenerate for ever a guilty race:—that woman was MARY.

From that time it was a tradition among the generations

* The word *Eden*, with the Arabs as well as among the Hebrews, is the name of the terrestrial Paradise, and of the Paradise of the elect. In Hebrew it signifies a place of delights; in Arabic, a place suitable for feeding flocks.

before the deluge, that a woman would come to repair the evil which the woman had done. This consoling tradition, which revived the hopes of a fallen race, was not effaced from the memory of men at the time of their great dispersion in the plains of Sennaar; they carried with them, beyond the mountains and seas, this sweet and distant hope, with the worship established by Noe, and the wreck of sciences and arts saved from the deluge.* Later on, when the primitive religion came to be weakened, and the ancient traditions were enveloped in clouds, that one of the Blessed Virgin and the Messias resisted, almost alone, the action of time, and rose above the ruins of the old creeds,—lost, as they were, in the fables of polytheism,—like that evergreen shrub which grows on the ruins of what was once Babylon the Great.†

* It is certain that the race of primitive men, which was wild, but not savage, were early acquainted with the arts analogous to their wants and pleasures. Scarcely do the children of Adam form little groups of men, but we see them establish public worship, manufacture tents, build cities, forge iron, cast bronze, invent musical instruments, and follow the course of the stars. The history of astronomy must be referred, according to Bailly, to a people before the deluge, of whom all memory has perished, and from whom some remains of astronomical science have escaped the general revolution. Lalande, who is afraid that this assertion should prove too much in favour of the sacred books, attributes the origin of this science to the Egyptians; but the Hebrews, who as neighbours, contemporaries, and ancient dwellers among the Egyptians, have a claim to arbitrate upon this question, decide for Bailly against his opponent, by informing us that the Egyptians owed their first knowledge of astronomy to traditions saved from the deluge.—(See Josephus, Antiq. of the Jews.)

† There is but one solitary tree found amidst the ruins of Babylon; the Persians give it the name of *Athele:* according to them this tree existed in the ancient city, and was miraculously preserved, on purpose that their prophet, Ali, son-in-law of Mahomet, might tie his horse to it after the battle of Hilla. It is an evergreen shrub, and so scarce in those countries that only one more is found of the same kind at Bassora.—(Rich's Memoirs.)

Indeed, if we traverse the different regions of the globe, if we search from north to south, from west to east, the religious annals of nations, we shall find the promised Virgin, and her divine parturition, to be the foundation of almost every theogony.

In Thibet, in Japan, and in one part of the eastern peninsula of India, it is the god Fo, who, to save mankind, becomes incarnate in the womb of a young woman betrothed to a king, the nymph Lhamoghiuprul, the most beautiful and most holy of women.

In China, the Emperor Hoang-Ti is reckoned among the *Sons of Heaven*, whose mother conceived by the light of a flash of lightning. Another emperor, Yao, contemporary with the deluge, had for his mother a virgin, rendered fruitful by a ray of light from a star. Yu, the head of the first Chinese dynasty, owed his life to a pearl,*—that emblem of light all over the East,—which fell from heaven to the chaste womb of a young virgin. Heou-Tsi, the head of the dynasty of the Tcheous, was born without prejudice to the virginity of his mother, who conceived him by divine operation one day when she was at prayer; and brought him forth without effort and without defilement, in a deserted cave, where oxen and lambs warmed him with their breath.† The most popular goddess of the celestial empire,

* "The pearl," says Chardin, "has everywhere a distinctive name; in the East, the Turks and Tartars call it *mardjaun*, a globe of light; the Persians, *marvid*, produce of light."

† We find in the *Chi-King* two beautiful odes on this marvellous birth of Heou-Tsi; and the glozes and paraphrases of the learned on these verses agree in explaining them in a way which makes the resemblance to the divine parturition of Mary still more striking:—"Every one at his birth," says Ho-Sou, "destroys the integrity of his mother, and causes her the most cruel sufferings. Kiang-Yuen brought forth her son without suffering injury or pain. This was because *Tien* (Heaven) would display its power, and show how much the Holy One differs from men."—"Having been conceived by the

Schingmou, conceived by simple contact of a water-flower: her son, brought up beneath the poor roof of a fisherman, became a great man, and worked miracles.

The Lamas say that Buddha was born of the virgin Maha-Mahai. Sommonokhodom, the prince, legislator, and god of Siam, in like manner owes his birth to a virgin, rendered fruitful by the rays of the sun. Lao-Tseu becomes incarnate in the womb of a virgin, black, *marvellous, and beautiful as jasper*. The zodiacal Isis of the Egyptians is a virgin-mother. That of the Druids is to bring forth the future Saviour.*

The Brahmins teach that when a god takes flesh, he is born in the womb of a virgin by divine operation; thus Juggernath, the mutilated saviour of the world,† and Chrichna, born in a grotto, where angels and shepherds come to adore him in his cradle, have each a virgin for their mother.

The Babylonian woman, Dogdo, sees in a dream a bright messenger from Oromazes, who lays magnificent garments at her feet; a heavenly light falls upon the countenance of the sleeping female, who becomes beautiful as the *Day-Star*. Zerdhucht, Zoroaster, or rather Ebrahim-Zer-Ateucht, ‡ the

operation of *Tien*," says another commentator, Tsou-Tsong-Po, "who gave him his life by miracle, he was to be born without prejudice to his mother's virginity."

* "Hinc Druidæ statuam in intimis penetralibus erexerunt, Isidi seu virgini dedicantes, ex qua filius ille proditurus erat (nempe generis humani Redemptor)."—(Elias Schedius, *de Diis Germanis*, cap. 13.)

† Juggernath, the seventh incarnation of Brahma, is represented in the shape of a pyramid, without feet and without hands. "He lost them," say the Brahmins, "because he wanted to carry the world, in order to save it."—(See Kircher.)

‡ Zer-Ateucht signifies "washed with silver:" this surname was given to Zoroaster, because, say the Ghebers, he proved his mission to a Sabean prince, who persecuted him, by plunging into a bath of melted silver.—(See Tavernier, t. ii. p. 92.)

famous prophet of the Magi, is the fruit of this nocturnal vision. The tyrant Nemroud,* informed by his astrologers that an infant, not yet born, threatens his gods and his throne, causes all the pregnant women in his dominions to be put to death: Zerdhucht, nevertheless, is saved by the ingenuity and prudence of his mother.† The Macenicans, who dwell in Paraguay, on the borders of the Lake Zarayas,

* This Nemroud, whom Tavernier calls Neubrout, is, as some say, Nimrod, the famous hunter; according to others, the tyrant Zhohac, of the Persians, king of the first dynasty of the princes who reigned immediately after the deluge. According to the author of *Mefathi alôloum*, Nemroud would be the same as Caïcaous, the second king of the second dynasty of Persia, called the Caïanides. The Persian historians give him a reign of nearly two centuries, which is certainly rather long. Some make him a wicked man, who had the strange fancy to ascend to heaven in a chest drawn by four of those monstrous birds called *kerkes*, of whom the ancient Oriental authors make mention in their romances. After wandering about in the air some time, he fell down again upon a mountain so violently, say the ancient legends of Persia, that it was shaken by it even to its foundation. According to the Persians, this Nemroud had Zerdhucht, whom they confound with Abraham, thrown into a burning furnace; according to others, Nemroud was by religion a Sabean, and it was he that first established the worship of fire.—(D'Herbelot, Bibliothèque Orientale, t. iii. p. 32.) The Jews claim for Abraham, the father and stock of their people, this persecution of Nemroud, the honour of which the Persians give to Zerdhucht, their lawgiver. St. Jerom relates an ancient tradition of the Jews, which declared that Abraham had been cast into the fire by order of the Chaldeans, because he would not adore it.—(Hieron., Quæst. in Genes.) Certain Jewish rabbins, much more modern, confirm this tradition: R. Chain ben Adda relates that Abraham, having met with a young girl who carried an idol about her, broke it to pieces; a complaint was immediately laid before Nemroud, who required Abraham to adore fire. The patriarch answered very sensibly, that it would be more natural to adore water, which extinguishes fire, the clouds which produce the water, the wind which collects the clouds, and man, who is a being more perfect than the wind. Nemroud, enraged at this bold answer, ordered Abraham to be cast into the fire, which spared him.

† See Tavernier, *loc. cit.*

relate that at a very remote period a woman of rare beauty became a mother, and remained still a virgin; her son, after working extraordinary miracles, raised himself in the air one day, in presence of his disciples, and transformed himself into a sun.*

Let all the scattered fragments of these mutilated creeds be collected together, and we shall reconstruct, in almost all its details, the history of the Blessed Virgin and of Christ. The Blessed Virgin, notwithstanding the royal blood which circulates in her veins, is of an obscure condition, like the mother of Zoroaster; like her also, she receives the visit of an angel bearing a message from heaven. The tyrant Nemroud, who was the worst of a number of very wicked princes, may pass for the type of Herod, and as resolutely seeks the death of the young Magian as the sanguinary spouse of Mariamne seeks the destruction of the infant Jesus: both let their prey escape. Born of a virgin who conceives him during fervent prayer, and brings him forth without defilement and without pain, in a poor stable, like the first-born of the noble and pious Kiang-Yuen, our divine Saviour lives in the midst of the poor classes, like the son of the Chinese goddess; angels and shepherds come to pay him homage, as was done to Chrichna, on the very night of his birth; then, after stilling the tempests, walking on the waters, casting out devils, and raising the dead to life, he achieves his triumphant ascension in presence of five hundred disciples, whose eyes, all dazzled, lose sight of him in a cloud, precisely as related by the savage hordes of Paraguay.

It is surely very strange that these marvellous legends, which have not been taken from the gospel facts, since they are incontestably more ancient, should form, when connected together, the actual life of the Son of God. Can truth then spring from error? What are we to think of these curious resemblances? Must we say, with the sneering philosophers

* See Muratori.

of the school of Voltaire, and a few German visionaries of rather more modern date, that the apostles borrowed these fables from the various creeds of Asia? But, not to speak of the jealous care with which the books reputed divine were in those times concealed in the impenetrable obscurity of the sanctuaries,—not to speak of the profound horror which the Jews professed of idolatrous legends, and their disdainful contempt for the learning of foreigners,—how should poor men of the lower class, whose whole knowledge was limited to steering a bark over the waters of the Lake of Gennesareth, and whose nets were still dripping with its fresh waters when they were promoted to the apostleship,—how should laborious artisans, obliged to work for their daily bread in the midst of their preaching, have turned over the sacred books of the Hindoos, Chinese, Bactrians, Phœnicians, and Persians? What likelihood was there that Simon Peter, the sons of Zebedee, or that austere disciple of Gamaliel, who said boldly at Corinth, the rich and learned Greek city, "I judged not myself to know anything among you, but Jesus Christ: and him crucified!" should have snatched from idolatry, which they were sent to destroy, some few of its old shreds, to join them on fraudulently to the life of Christ, so simple and so grand. Again, if the question were only of borrowing from the mythic legends of nations bordering on Palestine,—such, for example, as the Egyptians and Phœnicians,—however unjust the accusation, it would have had at least some colour of probability; but no! these brilliant points which go forth from the womb of the darkness of idolatry to form, like so many little stars, the glory of the Son of the Virgin, come from places the most remote and least known of the earth. To say nothing of that Gaul, with its impenetrable forests, which concealed, at the western extremity of Europe, its mysterious doctrines under the shade of oaks; of the Great Indies, so imperfectly known under Tiberius; of that Serica, with its towers of porcelain, whose far-distant provinces did not tempt even the greedy Romans,*—how could the apostles have communicated with far distant America, separated from the old continent by its green girdle of waves, and lost like a pearl amidst the waters?

But I will suppose that the apostles had—no matter how—a knowledge of these ancient myths scattered over every part of the globe. I go further: I admit, setting aside the native simplicity, the blood-sealed testimony, the exalted sanctity of these divine men—I admit that, carried away, as Rousseau says, by the ardent glory of their Master, it did occur to their thoughts, for a moment, to embroider the texture of the gospel with certain fabulous circumstances; even so, the thing would have been beyond their power. With what face, for example, could they have attributed to that Herod whom all Jerusalem had known, whose glorious and tragical reign every one knew by heart, an atrocious deed revived, without the least probability, of some unknown king of Persia, who, perhaps, never had any existence but in the imagination of the reveries of the Magi? If the massacre of the innocents had been a story *fabricated* or *copied* by the apostles, can any one believe that the Bethlehemites, having such means of knowing what passed in the holy city, the lofty towers of which they saw in the horizon, would not have strongly protested against this audacious falsehood; that those subtile Pharisees, who had sought to ensnare Jesus himself in his speech, would have let it pass current without refutation; or that the Herodians would have endured with patience to have so black a stain falsely imprinted upon the renown of a prince of whom they had almost made a god,† and who had loaded them with riches and honours?

* It was in the reign of Augustus that the Roman people received the first embassy from the Seres, whom we now call the Chinese: the ambassadors declared that they had been three years on their journey.

† The flatterers of Herod I., dazzled with the grandeur and magni-

If all were silent, it was because the thing was too well proved, too public, too recent as yet to leave the field open to contradictions; it was because, at two hours' journey from Jerusalem, were the mothers of those martyrs who had paid with their young lives for the honour of having been born at the same time with Christ; it was because whole villages had seen the murderous steel glitter, and heard the cries of death; it was because, at the first attempt to charge the Christians with falsehood, a whole population would have started up to exclaim, "But we ourselves were there!"*

It is the same with the divine parturition of Mary, with the visit of the shepherds sent by the angels, the glorious resurrection, and, in fine, with all the prodigies which signalised the coming of Christ. The apostles wrote even in the lifetime of those who had figured in the scenes which they related, and, before they consigned to writing those prodigies

ficence of that prince, maintained that he was the *Messias*. This it was that gave rise to the sect of the Herodians, of whom so much is said in the gospel, and whom the pagans knew, since Persius and his scholiast tell us, that even in the time of Nero, the birthday of King Herod was celebrated by his followers with the same solemnity as the Sabbath.

* "Neither Josephus nor the rabbins speak of the massacre of the innocents," says Strauss. "Macrobius, who lived in the fourth century, is the only one who says a word about the massacre ordered by Herod." Strauss is mistaken: the Toldos, whence Celsus derived some of the facts injurious to Christianity which he has interspersed in his writings, speak positively of it, and this fact is in the Talmud. See how Bossuet answers those who deny the gospel fact, and never was answer more decisive: "Where now are they," says he, "who, to secure their faith, would have it that the profane historians of the time ought to have made mention of this cruelty of Herod as well as of others? As if our faith ought to depend on what the affected negligence or policy of the historians of the world made them say, or leave unsaid, in their histories! Let us leave all such feeble ideas; human views alone would have sufficed to prevent the Evangelist from bringing discredit upon his holy gospel, by recording therein a fact so public, if it had not been so certain."

of the Messias, they had boldly preached them in the very temple of Jehovah, before that immense multitude of Hebrews from every province, who repaired thither to sacrifice, or to bring in the first-fruits; which would have composed the most dangerous audience in the world for them if they had spoken falsely.

So far from fearing contradictions, which would not have been wanting in case of imposture, St. Peter speaks to this numerous assemblage like a man sure of the adhesion of them all; he is not afraid to appeal to the still recent recollections of those who hear him; he affirms those miracles which marked the mission of the Son of Mary with the seal of the divinity, even before the great council of the nation, which contributed its utmost to the crucifixion of Jesus. And the senators of Israel, terrified and furious, ordered St. Peter and St. John to be scourged, to compel them to keep silence; but they do not deny—the Talmud owns it—those prodigies, which they stupidly attribute to magic. Accordingly, they do not say to the apostles, when dragged before them by the keepers of the temple, "You are dreamers or liars." They say to them, with an agitation which sufficiently proves their secret fears, "Hold your peace! would you have the people stone us?" To which these two men, simple in heart, but great in soul, resolutely answer, "We will not hold our peace! God commands us to speak, and it is better to obey him than men." Imposture is not thus fearless.

After examining the acts, the character, and position of the apostles, every impartial man will be forced to admit that they were neither deceivers, nor deceived, and that they are no way concerned in those coincidences which are remarked between the gospel facts and the traditions of ancient nations, more or less mixed up with fables.

But then, how are these analogies to be explained? Is it a game of chance, an accidental concurrence?

It has not happened by chance that the mystery of the Incarnation of a God in the chaste womb of a Virgin is one of the fundamental points of belief in Asia; it is not merely accidental that the privileged women who bear in their wombs this emanation of the divinity are always pure, beautiful, holy; that they have names glorious and full of mystery, which signify in all the ancient tongues, *beauty expected, virgin immaculate, faithful virgin, felicity of the human race, polar star;* and that they are so like each other, that one would say that they were moulded after some remote pattern, concealed from us by the night of time. In fine, it is not by mere chance that a ray of light unites the divine nature with the human.

These opinions, where we recognise the stamp of the primitive times, evidently go back to the infancy of the world. The antediluvian patriarchs,—that chain of aged men who lived as long as the cedars,—seeking to form an idea of that woman, blessed among all others, whose miraculous maternity was to save the human race, figured her to themselves under the features of Eve before her fall; they gave to her a majestic and sacred beauty, which could create no other sentiment in the souls of the children of men than that of religious veneration; they made her a lovely star, with a soft, mysterious, chaste, and veiled light, the rising of which was to precede that of the Sun of Justice.

The means by which God causes fecundity to descend into her virginal womb, agree in a striking manner among the different nations of the world. Take a view of all the ancient religions, you will see in them a sacred fire. Now fire was, among the Persians, the terrestrial emblem of the sun, and the sun itself was but the dwelling of the Most High—the glorious tent of *the God of heaven.**

The Hebrews, who shared this belief, acknowledged the

* The Persians suppose that the throne of God is in the sun, says Hanway, and hence their veneration for that luminary.

divine presence, or *Schekina*, in the luminous cloud which hovered between the cherubim of the propitiatory; and believed that God was clothed with light as with a garment, when he manifested himself to men on solemn occasions. It was the opinion of the synagogue, and the tradition of the temple said, that in the midst of the bush of wild roses, which burnt without being consumed on Mount Horeb, where Moses, that great shepherd of men, was feeding at the time the Arabian flocks of his father-in-law, a very beautiful face was distinguished, resembling nothing that we see here below; and that this celestial figure, which was brighter than a flame and more brilliant than lightning, was undoubtedly the image of the eternal God.* After this, it is not difficult to understand the grounds of the opinion, generally spread, that a luminous ray was to bring fecundity to the womb of the Virgin *reparatrix*, who was the expectation of nations.

With this graceful tradition of a pure virgin admitted to celestial nuptials, surrounded by mystery impenetrable, was connected the tradition of a God Saviour, born of her womb, who was to suffer and die for the salvation of the world.† This tradition was not perpetuated, like the other, by means of brilliant and poetical images, but by terror, which resists in a different way from poetry all attempts to efface it. The bloody sacrifice, which we find established, from the most distant times, among almost all nations, had no other object than to preserve among men the remembrance of the promise of the immolation of Calvary: it is easy to prove it.

Worship, that manifestation of love, that homage of gratitude, which Adam and Eve were bound to pay to God immediately after the benefit of their creation, consisted, no doubt, in Eden, of innocent prayers and offerings of fruits

* Philo, Life of Moses.

† This tradition is found in the sacred books of China.—(See the work of F. Prémare, entitled, Selecta quædam vestigia præcipuorum Christianæ religionis dogmatum ex antiquis libris oruta.)

and flowers alone.* But when, ungrateful as they were! they had broken the precept of easy observance, which the Lord had imposed upon them as a sweet yoke, and solely to make them sensible that they had a Master,—when they had lost, with the immortalising fruits of the tree of life,† their talisman against death,‡ and they descended from the charming slopes of Eden to a land bristling with brambles and

* Porphyr., de Abst., lib. ii.

† God could attach to plants certain natural virtues with reference to our bodies, and it is easy to believe that the fruit of the tree of life had the power of renewing the body by an aliment so well proportioned and so efficacious, that by making use of it, men would not have died.—(Bossuet, Elev. sur les Myst., t. i. p. 231.)

‡ Man was never immortal in this world in the same way as the pure spirits, for a body formed from dust must naturally return to dust; he was so by a favour unexampled, and granted conditionally, which exalted him and maintained him in a position very superior to his proper sphere. Immortality here below was never acquired by man by right of birth; every terrestrial body must perish by the dissolution of its parts, unless a special will of the Creator opposes this: such divine will was manifested in favour of our first parent. God planted, in the delightful garden where he had placed mortal man, the tree of life—a plant of heavenly origin, which had the property of repelling death, as the laurel, according to the ancients, repels lightning. To this mysterious tree was attached the immortality of the human race; afar from this protecting tree, death recovered his prey, and man fell back from the height of heaven into his miserable coating of clay.—(Aug., Quæst. Vet. et Nov. Test., q. 19, p. 450.) No one, I imagine, will call in question that God acted upon his just right in banishing Adam from the earthly Paradise after his disobedience; but banishment involved the sentence of death upon man and his posterity; without the tree of life, he was no longer anything better than a frail and perishable creature, subject to the laws which govern created bodies: when the antidote fails, it is plain that poison kills. Again become mortal, Adam begot children like himself: the children must follow the condition to which their father had fallen. In this God did the human race no wrong; we are mortal by our nature; he has left us such as we were. To withdraw a gratuitous favour, when the subject of such favour tears up with his own hands the deed which confers it upon him, is not cruelty, it is justice.

thorns, of which they were obliged to open the virgin soil for their support,—they added to the wild fruits and flowers, produced by the land of exile, the firstlings of their flocks. This deserves attention. Adam, who to perfection of form added a soul intelligent and exalted, in which the Lord had planted the germ of every virtue and every science, could not be without humanity. His fatal complacency towards Eve exhibits him to us as loving even to weakness, and thereby susceptible in the highest degree of soft and benevolent affections. How came it then into his mind that the Creator could be pleased with the violent death of his creature, and that an act of destruction could be an act of piety?

The immolation of animals, which has not the smallest connection with the vows and prayers of man, and which the exclusively vegetable diet of the primitive patriarchs left without any other object but murder, must have stirred up in the head of the human race a thousand feelings of natural repugnance. For a long time these poor creatures, deprived of reason, but capable of attachment, had composed in Eden the court of the solitary monarch; then he sat with them at the same table, slept on the moss of the same bank, quenched his thirst at the same fountain, and his prayer ascended to heaven at sunrise and sunset together with the warbling of the birds, who seemed also to be singing their morning or evening hymn. These companions of his happy life, involved in his misfortune, shared in his banishment: * some, yielding

* We know not exactly the time which Adam and Eve remained in the earthly Paradise; yet this abode must have been of some duration, and thus Milton understood it, whom we do not quote here in his character of a poet, but as a profound orientalist. If we recollect, moreover, that it was in Eden that Adam learned to distinguish and call by their names all the birds of the air, all the beasts of the earth, all the fishes which swim in the waters; that there he learned the virtues of plants, and what God thought proper to teach him of the course of the stars, we shall conclude that this was not the work of

to savage instinct, which had not declared itself in Paradise, fled into the depths of deserts and the hidden caves of mountains, whence they soon declared war unto death against their old master; others, inoffensive and gentle creatures, settled round about the grotto of their lord, to whom they offered their milk, their labour, their fleeces, and their melodious concerts, to satisfy his wants and charm away his sufferings. Well, it was among the ranks, not over numerous, of these humble friends, who had remained faithful to him in his distress, that Adam chose and marked out his victims; it was in the throat of the heifer which exhausted its udder to feed him, of the dove which took shelter in his bosom when the vulture hovered in the air, of the lamb which left its flowery pasture to come and lick his hand, that he had the heart to plunge the knife. Ah! when man, unskilled as yet in killing, stretched at his feet a poor creature, gentle and timid, which struggled in a tide of blood amidst the chokings of agony, he must have stood pale and dismayed, like the assassin after his first murder! This thought came not from him; it was not an act of choice, but of painful obedience. Who imposed it? He alone to whom it belongs to dispose of life and death—God.

Adam committed a fault so enormous by its aggravating circumstances and disastrous consequences, that to express

one day. The Persians and Chinese make the first man dwell in Paradise for several centuries. According to the opinion of the Arabs and rabbins, he remained there only half a day; but this half day of Paradise is equivalent, according to them, to five hundred years; for one day of Paradise answers to a thousand years. This space of time is too long, according to our ideas. It is commonly believed that Cain, whose birth is closely connected, in Genesis, with the expulsion of his parents, was born in the year 13 of the creation, which would fix the abode in Paradise at about twelve years. This term, though rather short, would have sufficed for the first man to establish his authority over the animals subject to his sceptre, and to attach him to his humble subjects by the bonds of habit.

its full enormity, the Hebrew tradition relates that the sun was darkened with horror.* Satan attacked him in his strength, at the time when he knew nothing, as yet, but good; in the most beautiful abode of the earth, under the recent impression of the immense benefit of his creation, free, happy, tranquil, immortal, and capable of resisting if he had only pleased. From this high position it was that he fell into the frightful abyss of disobedience and ingratitude. The justice of God demanded a punishment proportioned to the offence: man was condemned to die a double death; and there was no hope for the human race, if a divine Being, predestined before the birth of time to the work of our redemption, had not undertaken to satisfy for us all. From that time he was called the Messias, and revealed as a Saviour at that very moment when the voice of God, "that voice which breaketh down the cedars," pronounced the sentence of the three guilty ones. "Because thou hast done this," said God to the serpent seducer, who proudly lifted up his head from our ruin, "the seed of the woman, that is, a fruit produced from her, shall bruise thy head."

The Hebrew tradition adds that God, moved by the repentance of our first parents, revealed to them by an angel that a just man should be born of them, who should destroy the pernicious effects of the fruit of the tree of knowledge,†

* It is in memory of the sin of Eve, at the sight of which, according to the Jews, the sun withdrew his light, that the Jewish women are specially commanded to light lamps, which burn in every house during the night of the Sabbath. "It is just," say the Hebrew doctors, "that the women should rekindle the torch which they have extinguished, and that they should be burthened with this punishment in expiation of their sin."—(Basnage, liv. vii. c. 13.)

† It is generally supposed among Christians, that the tree of knowledge was an apple-tree; the Persians, on the contrary, maintain that this fatal tree was a fig-tree. In our days, the German Eichhorn makes it a species of manchineel. "Making due deduction from the marvellous which surrounds the fall of man," says the rationalist

by means of a voluntary oblation, and that he should be the salvation of those who should place their hope in him.* On the other hand, the Arabian traditions inform us that God, who is indignant and merciful, was pleased to make known to man the mode of imploring his pardon. This worship, revealed by God, was certainly sacrifice, a ceremony at once commemorative, expiatory, and symbolical, by which man confessed that he had deserved death, and by substituting innocent victims in his stead, recalled perpetually to his remembrance the great victim of Calvary.

Thus then the institution of the bloody sacrifice, which was no human invention, reposed in reality upon a thought of the divine mercy; since it perpetuated among all nations that tradition of the Messias, without which the work of redemption would have been a benefit lost.

God matures his counsels in the course of ages, for a thousand years are with him as one day; but man is eager to obtain, for man endures but a short time. It appears that Eve had concluded, from the words of the angel, that she should be the mother of this Redeemer promised to her, and that in this thought she showed transports of extraordinary joy in bringing forth Cain,† whom she took for her Saviour. Undeceived by the perverse inclinations which he showed, she transferred her hopes to Abel, that so much beloved son, whose name recalls to mind the mourning and tears of his mother; ‡ then to Seth; but in vain, for the gates which

writer, "the fact remains that the constitution of the human body was, at first, vitiated by the use of a poisonous fruit."—(Eichhorn's Argeschichte.)

* Basnage, liv. vi. c. 25, p. 417.

† Cain is called *Cabel* by all the Arabic authors; this name, which means *the first*, is perhaps his proper name. The surname of Cain, which signifies *traitor*, may have been given to him afterwards.—(Savary, in a note to c. 5 of the Koran.)

‡ Abel, which the Arabs write *Habel*, is, according to them, only the surname of that youthful shepherd who was the first type of Jesus

angels guarded with fiery swords opened to her no more.* The just of the race of Seth, those pure and contemplative men, whom the Scripture calls the sons of God, and whom the Assyrian legends call *genii*, flattered themselves a long time with the same hope, for the Jewish tradition represents them to us as wandering about the heights bordering on the garden of Eden,† the gigantic cedars ‡ of which they admired with sighs, and where they flattered themselves that one of their just ones would enable them again to enter. But it was not the name of a virgin of the primitive times which was written in the immutable decrees of the Eternal; and the earth, yet trembling under the divine malediction, stood in need of being washed as by the ablutions of a baptism, before the feet of Him who was to bring good tidings on the mountains should leave upon them their sacred impression.

Christ. In fact, it puts us in mind of that sorrowful event which threw the family of Adam into mourning, and properly signifies, says Savary (*loco citato*), "He has left by his death a mother in tears." Josephus, in like manner, says that the name of Abel signifies mourning.—(Antiq. Jud., p. 4.)

* See Basnage, liv. vi. c. 25.

† The Arabic traditions place the terrestrial Paradise in that beautiful valley of Damascus which the oriental poets designate by the name of the Emerald of the Desert. Its admirable situation, its beauty, its fertility, justify this idea; and a learned commentator on Genesis has not hesitated to consider this beautiful site as that of the garden of Eden, although the names of the Euphrates and the Tigris indicate a rather different situation. In support of this Arabic tradition there is shown, at half-a-day's journey from Damascus, a high mountain of white marble, overshadowed by beautiful trees, where there is a cavern, which is looked upon as the dwelling of Adam, Abel, and Cain; there is also seen the sepulchre of Abel, which is much respected by the Turks: the place where the fratricide was committed is marked by four columns.—(D'Herbelot, Bibliothèque Orientale, pp. 772 and 780; F. Pacifique, in his Commentaires sur la Bible.)

‡ The great cedars of Eden have remained traditionally in the memory of the Hebrews, who have made the terrestrial Paradise their paradise. In most of their epitaphs we read these words—"He has

When the earth had absorbed the waters of the deluge, and the winds had dried it up, the new family of mankind, which revived under favourable promises, were eager to re-establish the worship practised by Enos. Noe added to it the seven precepts which bear his name, without forgetting those historical and religious traditions which his long existence before the flood had enabled him to collect. He told of man being formed of the earth, of his rebellion, his fall, his future restoration, for which the world would be indebted to the miraculous parturition of a new Eve. At the sight of the bloody sacrifices offered for the unexpiated fault of their first fathers, he taught his descendants to lift up their eyes to a more august victim, seated at the right hand of Jehovah in the starry heights of heaven,—a victim of which the oblation of heifers and lambs was but the figure.*

The nations at first faithfully preserved these primitive notions, which are constantly met with as the foundation of all creeds.† They built altars at the confluence of rivers, in

gone down into the garden of Eden, to those who are among the cedars."—(Basnage, t. v. liv. vii.)

* "The old law bears throughout the character of blood and death, as a figure of the new law established and confirmed by the blood of Jesus Christ."—(Bossuet, Elev. sur les Myst., t. i. p. 428.)

† The Indians, Chinese, Peruvians, and Hurons, acknowledge that the first man was formed from the earth. The Brahmins, who make enchanting pictures of their *choream* (paradise), place in it a tree the the fruit of which would confer immortality, if it were allowed to eat of it. The Persians relate that the evil genius Ahriman seduced our first parents under the form of a *snake.* The history of the woman deceived at the foot of a tree, of the anger of God, and of the first fratricide, was a tradition among the Iroquois. The Tartars attribute our fall to a plant as sweet as honey, and of marvellous beauty; the Thibetans, to the fault of having tasted the dangerous plant *schimæ*, sweet and white as sugar: the knowledge of their state of nudity was revealed by this fruit. The tradition of the woman and the serpent was equally known in Mexico, &c.—(See Le Christ devant la Siècle, by M. Roselly de Lorgues, c. 9.)

the shade of forests, on the summits of mountains, on the shores of the green ocean, and on the sandy downs where the wormwood expands its leaves to the winds of the desert. The soft moonlight from the beginning lighted those rustic temples, which had no other boundaries than the horizon, no other ceiling than the sky with all its stars. At that far distant period, God was worthily adored, and with ideas so exact, so sublime, so uniform, and so simple, that they evidently could be traced up to himself.

Nevertheless, an element of superstitious terror,—founded upon the terrible and recent remembrance of the drowning of the globe, a remembrance visible, traces of which are found in most of the religious festivals of antiquity,*—like a principle of destruction, crept into the post-diluvian worship. Herded together on the elevated plains of Caucasus, and the mountains of Armenia, the descendants of Noe had long refused, with an obstinacy which the authority of Noe himself had been unable to conquer, to go down again into the plain; so much did they dread a second deluge! In vain did the rainbow display in the cloud—as if to remove all fear from the children of men—its soft and benign colours, where the green of the emerald united with the blue of the sapphire; this happy prognostic, this beautiful sign of a God appeased, diminished, but could not banish, a terror which had taken deep root: the tower of Babel is the proof. This gigantic monument of human pride concealed beneath its insolent defiance an immense amount of fear. It was as a fortress of refuge against the occurrence of a new deluge, which that race, which began already to be corrupt, felt that it again deserved. And when the confusion of tongues forced the descendants of Noe to disperse,—when they saw their precaution, offensive as it was to the sworn clemency of the Lord, turn to their confusion,—they were only the more disposed to be alarmed afresh.

* See Boulanger, Antiq. devoilée.

It must be owned, as some excuse for them, that the earth presented at that time a spectacle but little encouraging; the whole economy of creation was in confusion. The rivers, straying out of their courses, formed immense fens of water and putrid marshes* in the vast plains which before the deluge were rendered full of animation by the graceful tents of the shepherds. The cedars lay extended along the sea-shores, whilst the spoils of the ocean were found on the summits of high mountains eternally covered with snow. Nothing was seen on all sides but towers levelled with the turf,† and towns silent and in ruins. The ploughshare everywhere struck against bones and rubbish. The vengeance of provoked heaven had weighed heavily upon the human race, in a manner so overwhelming, that man, whose heart was still beating with fear at the remembrance of the perils which he had encountered, felt more disposed to dread his sovereign Master with great fear, than to love him with confiding affection: he was afraid of God! He distrusted his promises and his goodness. Like the shipwrecked man who is drowning, he sought eagerly around him for something to help him, which might interpose and conjure in the hour

* History has preserved us proofs of this displacement of rivers after the deluge. We read in Strabo, b. ii., that the Araxes, which waters Armenia, was still without any outlet, and inundated the country, when Jason, the chief of the Argonauts, opened a subterranean channel, by which the Araxes flowed into the Caspian Sea. In the celebrated *Chou-King* of Confucius, the Emperor Yao says that the waters, which formerly rose up to heaven, still bathed the feet of the highest mountains, and made the plains which they overflowed incapable of cultivation.—(Freret, Chron. des Chinois, 1ère partie.)

† The tower of Babel, so near to the great deluge, may give some idea of antediluvian architecture; they had employed in it brick and bitumen. If, as everything leads us to believe, this immense tower resembled the ancient and famous tower of Bel, at Babylon, it was surrounded by a staircase outside, of gentle ascent, which rose spirally to the platform, and gave this edifice the appearance of seven towers heaped up, one upon another.

of need that sacred, but terrible wrath. Noe had spoken of a Being powerful and divine, whose tender love for men was infinite, who was to plead their cause before the Eternal, and take their crimes upon himself; but who was this anxiously desired Mediator, this powerful friend? He was no longer known. The descendants of Sem thought they had found him in the stars which charmed their solitary vigils, and which they supposed to be animated by celestial intelligences; * they entreated those intelligences to protect them, and lighted fires on the heights of mountains in their honour.†

This was the origin of Sabeanism, which degenerated into idolatry, when the reprobate race of Cham, attaching themselves to the material object, adored fire, water, earth, agitated air; and, insolently deriding the worship practised by Noe, who knew nothing of images, consecrated statues of silver to the moon, and statues of gold to the sun.‡

* It is a very ancient belief in the East, that the stars are living creatures; the Jewish doctors had fallen into this error, which was of much older origin than their people. Philo said that the stars were intelligent creatures, who had never done any harm, and were incapable of any. According to Maimonides, the stars knew God who made them, knew themselves, and their actions are always good and holy.—(Philo., de Mundi Opificio, de Gigant., de Somniis; Maimonides, More nevochim, pt. ii. c. 4, p. 194, et de Fundam. legis, c. 3, § 11.) The modern Persians still sacrifice to the angel of the moon.

† According to R. Bechai, the Sabeans did not adore the sun; they only lighted fires on the earth to thank God for the torch which he lighted up for them in the heavens; and when they looked at the stars, they besought the angels whom God has placed there, to move them to be favourable to them.—(R. Bechai, Comm. in Genes., c. 1.) The fires still lighted in almost every country in Europe, and which in France are called fires of St. John, are remnants of Sabeanism.

‡ The ancient Arabs, descended from Cham, despised Noe because he did not serve images; they consecrated statues of silver to the moon, and statues of gold to the sun; they divided the metals and climates among the stars; they believed that they have great influence

As time went on, the darkness thickened; religious systems were loaded with rites; the worship of the true God was gradually mixed up with that of the stars and the elements; the invention of hieroglyphics completed the confusion; and the few truths which escaped the subversion of religious belief were mysteriously hidden in the recesses of idolatrous sanctuaries, like sepulchral lamps, which burn only for the dead. They were withdrawn assiduously from the multitude,* who lavished their senseless adorations on stones, trees, rivers, mountains, and animals, a still more degrading worship, and which ended by placing their vices and passions in heaven. Then it was that impostors, speculating upon human credulity, confounded or purposely broke the thread of patriarchal traditions which already hung so loosely together, and audaciously substituting remembrance for hope, assembled around the cradles of their fabulous kings, their false prophets and powerless divinities, the wonders of the Incarnation of the WORD, and the primitive revelations of his exalted and tragical destiny.

Thus, we maintain, those analogies are explained which at first appear incomprehensible.

All the nations of polytheism, however, did not take the mystery of the Messias for an accomplished fact. The Druids, immediately before the Christian era, still erected, in the dark forests of Gaul, an altar to the Virgin "who was to bring forth." The Chinese, taught by Confucius, who

over things which are devoted to them, and to the images consecrated to them.—(Maimonides, More nevochim, pt. iii. c. ii. p. 423.)

* Plato, speaking of the God who formed the universe, says that he is forbidden to make him known to the people. The books of Numa, written upon the bark of the birch-tree, and found in his tomb many ages after his death, were secretly burnt as dangerous to polytheism. The Brahmins, who, if certain travellers are to be believed, have a sublime idea of the Divinity, make the Hindoos nevertheless adore the most hideous idols that ever existed. The true religion alone has treated men as immortal and rational creatures.

had himself found this oracle in ancient traditions, expected the "HOLY ONE, born of a virgin and Son of God, who was to die for the salvation of the world,"* in the western regions of Asia, and sent after him, by a solemn embassy, less than half a century after the death of the Man-God. The Magi, on the faith of Zerdhucht, studied the constellations to find there the star of Jacob, which was to guide them to the cradle of Christ.† The Brahmins sighed after the *avatar* ‡ of him who was to "purify the world from sin," and prayed for him to Wichnou, as they laid upon his altar, sparkling with precious stones, odoriferous tufts of basil, the favourite plant of the Indian god. The proud sons of Romulus, those idolaters by pre-eminence, who had created whole legions of gods, read in those books of the Cumean Sibyl, contemporary with Achilles and Hector, so jealously and politically guarded, "the virgin, the divine child, the adoration of the shepherds, the serpent vanquished, and the golden age restored to the earth." In fine, towards the time of the Messias, all the nations of the East were in expectation of a future Saviour; and Boulanger, who thought better of it on his death-bed, after showing how general this expectation was, illogically calls it an universal chimera.§

* According to the ancient sages of China, says the learned Schmitt, the Holy One, the miraculous man, will renew the world, change the manners, expiate the sins of the world, die overwhelmed with grief and opprobrium, and open the gates of heaven.—(See Redempt. du genre humain.)

† Abulfarage (Historia Dynastiarum) says that Zerdhucht foretold to the Magi the birth of the Messias, born of a virgin; he added that, at the time of his birth an unknown star would appear, which would conduct them to his cradle, and he commanded them to carry him presents. Sharistani, a Mussulman author, relates in like manner a prophecy of Zerdhucht, relating to a great prophet who should reform the world, as well in the matter of religion as in that of justice, and to whom the princes and kings of the earth should be subject.

‡ *Avatar*, the fabulous incarnation of a Hindoo divinity

§ "An unanimous testimony is of the greatest weight," says

But what were these pale glimmerings, too weak to dissipate the darkness of idolatry, compared with the stream of light which illuminated the elect people of God? We are struck with astonishment at the sight of this chain of prophecy, the first link of which hangs on to the infancy of the world, while the last is fastened to the tomb of Christ.* The threat of Jehovah to the infernal serpent includes, as we have already observed, the first of the oracles relating to the Messias. We have also said, and the Jewish traditions confirm it, that this oracle was more particularly explained, in the sequel, to the exiles of Eden, when they were reconciled to heaven by repentance.† Noe, who was constituted by God heir of the faith,‡ transmitted these revelations to Sem; and Sem, whose long life nearly equalled those of his ancestors, might have repeated them to the father of the faithful. Then it was that a mysterious benediction, which comprised the promise of the Messias, announced that the blessed germ promised to Eve should be also the germ and offset of Abraham. The primitive traditions are soon succeeded by the grand prophecy of Jacob. The dying patriarch, who has beheld in spirit the condition of the twelve tribes when they shall have been in Palestine, announces to his sons, assembled round his death-bed, that Juda has been chosen, among all his brethren, to be the stock of the kings of Israel, and the father of that *Shiloh* so often promised, who is to be the King of kings, and the Lord of lords. The coming of Christ is designated in a precise manner: he shall spring up from the midst of the ruins

Bernardine de St. Pierre, "for there cannot be upon the earth an universal error."—(Etudes de la Nature, étude viii. p. 398.)

* It is a tradition taught in the synagogue, and admitted as true by the Church, that all the prophets, without one exception, prophesied solely for the time of the Messias.—(St. Cypr. de Vanit. Idol.)

† Basnage, t. iv. liv. vii.

‡ Epist. St. P. ad Hebr. ii.

of his country, when the *schebet* (the sceptre, the legislative authority) shall be in the hands of the stranger.*

The prophet saved from the waters, who was divinely called to collect and consign to writing the history of the first ages and ancient traditions of the human race,—traditions, the memory of which was still fresh among the nations,—does not fail to lend the support of his imposing testimony to the prophecy of Jacob: "The Lord thy God," said he, speaking to the people of God, "will raise up to thee a prophet of thy nation, and of thy brethren, like unto me: him thou shalt hear. And he that will not hear his words which he shall speak in my name, I will be the revenger." †

* Christians apply this revelation of Jacob to the Messias, and prove from it to the Jews that he must have come long ago, since for eighteen centuries their tribes have been intermixed, their sacrifices abolished, their political existence extinct; that they no longer possess a territory, nor princes of their nation, and that in all the places where they are dispersed they submit to the laws of foreign nations. To elude the force of this argument, the Jews maintain nowadays, that the word *schebet*, which we translate by sceptre, equally signifies the rod which chastises the slave; and they set out from this to maintain that, even if this oracle did refer to the Messias, all that could be concluded from it would be that their chastisement would endure till his coming, who was to deliver them from it. In fine, they deny that the word *Shiloh* can be translated Messias. But their ancient books contradict them; this prophecy is understood of the Messias in the Talmud; and this is how the Paraphrase of Onkelos explains this passage: "Juda shall not be without some one invested with supreme authority, nor without scribes of the sons of her children, till the Messias shall come." Jonathan, to whom the Jews assign the first place among the disciples of Hillel, and whom they reverence almost as Moses, translates *schebet* in the same way by principality, and *Shiloh* by Messias; the Paraphrase of Jerusalem also adopts this opinion. Thus the most ancient, most authentic, and most respectable commentaries among them supply victorious arms wherewith to combat them.

† Hence comes that hope of a new law which the Jews expect with the Messias, a law which they place far above that of Moses. "The law which man studies in this world is but vanity," say their doctors,

Now the synagogue always understood this very clear text as referring to the Messias: St. Philip applies it, without hesitation, to our divine Redeemer when he says to Nathanael, "We have found him of whom Moses in the law and the prophets did write, Jesus the son of Joseph of Nazareth."

Towards the end of the mission of Moses, and whilst Israel were still encamped in the desert, Balaam, whose curses a Moabite prince had bargained for in the Valley of Willows,* came in his turn to confirm the expectation of the Messias, and to designate in a clear and precise manner the great epoch of his coming. Standing upon the rocky summit of Phogor, surrounded by victims slain for a sacrifice of hatred, in sight of the accursed lake and the barren mountains of Arabia, the soothsayer from the banks of the Euphrates, moved by the spirit of God, perceives, as with the eye of a dream,† a wonderful vision; his expressions, interrupted by solemn pauses, are thrown out without order and without art upon the winds of the mountains, like fragments of some mysterious conversation held in a low tone with powers invisible: "I shall see him, but not now. I shall behold him, but not near. A star shall rise out of Jacob,

"in comparison with that of Moses."—(Medrasch-Rabba, in Eccl. xi. 8.)

* The plain of Babylon, intersected by rivers and canals, and on that account very marshy, abounded in willows. Hence it is called in Scripture the "Valley of Willows."

† If we did not know that the prophecy of Balaam is very ancient, the very manner in which it is made would sufficiently indicate it. Balaam, the Chaldean astrologer, does not prophecy like the *seers* of Juda; he requires a vast horizon, whence he perceives at once the earth, the sea, and the sky; he expresses himself like a man who relates to himself the things that he sees at the moment when he speaks, and which make the strongest impression upon him. This kind of prophecy somewhat resembles what the Scotch highlanders call *second sight*.

and a sceptre shall spring up from Israel, and shall strike the chiefs of Moab." Incoherent words are followed by a magnificent but gloomy picture of the conquests of the kingly people. It is not without purpose that the prophetic vision exhibits Rome at the highest point of its colossal power; then it is that Christ is to visit the earth, and immolate himself for us upon the disgraceful tree. The prophet paints this epoch of blood in strong colours; one would say that cities and empires yet unborn present themselves to him on the mirage of the desert. He beholds the fleet of the Cæsars leaving the ports of Italy, and directing its prows, favoured by victory, towards the flat shores of the Syrians; he sees the ruin of that Judea which is not to be in existence till long after, and where the people of God as yet possess nothing but a few sepulchres which they can call their own; in fine, he follows with his eye the fall of the Roman eagle, seven hundred years before the birth of the sons of Ilia, and when the wild goats of Latium are browsing peacefully upon the shrubby declivities of the seven hills.

Ages roll on, and other ages after them, without any other promises from Jehovah; but the oracles relating to the Messias are confided to tradition, which retains them faithfully, or deposited in the sacred law. Israel maintains an obscure contest, but one incessant and furious, against those idolatrous nations which surround and press upon his tribes; at times he gives way to that strange propensity which draws him into idolatry, and then the fatal sword of the Amorrhite and the Moabite is unconsciously drawn in the Lord's cause, and avenges unintentionally the injury done to the God of Jacob. But during these varied fortunes, the people do not forget the coming of Christ; they live in the faith of the Messias; in default of new revelations, their very life becomes prophetic. Institutions, political and religious, local customs and private manners all tend to the same object, all flow from the same source, all are connected with the generation of the SAVIOUR, born of a virgin of Juda. It was the coming of the Messias, which the prophet Samuel came to pray for on his knees, in the holy of holies, before the *Schekina*, his bright and divine emblem; as did also the high priests, who succeeded one after another, later on, in the temple of Solomon. It is with the expectation of the Messias that that law of Deuteronomy is connected, which provides that the brother shall raise up a heir to his brother who has died without children, that his name may be preserved in Israel. It is that lost hope of being related one day, more or less remotely, to that heavenly envoy, which causes that young and meek virgin of Galaad to lament on the mountains of Judea, who carries with her no other regret to the blood-stained sepulchre where her father's race has become extinct.* It is to this belief, so general among the Hebrews, that the Thecuite woman alludes, when denouncing to King David the secret plot which was contriving against her sole surviving son; she poetises her fears as a mother, and at the same time a Jewish matron, by that touching sentence, "My lord, they seek to quench my spark which is left!"

Nothing but the present incredulity of the Jews could equal in depth the faith of their ancestors. The great concern of those men of ancient times was the coming of the Messias; those who died at a period still so remote from that in which the divine promises were to be accomplished, died in the firm persuasion that they would be one day fulfilled;

* Some rabbins maintain that the daughter of Jephte was not sacrificed, but merely condemned to perpetual celibacy. This assertion is contradicted by that text of Scripture which says: "That from year to year the daughters of Israel assemble together, and lament the daughter of Jephte, the Galaadite, for four days."—(Judges xi. 40.) People do not mourn for a person living. Flavius Josephus also affirms the immolation of the daughter of Jephte.—(Ant. Jud., t. ii. lib. v. c. 9.)

on the threshold of eternity they hailed that hope from afar off, as Moses, the great prophet, hailed, with a sigh, that "land of milk and honey" which the Lord closed against him.

From the time of David, and under the kings his children, the thread of prophecy is joined again, and the mystery of the Virgin and the Messias is more than ever declared by predictions magnificent and clearer than the sun.

The holy king, whom the God of Israel had preferred to the race of Saul, sees the virginity of Mary, and the extraordinary birth of the Son of God. *Thy birth*, says he, not defiled, like that of the children of men, *shall be pure as the morning dew*. Then, lifting up his eyes on high, he beholds Him whom God has given him for his son according to the flesh, seated on the right hand of Jehovah, on a throne more durable than the heavens and the stars.

In the earlier prophecies, the Blessed Virgin, though always pointed out, was nevertheless a little in the shade, and, so to speak, in the background of the picture; but from the days of David, the radiant form of Mary no longer presents features so irregular, and she who was to cause the blood of Abraham, of Jacob, and of Jesse the Just to flow in the veins of the God-Man, is delineated more exactly. David had spoken of her virginal parturition. Solomon delighted in tracing her image with sweet strokes of the pencil, which leave far behind the graceful descriptions of the peris of the East, those smiling and airy divinities which cross the dreams of the shepherd of Arabia. He sees her rising up in the midst of the daughters of Juda, "as a lily among therns;" her eyes are sweet and soft, "like those of doves;" from her lips, red "as a scarlet lace," proceeds a voice pure and melodious, like the sound of harps exciting Israel to the combat; her step is light "as the smoke of perfumes," and her beauty rivals in splendour "the rising moon." Her tastes are simple and full of poetry; she loves to stray in the fresh valleys, "where the vines are in blossom," and the figs appear in knots, like emeralds, on the leafless branches; her eyes perceive the red buds of the pomegranate, the tree of Paradise,* and she delights in listening to the plaintive strain of the turtle. Silent and retired, she withdraws from the sight of all, and hides herself in her dwelling, like the dove "which makes its nest in the clefts of the rock." She is chosen for a mystical hymen, in preference to the virgins and queens of all nations; a crown is promised to her by Him "whom her soul loveth," and the happy band which unites her to her royal spouse "is stronger than death."†

Elias, in prayer on Mount Carmel, to obtain the end of that long drought which for three years parches the earth and dries up the springs, discovers the promised Virgin, under the form of a transparent cloud, which rises from the bosom of the waters to announce the return of rain. The blessings of the people hail this favourable augury,‡ and the prophet, who penetrates into divine things, builds an oratory to the future Queen of Heaven.§ Isaias declares to the house of David, whose chief, Achab, trembles under the threats of the stranger, "like a forest beaten down by a tempest," that God will give an encouraging sign of the

* The orientals give the pomegranate the name of "fruit of Paradise."

† All the holy fathers notice that the "Canticle of Canticles" is only a continued allegory of the Mother of God.

‡ When rain falls in Palestine, there is general joy among the people; they assemble in the streets, they sing, they are full of agitation, and cry out as loud as they can, "O God! O blessed!"—(Volney, Voyage en Syrie.)

§ The oratory which Elias erected on Mount Carmel was dedicated by him to the Virgin who was to bring forth, *Virgini pariturœ*. This chapel was called *Semnœum*, which means a place consecrated to an *empress*, who can be no other than Mary, the *Empress* of heaven and earth.—(Hist. du Mont Carmel, succession du Saint Prophète, c. 31.)

future condition of Judea—a future to be yet long and glorious. "A virgin shall conceive;* she shall bring forth a son, and his name shall be called *Emmanuel*, that is, God with us. This child, miraculously given to the earth, shall be an offset from the stock of Jesse, a flower sprung from his root.† He shall be called God, the Mighty, the Father of the world to come, the Prince of peace. He shall stand for an ensign of people, him the Gentiles shall beseech, and his sepulchre shall be glorious."

* This great oracle of Isaias has been the subject of a long and perplexing dispute between the Jews and the Christians. The rabbins, who have commented on the text since Jesus Christ, anxious to change the nature of the proofs which condemn them, and obscure the words of the prophet, have contended that the word *halma*, which is found in the Hebrew text, signifies merely a young woman, although the Septuagint has translated it by *virgin*. The fathers have triumphantly refuted this objection. "The seventy interpreters," says St. John Chrysostom, "are they who most deserve credit; they made their version more than a century before Jesus Christ; they were many together; their time, their number, and their union render them far more worthy of credit than the Jews of our days, who have maliciously corrupted many places of the holy Scriptures."—(St. Joan. Chrys., Serm. 4, c. i.) St. Jerom, the most profound Hebrew scholar of all the interpreters and all the commentators of Scripture, pronounces, as he says, without fear of contradiction from the Jews, that *halma*, wherever the word occurs in the divine Scriptures, signifies exclusively a virgin in all her innocence, and nowhere a married woman.—(Comm. St. Hieron. in Is., lib. iii.) Luther, who made so deplorable use of really great learning, cries out with the fury and vehemence for which he is so well known: "If any Jew or Hebraist can show me that *halma* signifies in any place *a woman of any kind*, and not a virgin, he shall have from me one huudred florins, if please God I can find them."—(Œuvres de Luther, t. viii. p. 129.) Mahomet himself has borne testimony to the virginity of the Mother of God. "And Mary, daughter of Imram, who has kept her virginity; and we have sent of our spirit into her, and she has believed the words of her Lord and his Scriptures."—(Koran, Surate 66.)

† Jesse, called also Isai, was the son of Obed and father of David. His memory is in high veneration among the Hebrews, who regard im as an accomplished just one.

The mystery of the Messias was entirely unveiled to the prophets; some of them see Bethlehem rendered illustrious by his birth; others foretell his triumphant entry into Jerusalem, and even describe the peaceful and slow-paced animal on which he rides. They see him enter the temple, that sacred priest according to the order of Melchisedech; they know the number of pieces of silver which the butchers of the synagogue will drop into the hand of the base wretch who sells his master to them;* they see the punishment of slaves, the draught of gall offered to the agony of a God, and the robe, woven by the hands of a Mother, cast lots for by rude soldiers; they hear the nails which tear the bleeding flesh, and are driven with a harsh, rough sound into the accursed wood. And then the scene changes, like those pictures of Raphael, where the subject begun upon the earth is continued beyond the clouds. The Man of Sorrows, the humble Messias, whom his own relations have treated with scorn, whom his own people have not known, looks down from the highest heavens upon his prostrate enemies: all the nations of the earth remember their God, forgotten for so many ages! The nations rally at the standard of the cross, and the empire of Christ shall have no bounds but those of the world. Nothing is wanting to the completion of the prophecies: Jacob has determined the coming of the *Shiloh* at that precise moment when the Jews shall cease to be governed by their own laws, which implies the ruin of a state; Balaam adds that this ruin will be the work of a people come from Italy, and the satrap Daniel reckons up precisely the weeks which are to elapse to that time.

"All that happens in the world has its sign before it," as

* This, passage, in which God himself states the exact number of pieces of silver of this infamous compact, bears the impress of bitter and terrible irony. "And the Lord said to me: Cast it to the statuary, a goodly price that I was priced at by them. And I took the thirty pieces of silver," &c.—(Zach. xi. 13.)

a man of genius has said, who now remains so solitary and so formidable beneath his tent. "When the sun is about to rise, the horizon is tinted with a thousand colours, and the east appears all on fire. When the tempest comes, a dull murmur is heard on the shore, and the waves are agitated as if by themselves." The figures of the Old Testament, as the fathers of the Church acknowledge, are the signs which announce the rising of the *Sun of Justice* and of the *Star of the Sea*. To Christ, the Son of God, belongs power; to Mary, grace and merciful goodness. She is the tree of life replanted in the abodes of men by the hands of God himself, and the earnest of a happiness preferable to that which our first parents enjoyed in Eden; the dove of the ark which brings the olive branch to the earth; the fountain sealed up, the waters of which have not been defiled by anything impure; the fleece which receives the dew from heaven; in fine, the frail and odoriferous bush of wild roses through which Moses perceived the Deity—the bush, which so far from being consumed by fire, which destroys all things, was in some measure preserved by it, and lost neither leaf nor flower from contact with the heavenly flame.*

Like that enchanting figure which an antique painter formerly composed, by borrowing a thousand scattered traits from the most beautiful women of Greece, the chaste spouse of the Holy Ghost repeated in her single person all that the most celebrated women of the old law had offered to the admiration of their contemporaries. Beautiful as Rachel

* Philo, who has made this remark, and who discovers in this burning bush a mysterious allegory, applies it erroneously to the Jewish nation by forced resemblances. Josephus, who sought in like manner to understand this mystery, has succeeded no better. Those wild roses, emblematical of chaste virgins who diffuse their modest perfume in solitude, and whom the contact of the Divinity causes to shine without prejudice to the holy purity of their white and delicate blossom, are the most striking image of Mary, that mystical Rose of the new law.

and Sarah, she knew how to unite the prudence of Abigail with the courageous resolution of Esther. Susanna, chaste as the flower of which she bore the name;* Judith, whose crown of lilies was stained with the blood of Holophernes;† Axa, whose hand was the prize for a conquered city; and that mother, so great and so unfortunate, who saw all her sons die for the law,—were but faint images of her who was to unite in herself all the perfections of woman and angel.

After an expectation of four thousand years, the time marked out by so many prophecies arrives at last; the shadows of the old law disappear, and Mary arises in the horizon of Judea, like the star which is the harbinger of day.

CHAPTER II.

THE IMMACULATE CONCEPTION.

A WOMAN destined from all eternity to be the means of saving the world by deifying our nature, and to contain in her chaste womb HIM whose "tabernacle is the sun, and who bows the heavens beneath his feet"—a woman expected from the creation of the globe, revealed by God himself in Paradise, and the avowed end of all the holy generations who have succeeded one after the other from the days of the patriarchs,‡ can be no ordinary creature, and must have

* The name of Susanna signifies *lily*.—(Favyn, ii. 2.)

† The ancients attributed to *lilies* the power of neutralising enchantments and averting dangers. "Judith bound her forehead," say the rabbins, "with a wreath of lilies, that she might make her way into the tent of Holophernes without fear."—(Comm. RR. in Judith.)

‡ According to St. Augustin, the progeny to which all the patriarchs aspire is Jesus Christ, and Jesus Christ in Mary, to whom alone their fecundity could extend. "And in fact," says he, "if

prerogatives superior to humanity. The pious belief in the immaculate conception of Mary flows from this feeling of reverence. Descendants of an unfortunate head,—degraded by our rebellious father, disgraced by the sentence which condemns him instead of receiving from him the life of grace, we have received from him the death of sin, and, by a fearful destiny, we are condemned before we are born. This misery, inherent in the human race, cursed as one man in its origin, is common to all, and the Scripture has made no exception in favour of any child of Adam; but the piety of the faithful could not bear the idea that the Mother of God should be subject to the disgraceful condemnation which marks us with the seal of hell in the wombs of our mothers; they have been persuaded that the Sovereign Judge must have suspended the general effect of his severe law in favour of her who came into the world for no other purpose than to contribute to the accomplishment of the most secret, most incomprehensible of the counsels of God—the incarnation of the Messias. Notwithstanding the silence of the gospel, it has been generally believed that the Virgin, with a view to her divine maternity, was held back, as it were, on the brink of the abyss which the fatal disobedience of our first parents opened under our feet, and that her conception was immaculate as her life.

This belief, which the Greeks borrowed from Palestine, and adopted with enthusiasm,* led to the institution of the

nature in all her efforts tends to Jesus Christ, who is the Lord of ages, it is not that she flatters herself that she shall attain to the son of God by her own power alone; the extent of her power stops at the humble Mary, who is to bring forth the blessed germ, not by the power of her forefathers, but by the virtue of the Most High."—(St. Augustin, 5, contr. Jul. 9.)

* We read in the Menologies, so ancient in the use of the Greeks, these words, which clearly set forth their belief in the mystery of the immaculate conception:—By a particular providence, the Lord was pleased that the Blessed Virgin should be as pure, from the first

Feast of the Immaculate Conception, which was celebrated with great pomp at Constantinople as early as the sixth century.* In the West, on the other hand, this doctrine met with opponents, and powerful ones; for St. Anselm, St. Bernard, St. Bonaventure, St. Thomas of Aquin, Albert the Great, and many other learned and wise personages, all great theologians, and what is more, very devout to Mary, maintained that she had been conceived in sin, and subject to the general law,† although shortly after she had been entirely purified from it, by a special and surpassing favour, which began her glorious state of Mother of God.

But the belief in the immaculate conception of the holy Virgin prevailed in the end over the opinion of the great doctors of the middle ages; what the eagles of the schools had not seen was discovered to the unlearned. The writings of the apostles and doctors were turned over afresh; what they have bequeathed to us from age to age concerning the grandeurs of Mary, was more scrupulously examined, and this research caused strong light to fall on this obscure point of the history of the Mother of Christ.

And, in fact, when we go back to the apostles, we already see the title of most holy and *immaculate* applied to Mary.‡

moment of her life, as it became her who was to become worthy to conceive and bring forth Jesus Christ, the Word made flesh."

* St. Andrew of Crete makes mention of this Feast of the Immaculate Conception, the office of which had been composed by St. Sabbas, to which St. Germanus, Patriarch of Constantinople, added an antiphon.

† The adversaries of the immaculate conception glory in reckoning in their ranks St. Anselm, St. Bernard, St. Bonaventure, St. Thomas, Albert the Great, &c. Great as these names are, we must not allow ourselves to be dazzled by them; for by comparing these doctors with themselves, we find that they positively maintained opinions both *for and against*, which shows that their opinion was not decided on this point, or else that they had strange distractions.

‡ St. James the Great and St. Mark, in their Liturgies.

The apostle St. Andrew, quoted by the Babylonian Abdias, expresses himself in these terms:—"As the first Adam was made of the earth before it was cursed, so the second Adam was formed of virgin earth which was never cursed."

The saints and martryrs who lived in the third century, St. Hippolytus,* Origen,† St. Dionysius of Alexandria,‡ give to the holy Virgin the qualification of "pure," and "immaculate." St. Cyprian § is more precise, and says plainly that "there is a very great difference between the rest of mortals and the Virgin, and that all she has in common with them is their nature, and not their fault.

In the fourth century St. Ambrose, who compares the Virgin to "a straight and shining stem, where there was never found the knot of original, or the bark of actual sin;"‖ St. John Chyrsostom,¶ who proclaims her "most holy, *immaculate*, blessed above all creatures;" St. Jerom,** who poetically makes her "the cloud of the day which never knew darkness;" St. Basil,†† whose footsteps the defenders of the immaculate conception have always gloried in following,—have never varied as to that purity of the lily which applies so well to the queen of angels.

In the fifth century, St. Augustin‡‡ cannot bear that even the name of Mary should be mentioned when there is any

* St. Hipp. in an oration "On the Consummation of the World."

† Orig. Hom. in St. Matt.

‡ St. Dion. in an epistle mentioned in the Biblioth. des PP.

§ St. Cypr., de Nat. Virg.

‖ "Virgo in qua nec nodus originalis, nec cortex actualis culpæ fuit."—(St. Ambr., de Inst. Virg., c. v.)

¶ St. J. Chrysostom, in his Liturgy.

** Commentaries of St. Jerom on Ps. lxxvii. "Deduxit eos in nube diei: nubes est beata Virgo, quæ pulchre dicitur nubes diei, quia non fuit in tenebris, sed semper in luce."

†† St. Basil, in his Liturgy.

‡‡ It must be observed that St. Augustin was then defending the doctrine of original sin against the Pelagians.

question of sin; and St. Peter Chrysologus* affirms that "all have been saved in the Virgin."

St. Fulgentius, who lived at the beginning of the sixth century, says that the "holy Virgin was entirely excepted from the primeval sentence."† "It is wrong," says St. Ildefonsus,‡ Archbishop of Toledo, who flourished in the same century, "to seek to subject the mother of God to the laws of nature; it is manifest that she was free from original sin, and that she removed the malediction of Eve." St. John Damascen,§ speaking expressly of her conception, says that she was "pure and *immaculate.*" In the ninth century Theophanes, Abbot of Grandchamp; in the tenth, St. Fulbert, Bishop of Chartres; towards the middle of the eleventh, Yvo,‖ one of the most shining lights of that time, and a little later, St. Bruno,¶ founder of the Carthusians, are evidently in favour of the immaculate conception of the Blessed Virgin.

Islamism itself declares for the immaculate conception, and the Arab commentators on the Koran have adopted, in their way, the opinion of those Catholic divines who have declared themselves for that doctrine. "Every descendant of Adam," says Cottada, "from the moment of his coming into the world, is touched in the side by Satan: Jesus and Mary,

* St. Peter Chrysol., de Annunciat., Serm. 140.

† St. Fulg., Serm. de laudibus Mariæ.—Serm. de duab. nat. Jesu Christi.

‡ St. Ildefonsus, in his book De Virginit. Mariæ.

§ St. J. Damascen, De Nativ. Mariæ., Or. 1a.

‖ The two holy bishops of Chartres, Fulbert and Yvo, declared themselves in favour of the immaculate conception. Yvo maintained it in the pulpit, and Fulbert says in his Paraphrase on the Angelical Salutation to the Virgin, "Ave, Maria, electa et insignis inter filías, quæ immaculata semper extitisti ab exordio tuæ creationis, quia paritura eras Creatorem totius sanctitatis."

¶ St. Bruno, in his explanation of these words of Ps. ci., "Dominus de cœlo in terram aspexit," which he applies to the Blessed Virgin.

however, must be excepted; for God placed a veil between them and Satan, which preserved them from his fatal contact."

These testimonies in favour of the immaculate conception of Mary become more feeble and less abundant in the twelfth and thirteenth centuries; few authors of note wrote then in this sense, and many men eminent for their learning and sanctity maintained the contrary opinion. To make up for this, the Feast of the Conception of the Virgin was established in several kingdoms.

William the Conqueror established this feast in Normandy as early as 1074; and from the reign of Henry I., his son, King of England and Duke of Normandy, it was celebrated at Rouen with extraordinary solemnity. "It was instituted," say the ancient chroniclers, "on account of the holy apparition made to an abbot worthy of credit, who had encountered the perils of the sea during a tempest." An old history of the antiquities of Rouen adds, that "from the very time of the institution of the feast, an association was founded of the most respectable personages of the town, who still elect every year one of their number to be the prince of the confraternity, who, holding the *puy*, or platform for all speakers, in all languages, gives excellent and valuable prizes to those who most elegantly, faithfully, and appropriately shall have celebrated the praise of the Virgin Mary on the subject of her holy conception, by hymns, odes, sonnets, ballads, royal songs, &c.*

Thus the Virgin, full of grace, presided over the revival of poetry, and her immaculate conception furnished pious subjects for the country of the minstrels.

From Normandy the Feast of the Conception of the Virgin came amongst the English. The first council of Oxford,

* Antiquités et Singularités de la ville de Rouen, by N. Taillepied, D.D.

held by Stephen Langton, Archbishop of Canterbury, in the year 1222, places it in the number of holidays kept without servile work. In France, in the year 1288, a bishop of Paris, Renoul de Hombiere, left by his will a considerable sum to found the office of this Feast of the Holy Virgin, which was introduced at the same time in the Lyonnais. In fine, a manuscript martyrology of the thirteenth century, found in the library of the Dominicans of Dijon, marks the Feast of the Conception of Our Lady, on the 8th of December; "which shows plainly enough," say the learned Benedictines who have read this ancient MS., "that this feast was already celebrated almost everywhere in the Church in the time of St. Dominic."

The doctrine of the immaculate conception had been banished from the pulpits and schools for a long space of time, when certain divines who had been convinced that this belief came down from the highest and purest sources of Christianity, undertook to revive it. The Fransiscans, who first began to make public profession of it by writing* and word of mouth, supported it by reasons so strong and convincing that not only the mass of the faithful, but the most learned bodies in Europe adhered to it with enthusiasm. The Sorbonne, which was then called the "firmament of science, the support of truth and piety in the Church of God," ordained that all who should be promoted to the degree of doctor should engage upon oath to maintain this religious belief.† This

* Montfaucon, who travelled through Italy about the year 1698, having paid a visit at Pavia to the library of the Chevalier Beleridus, renowned for his piety, was much surprised to see that this immense collection of books was entirely composed of treatises written by the Franciscans in defence of the immaculate conception.

† The decree of the Sorbonne is as follows:—"We decree and declare that no one shall be admitted in future into our faculty without promising on oath to defend all his life this doctrine of the immaculate conception." "Statuentes ut nemo deinceps huic nostro

was done successively by the universities of Mentz, Cologne, Valentia, Alcala, Coimbra, Salamanca, and Naples.

Among those religious orders who did honour to France for so many centuries, the Dominicans alone, or nearly alone, showed themselves hostile to the pious doctrine of the immaculate conception; but the learned Benedictines, who are held in veneration by the Protestants themselves for their immense scientific labours; the Carthusians, the Carmelites, the Order of St. Augustin, of Cluny, of Citeaux, of the Premonstratensians, and a multitude of others, whom it would be tedious to enumerate here, adhered with enlightened piety, ardent zeal, and profound conviction to the doctrine of the immaculate conception.

Councils have been favourable to this belief. That of Basle, in its session of 27th of September, 1429, says that "the doctrine which teaches that the glorious Virgin Mary was conceived without sin is a pious doctrine conformable to the worship of the Church, to Catholic faith, to right reason, and to Holy Scripture.* The Council of Avignon confirmed, in 1457, the decree of the Council

collegio adscribatur, nisi se hujus doctrinæ assertorem semper pro viribus futurum, simili juramento, profiteatur."

* "There has arisen in this holy council (that of Basle) a difficult question on the conception of the glorious Virgin Mary, Mother of God, and on the commencement of her sanctification; some saying that her soul was for some time, or at least for some moments, actually subject to original sin; others maintaining, on the contrary, that the love which God had for her extended to the first moment of her creation; that the Most High, who himself established her, and the Son, who formed her to be his mother upon earth, loaded her with singular and extraordinary graces; that Jesus Christ redeemed her in a superior and quite peculiar manner, by preserving her from the original stain, and sanctifying her in the first momont of her conception. Having therefore examined discreetly the reasons and authorities which, for several years, have been alleged on one side and the other, in the public acts of this holy council—having moreover given attention to many other things on the same subject—

of Basle; and in their session of 1564* the fathers of the Council of Trent declared that in the decree which they had made in 1546, on original sin, they had never intended to include the blessed and *immaculate* Mother of God.

Notwithstanding the prudent reserve which the Holy See prescribed to itself in an affair where famous doctors and illustrious divines appeared on both sides, it could not help making it appear to which side its sympathies leaned. From the year 1483, Pope Sixtus IV. had expressly forbidden any disputation in pulpits and schools upon the conception of Our Lady.† This might be taken for a simple act of neutrality if this pontiff had not approved of the Office of the Conception, composed by a religious of Verona, and granted an indulgence of a hundred days to all who should assist at

all being weighed and maturely considered, we decide and declare that the doctrine which teaches that the glorious Virgin Mary, Mother of God, by a special favour, and by a prevenient and operative grace, was never subject to original sin, but that she was always holy, immaculate, and exempt from all sin, original and actual; we declare that the doctrine which teaches all this is a pious doctrine, conformable to the worship of the Church, to the Catholic faith, to right reason, and to the Holy Scripture; and that as such it ought to be approved, held, and followed by all Catholics, so that it may not be lawful for any one henceforth to preach or teach the contrary. Renewing, moreover, the institution of the Feast of the Holy Conception, which, by an ancient and laudable custom, is celebrated on the eighth day of December, both at Rome and in other churches, we will and ordain that this feast be celebrated on the same day, under the name of the Conception of the Virgin, in all churches, monasteries, and communities of the Catholic religion, and that the faithful express themselves upon it in canticles of praise and joy." The council attaches even indulgences to this solemnity.

* "Declarat hæc sancta synodus non esse intentionis suæ comprehendere in hoc decreto, ubi de peccato originali agitur, beatam et IMMACULATAM Dei genitricem."—(Concil. Trid. Sess. v. 1546.)

† See the Constitution of Sixtus IV., which begins by "Grave nimis."

it.* The successors of this great pope uniformly trod in the path which he had struck out and followed. In 1506, Cardinal Ximenes established in Spain, with the consent of Pope Julius II., a confraternity of the Conception. The same pope confirmed by a brief dated 17th of September, 1511, an Order of religious women, founded under the same title by Innocent VIII.† In the hymns which Żachary, Bishop of Gordia, composed by order of Leo X. and Clement VII., it is said that Our Lady was created in a state of grace. In 1569 Pope Pius V. granted permission to the Franciscans to celebrate the Office of the Immaculate Conception, attaching to it the same indulgences as to the feast of the Blessed Sacrament. Paul V., by a bull in the year 1616, forbid any one to maintain, in public lectures, the contrary opinion to that of the immaculate conception; and Gregory XV., in 1622, extended this prohibition even to private discourses and particular conversations. It only remained for the popes to celebrate this feast in Rome itself, and this was done by Alexander VII. in 1661. It results from this conduct of the Holy See that all its sympathies are on the side of the doctrine of the immaculate conception. Nevertheless, it would not condemn the contrary opinion, doubtless out of regard for high and holy names.

One voice of immense weight, the great voice of Bossuet, has been heard in this cause; the *buckler of religion* has been nobly held up before the Blessed Virgin. "The opinion of the immaculate conception," says he "has an indescribable power to persuade pious souls. Next to the articles of

* See the Constitution of Sixtus IV., beginning with "Cum præexcelsa . . . Extrav. Commun."

† In this Order of the Immaculate Conception, each sister consecrated herself expressly to this mystery by these words, which are by no means ambiguous: "I, Sister N——, for the love and service of Jesus Christ our Lord, and of the immaculate conception of his Blessed Mother, promise," &c.

faith, I see hardly anything more certain. Hence I am not surprised that this school of divines of Paris should oblige all her children to defend this doctrine. For my own part, I am delighted in these days to follow up her intentions. After having been fed with her milk, I willingly submit to her decrees, and the more so as they are, as it appears to me, the will of the Church: she has a most honourable opinion of the conception of Mary; she does not oblige us to believe it to have been *immaculate*, but she gives us to understand that such belief is pleasing to her. There are things which she commands, in which we make known our obedience; there are others which she insinuates, where we may testify our affection. It becomes our piety, if we are true children of the Church, not only to obey the commandments, but to bend to the smallest signs of the will of a mother so good and so sacred."*

Devotion to the immaculate conception of the Virgin was popular in Western Europe from the middle ages—that is certain; and since then it has made immense progress: but be it said, without offence to France and Italy—those two nations so eminently devout to the Virgin—Spain has shown the greatest zeal and ardour in the propagation of this doctrine. The church of Spain, protesting against the pretensions of the church of Normandy, which claims the institution of the Feast of the Immaculate Conception of Our Lady in the West, professes to have celebrated it in the seventh century;†—what is certain is, that in 1394, Don John I. of Arragon, who instituted it, by his royal authority, in the several provinces of Spain which had shaken off the yoke of Islamism, affirms that many of his predecessors had

* Bossuet, On the Conception.

† "La Iglesia Española fué la primera que celebró la Inmaculada Concepcion de la santisima Virgen; cuya festa tuvo lugar en ella desde el siglo septimo."—(El maestro Villados, en el cap. *de los Festiv. Ecles*, t. i. part 2.)

celebrated this feast before him*. We shall not decide between the two churches; but if the church of Spain has only doubtful claims to the institution of this feast of Mary,

* The following is the decree of Don Juan I., of Arragon:—

"We, Don Juan, by the grace of God King of Arragon and Valentia, &c.—Why are some persons astonished that the Blessed Mary, Mother of God, should have been conceived without original sin, while we doubt not that St. John Baptist was sanctified in his mother's womb by that same God, who, coming from the highest heaven, and from the throne of the most Holy Trinity, was made flesh in the blessed womb of a virgin? What graces do we think the Lord could refuse to the woman who gave birth to him by the splendid prodigy of her fruitful virginity? Loving his mother as he loves her, he must have surrounded her conception, her nativity, and the other phases of her life, with the most glorious privileges.

"Why call in question the conception of a virgin so privileged, and of whom the Catholic faith obliges us to believe grandeurs and wonders which we cannot sufficiently admire? Is it not a much greater subject of admiration for all Christians to see that a creature has given birth to her Creator, and that she became a mother without ceasing to be a virgin? How then shall the human mind suffice to praise this glorious Virgin, whom the Almighty predestined to possess, without the least corruption, the advantages of the divine maternity, conjointly with the glory of the purest virginity; and to be exalted above all the prophets, all the saints, and all the choirs of angels, as their queen? Could there then have been wanting any purity and any grace to that excellent Virgin in the first moment of her conception, so that the stain of original sin might have been imputed to her—her to whom the angel of the Lord sent from heaven spoke these words, 'Hail, Mary, full of grace! the Lord is with thee; blessed art thou among women!' Let then those who speak thus improperly hold their peace: let those who have nothing but vain and frivolous arguments to propose against the immaculate conception, so privileged and so pure, of the Blessed Virgin, be ashamed to publish them, because it was fitting that she should be endowed with so great purity, that next to that of God, none like it could be imagined. It is indeed fitting that she who had for her Son the Creator and Father of all things should have been, and should be ever, most pure and most perfect, having from the beginning and before all ages, by an eternal decree of God, been chosen among all creatures to

which was called in France and England *the Feast of the Normans*, she cannot be denied the honour of having been the first to erect churches and altars under the title of the

contain in her womb Him whom the whole world and the whole immensity of the heavens cannot contain.

"But we, who among all Catholic kings have received from this Mother of Mercies so many graces and benefits without having deserved them, we firmly believe that the Conception of this Blessed Virgin, in whose womb the Son of God vouchsafed to be made man, was entirely holy and immaculate.

"Thus we honour with a pure heart the mystery of this immaculate and blessed conception of the most holy Virgin, Mother of God; and we, and all those of the royal family, celebrate the festival of it every year with solemnity, in the same manner as our most illustrious predecessors of glorious memory have celebrated it, having had established for it a perpetual confraternity. Wherefore we ordain that this Feast of the Immaculate Conception shall he celebrated annually for ever, with great solemnity and respect, in all the kingdoms of our obedience, by all the Catholic faithful, whether religious or secular, priests or others, of whatever state or condition they may be; and that henceforth it shall not be lawful, and we even forbid all preachers, and all those who publicly lecture on the gospel, to say anything, to publish and advance anything, which in any way whatever might prejudice or be injurious to the purity and sanctity of this blessed conception; but, on the contrary, we ordain that preachers and other persons who have had opposite opinions shall keep strict silence, since the Catholic faith does not place us in any necessity of maintaining and professing the contrary opinion: and that others who hold our holy and salutary opinion in their heart shall publish it in their discourses, and eagerly testify their devotion by celebrating, by the praises of the Most High, the glory and honour of his holy Mother, who is the Queen of Heaven, the gate of Paradise;—she who has care of our souls, the secure haven of salvation, and the anchor of hope of all sinners who have confidence in her. By the tenor of these presents we expressly establish, in perpetuity that if it happens in future that any preacher, or any other person among our subjects, of what state or condition soever he may be, does not observe this ordinance, without any necessity for any other decree from us, let him be banished from his convent or house; and while he remains in this contrary opinion, let him depart as our enemy from the whole extent of our kingdoms. Willing also and ordering, of our

Mystery of the Immaculate Conception. As early as the year 1525, the Spaniards of Mexico placed the splendid cathedral of Puebla de los Angelos under the invocation of the immaculate Virgin, whose holy image glittered with precious stones upon an altar of massive silver, surrounded by a forest of elegant columns, with plinths and capitals of burnished gold. The faithful of Mexico erected an altar and a statue to her in their metropolitan church with true Peruvian magnificence. A little later, the Mexican cathedrals of Merida, Maracaïbo, and Nabana, were founded under the invocation of the immaculate Virgin, and Peru did not remain behind. This striking adherence to the doctrine of the conception without sin was yet not sufficient for the zeal of the people subject to the dominion of Spain; in 1618 the Viceroy of Naples, his court and army, made a vow, in the Church of Our Lady the Great, to believe and defend the immaculate conception of the Virgin. A memorial column, surmounted by a magnificent statue of Our Lady, with the symbolical signs of her victory over original sin, was erected in testimonv of this public engagement thus chivalrously contracted.

knowledge and mature deliberation, under pain of incurring our anger and indignation, all and each of our officers, who are on this side and beyond the sea, those who are there now and who shall be there hereafter, to keep and cause to be kept with great diligence and respect our present edict, as soon as they shall have cognizance thereof; and that each, in his district, shall cause it to be published correctly, solemnly, and with sound of trumpet in all the usual places, so that no one may plead ignorance of it; and that the devotion of the immaculate conception of the most Blessed Virgin, which Christians have long cherished in their hearts, may more and more increase; and that those people of an opposite opinion may no more in future be heard to open their mouths. In testimony of which we command these presents to be expedited, authorised by our seal, which is attached to them.—Given at Valentia, on the 2nd of February, the day on which we celebrate the Feast of the Purification of this most holy Virgin, in the year of Our Lord 1394, and the eighth of our reign."

The Spanish nation, which has always particularly signalised itself in this devotion, has so thoroughly adopted it, that not a single preacher mounts the pulpit without prefacing his sermon with a profession of faith in the conception without stain,* and that it has been introduced even into the familiar forms of speech pronounced when people meet.†

Finally, in 1771, while the destructive blast of philosophy violently shook the belief of Christians in France and several other countries of Europe, the King of Spain, Charles III., instituted an order in honour of the Virgin conceived without sin, and solemnly declared her, with the concurrence of the Cortes, and a brief from the Holy See, "Universal Patrona de Espana è Indias."‡

In France, in spite of the licentiousness and infidelity which the flood of revolutions left behind it as it subsided, this belief gains ground, and penetrates even to the most secluded hamlets. The diocess of Paris is especially distinguished for its zeal in embracing this pious belief, which flourishes beneath the protecting shade of its archbishops,§ and which is

* "Alabado sea el santisimo Sacramento del altar, y la inmaculada concepcion de la Virgen Maria, concebida sin pecado original en el primer instante de su ser natural."

† In going into a Spanish house, the first words which visitors pronounce, before they wish "Good day," are these, "Ave Maria purisima;" the masters of the house immediately answer, "Sin pecado concebida, santisima."

‡ "Por la devocion que desde nuestra infancia hemos tenido à Maria santisima en su misterio de la inmaculada concepcion, deseamos poner bajo los divinos auspicios de esta celestial protectora la. . . . . Nueva Orden, y mandamos que sea reconocida en ella por patrona . . . . ."—(Leg. 12, t. iii. lib. vi., Noviss. Rec.)

§ "C'est un fait que nous sommes jaloux de constater, et nous desirons que la connaissance en parvienne jusqu'aux lieux les plus reculés du monde Catholique: dans notre diocèse cette dévotion a jeté avec le temps des racines de plus en plus profondes, et les malheurs sont encore venus l'affermir, l'accroître, et l'étendre avec un merveilleux progrès."—(See the Mandement of the Archbishop of Paris,

confirmed by the supernatural things related of the miraculous medal struck in honour of the mystery of the immaculate conception.

If the tradition of the apostles, the favourable disposition of the Church, the authority of councils, the adherence of universities and religious orders, the assent of kings and nations, the dedication of temples and altars, the foundation of offices, the institution of confraternities and of royal orders may be taken into account in a controversy which has astonished the very pagans,* the cause of the immaculate conception of Mary, so long before the tribunal of Catholic opinion, appears to us to be won; and we do not believe that it would be rash to suppose that God, preserving his divine Mother from the original stain, may have said to her, as Assuerus said to Esther, "This law is not made for thee, but for all others."

Addition by the Translator.

[The foregoing chapter was written by the author before the ever memorable 8th of December, 1854, when it was solemnly defined by the infallible authority of the Catholic Church, that "it is A DOGMA OF FAITH that the most Blessed Virgin Mary, in the first instant of her conception, by a singular privilege and grace of God, in virtue of the merits of Jesus Christ, the Saviour of the human race, was preserved exempt from all stain of original sin."]

on occasion of the consecration of the Church of Notre Dame de Lorette.)

* "What then!" exclaimed Julian the Pelagian, addressing himself to a bishop who maintained the universality of original sin, "what then! do you subject the birth of Mary to the empire of the devil?"—(St. Aug., lib. iv. Op. imperf.)

CHAPTER III.

BIRTH OF MARY.

TOWARDS the decline of the religion and affairs of the Hebrews, at the time marked out by the prophets, and when the regal sceptre was in the hands of a stranger, according to the grand prediction of Jacob, there was at Nazareth, a town of lower Galilee, not far distant from Mount Carmel, a just man, named Joachim,* of the tribe of Juda, and of the race of David † through Nathan; his wife—who, according to the opinion of St. Augustin, was of the priestly tribe ‡ —was called Ann, a name which signifies in Hebrew *gracious.*§

They were both just before Jehovah, and walked in his commandments with a perfect heart; || but the Lord seemed

* One of Mary's historians, Christopher de Castro, has found—after the Rabbins, St. Hilary, and other fathers of the Church—that the father of Mary had two names, Heli and Joachim. The Arabs and Mussulmans know him by that of Amram, son of Matheus, and distinguish him from another Amram, father of Mary, the sister of Moses.—(D'Herbelot, Bibliothèque Orientale, t. ii.)

† According to the Proto-gospel of St. James and the Gospel of the Nativity of Mary, Joachim was of the race of David. Justin, who flourished only fifty years after the death of St. John the apostle, who was born in Palestine, and who had been able to collect the traditions yet recent, says, in like manner, that Mary descended in a right line from King David.

‡ St. August., De consensu Evangel.

§ The Mahometans, inheritors of the Arab traditions, knew the blessed mother of the Holy Virgin under her proper name, which is Hannah; she was, according to them, the daughter of Nakhor, and the wife of Amram.—(D'Herbelot, Bibliothèque Orientale, t. ii.)

|| St. Ann and St. Joachim were publicly honoured in the Church in the early ages. St. John Damascen highly eulogises their virtues.

to have turned away from them the light of his countenance, for one great blessing was wanting to their life: they were without children, which made them sad, because in Israel sterility was a reproach.

Joachim, who loved his wife for her wonderful meekness and eminent virtues, would not add to her misfortune by giving her a bill of divorce, which the law at that time granted so easily;* he kept her in his house, and this pious couple, humbly resigned to the divine decrees, passed their days in labour, prayer, and almsdeeds.

So many virtues could not fail of their reward: after twenty years of barrenness, Ann conceived, as it were by miracle, and brought forth that blessed creature who was more perfect, more holy, and more pleasing in the eyes of the Lord than all the elect put together.

It was about the beginning of the month of *Tisri*,† which is the first of the civil year of the Jews, while the smoke of holocausts ascended to heaven for the expiation of the sins of the people, that the predestined Virgin was born who was

The Emperor Justinian I. had a church built at Constantinople under the invocation of St. Ann, about the year 550. The body of the saint was brought, it is said, from Palestine to Constantinople in 710.—(See Godescard, t. v. p. 319.) Luther was very devout to St. Ann before his heresy; it was to that saint that he promised to embrace the monastic state, before the corpse of one of his comrades, who was just killed by lightning before his eyes.

* It was the Pharisees who had introduced this abuse of divorce, so strongly condemned by our Lord (St. Matt. xix. 8): they taught that a wife might be put away for the most trifling causes; for example, for having over-dressed the meat for her *master of the household*, or merely for not being handsome enough. This was the opinion of Hillel and Akiba.—(Basn., liv. vii. c. 22.)

† The 8th of September, according to the teaching of the Church. —Baronius makes Mary born in the year of Rome 733, twenty-one years before the common era, on the 8th of September, on a Saturday, at daybreak. Le Nain de Tillemont says that the Virgin was born in the year 734: this opinion is most followed.

to repair the primeval transgression. Her birth was silent and unknown, like that of her divine Son; her parents were of the people, although descended from a long succession of kings, and led, to all appearances, an obscure life: this mystical Rose, which St. John saw later on clothed with the sun as with radiant garments, was to expand to the burning wind of adversity, upon a stem poor and despoiled.†

The cradle of the Queen of angels was neither ornamented with gold, nor covered with Egyptian counterpanes richly embroidered, nor perfumed with spikenard, myrrh, and aloes, like those of the Hebrew princes; it was composed of flexible twigs, and swathing bands of coarse linen compressed the little arms which were one day so tenderly to nurse the Saviour of the world. The children of kings, while still wrapped up in their swaddling clothes of purple, see the great men of the state bow their heads before them, and say to them, My lord! The woman who was the Spouse and the Mother of God, gave her first smile to some poor women among the people, who perhaps said sorrowfully to each other, as they thought of the unfortunate and despised condition to which men had condemned them, Here is one slave more!

* This is what the Turks relate of the birth of the Blessed Virgin:—The wife of Amram (Joachim) said to God, "O Lord, I have consecrated to thee by vow the fruit of my womb; receive it with goodness, O thou who knowest and understandest all things." When she had brought forth, she added, "O Lord, I have brought a daughter into the world; I have named her Miriam (Mary), I place her under thy protection, her and her posterity, that thou mayest preserve them from the artifices of Satan."—(The Koran, ch. 3.)

† Isaias had foretold it: saying, "There shall come forth a rod out of the trunk of Jesse;" for this word trunk, in the Hebrew expression, as St. Jerom observes (on Is. c. ii.), signifies a trunk without branches and without leaves, to denote, continues this holy doctor, that the august Mary was to be born of the race of David, when that family should have lost its splendour, and should have fallen away from it entirely.

In Israel, they gave the child on the ninth day after its birth, in the midst of the assembled family, the name which it was to bear among men: the daughter of Joachim received from her father the name of Miriam (Mary), which is translated from the Syriac by *lady, sovereign mistress*, and which signifies in Hebrew, *star of the sea.*

"And, surely," says St. Bernard, "the Mother of God could not have a name more appropriate, nor one more expressive of her high dignity. Mary is, in fact, that beautiful and brilliant star which shines upon the vast and stormy sea of the world."

This divine name conceals within itself a powerful charm, and one of such marvellous sweetness, that we have but to pronounce it, and the heart is moved; only to write it, and the style is adorned. "The name of Mary," says St. Anthony of Padua, "is sweeter to the lips than a honeycomb, more flattering to the ear than a sweet song, more delicious to the heart than the purest joy."*

Eighty days after the birth of a daughter, the Jewish woman was solemnly purified at the temple where she brought her first-born child. In conformity with the law of Moses, she then offered to the Lord a lamb, or two turtle-doves; the two turtle-doves were the sacred offering of the poor: they were that of the spouse of Joachim.

But the gratitude of the pious mother went beyond the customary sacrifice: the worthy rival of Anna, the wife of Elcana, she offered to the Lord a victim more pure, a dove more innocent than those which had just fallen gasping and bleeding under the knife of the sacrificing priest: she had no votive crown of most pure gold to hang up on the partition wall of the temple:† she laid at the feet of the Most High the crown of her old age—the infant with which He had

* "Nomen Virginis Mariæ, mel in ore, melos in aure, jubilum in corde," says poetically St. Anthony of Padua.

† Macch. lib. iv.

blessed her life; and she solemnly engaged to bring her daughter again to the temple, and consecrate her there to the service of the holy place, as soon as her young reason should be able to distinguish good and evil. The father of Mary ratified this vow, which then became of obligation.*

When the ceremony was finished, the couple returned to their native province,—that province barren of great men, from which Israel was far from expecting a prophet,†—and re-entered their humble dwelling, ever open to the needy and the stranger. There it was that the child of benediction became, from her early years, the delight of her family, and rose up like one of those lilies of which Jesus proclaims the beauty, and which, as St. Bernard poetically says, have the odour of hope—*habens odorem spei.* According to the custom of the women of her nation, Ann would feed her daughter at her own breast.‡

Mary's reason, like the daylight of the favoured regions of the sun, had scarcely any twilight, and shone forth from the most tender age. Her precocious fervour, the wisdom of her discourse, at a period of life when other children enjoy as yet but a mere physical existence, led her parents to

* There were two sorts of vows among the Jews: the first, *neder*, was a simple vow, after which what had been vowed to the Lord might be redeemed (such was that of Ann, the mother of Mary); the second, *cherem*, was a vow of indispensable obligation, by which all right to the thing promised was given up absolutely and irrevocably. Every Israelite might thus vow what belonged to him,—houses, lands, beasts, children, slaves, &c.,—and the things devoted could neither be sold nor redeemed, at any price whatever.

† "Can any good come out of Nazareth?" asked Nathanael of those who spoke to him of Christ. "Because this place was small and contemptible," says St. John Chrysostom, "and not only this place, but the whole of Galilee."—(Serm. ix. in St. Matt.)

‡ In Judea, women did not often give up suckling their children; we reckon but three nurses in the whole Scripture—the nurses of Rebecca, Miphiboseth, and Joas; it must be observed, moreover, that Rebecca was a stranger, and that the others were princes.

judge that the hour of separation was come: and when Joachim had offered to the Lord, for the third time from the birth of his daughter, the first-fruits of the harvest, and produce of the small inheritance of his fathers, the pair, grateful and resigned, took the road to Jerusalem, to deposit, in the sacred enclosure of the temple, the treasure which the Holy One of Israel had given them.

CHAPTER IV.

THE PRESENTATION.

The Cison proudly rolled its red waters, swelled by the equinoctial storms,* and the great mountains of Galilee began to be covered with snow, when the parents of Mary began their journey to Jerusalem. We are ignorant of the motive which induced them to leave their native province during the rainy season. Perhaps it was the desire to assist at the great solemnities of the Dedication; perhaps they merely regulated their departure by the epoch of the service of Zachary, whose priestly functions called him to the temple only at regular times.†

* The Cison is a small river, which runs between Nazareth and Mount Carmel; insignificant and impoverished during the summer, like all the streams of water of Palestine, it becomes considerable during the rainy season. The troops of Sisara, the general of the army of Jabin, were drowned in this overflowed river in the attempt to force a passage.

† According to the order established by David, the priests were divided into twenty-four classes, or turns, each of which served its week. Each class was subdivided into seven parts, which had each their week in turn to officiate; each part of this subdivision had that portion of the service which was assigned to him by lot.—(1 Paralip. c. xxiv.) Zachary was of the turn or service of Abia.—(Prid., Hist. of the Jews.)

Obliged to make a journey of several days, during the inclement season, with a child quite young, the prudent and pious travellers did not make their way towards the holy city by the wild and rocky road which winds across the arid flats, the foaming torrents, and the deep ravines of the mountains of Samaria: there winter ruled with all his frosts. They descended, by the shrubby slopes of Carmel, into the charming and fertile plains which stretch out between the mountains of Palestine and the coasts of Syria, a land happy and forward, the temperature of which is so mild that the orange-trees blossom there in the heart of winter, and the flowers of May expand in the month of December.* After leaving behind them the rich pastures where formerly rose the tents of Issachar, a tribe of shepherd astronomers,† whom the burning breath of the Lord's anger had dispersed, like a handful of light straw, even to the wild and mountainous regions of Media;—after having admired, as they passed, the hills covered with palm, banana, and pomegranate-trees, which once formed the smiling inheritance of

* Volney saw orange-trees bearing fruit and flowers in the open air, in the month of January, on the coasts of Syria. "With us," he says, "nature has divided the seasons by months; there, one may say that they are separated only by hours. If we are annoyed at Tripoli by the heats of July, six hours' march transports us upon the neighbouring mountains to the temperature of March. On the other hand, are we incommoded with the frost of December, in the midst of the mountains, one day's march brings us back to the shore among the flowers of May."

† St. Jerom assures us that the children of Issachar were the learned men who calculated times, and set down the feasts.—(Hieron., Quæst. in 1 Paralip. 112, p. 1390, et in Genes. 49.) This tradition is conformable to that of the rabbins, who affirm that those of the tribe of Issachar applied themselves assiduously to this knowledge of astronomy. — (Maimon., in Kiddosch. hachodesh, et Zachuth, in Juchasin.) In fine, the Scripture authorises this tradition, since it relates that the children of Issachar were expert in the science of the times, so as to order what Israel should do.—(1 Paralip. xii. 32.)

the sons of Joseph—a fine and warlike race, famous for their skill in shooting with the bow;—the travellers from Galilee went along by the side of the narrow stream of the Gaas, the willows of which love the bank; passed through the groves of Ramatha, a beautiful town, like a cameo fallen into a basket of roses; and reached at length the borders of the ancient territory of the Jebusites. There the aspect of everything was changed: no more flowers, no more verdure, no more odoriferous breeze wafting afar the sweet scent of the lemon-tree; barren rocks, deep ravines where the wind forced its way with lugubrious moanings; abrupt and bare mountains, resounding with the hoarse cries of the eagle: in a word, the grandest, most melancholy, most desolate, and most sterile land that could be seen.

The little caravan had followed, for some time, a stony path tracked along the flat of an arid mountain, when Joachim, stopping on a sudden at an abrupt turn, stretched out his arms towards the south with a movement of religious enthusiasm mixed with national pride. The object which he thus pointed out to the notice of his companions was worth remarking, for nothing more magnificent or more extraordinary existed at that time in Asia. It was a city of thirty-three stadia in circumference, enclosed in stone, like a ruby of Beloutchistan; a town of marble, cedar, and gold, its splendour having something in it sad, wild, and suspicious, which denoted an uneasy authority, permanent fears of some foreign power, and a state of things full of contrasts. There were seen in it enormous towers, magnificent as palaces, and palaces fortified like citadels. Its temple, glittering with gold, which shone brilliantly upon the narrow flat surface of the highest of its mountains, like the orb of the full moon when it skirts the snowy summits of Libanus,*

* The exterior front of the temple was entirely covered with plates of gold, so thick that as soon as daylight appeared, it was as dazzling as the rays of the rising sun. As for the other sides, where there was

was a fortress almost impregnable, which kept the *holy people of the Lord* in awe; while the tower Antonia, from the top of its four elegant turrets of polished marble, kept an overshadowing and continued watch over the court of the temple. A triple enclosure of walls of enormous stones, in which were encrusted ninety forts, bound the sides of this city, which was surrounded by dark valleys of dizzying depths and rocks inaccessible. This proud and warlike city, which seemed to have been transported by magic from the fabulous regions of Ginnistan,† beneath the cloudless sky of Palestine; this paradise of the Jews (*Ghangh-dix-houcht*), so poetically regretted on the banks of the Euphrates; the city of David and of the Machabees; this Jerusalem, which, in its abject slavery, all the East still salutes with the antique name which the father of Mary then gave it—*el Cods!* (the Holy.)

The parents of the Virgin entered the capital of Judea by the gate of Rama, upon which fell the shadow of a tower,‡ so high that from its flat top were seen Mount Carmel, the Great Sea, and the Mountains of Arabia. The green standard of Judas Machabeus was still flying there with its

no gold, the stones of them were so white, that this superb mass of building looked at a distance like a mountain covered with snow.—(Josephus, de Bello, lib. v. c. 13.)

* "Extrema rupis abrupta; et turres, ubi mons juvisset, in sexaginta pedes, inter devexa, in centenos vicenosque attollebantur; mira specie, ac procul intuentibus pares."—(Tacit. Hist. lib. v.)

† Ginnistan, which the marvellous traditions of the Assyrians and Arabs place at the foot of Mount Caucasus, and on the borders of the Caspian Sea, was the abode of the Peris—a beautiful and fabulous race, which much resembles that of our fairies. These powerful beings, born before the deluge, disposed of the elements, and created everything that could afford them pleasure. Their capital city which they had carefully fortified, to defend it from the attacks of the Dives, who were wicked and formidable genii, was of marble, gold, rubies, and diamonds.

‡ The tower Psephina.

religious device; but the soldiers who surrounded it no longer understood it; for they were Thracians, Galatians, Germans, and the fair children of Gaul, whom Herod, who feared the Jews and depended upon foreigners, took into his pay, and who were detested at Jerusalem almost as much as himself.

The travellers next followed certain winding and gloomy streets, lined with heavy square houses, without windows, with terrace roofs, which stood in melancholy lines, like citadels; and they stopped in the eastern part of the city before a house of modest appearance, which tradition points out as the dwelling of St. Ann.*

After a purification of seven days, according to the custom of those who came to sacrifice in the temple,† Joachim provided himself with the lamb which he was to offer to the Lord, clothed himself in white,‡ collected together some of the relations and friends whom he had in Jerusalem, and ascended at the head of them to the temple *with as much ardour as he would have gone up to the assault of a place in battle.*§

* A monastery has been erected over this house of St. Ann; this monastery has been turned into a mosque. Under the Christian kings it was inhabited by religious women.—(See Itin. de Paris à Jérusalem, t. ii. p. 211.)

† It was not merely necessary to be presented in the temple with the victim: the law required that the person should remain outside for seven full days, and be solemnly purified on the third and seventh day with ashes and hyssop: that done, they might sacrifice.—(Philo, Tract. de Sacrific., c. 3.)

‡ According to the rabbins, the sacrifice was of no avail when he who offered it was not clothed in white garments.—(Basn., liv. ix. c. 4.)

§ This was of obligation; the Hebrews were to go up to the temple with as much ardour as *a soldier to an assault;* they found this pretext in the 55th Psalm, where David said that he went to the house of God as to a strong city. (See Basn., Hist. des Juifs, liv. vii. c. 17.)

This temple of the God of hosts, where the Virgin then presented herself, like the dove of the ark with the olive branch, had undergone numerous vicissitudes. One of the ancestors of Mary, the wise son of King David, had made it the wonder of the East. He had lavished about it the gold of Ophir, the perfumes of Saba, the cedar of Libanus, the brass which the fleets of Tyre—that queen of the seas, whose merchants were princes—had gone in quest of to barbarous regions, and silver, so common at that time that it had become of little value; but this splendour had passed away like a vision of the night, thanks to the burning avarice of the people of Egypt and Chaldea. Despoiled twenty times over, but always re-established with magnificence, it had risen again from its ruins under Zorobabel, who had rebuilt it, sword in hand, in spite of the efforts of a multitude of jealous nations. Nevertheless, the second temple, notwithstanding its unheard-of richness, was every way inferior to the other in grandeur as well as in holiness. It was in vain that the Jews poured out there with a liberal hand *the strength of the corn and the blood of the vine;* that streams of gold arriving from all points of the horizon came to feed incessantly its sacred treasury; that pagan kings, confessing the awful sanctity of the God of Israel, sent thither the most magnificent offerings.* Nothing of all this could supply for the absence of the ark, with which had disappeared the tables of the law—that is to say, the will of God, written by himself by the glare of the lightening on Mount Sinai; the

* In Josephus may be seen the detailed description of the magnificent table of massive gold incrusted with precious stones, and the no less splendid vessels which Ptolemy Philadelphus gave to the temple; almost all the princes of Asia had enriched it with their gifts, and about the time of the Presentation of the Virgin, the Empress Livia sent thither, in her own name and in the name of Augustus, magnificent vessels of gold.—(Josephus, de Bello, lib. ii. c. 17; Philo, ad Cajum.)

rod of the almond-tree which had miraculously blossomed; the most ancient title of the sons of Aaron to the office of high priesthood; and the manna of the desert, which, by the miracle of its long preservation, confirmed so many ancient prodigies wrought for the deliverance of Israel. These precious things were lost, as well as the sacred fire, which the breezes of the holy mountain alone could enkindle on the brazen grate of the altar of holocausts; and the oil of unction, composed by Moses, whence the priests and kings derived their noble title of the anointed of the Lord. What was still more to be regretted, was that the *Schekina*, that white cloud which attested the divine presence, had never shown itself in the second temple, and that even the stones of the *rational*, that last and brilliant oracle of the God of hosts, had lost their prophetic lustre.* This is what filled the hearts of the sons of Aaron with bitterness, when they compared the house of Zorobabel with the temple of the son of David; this made the doctors of the law say that the fulfilment of the celebrated prophecy of Aggeus was hopeless, unless the Messias himself should appear bodily in the second temple.

After passing that magnificent gate of Corinthian brass, which twenty Levites could hardly close at night, and which opened of itself four years before the destruction of Jerusalem, to the great consternation of the deicidal people whom this gloomy presage filled with terror,† Mary and her parents found themselves in a vast enclosure paved with black and white stones, and surrounded by tall porticoes, which in

* God employed the precious stones which the high priest wore upon the *rational* to foretell victory; for, before the army took the field, there shone forth from them so bright a light, that the people knew thereby that his sovereign Majesty was present, and ready to assist them; but when I began to write this, the *rational* had ceased to give this light for two hundred years.—(Fl. Joseph., Ant. Jud., lib. iii. c. 8.)

† Joseph., de Bello, lib. vi.

time of war served as ramparts.* A crowd of strangers and people of the nation, whose brilliant costumes of opposite colours reminded one of an immense parterre of tulips, were walking and conversing in this forum of Jerusalem, which was not reputed sacred, and which was called the Court of the Gentiles, because idolaters could not advance farther under pain of death.†

At some distance from the crowd, under the porch of Solomon, the haughty aristocracy of Israel, clothed in purple and scarlet, or wearing those long Babylonian robes embroidered with flowers of gold, were waiting for the hour of prayer, keeping aloof from the foreigners with a haughty reserve, considerably mingled with contempt. Joachim, who was equal to the princes of his nation in nobility of race, although he had not their wealth, directed his steps that way, sure of being well received; for those Jews, so disdainful towards the Gentiles,‡ loved each other as brethren, especially when they belonged to the same lineage. Scarcely had they perceived them, when a number of illustrous ladies, warriors, and great lords of the family of David advanced to meet them, and after the customary salutations, they joined the family from Galilee, as if to form an honourable train of attendants for Mary.§ The fathers who relate this circumstance, have piously believed that these great personages, the flower of the Jewish nobility, were not found there by mere chance, but that God, who would provide a triumphal

* Tacit., Historiarum, lib. v.

† Joseph., de Bello, lib. v. et vi.

‡ Basnage remarks that at the time of Jesus Christ the Jews regarded the Gentiles as dogs, and hated them mortally. "If the idolaters drown themselves, the doctors taught, they must not be pulled out of the water, nor succoured; the only favour that can be done them is not to plunge them deeper into the water, down the precipice, or in the well, if they have fallen in."—(Basn., liv. v. c. 25.)

§ "Primarios quoque Hierosolymitas viros et mulieres interfuisse huic deductioni, succinentibus universis angelis."—(Isid. de Thess.)

entry into his temple for the future Mother of the Messias, had divinely inspired them with the resolution to come thither.

From the midst of the Court of the Gentiles arose two other enclosures—both sacred—which composed the temple. Seen from below, this majestic and splendid edifice presented a quadrangular mass of building, the walls of which, white as alabaster, were pierced with ten superb gates, covered with thick plates of silver and gold. As the temple, properly so called, crowned the summit of Mount Moria,—a site appropriate for the habitation of the *God of the hills*, —the ground was a continued ascent, and the walls were completely surrounded by marble steps, which somewhat diminished their height.

After ascending the steps of the temple, the group already purified, in the midst of whom was that blessed child who was to be consecrated to God, stopped for a moment on the small platform of Chel.* There the Pharisees displayed their *tephilim*,† and wound round their foreheads, bowed down,‡ a lappet of their *taled*, of white and fine wool,§ ornamented with purple pomegranates, and little cords of the colour

* The *Chel*, was a space of ten cubits between the Court of the Gentiles and that of the women.

† The *tephilim* were small pieces of parchment on which were written, with ink made on purpose, four sentences of Scripture; the Jews wore them at the bend of the left arm, and in the middle of the forehead. These *tephilim* or *phylacteries*, were much in use at the time of Jesus Christ, for they made of them marks of distinction, which drew upon them his reproaches.—(Basnage, Hist. Juifs, liv. vii. c. 17.)

‡ The Pharisees walked always with their heads down, to affect a more humble countenance; and sometimes even with their eyes shut, to avoid seeing what might prove a temptation: thus it very often happened that in passing through the streets they ran their heads against the walls.—(Basn., liv. iii. c. 3.)

§ *Taled*, a sort of square cloak which the Jews wore in the temple to make their prayer; some wound it round their necks, others

of the hyacinth. The brave captains of Herod half concealed their shining cuirasses beneath their long mantles, and the daughters of Sion enveloped themselves more closely in the folds of their veils of purple, sky-blue, or Syrian gauze, with flowers of gold, out of respect for the holy angels who had the charge of guarding the sanctuary.* This done, they entered the temple by the oriental gate, the most beautiful of all,—that one which poured streams of liquid gold when the Romans, unable to force it by the aid of iron, opened it by means of fire.†

In our cold northern regions, vast edifices are requisite to protect us from the injuries of the weather; thus we have immense cathedrals, capable of containing whole populations; but in ancient Asia the temples were almost exclusively for the use of the priests: the people used to pray outside. In Israel the *engdah*, or sacred assembly, was usually held in the court of the women: the second division was so called because the Jewish women, whom the severity of the old law made like to slaves, could not advance farther. Separated from their children and their husbands, who remained in the area of the court, or under the arcades of the peristyle during the ceremonies of religion, they prayed separately in upper galleries, with their heads humbly bent towards the house of Jehovah, of which they could see at some distance the magnificent roof of cedar, bristling all over with pinnacles of gold.‡

covered their heads with it; this latter custom was the most general. —(Basn., t. v. liv. vii. c. 17.)

* Ideo debet mulier potestatem habere supra caput propter angelos. —(1 Ep. S. Pauli ad Corinth. ch. xi. v. 10.)

† Josephus relates, that when Titus ordered fire to be set to the gates of the second enclosure of the temple, the gold and silver ran down from them like water from a fountain.—(De Bello, c. 23.)

‡ This precaution had been taken in order to prevent the pigeons and doves, which were very numerous at Jerusalem, from resting in their flight on the roof of the temple, and defiling it.

The ceremony of the Presentation certainly took place in the court of the women, and not in the actual interior of the sanctuary, where some authors have located it. It began by a sacrifice. The gate of Nicanor, silently rolling on its brazen hinges to let the victim pass in, showed a perspective view of the farthest space, quite like a marvellous vision of that Eden so much regretted, whose golden palaces, overshadowed by lofty cedars, were the habitations of the Just, as the Pharisees taught.* Through the marble columns of a superb portico, from the top of which hung down the gigantic branches and pendant clusters of a golden vine, was discovered an edifice which seemed at first sight to be of massive gold, so strong was the glare which was cast by so many dazzling plates covering its *façade* of a hundred cubits beneath the pure and powerful light of the sun of Asia. An incredible number of votive offerings, where ears of wheat, lilies, pomegranates, vine-leaves formed of emeralds, topazes, carbuncles, and rubies, according to their colours, were intermingled, were fastened to the temple by golden cords; and when the rushing wind of the mountains began to blow, they might have been taken for real flowers, such was their exquisite workmanship and perfect imitation. At different distances were seen banners shot through with arrows, and stained with idolatrous blood, which the Asmonean princes, heroes of imperishable memory, had won from the Greeks of Syria in the glorious wars of independence, and consecrated with their priestly and warrior hands to the God of hosts. Herod, a cruel prince, but a valiant captain, had added to

* The Jews believed that the souls of the saints go into the garden of Eden, the entrance of which is forbidden to the living by the angel of death. They are magnificent in the description of this locality, where they place palaces built of precious stones, and rivers of perfumed waters. In hell, on the contrary, a river of fire falls upon the damned, who suffer the extremes of heat and cold.—(Maimonides, Menasses, &c.)

them the standards lately taken in his fortunate expeditions against the Arabs; and the sight of these trophies of arms filled with patriotic pride and warlike ardour those Hebrew hearts who cared so little for death, when they had to fight for what was dearer to them than gold, their families, or their life—the temple!

The priests and Levites assembled in the last compartment received from the hands of Joachim the victim of *prosperity.** These ministers of the living God had not their foreheads bound with laurel or green smallage, like the priests of the idols; a kind of mitre of a round shape, of very thick linen cloth, a linen tunic, long, white, and without folds, fastened with a broad girdle, embroidered with hyacinth and purple, composed the priestly costume, which was worn only in the temple. One of the priests took the lamb, and after a short invocation of the God of Jacob, slew it, turning its head towards the north; the blood, which flowed into a brazen vessel, was poured out here and there around the altar. When these first rites were terminated, the priest laid out upon a golden plate a portion of the flesh of the victim, still quivering, and part of the entrails, which the Levites had carefully washed in the fountain-court; he wrapped up the oblation in a double covering of fat, covered it with incense, threw upon it the salt of the covenant, then, ascending barefooted the gentle rise which led up to the platform of the brazen altar, he there deposited the offering upon the billets of wood, perfectly sound and stripped of their bark, which fed the sacred fire. The rest of the victim, except the breast and the right shoulder, which belonged to the priests, was returned to the husband of St. Ann, that he might make a feast with it for his friends and relatives, according to the custom.†

* Whether a favour was asked of God, or he was thanked for one obtained, it was called "a sacrifice of prosperity."

† This feast, reputed sacred, might be kept for two days together;

The last sounds of the trumpets of the priests were dying away along the porticoes, and the sacrifice was still burning on the brazen altar, when a priest came down into the court of the women to conclude the ceremonial. Ann, followed by Joachim, carrying Mary in her arms, came forward with a veil over her head, towards the minister of the Most High, and if we may believe an Arab tradition which Mahomet himself has recorded in the Koran, she presented to him the young handmaid of the Lord, saying, with a voice full of emotion, "I come to offer you the present which God has made me." *

The priest accepted, in the name of God, who makes the womb of mothers fruitful, the precious deposit which gratitude confided to him, and blessed Joachim, as well as his pious company; † then stretching out his hands over the assembly, which bowed down over the pontifical benediction, ‡ "O Israel," said he, "may the Lord direct his light

but the law expressly forbad anything to be reserved from it for the third day, and it must be given even to the last morsel to the poor, for two reasons, says Philo: the first, because, as the victim belonged to God, who is in his nature liberal, it was his will that the needy should partake of it; the second, to hinder avarice, *which is a vice of slaves*, from creeping in, and dishonouring a holy practice.—(Philo, Tract. de Sacrif. c. 2.)

* According to a Mahometan tradition, when St. Ann had given birth to the Blessed Virgin, she presented her to the priests, saying these words, which are also found in the Koran: "Dhouncon hadih alnedhirat," that is "Behold the offering which I make you." Hossein Vaëz adds to these words in his Persian paraphrase, "Kih es an Khodii," which means, "For it is a present which God has made me," or, still more literally, "For it is from this present that God is to come."—(D'Herbelot, Bibl. Orient. t. ii. p. 620.)

† Heli blessed Elcana and his wife, and he said to Elcana, "The Lord give thee seed of this woman, for the loan thou hast lent to the Lord. And they went to their own home."—(1 Kings i. 20.) See F. Croiset upon this ceremony.—(Exercises de Piété, t. xviii. p. 48.)

‡ While the pontiff gave the blessing, the people were obliged to place their hands over their eyes and hide their faces, because it was

towards thee—may he make thee to prosper in everything, and grant thee peace!" A canticle of thanksgiving, harmoniously accompanied by the harps of the priests, terminated the Presentation of the Virgin.

Such was the ceremony which took place, in the latter days of November, in the holy temple of Sion. Men, who usually stop at the surface, beheld nothing but a young child, very beautiful and wonderfully fervent, consecrated by her mother to that God who had granted her to her prayers and tears; but the angels of heaven, who hovered over the sanctuary, discovered in that weak and gentle creature the Virgin of Isaias, the spouse of whom Solomon had sung the mystical espousals, the celestial Eve who came to impart to a fallen race the hope of a glorious immortality. Penetrated with joy to see at length the aurora shine forth of the day of the Messias, "they united," say certain ancient authors,* "with this feast of earth, and covering the young descendant of David with their white wings, they scattered under her feet the odoriferous flowers of Paradise, and celebrated her entry into the temple with melodious concerts."

What passed then in the soul of Mary, in that soul sweetly expanded to the breath of the sanctifying Spirit, where all was peace, pure love, and light? By what sacred ties did she unite herself to HIM, who had preferred her to the virgins and queens of so many nations? This is a secret between herself and God; but we may reasonably believe that never was oblation more favourably received; and St. Evodius of Antioch, St. Epiphanius of Salamis, St. Andrew of Crete, and a multitude of Latin fathers, agree in considering the consecration of the Virgin as the most pleasing act

not lawful to behold the hands of the priest: the Jews imagined that God was behind the pontiff, and looked upon them through his outstretched hands; they did not dare to lift up their eyes to him, "for no one can see God and live."—(Basn., liv. vii. c. 15.)

* St. Andrew of Crete, and St. George of Nicomedia.

of religion in the sight of God which man had hitherto performed.

The name of the priest who received the Blessed Virgin among the number of daughters of the Lord is not known; St. Germanus, patriarch of Constantinople, and George of Nicomedia, incline to the belief that it was the father of St. John the Baptist: the ties of relationship which connected Zachary with the family of Joachim, the high rank which he then occupied in the priesthood,* and the tender affection which Mary cherished for him and for Elizabeth, impart to this supposition a high degree of probability.

Be this as it may, the blessed daughter of Joachim was solemnly admitted into the number of the *almas*, or young virgins, who were brought up under the sacred shadow of the altar.

That Mary spent her best years in the temple is proved by apostolic tradition, by the writings of the fathers, and the opinion of the Church, who is not used to sanction doubtful facts;† nevertheless, certain heretics have allowed themselves to treat this circumstance as fabulous, and some Catholic authors themselves have considered it an obscure

* The Jews believed that St. John Baptist was much greater than Jesus Christ, because he was the son of a *high priest*.—(St. J. Chrysost., Serm. 12, in Matt.)

† In 1373, Philip de Maziere, a French nobleman, chancellor of the King of Cyprus, came to the court of Charles V., and related to him that in the East, where he had lived a long time, the Feast of the Presentation of the Blessed Virgin was annually celebrated, in memory of her having been presented in the temple at the age of three years. Philip added, "I reflected that this great feast was not known in the Western church, and when I was ambassador from the King of Cyprus to the pope, I spoke to him about this festival, and presented him the office of it; he had it carefully examined by the cardinals, prelates, and doctors of theology, and permitted the feast to be celebrated." The Greeks kept it early under the title of the "Entrance of the Blessed Virgin into the Temple:" mention is made of it in their most ancient martyrologies.

point, concealed beneath the veil of olden times, which it was very difficult to clear up. The denials of the former surprise us but little, but the circumspection of the others is strange indeed; for if ever a Christian tradition possessed a character of authenticity it is this. St. Evodius, who was the first to relate, in an epistle entitled *Lumen*, which Nicephorus has preserved for us, this glorious circumstance of the infancy of the Virgin, flourished at the very time of the apostles and of the Mother of God. He was Bishop of Antioch, a town of Syria, to which both Jews and Christians resorted; and the temple where the newly-formed faithful followed, with profound veneration, the traces of the Son of God and his divine Mother, still subsisted in all its glory. This tradition, which came from the church of Jerusalem,—a church composed of the first disciples of Jesus Christ, among whom were found a number of relatives of the Virgin and of St. Joseph,—was consecrated very early by a religious memorial; a demonstrative proof in the eyes of Protestants themselves.* In fine, the greater number of the fathers,† and especially St. Jerom, who lived in the midst of the sites of our redemption, and where the traditions were yet recent, have recorded it, and held it to be true. This traditionary belief may therefore be ranked in the number of the best established facts of history.

* Gibbon himself could not help acknowledging the authenticity of the religious traditions in Palestine. "They (the Christians) fixed, by *unquestionable* tradition, the scene of each memorable event" (c. xxiii.): an avowal of considerable weight in the mouth of a writer so well informed as the English historian, and a man at the same time so little disposed in favour of religion. According to M. de Chateaubriand, if there is anything well proved upon earth, it is the authenticity of the Christian traditions at Jerusalem.

† St. Epiphanius, St. Gregory of Nyssa, St. Gregory of Nazianzum, St. Germanus, patriarch of Constantinople, George of Nicomedia, St John Damascen, &c.

CHAPTER V.

MARY IN THE TEMPLE.

In the fortified enclosure of the temple, on that site where the Christians erected an oratory, of which the companions in arms of Godfrey made a church with a gilded cupola, under the invocation of the Blessed Mary,* which the brave Knights Templars often took delight in ornamenting with spoils of the Saracens, arose that part of the religious edifice which had been consecrated to the virgins who were dedicated to the Lord: it was thither that Zachary led his young relative.†

* The mosque of Omar (*el Aksa*) represents to the Christians the ancient temple of Solomon; *el Sakhra* (the rock) is built on the place where Mary lived from the age of three years till her espousal with Joseph. This place was at that time an appendage to the temple of Solomon, as *el Sakhra* is now to the mosque of Omar. Before the crusades, *el Sakhra* was only a chapel; the Franks added to it a church, which they surmounted with a gilt cupola. When the conquerors threw down the great cross which glittered on the cupola of the *Sakhra*, the cries of joy of the Mussulmans, and the cries of grief of the Christians, were so great, says an Arab author, that it seemed as if the world was going to be destroyed.—(Correspondance d'Orient, t. v.) According to Schonah, there arose a great tumult in the city, which Saladin was obliged to suppress in person.

† St. Germanus affirms that it was Zachary who undertook to place the Virgin in the temple. The Arab traditions relate, in like manner, that God gave the Virgin in charge to Zachary, *ouacafalha Zacharia*. The Koran, in the *Surate* which treats of the family of Amram, adds to this fact a marvellous legend picked up among the Christian tribes in the desert. It says that Zachary, who went from time to time to visit his young relative, never did so without finding near her a quantity of the finest fruits of the Holy Land, and always out of season, which obliged him at length to inquire of Mary whence all these fine fruits came. Mary answered, "*Hou men and Allah ïarzoe*

Although virginity in Israel was only a temporary virtue, and had soon to give place to conjugal virtues, it was not without privileges and without honour. Jehovah loved the prayers of chaste children, of pure virgins; and it was a virgin, and not a queen, whom he had chosen to bring about the redemption of the human race. Thus, when the *seers* of Juda unfolded to the elect, but oft chastised people, the prophetic picture of their miseries, or their victories, they always introduced in it a virgin, either smiling or in tears, to personify provinces and cities. In the wars of extermination, in which the broadsword of the Hebrews cut down the women, children, and old men of Moab, the virgins were spared; and the high priest, who was forbidden by a severe law to pay funeral honours to the friend *whom he loved as his own soul*, and even to the prince of his people, might assist without being defiled at the funeral of his sister if she had died a virgin.*

The virgins, or *almas*, took part in the ceremonies of the Hebrew worship before that worship had a temple. We see them, under the guidance of Mary, the sister of Moses, celebrate with dances and canticles the passage of the Red Sea.† These dancing choirs of young women, transplanted from Egypt into the desert, continued a long time among the Hebrews. The virgins of Silo, who seem to have been, in the time of the Judges, more especially consecrated to the service of Adonai than the other daughters of Israel, were dancing to the song of canticles and the sound of harps, at a short distance from the holy place, during a feast of the

man ïascha begaïr hissa," (All that you see comes from God, who provides what he pleases, without count or number.)—(D'Herbelot, Bibliothèque Orientale, t. ii. art. Miriam.)

* Levit. xxi. 3.

† Mary and *her young companions* (les almas) sung canticles at the passage of the Red Sea, accompanying themselves with timbrels.—(R. sal Yarhhi. Exod. xv.)

Lord, when the Benjaminites carried them off. This serious event did not put an end to this custom, which ceased only at the disastrous epoch when the ark was lost and the first temple destroyed.*

All the *almas* were probably admissible to these sacred choirs, when their reputation was not tarnished with any stain; but among them a chosen portion are distinguished, who are grouped about the altar, with greater fervour and perseverance. While the ark of God was still encamped in tents, *the women who watched and prayed at the door of the tabernacle* offered to God the brazen mirrors which they had brought from Egypt. They were doubtless pious widows, who had refused to form new engagements in order to attend more uninterruptedly to heavenly things, and *almas* devoted by their parents to the service of the sanctuary, who had been placed under the protection of these virtuous women. St. Jerom thus understands this passage of Exodus.

As the vow of parents could generally be redeemed, and as the redemption, fixed at a moderate sum,† was always effected at the end of a few years,‡ these temporary vows

* These sacred dances, which brought to mind the passage of the Red Sea, and which were accompanied with hymns of praise, were considered among the Jews as a practice of so great piety, that we find them even among the severe therapeuts. "The sacred dance of the devout therapeuts," says Philo, "was composed of two choirs, one of men, the other of women,—the union of both was very harmonious and real music, because nothing was heard but very fine words, and the grave and decorous dancers had no other object than the honour and service of the God of Israel."—(Philo, de Vita cont.)

† Moses had fixed the ransom of this vow, by an express law, at a sum of fifty sicles at most. The sicle of silver weighed four Attic drachms, and was worth about fifteen pence of English money.

‡ The children, in this sort of bondage, retained their rights to the paternal inheritance, and could ransom themselves, if their parents did not redeem them.—(L'Abbé Guenée.) Josephus (Ant. lib. iv.) remarks that men and women who, after consecrating themselves voluntarily to the ministery, wished to break their vows. paid to the

were called a loan made to the Lord.* "I have lent him to the Lord," said Anna, when she took her little Samuel to Silo.†

After the return from the captivity, the influence of the Persians, who banished women from their religious solemnities,‡ told upon the institution of the *almas;* they ceased to form, in some degree, a body in the state, and to take an ostensible part in the ceremonies of worship. Under the pontiff kings, they lived in seclusion, and their days passed in so profound a retreat, that when they ran in dismay to the high priest Onias, at the time when the sacrilegious attempt of Heliodorus threw all Jerusalem into commotion, the Jewish historians considered the fact so unusual and wonderful that they recorded it in their annals.§

There were then, whatever some may have said, certain virgins attached to the service of the second temple at the time of the presentation of Mary; the institutions of the primitive Christians attest it,|| and St. Ambrose, St. Jerom, and before them the proto-gospel of St. James, have affirmed

priests a certain sum, and that those who were unable to pay placed themselves at the discretion of the priest.

* F. Croiset, Exerc. de Piété.

† Id circo et ego commodavi eum Domino.

‡ At Bombay, the descendants of the Persians have a temple consecrated to fire. They come in crowds upon the platform, with their brilliant white costumes and coloured turbans, to salute the rising of the sun, or to offer their homage to his last rays, by humbly prostrating before him. Their wives do not appear at that time; it is the hour when they go to fetch water from the wells.—(Buckingham, Picture of India.)

§ Macch. i. 2.

|| It is known that the primitive Christians, particularly those of Jerusalem, who were of Hebrew origin, preserved some institutions of the old law; of this number was that of virgins and widows, who are found attached to the primitive churches to exercise various good works in use by the sex.—(See Fleury, Mœurs des Israelites et des Chrétiens, p. 115.)

it. But what passed during the abode of the Virgin in the temple? What were, at this interesting time of her life, her tastes, her habits, her practices of devotion? On this subject, there remain but few authentic documents. A traditionary life of the Mother of God, which St. Epiphanius, who lived in 390, considered then as very ancient, no doubt entered into those details, but it is lost. The gospel of the infancy of the Virgin, and of St. Jerom, though both inform us of the admission of Mary among the daughters of the Lord, confine their indications almost entirely to this fact. To fill up this vacant space of a history which God seems to have been pleased to envelop in clouds, we have nothing more than a few uncertain lines, some mutilated pages of the fathers, of which it is difficult, even by putting them carefully together in order, to make a satisfactory outline. No matter; like the Indian artisan, who joins together a broken piece of cloth, thread by thread, and who patiently endeavours to join the ends again by unravelling, tying together, and letting his shuttle glide with infinite precautions along this woof, worn out and easily broken, we shall apply laboriously to the work, and collect together the scattered shreds of the precious web of the life of the Virgin, to reunite the tissue, if it be practicable. With the persevering patience of Banian, we shall endeavour, not to make up a conjectural affair, which our profound respect for our subject would forbid, but to give, by the help of the best authorities and a long study of the manners of the Hebrews, the most precise idea, and that approaching as near as possible to the truth, of the almost cloistered life of Mary in the temple.

Some old legendary writers have delighted in surrounding the early childhood of the Virgin with a number of prodigies: we pass over in silence these marvellous events, which are not sufficiently proved; but what we ought to call attention to, is an inaccurate assertion, or rather an inadmissible one, which has been adopted confidently and without examination by some holy personages and religious writers.* From the Virgin's having always been sanctity itself, which no one disputes, it has been inferred that she must have been placed in the most sanctified part of the temple, that is, in the HOLY of HOLIES, which is materially untrue. The HOLY of HOLIES, *that* impenetrable sanctuary of the God of hosts, was closed against the whole of the Hebrew priesthood, except the high priest, who went into it only once a year, after a number of fasts, vigils, and purifications. He did not present himself there without being enveloped in a thick cloud of perfumes, which interposed between him and the Divinity, "whom no mortal could see without dying," says the Scripture; in fine, he remained there only a few minutes, during which the people, prostrate with their faces to the ground, uttered loud sighs, for fear that he should there die. He himself afterwards gave a great feast to his friends, to rejoice with them for having escaped a danger so pressing and formidable.†

After this, let any one judge if it be possible that Mary was brought up in the HOLY of HOLIES!

The local traditions of Jerusalem protest no less loudly than common sense against this opinion, thrown out at hazard: the *Sakhra*, which was originally a Christian church, built on the site of the apartments of the Virgin, is a distinct appendage of the mosque of Omar, and is not enclosed within that edifice; yet the mosque of Omar is built on the very place where the temple stood.

F. Croiset, in his Exercises de Piété, has not adopted this opinion; but, unwilling to reject it altogether, he has attempted a sort of compromise. According to him, the Mother of God was not brought up in the HOLY of HOLIES, but the priests, struck with her admirable virtues, permitted

* St. Andrew of Crete, George of Nicomedia, &c.

† Prideaux. Basnage, Histoire des Juifs, liv. v. c. 16.

her to go and pray there from time to time. The Jesuit father has forgotten several things in adopting this *mezzo-termine*: first, that woman, among the Hebrews, was a being reputed unclean, likened to a slave, and hardly bound to pray at all;* one who was banished to an enclosure which she could not pass beyond, and that the interior of the temple was a forbidden place to her, even if she were a prophetess or the daughter of a king. Secondly, that the priests could not grant to Mary a privilege which they did not enjoy themselves, and that, moreover, it would have been exposing her to certain death.† Lastly, even supposing none of these prejudices and fears to have existed among the priests of Jehovah, they would not have suffered any one, on any account, to go into the HOLY of HOLIES, considering that it was important to withhold from the people the knowledge of the disappearance of the ark, which had been lost in

* The impurity of the woman, according to the Rabbins, dates from the seduction of Eve by the serpent, and cannot be expiated but at the coming of their Messias. Prayer is not so obligatory upon her as upon man; she is not even bound to the greater part of the positive *commandments*; in fine, the Jews still say, in their morning prayer, "Blessed be thou, O Lord, King of the universe, for not having made me be born a woman." The woman in her humiliation says, on her part, with sorrowful resignation, "Blessed be thou, O Lord, who hast made me what thou hast pleased."—(Basnage, Hist. des Juifs, liv. vii. c. 10, p. 169.)

† "The sanctuary is a place so holy," says Philo, "that there is no one among us but the high priest alone who is allowed to enter it, and that only once in the year, after a solemn fast, to burn perfumes there in honour of God, and humbly to beg of him that this year may be happy to all mankind. If any one, not only of the common people of our nation, but even one of the chief priests, dared to go in thither, or if the high priest himself went in twice a year, or more than once on the day when he is allowed to do so, it would cost him his life, without any possibility of saving him, so strictly has Moses, our legislator, commanded us to reverence this place and render it inaccessible."—(Philo, ad Cadjum, c. 16.)

some obscure cavern of the mountains of Judea ever since the days of Jeremias.*

This second version, therefore, is no more admissible than the first.

The education which Mary received in the temple was as carefully provided as was compatible with the knowledge of the time and the manners of the Hebrews; it turned principally on domestic work, from which the wife and daughter of Augustus Cæsar did not think themselves exempt in their imperial palace, and in the midst of the luxuries of Rome.† Brought up in the strict observance of the laws of Moses, and conforming to the customs of her nation, Mary rosè at the song of the bird, at the hour "when the bad angels are silent, and when prayers are heard most favourably." ‡ She dressed herself with extreme decency, out of respect for the glory of God, who penetrates everywhere, and beholds the actions of man, even in the darkest night; then she thanked the Lord for having added another day to her days, and having preserved her during her sleep from the snares of the evil spirit.§ Her toilet was not long, and there was no refinement about it; she wore neither pearl bracelets nor gold chains "inlaid with silver," nor purple tunics, like the daughters of the princes of her race. A robe of hyacinth blue, of soft and velvet-like appearance, like that flower of

* The Jews are not agreed as to the fate of the ark after the ruin of their first people: some will have it that Jeremias hid it in a cavern in the mountains, the entrance to which it had never been possible to find again; others say that the holy King Josias, admonished by Holda, the prophetess, that the temple would be destroyed soon after his death, had this precious deposit placed in a subterranean vault which Solomon had had constructed.

† Augustus never wore any other garments but those woven by his wife or his daughter; and Alexander the Great, by his mother and his sisters.

‡ Basnage, liv. vii. c. xvii. p. 309.

§ Basnage, *loco citato*

the field—a white tunic confined by a plain girdle, with the ends hanging free—a long veil with its folds inartificially but gracefully arranged, and so formed as quickly and completely to cover the face—and, lastly, shoes to match the robe, composed the oriental costume of Mary.*

After the customary ablutions, the Virgin, her companions, and the pious women who were responsible to the priests and to God for this sacred deposit, proceeded to the tribune surrounded with balconies,† where the *almas* seated themselves in the place of honour.‡ The sun was beginning to gild with his early rays the distant mountains of Arabia, the eagle was soaring in the cloud, the sacrifice burned upon the brazen altar to the sound of the morning trumpets, and Mary, with her head bowed down under her veil, after repeating the eighteen prayers of Esdras, besought of God, with all Israel, the Christ so long promised to the earth, and

* The Annunciades of Genoa wore in the sixteenth century the costume of the Blessed Virgin, that is to say, *white below, and sky blue above, that such a habit might cause a continual remembrance of her. The slippers of the choir nuns in like manner are covered with leather of sky-blue colour.*—(Rule of the Annunciades of Genoa, c. 2.) M. de Lamartine found in those Eastern regions, where everything seems unchangeable, the costume of Mary in that of the women of Nazareth. "They wear," says the traveller poet, "a long tunic of sky-blue, fastened by a white girdle, the ends of which hang down to the ground; the full folds of a white tunic gracefully fall over the blue." M. D. Lamartine traces back this costume to the times of Abraham and Isaac, and there is nothing improbable in this supposition. We see but a very slight difference between the costumes adopted in the sixteenth century from the traditions of Italy, and that which the French traveller found in the very places themselves.

† In the feast of the drawing of the waters, the men were placed above the galleries, which went all round the peristyle of the women.

‡ Origen, St. Basil, St. Gregory of Nyssa, and St. Cyril have preserved to us the tradition which assigns to the virgins of the temple an honourable and separate place in the peristyle of the women

so slow to come. "O God! may thy name be glorified and sanctified in this world, which thou hast created according to thy good pleasure; *let thy kingdom come:* may redemption flourish, and may the Messias come speedily."*

And the people answered in chorus, "Amen! amen!" Then they sung the concluding verses of that beautiful psalm attributed to the prophets Aggeus and Zacharias:—

"The Lord looseth them that are fettered: the Lord enlighteneth the blind.

"The Lord lifteth up them that are cast down; the Lord loveth the just.

"The Lord keepeth the strangers: he will support the fatherless and the widow; and the ways of sinners he will destroy.

"The Lord shall reign for ever: thy God, O Sion, unto generation and generation."†

The reading of the *schema*‡ and the blessing of the priest concluded this public prayer, which was made at night and morning.§

* This prayer, which is called *Kaddisch,* is the most ancient of all those which the Jews have preserved, and as it is read in the Chaldaic tongue, it is believed to be one of the prayers which had been made after the return from Babylon.—(Basn., liv. vii. c. 17, p. 314.) Prideaux affirms that it was used long before our Lord's time, and that the apostles often offered it with the people in the synagogues. It was recited often in the service, and the assembly were obliged to answer *Amen* several times.

† Leo of Modena. Maimonides.

‡ Leo of Modena, c. 11, p. 29. By the *schema* is understood three different sections of Deuteronomy and Numbers. It is a kind of profession of faith which is recited night and morning, by which they confess that there is but one God, who delivered his people out of Egypt.

§ It is certain that the Blessed Virgin must have assisted very often at the public prayers of morning and evening: these prayers were considered more efficacious than others, and there are even Hebrew doctors who maintain that God hears none but these.

After fulfilling this first religious duty with indescribable fervour, Mary and her young companions resumed their accustomed occupations. Some turned swiftly with their active fingers spindles of cedar or ithel,* others worked in purple, hyacinth, and gold upon the veil of the temple, or the rich girdles of the priests; while groups, bending forward over a Sidonian loom, were employed in executing the varied designs of that magnificent tapestry for which the valiant women deserved the praises of all Israel, and which Homer himself has extolled.† The Virgin surpassed all the daughters of her people in these beautiful works, so highly appreciated by the ancients. St. Epiphanius informs us that she excelled in embroidery and in the art of working in wool, fine linen, and gold; ‡ the Proto-Gospel of St. James exhibits her to us seated before a spindle of wool dyed purple, which turned round under her light hands like the quivering leaf of the aspen-tree; § and the Christians of the East have perpetuated the traditionary opinion of her unrivalled skill in spinning the flax of Pelusium,|| by giving the name of the *Virgin's thread* to those webs of dazzling whiteness, and

* The *ithel* is a species of acacia. which grows in Arabia; it is of a fine black, and resembles ebony: it is thought to be the setim wood of Moses.

† See the Iliad, lib. vi.

‡ In the middle ages, in memory of the Virgin working in linen, the weavers had placed themselves under the banner of the Annunciation. The manufacturers of gold brocade and silk stuffs had for their patroness *Our Lady the Rich*, and bore her image on their banner, heavy with magnificent embroidery.—(Alex. Monteil, Hist. des Français des divers états.

§ The church of Jerusalem had early consecrated this memorial by numbering among its treasures the spindles of Mary. These spindles were sent afterwards to the Empress Pulcheria, who placed them in the church of Hodegos, at Constantinople.

|| The vestments which the high priests wore in the morning were, says the Misnah, of fine linen of Pelusium, a town of Egypt, where the flax was exquisite.

texture almost vaporous, which hover over the deep valleys in the damp mornings of autumn. The serious and pure wives of the first faithful, in remembrance of these domestic occupations, which the Queen of angels did not disdain, never failed to consecrate to her a distaff surrounded with little bands of purple, and supplied with spotless wool.*

But the talents and knowledge of the Virgin were not confined to this. St. Ambrose attributes to her a perfect understanding of the sacred books, and St. Anselm maintains that she knew perfectly that ancient Hebrew, the language of the terrestrial Paradise,† in which God traced with his potent finger, *on very thick precious stones,*‡ the ten precepts of the Decalogue. Whether Mary, by studying the idiom of Anna and Debora, had been initiated, during her solitary vigils, in the sublime conceptions of the *seers* of Israel, or whether she received from that sanctifying spirit, who had so richly endowed her, a breath of poetical inspiration similar to those harmonious breezes which lightly touched the Eolian harp of King David,§ still we cannot deny that the young prophetess, who gave to the new law its most beautiful canticle, must have known the sweetest and most sublime inspirations of

* This custom still exists in some villages of the north and west of France.

† According to the rabbins and commentators on the Bible, the language of the terrestrial Paradise was the ancient Hebrew.

‡ Hebrew tradition.—(Basn., liv. vi. c. 16.) According to some oriental authors, the tables of the law were of red rubies or carbuncles; but the most common opinion among the Arabs and Mussulmans is that they were emeralds, in the inside of which the characters were so cut as to be legible on every side.—(D'Herbelot, Bibliothèque Orientale, t. ii.)

§ According to an ancient Jewish tradition, David had a harp which played at night when a *particular breeze* blew. Basnage ridiculed these strings which sound of themselves at the night breeze, and openly treats this assertion as an *absurdity*. The invention, or rather the re-discovery of the Eolian harps, the magic sounds of which enchant the parks of the English, has justified the rabbins.

genius. Certainly, the woman who composed the *Magnificat* was no young girl of the ignorant common people, as some Protestant authors have not been afraid to say, and she combined with unequalled sanctity talents of the highest order. Nevertheless, this brilliant side of her intelligence was hardly perceived, so adroit was she in concealing it beneath her evangelical modesty. Knowing the delicate duties and true interests of her sex, she avoided display with extreme care, and passed along without noise, like a silent star, that pursues its course through the clouds. The rich treasures of her mind and heart have been but rarely and imperfectly revealed to the earth; they were the roses of Yemen, which the young Arab girl conceals beneath her veil, and the softened perfume of which is hardly perceived.

An ancient poet said with servility of Augustus that he was himself the work of several ages, and that, since the days of the creation, all the industry of nature had been put in request to produce him. What was an hyperbole carried to an absurd length in speaking of the sanguinary nephew of Cæsar, becomes a truth demonstrated when applied to the Virgin. Mary is the masterpiece of nature, the flower of the old generations, and the wonder of ages. Never had the earth seen, never will the earth see, so many perfections combined in a simple daughter of men. All was grace, holiness, grandeur in this blessed creature: conceived in the friendship of God, sanctified before her birth, she knew not those passions which disorder the soul, and sin which corrupts the heart. Attracted towards good by a sweet and natural inclination, by favour of her immaculate conception, her pure and innocent actions were like those coats of snow which are silently heaped upon the lofty summits of the mountains, adding purity to purity, and whiteness to whiteness, till a dazzling cone is raised, on which the light darts playfully, and which forces man to turn away his eyes, like the sun. It has not been given to any second creature to present such a life to the sovereign Judge of men; Jesus Christ alone surpassed her,—but Jesus Christ is the Son of God.

Mary entered the temple of God, like one of those spotless victims which the Spirit of the Lord had shown to Malachy. Beautiful, young, nobly born, and qualified to aspire to every position among a people who often placed beauty upon the throne,* she attached herself to the corners of the altar by a vow of virginity. By this vow, unheard of before, Mary *broke down the fence* which separated the old law from the new, and plunged so deeply *into the sea of the evangelical virtues*, that it might be said that she had already sounded almost all its depths when her divine Son came to reveal it to the children of men.

God does not change his ways abruptly; he announces, he prepares long before, the great events which are to change the face of the earth: a precursor was needed for the Messias, and he found him in the person of St. John the Baptist; a preliminary was requisite to the new law, and the virtues of Mary were to the gospel what a cool and cheerful dawn is to a fine day.

St. Epiphanius, quoted by Nicephorus, has left us a charming portrait of the Virgin; this portrait, sketched in the fourth century, from traditions now effaced, and manuscripts which we no longer possess, is the only one which has come down to us.

The Virgin, according to this bishop, was not tall of stature, though her height was a little above the middle size; her colour, slightly darkened, like that of the Sulamite, by the sun of her country, had the rich tint of ripe ears

* "It is neither climate, nor diet, nor bodily exercise which forms the beauty of the human form; it is the moral sentiment of virtue, which cannot subsist without religion. Beauty of countenance is the true physiognomy of the soul."—(Bernardin de Saint Pierre, Etudes de la Nature, étude 10.)

of corn; her hair was light, her eyes lively, the pupil being rather of an olive colour, her eyebrows perfectly arched, and of the finest black; her nose, remarkably perfect, was aquiline; her lips rosy; the shape of her face a fine oval; her hands and fingers long.

All the fathers eagerly attest, with one accord, the admirable beauty of the Virgin; St. Denis the Areopagite, who had seen the divine Mary, assures us that *she was a dazzling beauty, and that he should have adored her as a goddess, if he had not known that there is but one God.*

But it was not to this assemblage of natural perfections that Mary owed the power of her beauty; it emanated from a higher source. St. Ambrose understood it well, when he said that this attractive covering was but a transparent veil which let all the virtues be seen through it, and that her soul, the most noble and purest that ever was, next to the soul of Jesus Christ, was entirely revealed in her look. The natural beauty of Mary was but the remote reflexion of her intellectual and imperishable beauties: she was the most beautiful of women, because she was the most chaste and most holy of the daughters of Eve.*

God has made a palace of pearl-coloured shell for the pearl of the Green Sea;† but it is the pearl, and not its brilliant shell, which is set in gold, and with which the diadems of kings are incrusted. The fathers were not here mistaken; and accordingly, in what they have left us about the person of Mary, they have devotèd a considerable part to moral

* We know that David, Solomon, and the other kings of Juda, often placed upon their royal couch women of obscure condition; the celebrated Sulamite of Solomon was, it is said, a young country girl of the little village of Sulam, situated at a short distance from Jerusalem. In the time of Mary, Herod the Great had espoused Marianne, the daughter of a plain sacrificing priest, on account of her beauty.

† *Bahr-al-Akhdhar*, a name of the Persian Gulf.

beauties,—the only ones which are not the food of worms. We are about to collect the little precious stones which they have scattered over their writings, to compose with them a mosaic which may exhibit a second portrait of her who was, says St. Sophronius, "the garden of pleasure of the Lord."*

The greatest propriety reigned in all the actions of the Virgin; she was good, affable, compassionate, and never tired of hearing the long complaints of the afflicted. She spoke little, always to the purpose, and never did an untruth defile her lips. Her voice was sweet, penetrating, and her words had something unctuous and consoling, which shed calm over the soul. She was the first in watchings, the most exact in fulfilling the divine law, the most profound in humility, the most perfect in every virtue. She was never seen in anger; she never offended, afflicted, or railed at any one. She was an enemy to pomp, simple in her attire, simple in her manners, and never had a thought of displaying her beauty, her ancient nobility, or the rich treasures of her mind and heart. Her presence seemed to sanctify all around it, and the sight of her banished the thought of the things of earth. Her politeness was no vain formality, made up of words of falsehood: it was an expansion of universal benevolence which came from the soul. In fine, her look already discovered the Mother of mercy—the Virgin of whom it has since been said: "She would ask of God forgiveness even for Lucifer, if Lucifer himself asked for forgiveness."

Though very scantily provided with riches, Mary was liberal to the poor, and her young maiden alms often dropped unperceived into that chest which was fixed to one of the columns of the peristyle, into which Jesus at a later period saw the widow's mite fall. St. Ambrose makes known to us the pure and sacred source from which Mary derived her alms; she deprived herself of everything, granting only to

* "Vere Virgo erat hortus deliciarum in quo consita sunt universa florum genera et odoramenta virtutum."—(Sophron., Serm. de Ass.)

nature what she could not withhold from it without dying, and seemed to live, like the grasshoppers, upon air and dew.* Her fasts, which were frequent and rigorous, were in like manner beneficial to the poor. But the fasts of the Blessed Virgin were not like our fasts in the north, which last only for a morning, and are confined to the privation of certain kinds of food; they were an abstinence from everything, which began in the evening at sunset, and ended the next day at the rising of the stars.† All this time Mary denied herself all that could gratify her taste and her heart; she imposed upon herself the hardest work, the most disagreeable works of mercy, put on her poorest garments, slept on the ground, and did not allow herself, during these days of mortification and tears, which were often prolonged for weeks together, anything but a slender repast, composed of bread baked in the embers, bitter herbs, and a cup of water from the fountain of Siloe.‡ Her meditations were frequent, and her prayer so recollected, so attentive, so profound, that her soul seemed to dissolve in adoration before the Eternal.

* The ancients believed that grasshoppers lived on air and dew.—(Philo, de Vita cont., p. 831.) Homer, in the third book of the Iliad:—

. . . . *Τεττίγεσσι ἐοικότες ὅιτε καθ' ὑλῆν*
Δενδρέω ἐφεζόμενοι ὅπα λειριόεσσαν ἱεῖσι.

"Like grasshoppers, which, perched upon the trees, send forth a sweet sound, after sipping a little dew." "Grasshoppers feed only on dew."—(Theocritus, Idyl 4: —*μή πρῶκας σιτίζεται ὅσπηρ ὁ τέττιξ*;) "Does he not feed on dew, like the grasshopper?" And Virgil:—

"Dum thymo pascentur apes, dum rore cicadæ."

"While bees are fed on thyme, while grasshoppers on dew."

On this account Callimachus has called dew *πρώϊον τέττιγος εἶδαρ* "the food of the grasshopper."

† The Jews did not consider that day as a fast on which the sun did not set.

‡ Basnage, liv. vii. c. 18; Fleury, Mœurs des Israelites, p. 104.

The roaring of the tempest and the noise of the thunder, which used to make Cæsar take refuge in the subterranean vaults of his palace,* did not reach the ear of the young girl; completely absorbed in her religious duties, her soul was at the feet of the great Author of the universe, beyond the limits of the world and the region of storms. "Never," says St. Ambrose, "was any one gifted with a more sublime gift of contemplation; her mind, always in agreement with her heart, never lost sight of HIM, whom she loved more ardently than all the seraphim together; her whole life was but one continual exercise of the purest love of her God, and when the sun came to weigh down her eyelids, her heart still watched and prayed." †

Such were the virtues, such were the occupations of Mary in the temple; she shone there among her youthful companions like a rich diamond, which, set among other precious stones, eclipses them all by its brilliancy. Thus it happened that old men who had grown grey in the priesthood never passed by her without blessing her, and considered her as the richest ornament of the holy house.

CHAPTER VI.

MARY AN ORPHAN.

IT must be owned, though it be a strange thing, that the history of the Virgin is barren of facts and full of interrup-

* Augustus, if we may believe Suetonius, was afraid of thunder and lightning with a weakness scarcely excusable in a woman. At the least appearance of a storm, he went and hid himself under deep vaults, where the noise of the thunder and the flashes of lightning could not penetrate.

† St. Ambr., De Virg., lib. ii.

tions: one might compare it to the majestic ruins of some ancient city of the desert. Here, gigantic pillars, whose bases are as immovable as those of the mountains; there, porticoes which the Arab, fond of marvellous tales, proclaims as the work of the genii; farther on, temples buried in sand, which the imagination can still build up again; and then at intervals a plain of sand, bare and barren, which has not a single blade of grass for the camel of the Bedouin. Instead of the apostles,—who, it would seem, were too much taken up with the grand person of Christ to think of his earthly family,—the fathers have introduced us to the virtues of St. Ann: we have entered after them beneath her humble roof; we have been witnesses of her vows, of her fervent prayers, of the joys of her late maternity, of the effusion of her gratitude; but here the thread of tradition becomes so loose that it breaks continually, and the rest of St. Ann's life is almost entirely matter of conjecture. This mother, who had obtained her blessed daughter after so many fasts and prayers, who had surrounded her childhood with so much love, who had brought her in her arms to the Lord,* and deposited her with tears in his sanctuary, appears again upon the scene but for a moment,—and then it is to die. Still it is not to be supposed that the spouse of Joachim remained nine years without seeing Mary again. The exterior buildings of the temple, where children consecrated to the God of Israel were brought up, could not have been forbidden to mothers: a mother has also sacred and religious rights; all nations declare them inviolable, and moreover, the Scripture informs us that Anna, the wife of Elcana, freely visited her son at Silo, on solemn days, and that she never failed to bring a tunic woven with her own hands to the young prophet whom she had *lent* to the Lord. Anna had had after the birth of Samuel several children, whom she beheld growing up under her eyes like young olive-trees, and

* St. Alphonsus, Le Glorie di Maria, Disc. 3, p. 59.

who shared with the little servant of the tabernacle her maternal solicitude: St. Ann had none but Mary; * the sum of her happiness, the hope of her old age, the source of her joy on earth, were all centred in her. It is not then to be doubted that, in company with her spouse, she came to see her every time that her piety led her to the temple, and that she also sat up, by the light of her lamp at home, or by the white light of the moon, † to weave the virginal robes of her child.

It is believed that St. Ann and St. Joachim returned to their home after the presentation of Mary, and dwelt there some years before they settled finally in Jerusalem. Joachim, who was not an artisan, like Joseph, apparently cultivated the small property inherited from his forefathers, and enjoyed that happy mediocrity which has always been the ambition of sages, great men, and poets, in their moments of grumbling at fortune.‡ Churches have been erected at Sephoris, Nazareth, and Jerusalem, on sites which formed part of his patrimony; but the vineyard or field of his fathers must have been in the environs of Sephoris: this was the cause of his returning to lower Galilee. Joachim was a true Israelite, much attached to the law of Moses; he

* Some have given Ann another daughter, named Mary, born twenty years before the Blessed Virgin; this tradition has not been received by the Church.

† The Jewish women spun together during the summer by moonlight, since the Jewish doctors authorised a husband to repudiate his wife when the women who *spun by moonlight* spoke ill of her.—(Sotah c. 6, p. 250.) This custom of spinning by moonlight still continues in many southern countries.

‡ According to St. Gregory of Nyssa, the father of the Blessed Virgin was "an honourable citizen," of signal piety, and much fearing God. F. de Valverde assures us, on the testimony of some fathers of the Church, that enjoying easy circumstances, Ann and Joachim gave one part of their savings to the temple and the other to the distressed.—(Life of Jesus Christ, t. i. p. 46.)

went up to the temple at all the solemn festivals with his wife and some of his relations, after the custom of the Hebrews, and it is to be supposed that the desire of seeing his daughter increased his attraction for the ceremonies of divine worship. With what joy did his good and pious partner take her travelling veil to journey to the holy city! How long did those tracks which she saw winding across the mountains and plains appear to travel over! She reached by sight, she gained twenty times over in thought, before she arrived at them in reality, the bushes of nopals, the tufts of rose-bay, the masses of green oaks or sycamores which arose at intervals upon her journey; for when each of these points were gained, she was the nearer to her daughter,—her daughter, the gift of the Lord, the child of miracle, she whom an angel had proclaimed the glory of Israel! With what emotion must she have hailed, from the bottom of the valley, that tower of Antonia which arose, splendid and menacing, on its base of polished marble,* to protect the house of prayer! and how much must the sight of the temple, which contained her child and her God, have affected that tender and holy soul!

When the evening was come, and the trumpets of the priests called the people to the ceremony,† Ann hastened to adore God, and cast her eyes upon her daughter, whom she had not seen for whole months. The court, which had no ceiling but the sky, mingled the dazzling light of its chandeliers ‡ with the flickering light of the stars; thousands of

* The tower of Antonia might be considered as the citadel of the temple; it had been anciently the palace of the Asmonean princes. The rock on which it was seated was inaccessible on every side, and fifty cubits high, Herod had had it cased with marble from the foot to the summit, so that no one might be able to go up or down it.—(Joseph,, Ant. Jud., lib. xv. c. 14, and de Bello, lib. ii. c. 16.)

† The religious festivals of the Jews always began in the evening.

‡ These chandeliers were of gold, and fifty cubits high. The light which they diffused was seen, say the rabbins, who were born to

lights intersected each other beneath the portions adorned with fresh garlands;* and the princes of the priests passed through the crowd with their splendid ornaments, brought from the borders of India by the caravans of Palmyra.† From time to time, the insulated harmonies of harps seemed to accompany the low shrill sound, like the confused noise of the waves,‡ which a multitude of Hebrews made at their prayers, who had come from the banks of the Nile, the Euphrates, and the Tiber, to bend their knees before the only altar of the God of their fathers.§ Amidst this immense concourse of believers, national and foreign, Ann, who prayed fervently, raised her head but for a moment: it was when Mary and her young companions were passing along, white and veiled, with lamps in their hands, like the wise virgins of the gospel.

When the feast was over, Ann, after having blessed and embraced Mary, took the road of the mountains again with Joachim; she departed from Jerusalem with slow steps, without daring to look back, and carried with her happiness and recollections to last her all the time till the next festival.

When age and labour had worn out the strength of

exaggerate, to an incredible distance from Jerusalem, and even in the towns the houses were so well lighted that, without the help of their lamps, the cooks could pick out the different kinds of grain for their soups.—(Talmud. tract Succa., fol. 3.)

* These green garlands were put on during the Feast of Tabernacles.—(Basn., liv. vii. c. 16.)

† The dresses which the priests wore in the evening on solemn feasts came from India, and were very expensive.—(Basn., liv. vii; c. 15.)

‡ We know that the Jews and Arabs pray aloud.

§ While the temple existed, the Jews made it a particular point of devotion to repair thither. More than eleven hundred thousand persons perished at the destruction of Jerusalem under Titus, because they were assembled for the feast of the Passover, when it was besieged.—(Joseph., lib. vii. c. 17.)

Joachim, and he was no longer able to cultivate his paternal land by himself, he thought of coming to live near to his daughter; the holy couple finally quitted lower Galilee, and came to live at Jerusalem, in a quarter near the temple. Ann had then arrived at the summit of her wishes: she could serve the Lord in his holy house, and see Mary often. How many times, during the fine summer evenings, while turning her spindle on the terrace roof of her house, must she have let it slip out of her motionless fingers, while her maternal looks were thoughtfully fixed on the gold and cedar roof of the temple? "Where a man's treasure is," says the Scripture, "there is his heart."

St. Ann could have shortened the term of this painful absence, as the law of Moses would have accepted her compensation. She did not desire it: her gratitude towards God spoke more powerfully than her maternal tenderness; and when the voice of religion was heard, the cry of nature was appeased.

The Virgin had lived nearly nine years secluded in the temple,* when the first dark cloud came to sadden the sweet and serene sky of her young life; her beloved father, Joachim, the just man, fell seriously ill, and soon the symptoms of approaching dissolution were apparent. Alarmed at his situation, his relatives and friends hastened to afford him a thousand testimonies of affection and sympathy; for there reigned a great and laudable union among the families of Juda. The dying man benignantly smiled upon his friends and relations; like Jacob, he had long been a sojourner upon the earth, and it mattered but little to him that the wind came and overturned his tabernacle, for beyond this planet of earth, he beheld in spirit the happy regions where he was going to repose in the bosom of Abraham.

When the gradual exhaustion of his strength had given the aged man to understand that life was departing from him,

* F. Croiset, Exercises de Piété, t. xviii. p. 59.

he made aloud, in presence of all, the confession of his sins, after the manner of the Hebrews,* and offered up his death to the sovereign Judge in expiation of the faults inherent in our nature, from which the most just are not exempt. This duty fulfilled, Joachim asked for his daughter, to give her his blessing. Mary came; † her ardent prayers for the preservation of the author of her days had not been heard: the *jealous God* was pleased to dissolve by degrees the terrestrial attachments of the spouse whom he had chosen for himself, that she might no longer have any support upon earth but his.

Pious authors have been of opinion that at the moment when Joachim stretched out his hands in the attitude of blessing over his child, a revelation from above allowed him to see all at once the glorious destiny to which Heaven called his daughter: the joy of the elect was diffused over his venerable face; he dropped his arms, bowed down his head, and died.

The house then resounded with wailings and shrill cries; the women struck their bosoms and tore their hair; ‡ the men covered their heads with ashes and rent their garments;

* Confession among the Hebrews is of the highest antiquity; the Jews made it at the hour of death, not only *aloud*, but *before ten persons and a rabbin.* Aaron Ben-Berachia, in his book entitled Maavar Jobbok, where he treats of the art of dying well, and of the manner of assisting the dying, relates the manner of confessing sins, and the prayers of the agony. Abraham Ben-Isaac Laniado has also made a book entitled The Buckler of Abraham, a work esteemed by the Jews, in which he treats of the confession of sins.—(See also Basn. liv. vii. c. 24.)

† It was a custom which came down from the patriarchs, that children should receive the blessing of their dying father: Mary must have conformed to this custom; her retirement in the temple was not a monastic enclosure, and St. Joachim lived at that time in Jerusalem.

‡ St. Jerom remarks, that in his time, most of the Jews mangled their skin at the death of their near relations, and made themselves bald by tearing off their hair, which they sacrificed to death.

while certain Jewish matrons, moved by a principle of devotion and charity, extended a thick veil over the pale but serene countenance of the just man, whom it was no longer permitted to see in this world, and bent his thumb in his hand, which they left open, as a sign of being abandoned by all earthly things.

After washing the body with water mixed with myrrh and the leaves of dry roses, these pious women wrapped it up in a linen winding-sheet, which they bound round with bandages after the manner of Egypt. Then, having opened all the doors and windows of the house,* they lighted a brazen lamp with several lights near the corpse, the lamp of the dead, which cast its mournful reflexion over the funeral couch.

The next day a numerous train, in which were seen some flute-players,† stopped before the house of the dead. The relations made their way to the upper chamber, where Joachim had been laid forth, and deposited the corpse upon a litter,‡ which they took up upon their shoulders. They passed along the streets of Jerusalem, chanting funeral canticles, accompanied by the soft and plaintive sound of

* Dead bodies, among the Jews, defile and render unclean those who touch them.—(Misnah, Ordo puritatum.) "When the doors are shut, the house of the dead is regarded as a sepulchre, and consequently it is defiled; when the doors are open, on the contrary, the uncleanness departs."—(Maimonides.)

† Jesus Christ found minstrels who made a great rout at the door of a ruler whose daughter he had raised to life. Maimonides says, that the poorest Jew is obliged to hire two flute-players and a female mourner for the funeral of his wife, and that the rich must increase the number in proportion to their wealth.—(See also Fleury, Manners of the Israelites, p. 106.)

‡ These funeral litters were used long before coffins, which are still unknown to the Arabs, who bury their dead in a linen cloth only, which gives the jackals, who prowl about the cemeteries by night, the facility of disinterring corpses to devour them.

flutes, and above which were heard the loud lamentations of the mourners. Ann and Mary were present at the funeral, and walked with their heads down, among the matrons of their family, who shed streams of tears.*

The procession passed the sheep-gate, which afterwards, among the Christians, bore the name of the Gate of the Virgin. When they had arrived at the place of interment, the sound of the flutes, the canticles, and lamentations ceased for a short time, and he who conducted the mourning made this address to the corpse:—"Blessed be God who formed thee, fed thee, and has taken away thy life. O ye dead, he knows your number, and he will one day raise you up again. Blessed be he who takes away life and restores it!"†

A small bag of earth was laid upon the head of the dead man, then the sepulchre was opened,—a dark cave, which was called *the house of the living*,‡ where the patriarch was going

* Women and children assisted at the funerals of their husbands and fathers. The widow of Naim followed the corpse of her son; Joseph conducted the obsequies of his father; this custom still continues in Judea. The children of the Hebrews received the blessing of their parents, closed their eyelids, and accompanied them to the field of repose, to gather them to the bones of their forefathers. —(Salvador, Hist. des Institutions de Moïse et du peuple Hebreu, t. ii. p. 398.)

† Leo of Modena, Cont. des Juifs. Buxtorf, Syn. Hebr., p. 502.

‡ The sepulchre should have been called *the house of the dead;* but they gave it, on the contrary, the title of *house of the living*, to indicate that the immortal soul still lives after the separation from the body: this denomination is attributed to the Pharisees.—(Basn., liv. vii. c. 24.) The rabbins give an exact description of these sepulchres. They make the entrance to them very narrow, for usually a stone rolled up to the entrance sufficed to close them. They left a great space empty, where the bearers went in and deposited the coffin, before they set it in its place. They hollowed out a certain number of niches in the sides and at the end, in which they placed the bodies of each family. Tombs were greatly respected; it was not allowed to pass over them by making an aqueduct or a high-road through them, nor to go thither to cut wood, nor to lead flocks there to feed. They were

to sleep his last sleep, waiting for the other members of his family. Then cries arose from all sides, enough to wring the heart. Ann threw herself upon the mortal remains of her spouse, to pay him the last adieu, and soon she was carried off in a state of insensibility. After consigning to the earth the sacred remains of the just man, they rolled up to the entrance of the sepulchral cave an enormous stone, which no one must remove *under pain of excommunication.* The funeral cries began again, and the spectators, pulling up three several times a tuft of grass, and throwing it each time behind them, said in a mournful tone, "They shall flourish as the grass of the field!" These rites terminated the obsequies of the descendant of the kings of Juda, the father of Mary, the grandfather of Jesus Christ according to the flesh.*

The Blessed Virgin's heart was wounded by this first grief, which was the prelude to so many others; it was her apprenticeship to sorrow. Adversity reached her on the threshold of adolescence; the noble child did not shrink back on her way; she wept,—for her soul, like that of her divine Son, was never dry or insensible,—but she drained the bitter cup, saying to God, "O Jehovah, thy will be done!" The mother and daughter put on mourning after the manner of the Hebrews; they were clothed in a coarse camlet, tight, and without folds, which was called a hair shirt; the head and feet bare, the face hidden in a fold of their robes, keeping fast and abstinence,† they remained sitting on the ground

placed on the high-roads, in order to excite the remembrance of those who passed by, and preserve the memory of the dead.—(Lightfoot, Cent. Chorogr., c. 100.) In the gospel, we see that the tomb of Lazarus was a cave closed by a large stone.

* Salom. Ben-Virgæ, Hist. Jud., p. 193; Leo of Modena, Cont. relig. des Juifs: Basn., liv. vii. c. 25.

† Fasting was very severe among the Jews; they were obliged to be contented with certain kinds of pulse—beans, for example, or lentils, which were mourning diet. Eggs were allowed, for the form of an egg, being round, and in the shape of a globe, is the image of a

for seven days, giving way to tears with their relations, and praying for the soul of the deceased.* When the seven days were passed, Ann had lamps lighted in the synagogue; where she requested prayers for her husband, and added alms in proportion to her fortune. Mary, on her part, fasted every week, on the day on which she had become an orphan, and prayed every night and morning for the repose of her father's soul. These fasts and prayers for the dead continued for the space of eleven months.†

"Welcome, O misfortune, if thou comest alone," say the Greeks. This first affliction was followed by one still more poignant, and another mourning soon came to be mingled with the mourning for Joachim. Scarcely was the mortuary lamp extinguished in the sorrowful abode of St. Ann, when it became necessary to light it afresh; hardly were the tears dried up which the Virgin had shed for one of the authors of her days, when she had to deplore the loss of the other.‡ One evening, Mary, accompanied by some of her relatives, went down from the temple to the narrow and dark street where her mother dwelt. The red and feeble ray of a lamp gleamed across one of the narrow trellised windows of the humble dwelling. Before the threshold were grouped together in silence those women, who even to this day throughout the East bewail the dead as a means of earning their support; like birds of evil omen which forbode funerals, these unlucky creatures were on the look out for some family in tears, to come and hire their venal lamentations.§

man in affliction. Wine was no less forbidden than meat.—(Basn., liv. vii. c. 28.)

* During the days of mourning they recited the forty-ninth psalm.—(L. de Mod., Cont. des Juifs, p. 182. Lightfoot, in John, p. 1072.)

† Basnage, liv. vii. c. 11, p. 182.

‡ According to the best authorities, St. Ann and St. Joachim died at a short interval one from the other.

§ In the Levant women are hired to bewail the dead, who have no other means of earning their living. They are paid so much per

St. Ann exerted her failing strength to bless her daughter, recommended her pathetically to her kinsfolk, but above all to HIM who is the father of the orphan, and slept the sleep of the just.* Mary bent down in tears over the cold visage of her mother; her light hair mixed with the grey hairs of the departed: it seemed as if she would have brought her to life again with her tears; but the breath of God alone can reanimate the dead! After the first burst of this sorrow, which was so justifiable, she closed with her hands the eyelids of the saint, and gave her one long and sorrowful embrace,—the last adieu of her people.†

The grief of the young orphan was silent, profound, and nobly endured. Having no longer any other reliance upon earth but Providence, she took refuge in the bosom of God; thence, as from the recess of a tranquil bay, she heard the distant roaring of the storms of the world, and understood all the vanity of the things of life; the vanity of rank, of grandeur, of fortune, of beauty—things which glitter and pass away like the bubble upon the course of the wintry torrent, which itself disappears at the end of a season.

It is to this period of mourning, insulation, and solitary meditations, that a certian historian has judiciously attached the vow of perpetual virginity made by Mary;‡ it nowhere appears that this vow was known to Ann and Joachim, and without their consent it would not have been valid in the

hour, and they exert themselves to earn their salary by uttering the most piercing cries.—(Burckhardt, Voyage en Arabie, t. ii. p. 139.)

* Grave historians affirm that the Virgin was present at the death of her mother, which is quite conformable to the manners of the Hebrews.

† This custom is very ancient; for Philo, recording the lamentations of Jacob for the premature death of his son, makes him say that he shall not have the consolation "to close his eyes, and give him the parting kiss."

‡ Descoutures, Vie de la Sainte Vierge, p. 27.

eyes of the law, either civil or religious.* It was after their death, then, that Mary chose the Lord for her portion, and consecrated herself by vow to his service, without any limitation of time, says Bernardin de Busto, and with the intention of never departing from the temple. Like the august head of her race, the Virgin found that "one day passed in the tabernacles of the God of Israel was better than a thousand other days," and she too would have preferred to be the last in the holy place, rather than the first in the tents of Cedar.

CHAPTER VII.

MARRIAGE OF THE VIRGIN.

WHETHER Joachim on his death-bed had placed the Virgin under the special protection of the priesthood; whether the magistrates who took care of the orphans had themselves chosen guardians for her in the powerful family of Aaron, to which she belonged on her mother's side; whether the guardianship of children devoted to the service of the temple belonged of right to the Levites, it is certain that after the death of the authors of her days, Mary had guardians of the priestly race. It is probable, and the Arab traditions affirm

* A young girl might make vows among the Jews, and she could even make a vow of virginity; but this vow was annulled by the authority of the father, because, being under the father's power, she could not violate the power which nature gives. All vows made by a young girl or a married woman, unknown to or contrary to the will of a father or a husband, were null.—(Num. c. xxx.) Some rabbins, however, maintain that it was necessary that the father or husband should annul them twenty-four hours after they came to know of them, in default of which they held good.—(Basnage, liv. vii. c.

it, that the cares of this guardianship were especially confided to the pious spouse of Elizabeth, to Zachary, who seemed designated by his high reputation for virtue, and his title of near relative,* for these duties of guardianship.† The eagerness which led the Blessed Virgin, two or three years later, to travel all through Judea, to offer her services and congratulations to the mother of St. John Baptist, and her prolonged stay in the mountains of Hebron, seem, in fact, to indicate a more intimate connection than that of mere relationship; the roof which sheltered Mary during so long a visit could not have been, according to the etiquette so rigorously observed among the Hebrews, any other than a roof as sacred as her paternal dwelling.

Whoever the priests may have been who were honoured with the guardianship of the blessed daughter of the saintly Ann, they scrupulously acquitted themselves of the obligations imposed by their charge, and when the Virgin had attained her fifteenth year, they thought of giving her a spouse worthy of her. This proposal of marriage threw

* The Jews, together with Celsus, Porphyrius, and Faustus, have taken this relationship as their ground for maintaining that the Blessed Virgin was of the tribe of Levi. The Catholic doctors oppose this opinion: they maintain that Mary was of the tribe of Juda, and of the family of David. In fact, St. Matthew teaches us that Jesus Christ is called the Son of David, according to the flesh: but he can be the son of David only through Mary, since he had no father among men. When it is asked how it can be that Mary, being of the tribe of Juda, should be cousin to St. Elizabeth, who was of the tribe of Levi, St. Augustin answers that there is nothing impossible in a man of the tribe of Juda taking a wife of the tribe of Levi, and that the Blessed Virgin, sprung from this marriage, should be the relation of Elizabeth on her mother's side. It is proved, moreover, that the prohibition to contract an alliance with another tribe, regarded none but orphans who were heiresses of the property of their fathers.

† The Koran, where many Arab traditions are found relating to Mary, says formally that Zachary took her under his protection.—(Koran, c. 3.)

Mary into extreme affliction; that soul so elevated, so pure, so contemplative, had foreseen the gospel, and virginity appeared to her the most perfect, holy, and desirable of all conditions. An ancient author, quoted by St. Gregory of Nyssa, relates that she excused herself a long time, with great modesty, from consenting to the determination announced to her; and that she humbly entreated her family to consent to her leading a life in the temple, innocent, hidden, and free from all ties, except those of the Lord. Her request caused great surprise in those who disposed of her lot. What she implored as a favour was sterility,—that is to say, reproach,—a state solemnly accursed by the law of Moses;* it was the celibacy of an only heiress,†—that is to say, the total extinction of her father's name,—a thought considered almost impious among the Jews, who looked upon it as a signal misfortune for their name not to be perpetuated in Israel. As to the vow of virginity, with which she had desired to bind herself for life, she would not have dared to ground any claim upon that, because it might be annulled by a decision advised by her family. It is well known that the woman was, "everywhere, and at all times," treated as a minor, before the promulgation of that immortal code which gloriously raised her from the *malediction of servitude.*

The entreaties of the Virgin found therefore but little sympathy among the priests of Jehovah; they had not attained to such virtues: and to these men of penetration and science, the angelical and all-holy soul of Mary was a book

* Origen remarks that the law attached a curse to sterility; for it is written, "Let him who shall not leave of his race in Israel be accursed."

† Mary was an heiress, because it appears congruous that the descendants from David, whence the Messias was to spring, should end by a sole heiress, who, becoming the mother of the eternal heir of the throne of David, should thereby crown and terminate his race.—(Oldhause.)

closed with seven seals of brass. Her thought, which was in advance of the age in which she lived, and opposed to the ancient prejudices of her nation, remained not understood, and all that she could allege, to save herself from embracing a state contrary to her dearest vows, availed her nothing. How indeed could she have convinced, since God himself was against her? Her marriage with a just man, who would bear witness to the purity of her life, free her from the importunities of the young Hebrews, who might have asked her hand even in the temple, as St. Augustin remarks,* and protect her and her divine Son in the hour of danger, entered into the secret views of Providence. It was the only means of concealing the mystery of the Incarnation from the malevolent investigations of a perverse world, who would have taken advantage of the prodigy to indulge in abominable conjectures, and would perhaps have carried their false zeal so far as to stone the mother of our Saviour, as they wanted afterwards to stone the sinful woman in the gospel; † for the Hebrews never reckoned mercy in the number of the virtues of their choice, and God himself reproaches them, by the mouth of his prophets, with having *a heart as hard as adamant.*

To these reasons, powerful, but hidden in the impenetrable obscurity of the counsels of God, was added another reason derived from the source of antediluvian traditions and national pride, which, of itself, would have left but little chance of success to the timid opposition of the Virgin. Perpetual chastity, which Christians have made the queen of virtues, was little better than nonsense among the disciples of Moses, who lived for so many ages in the anxious expectation of the *King-Messias* (Melech Hamaschiak). A young flower of the stem of Jesse, a daughter of David, was not at liberty to decline the yoke of hymen; she owed a son to the

* St. Aug., De Sancta Virg., c. 4.

† St. John Chrysost., Serm. 3, in Matth.

ambitious piety of her family, who would not have renounced, for all the treasures of the Great King, the hope of one day reckoning in the number of their members the liberator of Israel. This hope—which had supported the Jews when the Chaldeans, *mounted on horses swifter than eagles*, had violently broken down the ramparts which encircled Sion, and transplanted her people to the borders of the Euphrates—had been newly tempered into a fierce desire of vengeance, since the Romans had held dominion in Asia. The Hebrews hoped soon to see the day when the eagles would fly before the emerald-coloured standard,* and when the motto of the Macchabees † would wave victorious above that of the senate of Rome. Never had the accomplishment of the oracles relating to the Messias appeared so near, and the moment was not auspicious for obtaining the favour which the chaste young daughter implored.

According to the Gospel of the Nativity of Mary, and the Proto-Gospel of St. James, the guardians of the Blessed Virgin, without regard to her repugnance and representations, assembled together her nearest relatives, all being of the race of David and the tribe of Juda, like herself,‡ in order to proceed to the choice of the spouse whom they forced upon her. Among those who might aspire to her hand, were found a number of young Israelites,—some handsome and brave, others owners of fertile fields, vineyards, flocks, and groves of olive-trees. The captains of Juda would have added to the portion of Mary part of the spoils and slaves taken in their battles ; the Nabals of her

* The banner of Juda was green.—(Don Calmet.)

† This motto of the Macchabees contained these words: "Who is like to thee, O Eternal? *Mi camocha baehin, Jehovah?*"

‡ Every heiress to a property, and not daughters in general, as the Vulgate says, was bound to marry a man of her own family and tribe, and not her nearest relation, as Montesquieu has said, in order that inheritances might not be transferred from one tribe to another.

tribe would have covered her with stuffs from India wrought with gold and purple of Tyre twice dyed; while the sons of commerce who trafficked in the emeralds of Egypt, the turquoises of Iran, and pearls of the Persian Gulf, would have laid at her feet chains of precious stones, valuable bracelets, ear-rings of value equal to the ransom of a prince —in fine, all the magnificent and brilliant insignia of the servitude of the weaker sex. But these illustrious parties were weighed in the balance and found light. Disdaining the advantages of youth, beauty, high rank, fortune, and the glory of arms, the priests who were guardians of the Blessed Virgin, and the ancients of her house, fixed their choice upon a man advanced in age,* a decayed patrician, whose fortune had been absorbed by the political revolutions and religious wars of Judea, as a drop of rain is swallowed up in the sea, leaving him only his tools and his arms for labour; this man of low condition, though of great family, who was a widower,† according to the Proto-Gospel of St. James, and

* The Proto-Gospel of St. James, c. 2, and the Gospel of the Nativity of Mary, c. 8, books of which the contents have been approved, for the most part, even by the fathers of the Church, merely say that he was already old. St. Epiphanius gives Joseph eighty years at the time of his marriage; F. Pezron, fifty; and the Histoire divine de la Vierge, of Mary d'Agrada, thirty-three. The supposition of St. Epiphanius does not bear examination; it is, moreover, solemnly refuted by the law of the Hebrews, which forbids the alliance of a young woman with an old man, and classes it with things the most disgraceful.—(Basn., liv. vii. c. 21, Hist. des Inst. de Moïse.) Neither the high priests nor Joseph would have been willing to do a thing condemned by the law. The age attributed by Mary d'Agrada to St. Joseph does not agree with the opinion of the fathers: there remains that of F. Pezron, which appears the most probable.

† Several fathers have thought that St. Joseph was a widower when he was espoused to the Blessed Virgin. The Proto-Gospel of St. James, and the Gospel of the Nativity of the Virgin, assure us that he was a widower; St. Epiphanius says that he had four sons and two daughters; St. Hippolytus of Thebes calls his first wife

a bachelor according to St. Jerom, whose opinion has prevailed in the Church, was Joseph, the carpenter of Nazareth.

When we reflect on the rare beauty of Mary, the education which she had received in the temple, the great alliances of her family, her position as a heiress, which made her, among the Jews,—who portioned their wives, and received hardly anything from them,*—a desirable, and even brilliant match, we might well be astonished at this family decision, if the fathers had not assured us that Joseph was chosen by lot, and by the express manifestation of the divine will.† An ancient tradition, recorded in the Proto-Gospel of St. James, and mentioned by St. Jerom, relates that the candidates, after having prayed to Him *who presides over the lots*, deposited over-night in the temple each one his rod of almond-tree; and that the next day the dry and dead branch of Joseph, the son of Jacob, the son of Mathan, was found green and in blossom, like that which had before confirmed the priesthood to the sons of Aaron. The history of Mount Carmel testifies that at the sight of this prodigy, which destroyed his hopes, a young patrician, belonging to one of the most powerful families of Judea, and the possessor of a great

Salome: Origen, Eusebius, St. Ambrose, and many other fathers, have adopted the same opinion. Nevertheless, this opinion is the least followed, and it is commonly believed that St. Joseph had lived in virginity. This is the opinion of St. Jerom, who expressly says, writing against Helvidius: "We do not anywhere read that he had any other wife than Mary: *aliam eum uxorem habuisse non scribitur.*" St. Augustin leaves the question undecided; but St. Peter Damian affirms that the whole Church believes that St. Joseph, who passed for the father of our Saviour, was a virgin like Mary.

* At the time of contracting marriage, the wife received from her relations only things necessary for her attire. It was the husband who furnished the dowry.—(Salvador, Institutions de Moïse, t. ii. c. 1.)

† Evangel. de Nativ. Mar., c. 7: Protev. Jac., c. 8; Hier. in Dam., lib. iv. c. 5; Greg. Naz., hom. de S. Nat.; Niceph., lib. ii. c. 7.

fortune, broke his rod with every sign of despair, and ran to shut himself up in one of the caves of Carmel with the disciples of Elias.*

When the choice of the guardians was determined, it was announced to Mary, and this admirable young woman, accustomed to elegant occupations, brought up in the midst of the perfumes, melodious strains, and fairy magnificence of the holy house, did not hesitate to devote herself to a life of obscurity, to low and common employments, and painful cares, with the humble artisan presented to her by her relations. A divine inspiration, it is said, had made known to her that this just man would be to her no more than a protector, a father, a guardian of her chastity; † what more did she desire? The Lord had heard her prayer; by leaving her faithful to the vow which she had made, he gave her, over and above, the merit of obedience.

The marriage proposed between Joseph and Mary must have caused some surprise at Nazareth and at Jerusalem; for there was but little correspondence in the age, fortune, and condition of the future pair. It would be a mistake, however, to suppose that this union, which appears so strangely incompatible, was considered in Jewish society—a society of simple and primitive habits—as any flagrant, ill-sorted alliance. Without holding any distinguished rank in the state, the profession of an artisan was neither abject nor degrading in Israel.‡ We see in the genealogy of the tribe

* This young pretender to the Virgin, who is said to have been named Agabus, became afterwards celebrated for his sanctity, and a Christian.—(See Hist. du Carmel, c. 12.)

† Vie de la Sainte Vierge, by Descoutures, p. 49; Vie de Jesus Christ, by F. Valverde, t. i. p. 71.

‡ Artisans are still held in distinguished estimation in Judea. "In Palestine and in Syria," says Burckhardt, "the companies of artisans are almost as much respected as they were in the middle ages in France and Germany. A master artisan is quite on a level there, in rank and consideration, with a merchant of the second class; he

of Juda one family of workers in fine linen, and another of potters, whose memory is in honour; and the Scripture has handed down to posterity the names of Beseleel and Hiram. We know that St. Paul, brought up to the study of the law, the famous Pharisee doctor Hillel, and after them a great number of doctors, who, in the emphatic language of the rabbins, "sowed light amidst the holy nation," applied themselves to mechanic arts of a kind the least brilliant, and were not ashamed. Nay, more: every Israelite was an artisan; for every father of a family, whatever might have been his social position, was bound to make his son learn a trade, *unless*, said the law, *he wished to make a robber of him.**

The Jews, whose patrimony was locked up in the hands of foreigners, had no alternative, while waiting for the grand epoch which was to re-establish their fortunes, but to expatriate themselves, or to live in a poor way by the labour of their hands, in the bosom of their native mountains. Those who were led by the love of their country to adopt this latter expedient did not act in any way contrary to their dignity, and remained well fitted for any sort of employment. Israel had no castes, like Egypt and India; all its pride arose from its religious belief and its descent from the patriarchs. "To be descended from Abraham according to the flesh," says the eagle of Meaux, "was a distinction which naturally raised them above all others." In fact, the lowest of the

may take a wife of the respectable families of the city, and has generally more influence in his locality than a merchant whose fortune is three times as great as his own."—(Burckh., Voyage en Arabie, t. ii. p. 139.)

* Every man who does not give his children a profession, says the school of the Pharisees, prepares them for an evil life. "Be not a burthen to any one . . . . never say, I am a man of a quality, this employment is not suitable for me. Rabbi Johanan had learnt the trade of a skinner; Nahum that of a copyist of books: another Johanan made sandals; and Rabbi Juda knew the trade of a baker." —(Talmud, Tract. Kidouschim. Pessarh, Aboth; Soto.)

Hebrews considered himself a prince in comparison with strangers.*

Still there were among the Jews, as among the Arabs, some tribes more illustrious and certain houses more noble than others; the tribe of Juda, which bore the national standard at the head of the *thousands* of Israel in the day of battle, and from which the sceptre was not to depart till the coming of the Messias, had always had the pre-eminence; and the family of David was the first and most honoured among the families of Juda. Now Joseph, though poor, was of the race of David; the blood of twenty kings flowed in his veins, and it was Zorobabel, one of his ancestors, who brought back the people of God from the land of exile. From that time the glory of his house had gradually become obscured; his family had become confounded with the people, like those of Moses and Samuel; but his illustrious origin was known: in our days, the lowest of the Abassides, who vegetate in the heart of the Hedsjaz, are no less respected as the descendants of Aaron-el-Raschid, and no Arab family would disdain to contract an alliance with them.

The holy daughter of Joachim did not then lower herself as much as might be supposed by marrying the CARPENTER. But if we take a higher view of this union, which at first seems so ill-assorted, we shall discover that it was in reality a noble alliance. God did not give as a spouse to the Virgin after his own heart, a man whose whole merit consisted in his fields, his vineyards, his sicles of gold,—things which often change masters, and are no more inherent in the rich man than the garments which he puts off at night: he gave her a just man,—the most perfect of his works. The Lord is not taken with the vain baubles which dazzle the vulgar; in his eye all ranks are equal among poor creatures, who creep about the dust for a moment, to become in a short time the

* In losing their nationality, the Jews did not lose this opinion, which they still maintain.

food of worms. "Man judges by those things that appear," says the Scripture, "but the Lord regardeth the heart." If God chose the humble Joseph for the spouse of the Queen of angels, for the adoptive father of the Messias, it was because he possessed treasures of grace and sanctity, enough to excite the envy of the celestial intelligences; it was because his virtues had made him the first of his nation, and because he was placed much higher than Cæsar in the book of life, those heraldic annals of eternity. The Virgin was not confided to the most powerful, but to the most worthy; thus the ark, which the princes and valiant men of Israel did not dare to approach, for fear of being struck dead, drew down the benedictions of heaven upon the house of a simple Levite, under whose poor roof it was sheltered.

The espousals of Mary were celebrated with all the simplicity of ancient times. Joseph, in presence of the guardians and a few witnesses, presented her with a piece of silver, the value of which is not known,* saying to her, "If thou consentest to be my bride, accept this pledge." Mary, by accepting this gift, was solemnly engaged, and a sentence of divorce alone could from that day restore her liberty. The scribes drew up the contract; it was short, and but little interlarded with technical terms.† The husband promised

* Hillel and Schammay disputed warmly about the value of this piece of money at espousals, mentioned in the Talmud, without being able to come to an agreement.—(Basn., liv. vii. c. 21.)

† The following is the literal form of Hebrew marriage-contracts, which has come down from the most remote times, and which Joseph and Mary must have used:—"In the year . . . . the . . . . day of the month . . . . Benjamin, son of . . . . said to Rachel, daughter of . . . . 'Become my wife, under the law of Moses and of Israel. I promise to honour thee, to provide for thy support, thy food, thy clothing, according to the custom of Hebrew husbands, who honour their wives and support them as it is befitting. I give thee at once . . . . (the sum adjudged by the law), and promise thee, besides nourishment, clothes, and whatever shall be necessary for thee,

to honour his wife, to provide for her support, her food, her clothing, according to the custom of Hebrew husbands, and settled upon her a dowry of two hundred zuses (fifty crowns), a portion alike for the daughter of a prince as for the daughter of the people, but to which they were free to add anything in proportion to their fortune. After having secured this dowry upon all that he possessed, and even upon his mantle, which the law nevertheless did not allow him to recover till after her death,* Joseph signed the contract, to which Mary also added her signature. A short benediction to the praise of God terminated this ceremony, which must precede that of marriage by several months.

The nuptials of the Blessed Virgin were celebrated at Jerusalem, and the persons of the highest quality of her family made it a duty to appear at it with that splendour which is peculiar to the East, and which travellers from Europe never mention without admiration and astonishment, even the common people displaying on these occasions a degree of luxury absolutely unheard of.† Not to invite all their relations on so solemn an occasion would have been refusing to follow the ancient customs of their forefathers,—a thing impossible to suppose in that traditionary nation, which was as immutable in its customs as in its religious practices, as was said in all truth by the Jew Philo to the

conjugal friendship, a thing common to all the nations of the world.' Rachel consented to become the wife of Benjamin, who, of his full consent, to form a dowry in proportion to his own fortune, adds to the portion above-named the sum of . . . ."—(Institut. de Moïse.)

* Basn., liv. vii. c. 21.

† "In Europe we have no idea of the luxurious display made on similar occasions in the East," says F. de Geramb, in his Pélerinage à Jerusalem: "the nuptial dresses of almost all wives is of red velvet embroidered with gold; they add to it decorations of diamonds, fine pearls, &c." M. de Lamartine was equally astonished at the splendid costumes, and the profusion of precious stones displayed by the women of Syria at the weddings of their fellow countrywomen.

Emperor Caius; it would have been wanting, moreover, in all the proprieties of Hebrew society, and the presence of Mary at the marriage of Cana proves, on the contrary, that she conformed to them.

One fine day in winter,* at the time when the new moon rose slowly behind the mountains,† a long procession of women richly adorned was seen proceeding towards the habitation of Mary; the torches of resinous fir, borne by a number of slaves, made brilliant their golden girdles, their pearl network, the diadems of precious stones which they wore on their foreheads, and the diamonds of their Persian tiaras.‡ These daughters of Sion had kept up the use of paint, which was known as early as the time of Jezabel; their eyebrows and eyelashes were dyed black, and the tips of their fingers were red, like the berry of the eglantine.§ Introduced into the interior apartment, where the young and holy betrothed one was in company with certain pious matrons, who were her relations, they blessed God, who gave her a protector in the person of a spouse, and complimented her upon her marriage, in the joy of which they came to participate.

Belonging to Jewish society, where all the details of the dress of young brides was a biblical reminiscence with which

* In the middle of the sixteenth century, the Church permitted this feast to be kept; it is celebrated on the 22nd of January, the day on which it is said that the marriage of Mary and Joseph was celebrated. The city of Arras keeps this feast on the 23rd of January, and some churches in Flanders on the 24th of the same month.

† All days were not chosen alike for celebrating the marriages of the Israelites: the time of the new moon was usually fixed upon, and a Wednesday in preference to the other days of the week.—(Basn., liv. vii. c. 21.)

‡ Isaias, c. iii.

§ Throughout the East, the women stain the tips of their fingers with alkanna, *lausonia inermis* (Linn.) This plant is very plentiful in the Island of Cyprus.

it was not lawful to dispense, Mary was obliged to submit for a short time to the requirements of oriental luxury, though this luxury had no charms for her. Gold, pearls, rich tissue, are not in themselves things to be condemned; it is the thoughts of pride and vanity to which they give rise in weak heads and light minds, which are bad. Beneath garments heavy with embroidery and adorned with precious stones, Queen Bathildes was more humble than the women clad in coarse cloth with whom she lived in seclusion after her glorious regency; the chroniclers of the time have informed us of this with candour and simplicity.

Therefore, avoiding any show of negligence in her dress, which would have been taken very ill, since custom required of the married couple, as well as of their guests, a dress suitable to the occasion—as the gospel of the wedding garment would inform us, even if all the East, both ancient and modern, did not concur in the same—the young descendant of the kings of Juda was obliged to wear, on this occasion, rich and suitable costume, and authentic relics prove in fact that so it was.*

Her robe, which was preserved as a precious treasure in Palestine, whence it was sent to Constantinople, about the year 461, as Nicephorus informs us, was of a texture precious from its design and ornaments. The ground was of the colour of nankeen, with flowers blue, white, violet, and gold: it is now the sacred relic of Chartres.†

In memory of the ancient times and patriarchal manners

* There are in existence two tunics of the Blessed Virgin, the material of which is very precious. Chardin saw one in Mingrelia covered with flowers embroidered with the needle on a nankeen ground. This tunic is eight Roman palms long by four wide; the neck is narrow, the sleeves a palm long; it is kept in the Church of Copis.

† This tunic was given by Charles the Bald to the Church of Chartres, in 877: numerous miracles are attributed to it.

of her fathers, she wore, like Rebecca, ear-rings and bracelets of gold, the modest and indispensable present which Joseph was to send a few days before the ceremony,* and to which the wealthy Hebrews added necklaces of pearls and magnificent sets of diamonds. Instead of an indented crown of gold,† which was worn by the brides of the opulent classes, there was placed upon the light hair and tresses ‡ of Mary a simple garland of myrtle; in the spring time roses would have been added to it;§ her nuptial veil covered her from head to foot, and floated around her like a cloud.||

A canopy of precious materials awaited the future spouse outside; four young Israelites bore it.¶ Mary had to place

* The Christians of Damascus have kept up this custom. Some days before the nuptial festival, the bridegroom sends to his bride a pair of bracelets of gold, or set with diamonds, according to the fortune of the future spouse, a piece of stuff embroidered with gold, and 160 piastres for the expenses of the bath and the nuptial feast.—(Corresp. d'Orient, lettre 147.)

† The crown of the bride was usually of gold, and made in the shape of a tower, like that of Cybele; this custom was abolished during the siege of Jerusalem by Titus, but they kept up the crowns of myrtle and roses.—(Basn., liv. vi. c. 21.)

‡ Among the Hebrews, not even the dress of the women was independent of the empire of tradition. "The female hair-dressers were called in to dress the hair of young married women, because, said the rabbins, Jehovah himself curled the hair of Eve, when he united her to Adam in Paradise."—(Basn., liv. vii. c. 21, p. 393.)

§ Crowns of myrtle and roses were worn by the young betrothed women of the common people.—(Basn., liv. vii. c. 21; Misnah. Tit. Sotah, c. 9, sect. 14.)

|| These nuptial veils, embroidered with gold and silver, are still in use in Syria.

¶ The regulation of this nuptial pomp, which comes down from the earliest times, is still found in Egypt. Niebuhr thus describes an Egyptian marriage:—"The bride, covered from head to foot, walks between two women who conduct her beneath a canopy borne by four men. Several slaves go before, some of whom play on the tambourine, others carry fly-flappers, others sprinkle her with scented waters. She is followed by a number of women, and by musicians

herself under it between two matrons, one of whom, who stood on her right, represented her mother; the other was perhaps that Mary of Cleophas, whom some others have made the elder daughter of St. Anne, but who was only sister-in-law of the Blessed Virgin.* After them walked, to the sound of timbrels, flutes, and harps, playing in unison† airs of grave and simple melody, which, perhaps, were the same as those of the choirs of music of King David; the entire nuptial procession waving, in token of joy, branches of myrtle and palm.‡ The bridegroom, with his brow adorned with a singular crown, transparent as crystal, and peculiar to his people,§ advanced in the midst of a crowd of friends, who sung an epithalamium in imitation of the Canticle of Canticles of Solomon, that magnificent and mysterious nuptial song, the sublime metaphors of which have a hidden and divine signification. They celebrated the beauty of the new bride, whose "looks were like young palm-branches, and stature graceful and upright, like the branches of the erac, teeth white as a flock of sheep which come up from the

riding upon asses. The procession takes place in the night; some slaves carry torches."—(Niebuhr, Voyage en Arabie, t. i.)

* According to M. Pignot, a conscientious historian who made numerous researches on this subject, this holy woman was the wife of Cleophas, the brother of St. Joseph, and consequently sister-in-law to the Blessed Virgin.—(See Recherches historiques sur la personne de Jésus Christ et celle de Marie, p. 249.)

† The music of the Orientals is of a very different kind from ours; it is grave and simple, without any studied modulation: all the instruments play in unison, unless one or other should take a fancy to perform a continued bass by repeating incessantly the same note.—(Niebuhr, t. i. p. 136.)

‡ See Fleury, Mœurs des Israelites.

§ This crown, which contained, say the Jewish doctors, a mysterious lesson, was composed of salt and sulphur; the salt was transparent like crystal, and they traced various figures upon it with sulphur.—(Codex. MS. apud Wagenseil in Mismam, Tit. Sotah, adult. de uxore suspect., c. 9, sect. 14.)

washing, eyes mild, like the eyes of doves which sit beside the plentiful streams; they said that the sweet odour of her good name was like the perfumes which exhaled from her garments; that she was the lily of young virgins, and the object of the praise of women." Then, passing on to the eulogy of the bridegroom, they extolled his form, "majestic and imposing as Libanus, the sweetness of his voice, the urbanity of his manners;" and they added, "that he was distinguished from the crowd of men, even as the cedar is distinguished among all trees." Then, coming to more general and elevated considerations, they said that the spouse should be to his wife as "the nosegay of myrrh which she wears over her heart;" that she should pass through life leaning upon him, with no more care for other men than if she was passing through the desert; because "jealousy is as inflexible as death, and the lamps thereof are lamps of fire and flames." They added that tender affection was a thing so precious between married persons, that "the wealthiest man in the world, if he gave all his riches for it, ought still to consider that he had given nothing."

From time to time, the young men who closed the procession formed dances of the same kind as the sacred dance which was originally associated with religious festivals,* or they uttered, in token of rejoicing, those shrill and prolonged cries which are still in use among the Arabs,† and which a modern traveller, who lately went all over Syria, compares to those loud cries which the vine-dressers of the south of France utter from hill to hill during the vintage. All in the procession scattered among the poor, who loaded them with blessings, a quantity of small pieces of silver‡ bearing a

* Dancing, which at first was intended to imitate the movements of the stars, was mixed up with all the religious festivals of antiquity: it was, no doubt, of antediluvian origin, and must even have preceded the invention of musical instruments.

† See Niebuhr, *loco citato*.

‡ Basn., liv. vii. c. 21.

figure, either of a vine-leaf, or of three ears of wheat, which were the emblem of Judea.* The women of Israel, in groups along the way that the wedding couple passed, strewed palm branches under their feet, and from time to time they stopped the bride to sprinkle essence of roses upon her attire.† Mary was to have also her own day of triumph in Jerusalem.

When they arrived at the house where the wedding was to be celebrated, the friends of the bridegroom and the companions of the bride cried out in chorus, "Blessed is he that cometh!" Joseph, covered with his *taled*, and Mary with her veil, were seated under the canopy side by side; Mary took the right, because the psalmist has said, "Thy wife is on thy right hand,"‡ and turned towards the south.§ The spouse placed a ring on the finger of his partner,‖ "Behold, thou art my wife, according to the rite of Moses and of Israel." He took off his taled and covered his wife with it, in imitation of what passed at the marriage of Ruth, who said to Booz, "Spread thy coverlet over thy servant."¶ A near relative poured wine into a cup, tasted it, and then presented it to the bridegroom and bride, blessing God for having created man and woman, and instituted marriage. While the married couple put the sacred nuptial cup to their lips, they sung to the God of Israel a canticle containing six benedictions. After this, Joseph poured out the rest of the wine as a sign of bounty, and handfuls of wheat as a

* Some of these Jewish coins have been found of the time of the Machabees and of Herod; they do not bear the effigy of any prince, but only of ears of wheat and vine leaves.

† This custom was borrowed from Egypt, like many others.

‡ Ps. xlv. 10.

§ Basn., liv. vii. c. 21.

‖ It is said that this ring is at Perosa, where it is carefully preserved.—(Basn., liv. vii. c. 2.)

¶ See Buxtorf.

symbol of abundance: then a young child broke the cup in pieces.*

The whole assembly surrounding the new married couple with torches, blessed the Lord, and went forward into the dining-room, where they proceeded—according to a very ancient Bishop of Brescia,† who derives this Hebrew tradition from the time of Jesus Christ—to nominate a king of the feast, taken from the priestly race, who was to preside over the viands and the wine, and to oblige the guests to behave with all that decorum required by religion and propriety. Joseph and Mary rose also; but, before they followed their company, there were exchanged between them some secret words in presence of heaven and the stars, which declare the glory of the Most High.‡ "Thou shalt be as my mother," said the patriarch to the Blessed Virgin, "and I will respect thee even as the altar of Jehovah." From that moment they were no longer, in the eye of the religious law, any more than brother and sister in marriage, although their union might be fully maintained.§

* Basn., liv. vii. c. 21; Institut. de Moïse, liv. vii. c. 1, p. 336.

† Gaudent., Serm. 9. B. P., t. ii. p. 38.

‡ St. Thomas is of opinion that it was immediately after the celebration of their marriage that St. Joseph and the Blessed Virgin made a vow of virginity, by mutual consent.

§ This vow of continency in marriage, which has given occasion to so many impious sarcasms to the *philosophes* of the school of Voltaire, was not a thing unheard of among the Hebrews; only it was a vow dictated by passion and anger, while that of the two holy spouses was suggested by piety. If a husband said to his wife, "Thou art as my mother," it was no longer lawful for him to consider her but as such in marriage; and still more when he had introduced into his vow the altar of Jehovah, the temple, or the sacrifice. The wives sometimes did the same thing; and although these vows were not much approved, because they hardly ever came but at the end of fits of anger and curses, they were not less obliged religiously to fulfil them when they were made.—(Basn., liv. vii. c. 19, p. 352; Leo of Modena, Ceremon. et. cont. des Juifs, c. 4.)

The festivities, among which figured the religious ceremony of sacrifice, lasted seven days, as in the time of the patriarchs; the week of the nuptials being expired, Joseph and Mary, under the escort of a number of their relations, who formed around them a brilliant cavalcade, went again on their way to Galilee. The little caravan went forward to the sound of cymbals, and was not interrupted till near the fountain of Anathoth,* where those of Jerusalem took leave of the bride and bridegroom, with tears in their eyes, blessings in their mouths, and their hands laid solemnly upon their hearts. The Nazareans continued their journey; they crossed the mountains of Samaria, where the eagle from the height of his nest beheld them pass, indifferent to their presence. Sichem next presented itself to the travellers, with its evergreen groves, its streams of limpid water, and its majestic edifices rising above the foliage. They left behind them Garizim, with its red-tinted sides, where the ruins of the schismatical temple were observable, the disgraceful rival of the house of holiness, which John Hircanus delivered to the avenging flames, and which was to be replaced later on by a church dedicated to Mary herself; then the high summits of Mount Hebal; then Sebaste, which reared its new palaces under the protection of Augustus, and which Herod delighted servilely to embellish, as the only altar where he could sacrifice to the genius of Rome.

Towards the middle of the second day's journey they distinguished Mount Thabor, whose verdant head was traced upon the pale silvery sky of Galilee: and beyond it the high tops of Libanus, which hid their pointed tops of stone, covered with eternal snows, in the clouds. From the woody

* All the relations escorted the bride on horseback to the house of her husband, when he did not live at too great a distance from the place of their feasting; this custom still continues among the Arabs. We have made the nuptial caravan separate at Anathoth, a small town five leagues from Jerusalem, because it is the first halting place.

slopes of Hermon, where the goats browsed upon the tender shoots of the shrubs, they descended into the delightful plain, which was displayed like an immense basket of flowers, between hills covered with green oaks, myrtles, plots of vineyards, and magnificent woods of olive-trees. Fields of barley, wheat, clover, and doura in full verdure, gently waving with the breeze, warmed by the approach of a spring more speedy and genial than that of our western regions. A pure and golden light favoured this fertile land, where a vigorous vegetation was unfolding itself, and blue waters, which the summer would soon dry up, ran in silvery ribands in this new Eden. Here and there opulent villages appeared beneath high colonnades of palm-trees, and then, at different distances, on the rugged crest of a rock, a solitary fortress of soldiers, still national and entrusted with a mission entirely protective, measured their Damascus sabres only with nocturnal depredators, or the Arabs of the desert. This valley, with its charming freshness, and enclosed within a dark border of high mountains, was the valley of Esdrelon, at the extremity of which appeared a little city, seated with picturesque effect on the back of a hill, and which shone like a flower amidst the neighbouring hamlets: this smiling and beautiful town was Nazareth, the native town of the Virgin, the cradle of Christ!*

* The *philosophes* of the last century studiously laboured to depreciate Palestine; the impression which they have given of it still remains, and the state of poverty and depopulation of that country, which hardly breathes beneath the sabre of the Mussulmans, has often made them appear right in the eyes of superficial readers. Yet it is certain that with the exception of the environs of Jerusalem, the sterility or which has never been denied, the promised land of Moses is still found in that country, and especially in the part which formerly belonged to the Canaanites. We will give two descriptions of Galilee, written at the distance of eighteen centuries between them, in proof of this assertion. "Galilee," says Flavius Josephus, "is divided into upper d lower, both very fertile; the soil is at once rich and light

Doubtless, Mary could not behold again without emotion that city where she had first opened her eyes to the light. She had left it when quite a child for the splendid walls of the temple; she returned to it beautiful, young, accomplished, and a virgin on her return even as on her departure.

The travellers stopped at the house of St. Ann, an ancient and mysterious dwelling, partly hollowed out of the rock, like the prophetic grottoes of ancient times, and which was

abounding in pasturages, fitted for all sorts of produce, and covered with trees of all kinds; there are to be seen particularly large plantations of vines and olive-trees. It is watered by torrents, which fall from the mountains, by a great number of springs and rivulets, which afford a constant supply of water, and make up for that of the torrents, when the heats of summer dry them up. The goodness of the land is such, that it invites men to labour who are the least disposed to it. Thus every part is cultivated, and no tract of land is seen unproductive. The inhabitants are robust and warlike, the towns numerous, and so populous that the smallest can reckon as many as fifteen thousand souls."—(Joseph., de Bello, lib. ii. c. 2.) "If one desired to give an idea of the aspect of Galilee," says a modern traveller in his turn, "France would not serve to compare it with, but *l'Agro Romano;* round about Nazareth, as in the environs of Rome, there is everywhere the same brightness, the same formation of the soil. Nature is there sublime, like the gospel. Galilee is an abridged picture of the Holy Land, and when it has been seen under its day and night aspects, we understand what it was in the time of Jesus Christ. For an artist, Galilee is an Eden; nothing is wanting: neither the accidental advantages of the land of Judea, nor the bright solitudes of Palestine, nor the green fecundity of Samaria. Garizim and the Mount of Olives are not more sublime than Hermon and Thabor, nor are the blue shores of Ascalon more solemn than the odoriferous borders of the Lake of Tiberias, where the air vanishes beneath the light. The soil of Galilee presents to us everywhere history and miracles, traces of heroes and the footsteps of a God; and we feel as we contemplate Galilee from the heights of Thabor, that it was the country which the God-man inhabited, so much are religious recollections, the wonders of earth and heaven, commingled there interminably."—(Corresp. d'Orient, t. v.)

shortly to become more holy than the temple of Jerusalem, the very house of Jehovah.* The women of Nazareth greeted with blessings the arrival of the young bride, who advanced modestly, and veiled like the Rebecca of Isaac; and Mary, in the midst of the congratulations of those who had witnessed her birth, entered this peaceful paternal habitation, which seemed still perfumed with the sweet odour of the virtues of Ann and Joachim.

CHAPTER VIII.

THE ANNUNCIATION.

It is easy to imagine the tranquil and blessed life which the married couple led during the first months of their chaste union; the peace of God reigned in their humble dwelling, and work divided their time with prayer, which made it less laborious by sanctifying it. After an ancient custom, which still subsists among the Arabs and in a great part of the East, Joseph exercised his trade in a different place from that where Mary lived.† His workshop, where Jesus himself worked, was a low room of ten or twelve feet square: a stone seat outside offered rest to the passer-by, or the

* "There are still found at Nazareth," says F. de Geramb, "some houses like that of St. Joseph, that is to say, small, low, and communicating with a cave hollowed out of the side of a mountain."

† This house of St. Joseph is a hundred and thirty or a hundred and forty paces from that of St. Ann. The place is still pointed out, under the name of the *workshop of Joseph*. This shop had been transformed into a large church; the Turks have destroyed one part of it; but there remains a chapel where the holy sacrifice of the mass is daily offered.—(Pélerinage à Jérusalem, par le P. de Geramb.)

traveller, which was protected from the burning rays of the sun by a kind of awning of twisted palm-leaves.* There it was that the laborious workman formed his ploughs, his yokes, and rustic carts. Sometimes he built under his own inspection the huts of the valley; sometimes his arm, yet strong, cut down the tall sycamores and black turpentine-trees of Mount Carmel.† The pay which he received for so much fatigue was but small, and this little he shared with the poor.

His gentle and holy companion was not idle on her side; gifted with a mind enlightened, judicious, and wise, without regret for the past, without illusions for the future, viewing the world such as it is, and her own position in its true light, she piously conformed herself to it, and desired to fulfil its sacred obligations with religious exactitude. From the moment that she took possession of the house of her mother, she put on poverty as a garment of honour sent her from God, and became what it behoved her to be in the obscure condition to which Providence had reduced her—a young and simple daughter of the people. All the brilliant and fancy works belonging to the elegancies of life were at once laid aside, and replaced by the fatiguing cares and monotonous occupations of a poor household, where the mistress of the house has neither slaves nor servants. The delicate hands of Mary, accustomed to handle silken tissues, platted with leaves of the date-palm, or rushes pulled from the banks of the Jordan, the matting which covered the rough floor of her dwelling; her spindle was covered with coarse flax; she had

* These shops are still the same all over the Levant.—(See Burckhardt, Voyage en Arabie, t. i.)

† St. Justin, martyr (Dialog. cum Tryphone), records that Jesus Christ helped his adopted father in making yokes and ploughs. St. Ambrose (in Luc., lib. iii. 2) assures us that St. Joseph worked at felling and cutting out trees, at building houses, and other such work.

to grind the grains of wheat, barley, and doura,* the coarse and yellow flour of which she kneaded into round and thin cakes. Covered with her white veil, with an antique urn upon her head,† she went to draw water at a fountain at a little distance,‡ like the wives of the patriarchs, or to wash her blue robes in the running water of the brooks, like the princesses of Homer.

* The first mills that were invented were hand-mills. In Egypt, Arabia, Palestine, and even in Greece, they were turned by women. There is still shown at Mecca, in a fine house, which is believed to have been that of Khadidje, a hollow place, where it is said that Fatima, surnamed "the Brilliant," daughter of Mahomet, and wife of Ali, turned her own hand-mill when she was grown up.—(See Burckhardt, Voyage en Arabie.) The wives of the Arab sheiks have still this painful occupation allotted to them. Under the reign of the sons of Clovis, St. Radegundes, Queen of France, ground herself, *in imitation of the Blessed Virgin*, all the corn that she consumed during Lent.—(Le Grand d'Aussy, Hist. privée des Français.) The invention of water-mills is attributed to Mithridates. It is certain that they were in existence in his time. Among other proofs, is cited that fine epigram of Antipater of Thessalonica, of which the following is a translation:—"You women who have been hitherto employed in grinding our corn, let your arms rest henceforth, and sleep without care; the birds will no longer proclaim with their songs the break of day for you. Ceres has commanded the Naiads to do your work: they obey, and quickly turn a wheel which rapidly moves by itself the heavy millstones." The Romans did not bring water-mills to perfection till Constantine had abolished slavery.

† These urns are enormous earthen vessels, of a height out of all proportion. The women of Nazareth carry them on their heads, and beneath so great a weight, sometimes even with an infant in their arms, they walk with an activity quite astonishing.—(F. de Geramb, t. ii. p. 239.)

‡ This fountain is called in the country *the fountain of Mary*. Tradition relates that the divine Mother of Jesus went habitually to draw the water which she required, and to be convinced that it must have been so, it would suffice to consider that water is extremely rare at Nazareth. The road which leads to this fountain, where the pious mother of Constantine had had fine basins and reservoirs constructed, is bordered with nopals and fruit-trees.—(F. de Geramb, *loco citato*.)

Jesus Christ, witness of the laborious habits of this valiant woman, sometimes alludes to them in his parables; and these simple occupations of Mary are preserved in the gospel narrative, like a sea-weed in amber. We see, in fact, the industrious woman putting leaven into three measures of meal,* carefully sweeping her floor to recover something lost,† and economically mending an old garment.‡ When Jesus seeks a comparison, to recommend purity of heart, he draws it from the remembrance of her who carefully cleans "both the inside and outside of the cup;"§ and we suspect that his thought is of Mary when he praises the offering of the widow "who gives not of her abundance, but of her indigence." Thus the poet of Chios represents to us Justice under the features of his mother, a poor woman of the people, weighing exactly the wool which she is going to spin for the support of herself and her son, and remaining upright and just towards the rich, in the midst of deep misery.

At the approach of night,‖ when the birds seek a shelter beneath the foliage, Mary placed upon a neat polished table, the work of Joseph's hands, little loaves of barley and doura, savoury dates, butter, and cheese, dry fruits and herbs, which composed the frugal banquet of the descendant of the princes of Israel. These dishes, simply prepared, were the chief food of the ancient Hebrews,—a sober race, who knew how to be contented with bread and water when necessity required it.¶ As to the Virgin, she lived on so little that ancient

* St. Luke xiii. 21, and St. Matt. xiii. 34.

† Ibid., v. 36.

‡ Ibid., xv. 8.

§ St. Luke xi. 39, and St. Matt. xxv. 25.

‖ In Israel, those who kept regular hours eat after their work, and pretty late.—(Fleury, Mœurs des Israelites.) The principal meal of Joseph and Mary was about six o'clock in the evening.

¶ Fleury, Mœurs des Israel., p. 61.

authors, fond of the marvellous, believed that she was fed by angels.

When Joseph, fatigued with the labours of the day, returned at sunset to his little low apartment, he found his young companion hastening to offer him, by turns, warm water, which she had heated to wash his feet, and cold clear water from the fountain, in a vessel pure from all unclean contact,* for the ablutions before the repast. That grave and simple man, with his fine patriarchal countenance, where every passion was silent; that angelical young female all eager to serve him with the solicitude of a dear daughter, formed a group worthy of the golden age.†

Meantime, the hour marked out by the Eternal in his divine counsels for the Incarnation of his CHRIST had arrived. The angel Gabriel, one of the four‡ who are always before the face of the Lord, received a mysterious mission, which removed him, for a short time, from the kingdom of heaven. Clothed in one of those beautiful coverings of dense air, with which the pure spirits are surrounded when they would be perceptible to the gross senses of the children of men,§ the angel left behind him the golden palaces and the emerald walls of the heavenly

* There was among the Jews a multitude of precautions to be taken for the purity of the vessels in which they drew water, and in which they prepared their food; not only did they take care that they had not belonged to strangers, but they carried their scruples much farther, for a thousand circumstances rendered them unclean.—(Misnah, Ordo, Puritatum.)

† An ancient author makes the Virgin say, "Non dedignabar parare et ministrare quæ erant necessaria Joseph; and this is in perfect conformity with the customs still existing.

‡ "There are four angels who are hardly ever seen upon earth," say the rabbins, "because they are always round about the throne of God: these angels are, Michael, who is on the right; Gabriel, who is on the left; Uriel, who is before God; and Raphael, who is behind him."

§ St. Thomas of Aquin, Quæst. Univ. de creat. Spirit., Art. 6.

Jerusalem, the gates of which are twelve pearls,* and spread his vast white wings,† with his brow all radiant with benignant joy; for the holy angels are as glad at the happiness of men as the bad angels are at their ruin and sufferings.

After traversing the immeasurable deserts of the sky, of which the stars are the oasis, the angel who had foretold to Daniel the coming of the Messias, and who came to act for the accomplishment of that grand promise of God, directed his course, with the rapidity of thought, towards our little planet, which his piercing eye discovered at an immense distance, in the state of a nebulous star, which next shone with a feeble milky light; and which finally took the rotundity and tranquil light of the moon, whose phases it has.

As he approached this little globe,—which man has proudly divided into zones and hemispheres, and in which he bestirs himself, with insane ardour, to pick up a few bits of gold, which he makes his god,—the angel began to distinguish expanses of blue and shining water, surmounted with dark points like small submarine rocks: these were our oceans and our high mountains. The towns were not yet visible, nor men; they are so small! But at last, the earth, which had at first presented itself under a microscopic form, was gradually enlarged into vast countries covered with kingdoms, divided by deserts, and planted with forests. Arrived directly over Palestine, the angel from on high directed his look, as a benediction, down upon the beautiful town of Nazareth, and descending softly from the clouds like the falling stars, he came down gracefully, like a fine swan,

* Apocal., c. xxi. v. 21.

† The Jews represent the angels with wings, as do the Christians. The Koran gives a hundred and forty pairs of wings to the angel Gabriel, and says that he took but one hour to come from heaven upon earth.—(Legend of Mahomet.)

on his flight folding his wings upon the holy and [illegible] of Joseph, that carpenter of [illegible] [illegible] ancestors.

The sun was declining [illegible] promontory of Carmel, and would soon [illegible] the horizon of the sea of Syria, when the angel presented himself in the modest oratory of the Blessed Virgin.* As a faithful observer of the religious customs of her people, Mary, with [illegible] turned in the direction of the temple,† was then [illegible] evening prayer to the God of Jacob.‡ "Hail, [illegible] said the celestial envoy, bowing his [illegible] Lord is with thee; blessed art thou am[illegible]

Mary felt an involuntary trembling [illegible] apparition. Perhaps, like Moses, she fear[illegible] see God, and die; perhaps, as St. Am[illegible] virginal purity was alarmed at the sight of [illegible] who entered, like the rays of light, into that [illegible] cell where no man penetrated; perhaps it was the respectful attitude and the magnificent eulogy of the angel which disconcerted her humility. Whatever may have been the cause, the Evangelist relates that she was troubled at hi[illegible] and thought with herself what manner of sal[illegible] should be, seeking, but in vain, to understand [illegible] this astonishing visit, and the hidden [illegible] terious salutation.

* It is commonly thought that the visit of [illegible] Virgin took place towards the evening.

† The people of the East turn to a certain p[illegible] when they pray; it is what they call the K[illegible] towards the temple of Jerusalem, the Mahometans [illegible] Sabeans towards the south, and the G[illegible]

‡ The Jews prayed three times in the day, [illegible] rise; in the afternoon, at three o'clock, when th[illegible] and in the evening, at sunset. According to th[illegible] established morning prayer; Isaac, that of the af[illegible] that of the evening.—(Basn., liv. vii. c. 17.)

on his flight folding his wings, upon the holy and poor house of Joseph, that carpenter of Galilee, who had kings for his ancestors.

The sun was declining towards the lofty promontory of Carmel, and would soon set in the horizon of the sea of Syria, when the angel presented himself in the modest oratory af the Blessed Virgin.* As a faithful observer of the religious customs of her people, Mary, with her head turned in the direction of the temple,† was then making her evening prayer to the God of Jacob.‡ "Hail, full of grace," said the celestial envoy, bowing his radiant head; "the Lord is with thee; blessed art thou among women."

Mary felt an involuntary trembling at this marvellous apparition. Perhaps, like Moses, she feared that she should see God, and die; perhaps, as St. Ambrose thought, her virginal purity was alarmed at the sight of this son of heaven, who entered, like the rays of light, into that solitary cell where no man penetrated; perhaps it was the respectful attitude and the magnificent eulogy of the angel which disconcerted her humility. Whatever may have been the cause, the Evangelist relates that she was troubled at his saying, and thought with herself what manner of salutation this should be, seeking, but in vain, to understand the object of this astonishing visit, and the hidden meaning of this mysterious salutation.

* It is commonly thought that the visit of the angel to the Blessed Virgin took place towards the evening.

† The people of the East turn to a certain point in the heavens when they pray; it is what they call the *Kebla.* The Jews turn towards the temple of Jerusalem, the Mahometans towards Mecca, the Sabeans towards the south, and the Ghebers towards the rising sun.

‡ The Jews prayed three times in the day; in the morning, at sunrise; in the afternoon, at three o'clock, when they offered sacrifice; and in the evening, at sunset. According to the rabbins, Abraham established morning prayer; Isaac, that of the afternoon; and Jacob, that of the evening.—(Basn., liv. vii. c. 17.)

The angel, who perceived her trouble, said to her mildly, "Fear not, Mary, for thou hast found grace with God. Behold thou shalt conceive in thy womb, and shalt bring forth a son, and thou shalt call his name JESUS. He shall be great, and shall be called the Son of the Most High, and the Lord God shall give unto him the throne of David his father: and he shall reign in the house of Jacob for ever, and of his kingdom there shall be no end." At these words, which would have transported any other but Mary with immoderate joy, the chaste and prudent young woman thought of nothing but her pure white crown of virginity, which she desired to preserve at any cost, and asked how she could reconcile this magnificent prediction with the vow of virginity with which her life was linked.*

The modesty of a young woman is a thing so sacred in the sight of angels, that Gabriel, to remove all apprehension from Mary on that head, was not afraid to unveil a part of the mystery of the Incarnation. "The power of the Most High shall overshadow thee," said he, "and the Holy that shall be born of thee shall be called the Son of God."† Then, accord-

* Calvin, that proud heresiarch, who had Servetus burned, while he himself preached up toleration, has dared to calumniate the Virgin, taking his text from this answer, to accuse her of unbelief. St. Augustin had answered him long before. "The Virgin doubts not," said he, "*non quasi incredula de oraculo;* she only desires to be informed as to the manner in which the miracle is to be accomplished." St. John Chrysostom adds, "that this question is the effect of respectful admiration, and not of vain curiosity."

† This gospel narrative has been received by the Mussulmans themselves. This is how the Koran relates the interview of the Blessed Virgin and the angel:—"The angel said to Mary, God announces his Word to thee, he shall be called Jesus, the Messias, the Son of Mary, great in this world, and in the other, and the Confidant of the Most High; he shall make his word heard by men from the cradle to old age, and shall be of the number of the just.—My Lord, replied Mary, how shall I have a son? I know not man.—It shall be thus, replied the angel: God forms creatures at his pleasure; is it is

ing to the custom of the messengers of Jehovah, he would give her a sign which should confirm his words: "And behold," continued the angel, "thy cousin Elizabeth, she hath also conceived a son in her old age; and this is the sixth month with her that is called barren; because no word shall be impossible with God."

Sarah had laughed with incredulous laughter when an angel, in the guise of a traveller, seated in the shade of the great oaks which covered her tent, had announced a son to her, aged and barren as she was. Mary, to whom was announced a new prodigy, as Isaias declares, a thing without example under the sun, in fine, a virginal maternity, believed at once the divine promise, and, annihilating herself before Him who exalted her above all women, she replied, in a submissive voice, "Behold the handmaid of the Lord, be it done to me according to thy word." At these words the angel disappeared, and the WORD was made flesh to dwell among us.* Thus did the angel of light treat of our salvation with the new Eve, and the fault of the sinful Eve, who had conspired for our destruction with the infernal angel, was gloriously repaired; thus was a simple mortal exalted to the unequalled dignity of Mother of God, and being both virgin and mother, she confounded, by a new miracle, the two most opposite and sublime states of her sex. "Proceed no farther," says St. John Chrysostom, "seek nothing beyond what is said nor say, How did the Holy Ghost effect this in the Virgin? . . . . Enquire not, therefore, but receive what is revealed, and search not curiously into what is hidden."†

We have adopted the opinion of those doctors and theologians who maintain that Joseph was legally the husband

will that a thing should exist? he says, Be thou made, and it is made."—(Koran, c. iii.)

* The mystery of the incarnation was accomplished on the 25th of March, on a Friday evening, according to F. Drexelius.

† St. J. Chrys., Serm. 4, in St. Matt.

of Mary at the time of the Incarnation; yet this opinion is disputed, and among the authorities who assert that Mary was not yet the wife, but only the betrothed of Joseph, we find in the first rank the great St. John Chrysostom himself.* Nevertheless, according to the same father, Mary dwelt in the house of St. Joseph at the time when the angel appeared to her. "For," says this illustrious sacred orator, "among the ancients it was the custom generally to have the betrothed in the house, and this may be seen even now; and the sons-in-law of Lot lived with him."†

Notwithstanding the profound veneration inspired by St. John Chrysostom, the Church has not adopted his opinion. Moreover, the reference to the sons-in-law of Lot, with which he would strengthen his opinion, is badly chosen: the Scripture nowhere says that they lived with Lot, and everything leads us to think the contrary, since the patriarch was obliged to *go out of his house* in a moment of trouble and affright, while the most hideous commotion was fomenting in the city, *to speak to his sons-in-law that were to have his daughters, to arise and get out of the place, because the Lord would destroy the city.* Supposing even that the young men betrothed to Lot's daughters had formed a part of the family of this patriarch, whose flocks covered the hills and valleys of a whole province,—according to the manners of the times, these young men would have been nothing more on the banks of the Jordan than what Jacob was later on in Mesopotamia, active and vigilant servants, *day and night parched with heat and with frost.*‡ We nowhere see that they had their betrothed spouses in their tents; they lived under the protec-

* Descoutures is wrong in placing St. John Chrysostom in the ranks of those who maintain that Joseph was legally the husband of Mary at the moment of the Incarnation: this writer, who is in general judicious, probably quoted him on trust.

† St. J. Chrys., Serm. 4, in St. Matt.

‡ Gen. xxxi. 40.

tion of the patriarch, being only his principal shepherds: there is nothing in all this at variance with the manners of ancient Asia. An orphan, left alone, and living under the roof of her betrothed, the Blessed Virgin, on the contrary, would have been in a position quite exceptional. A generally received custom among the Hebrews could alone have authorised such a supposition, and all that we find in their code is a law expressly opposed to it.* St. Chrysostom, agreeing in this respect with the ancient theologians, himself informs us that God for a long time covered with a thick veil the miraculous maternity of Mary, to save her from a revolting suspicion, which would have been as dangerous to the divinity of the Son, as to that respect which the whole world owed to the Mother. But marriage alone could cover with its honourable mantle the mystery of the Incarnation, for mere espousals could not suffice for that purpose; and then, if Joseph and Mary had been only affianced at the time of the Incarnation of the Word, they would have been no more four months later, since the Evangelist informs us that Mary, after the Annunciation, *went with haste* to visit St. Elizabeth, and that it was not till her return from her journey to Hebron, which had lasted three months, that *she was found with child*,—an expression which indicates a situation visible to all. At this rate, the marriage of Mary would not have been celebrated till her maternity had become evident, proved, undeniable! What would both families have thought of it? What would have been said by all Nazareth, who would have hastened to witness the ceremony? To what outrageous reproaches would the pure Virgin have been exposed, among a people where female honour was a thing so sacred as to be infallibly avenged by murder? Would not the birth of the Messias—that birth which was to be pure *as the morning dew*, according to the poetical expression of David—have been thereby tainted and defiled? The Jews, par-

* Misnah, t. iii. de Sponsalibus. Selden, Uxor Hebraica.

ticularly the Jews of Nazareth, who showed such hostility to Jesus Christ, and called him the *son of the carpenter*, would they not have bitterly reproached him with the irregularity of his birth? If they did not do so, it was because they had apparently no hold on that side.

These, no doubt, are the reasons which have induced a number of illustrious divines to pronounce in favour of the marriage, notwithstanding the countenance which the opposite party found in the words of St. Matthew, words which seem to favour the other interpretation, but which nevertheless do not convey a meaning precise enough to remove the difficulty.* After all, the dispute never bore upon the prin-

* The verse which has divided the doctors is this: "Christi autem generatio sic erat: *cum esset desponsata mater ejus Maria Joseph, antequam convenirent, inventa est in utero habeus de Spiritu Sancto.* Those who dwell on the force of the words, say that the Virgin was only betrothed, because the Greek verb, which is a translation of the Hebrew expression of St. Matthew, means *desponderi*, to be promised, and because there is another term to signify to be married, as we find among the Latins *desponderi* and *nubere*, so that St. Joseph had not yet taken the Virgin home to his house; which they prove by those words of verse 20:—"*Noli timere accipere Mariam conjugem tuam: quod enim in ea natum est, de Spiritu Sancto est*," which they explain thus: "Take Mary for thy wife without fear, for what is born in her is born by the operation of the Holy Ghost." But to be translated thus it must have been *in conjugem tuam*. The opposite opinion, which is maintained by fathers, interpreters of considerable weight, and almost all theologians, finds wherewith to combat its antagonists in the second chapter of St. Luke; for, notwithstanding that the Virgin was already married to Joseph, the gospel uses the Greek term ὑπισχνεῖσθαι, which signifies *to be promised*, and says: "*Ut profiteretur cum Maria desponsata sibi uxore prægnante*, to be enrolled with Mary, his espoused wife, who was with child;" and in verse 19 of the first chapter of St. Matthew, St. Joseph is called *vir ejus*, her husband, and not her espoused. If St. Matthew calls the Blessed Virgin *sponsa*, spouse, although she was wife, it is not to say that she had not yet contracted marriage; it is merely to show, as one of the fathers remarks, that she had no more intimacy with her husband than if she had been only his betrothed.

cipal point: wife or betrothed, no one, among Christians, has ever doubted that the Mother of God was the purest and most holy of virgins; even the Mussulmans admit that *she was the spring and mine of purity.**

CHAPTER IX.

THE VISITATION.

MEANWHILE Mary, informed by the angel of the pregnancy of Elizabeth, resolved to go and offer her affectionate congratulations to her venerable relative. It was not, as heretics have dared to say, that the Virgin wanted ocular demonstration of the reality of this event, which was out of the ordinary laws of nature; she knew that nothing is impossible to God, and, moreover, could not suppose that a messenger of heaven would bring her from the Most High words of deception and falsehood. She went, not to be made sure, but because she was sure; she went with haste, because charity, says St. Ambrose, admits neither delays nor hindrances; and besides, good and kind as she was during her whole life, she longed to carry to relations whose protection had sur-

* The purity of Mary is so fully recognised by the Mussulmans, that Abou-Ishac, ambassador of the caliph at the court of the Emperor of the Greeks, holding a conference with the patriarch and certain Greek bishops, on the subject of religion, the bishops reproached the Mussulmans with many things which had been formerly said by the Mussulmans themselves against Aïschah, the widow of their prophet, which had stirred up divisions among them. Abou-Ishac answered them that they need not wonder at these dissensions, since among Christians opinions had been so divided on the subject of the glorious Mary, mother of Jesus, "who may be called," said he, "*the mine and fountain of all purity*, genab ismet mealo kon offet."—(D'Herbelot, Bibl. Orientale, t. ii. p. 620.)

rounded her childhood, and who had long looked upon her as their daughter, some little of that sanctification and those heavenly graces which flowed in her soul as inexhaustible springs of living water, from the time that she bore in her chaste womb the Creator of the world.

With the consent of St. Joseph, whose simple but elevated soul was in unison with her own, and who had but one heart and will with her, Mary left Nazareth in the season of roses, and went towards the mountains of Judea, where Zachary dwelt. The Scripture, which neglects details, and takes up the leading points of events, does not say whether the Virgin had any companions in this journey; some authors have thence inferred that she performed it alone, which is not at all likely. In fact, the distance from Nazareth to the town of Ain* is five days' march; part of Galilee, the hostile Samaria, and almost all the territory of Juda had to be passed through. Now the country is rugged with mountains, intersected by torrents, and interspersed with deserts.† The roads, which the Romans repaired at a later period, full of holes made by the heavy footsteps of camels, and covered with loose stones, threatened the traveller at every step with a fatal fall. When the evening came on, one must sleep in some caravansary, where nothing was to be found but a small place without provisions, and furnished with a plain rush mat;‡ for the primitive hospitality had marked by its

* Zachary lived at Ain, or Aen, two leagues to the south of Jerusalem. St. Helen had a church built on the site of his house.

† Although Judea was much more populous then than now, there still remained districts so barren as to be incapable of cultivation. The gospel makes mention of deserts but a short distance from towns where Jesus Christ went to pray.

‡ "There is no inn in any part of Syria and Palestine," says M. de Volney, "but the towns and most of the villages have a large building called Kervanseraï, which serves as a shelter for all travellers. These receptacles, always placed outside the walls of towns, are composed of four arcades, which enclose a square court which serves

gradual decrease the different phases of advanced civilisation among the Hebrews. In such a state of things is it to be presumed that a man full of days and experience, like Joseph, would willingly have exposed a young wife—beautiful, delicate, brought up retired from the world, and confiding as innocence itself—to dangers of all sorts, to every kind of inconvenience which a solitary journey presented? Such an assertion contradicts the history of the people of God, and the manners of Asia;*—a Jewish woman would never have trusted herself, without a respectable escort, such a distance from her house.

If St. Joseph, as F. Croiset thinks, could not accompany Mary, it is probable that the Mother of God joined some of her relations who were led by their piety to the holy city, with their husbands, or their servants, and that thence she pursued her journey under some safe protection. We always find her travelling thus in the midst of her own relatives, whether she goes to Jerusalem for the great solemnities, or follows the preachings of Jesus with the holy women at a much more advanced period of her life. "Though she could have had no better guardian than herself," says St. Ambrose, "she never appeared abroad without being faithfully escorted."†

When she arrived at the priestly city where the Levite and his happy wife dwelt, Mary was directed to their well-known house without allowing herself any time to rest. Elizabeth, informed by one of her slaves of the unexpected visit of her cousin, came to meet her with great signs of joy.

as a place for the beasts: there are in these places neither provisions nor furniture."

* No one travels alone in Syria; the people only go in troops and caravans; they have to wait till several travellers want to proceed to the same place. These precautions are necessary in countries exposed to the Arabs, like Syria and Palestine.—(Volney, Voyage en Syrie.)

† St. Amb., de Virginibus, liv. ii.

Seeing her approach, the young Virgin bowed, and laying her hand on her heart, said, "Peace be with thee," hastening to be the first to offer a salutation.* Elizabeth stepped back a little: the animated and friendly expression of her countenance had given place to profound respect; her features gradually brightened; it was evident that something unusual and prodigious was passing within her. The simple formulary of politeness which the Virgin had pronounced in her low and mild voice had overpowered her relation. All at once, the spirit of prophecy descended upon Elizabeth, and she cried out, "Blessed art thou among women, and blessed is the fruit of thy womb. And whence is this to me," she added, "that the Mother of my Lord should come to me? For behold, as soon as the voice of thy salutation sounded in my ears, the infant in my womb leaped for joy. And blessed art thou that hast believed, because those things shall be accomplished that were spoken to thee by the Lord."

The answer of Mary was the sublime, unpremeditated effusion of the MAGNIFICAT, the first canticle of the New Testament, and the finest in the sacred Scriptures:—

"My soul doth magnify the Lord: and my spirit hath rejoiced in God my Saviour.

"Because he hath regarded the humility of his handmaid: for behold from henceforth all generations shall call me blessed.

"For he that is mighty hath done great things to me, and holy is his name.

"And his mercy is from generation to generations to them that fear him.

* This salutation, which Jesus Christ often used, is still that of all the East. When the Orientals meet, after the ordinary salutation, "Peace be with you (*salem alaicom*)," they lay their hand on their heart. This salutation was in use in the time of Abraham.—(Savary, Note sur le c. ii. du Koran.)

"He hath showed might in his arm: he hath scattered the proud in the conceit of their heart.

"He hath put down the mighty from their seat, and hath exalted the humble.

"He hath filled the hungry with good things: and the rich he hath sent empty away.

"He hath received Israel his servant, being mindful of his mercy.

"As he spoke to our fathers, to Abraham and to his seed for ever."

Thus did the Virgin discern at once, by a supernatural light, those ancient prophecies and their perfect accomplishment, herself being a thousand times more enlightened and more privileged than all the prophets put together. "In this celebrated interview, and in this admirable conversation," says St. Ambrose, "Mary and Elizabeth both prophesied by the Holy Ghost, with whom they were filled, and by the merits of their infants."

The virgin sojourned three months in the country of the heathens, and spent this long visit at a short distance from the city of Ain, in the hollow of a shady and fertile valley, where Zachary had his country house.* It was then that the daughter of David, herself also a prophetess, and endowed with genius equal to that of the illustrious head of her race, could contemplate at leisure the starry heavens, the sonorous forests, and the vast sea, which, at the horizon rolled its waves, whether loud or peaceful, on the blue resounding shores of Syria. The Blessed Virgin did not look with indifference upon these magnificent scenes of creation. All the works of nature spoke to her of their great Author, and

* This country house was at a short distance from Ain, in a pleasant and fertile valley, which serves now as a garden to the village of Saint John. There had been built in this place, in honour of the Visitation, a church, which, in our days, is no more than a heap of ruins.

came gently to warm her soul after charming her eyes. The plain which vanished from her sight beyond the mountains of Arabia, the blue vaulted sky which is spread like a tent above the habitations of men, gave her some idea of the immensity of God the Creator; the golden harvests, the savoury fruits, the cool mountain spring, proclaimed to her his providence; the voice of the tempests, his power; the regular order of the heavens, his wisdom; and the care which He takes of the birds of heaven and the insects of the earth, his goodness.

In these excursions in the country, she sometimes rested by the side of a gushing fountain, the foam and noise of which she loved: this spring, called Nephtoa in the time of Josue, bears to this day the name of "Mary."*

At the back of the elegant *villa* of the Hebrew priest extended one of those gardens called a *paradise* by the Persians, the mode of laying out which had been borrowed by the captives of Israel from the nations of Cyrus and Semiramis: there were seen the finest trees of Palestine; and the groups of flowers scattered irregularly about the open spaces, the sweet perfume of the orange-trees, the streams of water which ran beneath the low bending branches of the willows, made its shades very charming. There the sweet converse of Mary made Elizabeth forget her fears for an event, the hope of which overpowered her with joy, but which her advanced age might render fatal. How religious must have been the conversation of these two women! The one young, artless, and ignorant of evil as Eve when she came forth from the hands of the Lord; the other full of days, and rich in long experience of the things of life; both deeply pious, and objects of the complacency of Jehovah; the one

* This fountain has so great an abundance of water that it irrigates the whole valley and renders it productive. Tradition relates that Mary sometimes came thither; it bore the name of *Nephtoa* in the time of Josue; it now bear that of the *Fountain of the Virgin.*

bearing in her womb, so long barren, a son who was to be "a prophet, and more than a prophet;" the other, the blessed germ of the Most High, the chief and liberator of Israel.

In the fine summer evenings, when the white light of the moon shone on the foliage, there was brought out beneath a large fig-tree, or under the green leafy branches of a thick vine,* the repast of the opulent family: the lamb fed in the deep valleys in the neighbourhood of Bethlehem, the kid of the aromatic mountains of Bethar, clean birds netted by the Israelite fowler, shell-fish caught by the fishermen of Sidon, milk, butter, and cheese, honeycombs; and then, in baskets of palm-leaves, pomegranates, figs, grapes from Galilee, with dates from Jericho,† which even figured on the table of Cæsar; there were also seen apricots from Armenia, plums from Damascus, pistachio nuts from Aleppo, water-melons from the banks of the Nile, and that sweet cane from the marshes of Egypt, which Herodotus speaks of as an exquisite eatable; lastly, the golden wine of Libanus, and the perfumed wine of Cyprus, which the steward kept in stone jars,‡ circulated in rich cups. Mary, temperate as ever in the midst of this abundance, was content with a little fruit and a cup of pure water. Frugality with her was no forced virtue, or an abstinence merely of circumstance; it was a virtue by choice.§

Some writers, to extol the humility of the Blessed Virgin,

* The Hebrews were fond of taking their meals in gardens, under trees, and in arbours; for it is natural, in hot countries, to seek air and coolness.—(Fleury, Mœurs des Israel., § xvii.)

† The dates of Syria and Judea are yellow and black, round, like apples, and very sweet. Pliny reckons forty-nine kinds of dates.

‡ The Jews established in the Yemen still make use of these jars.—(See Niebuhr, Voyage en Arabie.)

§ Her abstinence did not appear to be a fast: it was rather a custom, as it were, not to make use of food.—(F. Valverde, Vie de J. Christ, t. i. p. 6.)

which needs no extraneous commendation, have insisted that she rendered to Elizabeth the offices of a *servant*, and almost of a slave.

This is an evident inconsistency: Elizabeth would never have allowed a woman whom she herself had proclaimed the Mother of her Lord, and whom she had highly extolled above all the daughters of Sion, to lower herself in such manner before her. The holy spouse of Zachary* could not have wanted servants or slaves. By the consent of Christians and Jews, this family was distinguished, and the illustrious birth of St. John Baptist even cast something like discredit upon that of Jesus Christ, born of parents much less distinguished, and leading in poverty the common life of the people.

The attentions, therefore, which the amiable and gentle Virgin profusely paid to Elizabeth had nothing in them painful or servile; they were those delicate and forecasting attentions with which she would have waited upon her own mother, if heaven had spared her to her; and no doubt she often imagined that she beheld again the authors of her days

* Zachary was descended from Abia, father of the eighth priestly family. These ancient families were rare, several of them having settled in Persia after the captivity. Elizabeth was descended from Aaron and from David. The Jews reckoned John the Baptist far above Jesus, because he had passed his life in the desert, and was the son of a chief priest. Jesus Christ, on the other hand, born of a poor woman, appeared to them as one of the common people.—(S. Joan. Chrysost. in Matt., Serm. 12.) The Mussulmans have retained a high idea of St. John Baptist, whom they call *Jahia ben Zacharia* (John, the son of Zachary). Saadi, in his Gulistan, makes mention of the sepulchre of St. John Baptist, venerated in the mosque of Damascus; he said some prayers there, and records those of a king of the Arabs, who came thither on a pilgrimage. "The Caliph Abdalmalek wanted to purchase this church out of the hands of the Christians," says D'Herbelot, "and it was only after their refusal of four thousand dinars, or gold pistoles, which he had offered them, that he took possession of it by force."—(Bibliothèque Orientale, t. ii.)

in that affectionate, devout, and vnerable pair, who loved her with parental affection, and who showed towards her from the first interview, when her greatness was so marvellously revealed, a sentiment of admiration mingled with respect, which Mary humbly endeavoured to prevent, but which she did not succeed in destroying.

It is easy to understand, say the fathers, how many blessings were drawn down by the visit of Mary upon the priestly family who had given her so affectionate a reception. If the Lord blessed Obededom, and all that belonged to him, even so far as to make the holy king David jealous, for having had the ark of the covenant in his house for three months, what graces must have been drawn down upon Zachary and all belonging to him by the three months' abode of Her of whom the ark of the covenant was but the figure, though so holy and awful! "The purity in which St. John always lived," says St. Ambrose, "was an effect of that unction and that grace infused into his soul by the presence of the Virgin."

We know not precisely whether the Mother of God assisted at the lying-in of Elizabeth. Origon, St Ambrose, and other grave authors, ancient as well as modern, declare for the affirmative, and this opinion is very probable; for it would have been at least very extraordinary, after having spent so long a time with her relation, if Mary had abruptly left her in the hour of danger, and without any reasonable motive for so unseasonable and precipitate a departure. Custom required that all the matrons of the family should assemble round the new mother to rejoice with her in her happiness; the gospel informs us that they were not wanting to Elizabeth on this solemn occasion, and that the birth of St. John Baptist drew a large concourse of kinsfolk and friends to the house of his father. It is alleged that virgins were not generally found at these sort of gatherings, and this we can conceive; but Mary was married, which required of her those duties which became her, and which she could not omit without violating usages received from the time of the patriarchs. Some argue with as little reason, from the retired habits of the Virgin, to the conclusion that even the noise of the festivities which celebrated the birth of the precursor of Jesus Christ put her to flight like a young dove suddenly alarmed. Mary was quite able to reconcile her small inclination for the world with that exquisite sense of propriety attributed to her by the fathers, and her tender solicitude for her mother's niece: she must have remained beneath the roof of the priest until Elizabeth was out of danger: and then, escaping from that admiration which she never failed to excite, she left the mountains of Judea, after embracing and blessing the new Elias.*

A religious author observes that the blessed daughter of Joachim had hastened with all diligence to visit her cousin, but that she departed slowly, and as if with regret, from

* Those theologians who have embraced the contrary opinion to that of Origen and St. Ambrose, dwell upon that passage of St. Luke which does not speak of the *accouchement* of Elizabeth till after having brought the Blessed Virgin back into Galilee. It seemed to us that this deserved consideration: we therefore attentively examined the gospel of this evangelist; this minute examination convinced us that this reason is not conclusive; for it is the custom of St. Luke to make transpositions of this kind, and we can quote two others of the same nature. For example, after having followed up the preaching of St. John Baptist, and announced his imprisonment, St. Luke speaks, in the following verse, of the baptism of Jesus Christ, of the priority of which to the prison of the precursor, and his tragical death, there can be no doubt. When relating the adoration of the shepherds, St. Luke expatiates on the marvellous accounts which they gave of their journey to the cave of Bethlehem, and of the astonishment which these recitals caused; after which, taking us back without any transition to the interrupted scene of the adoration, he speaks of their departure from the stable. This is what makes us adopt the doctrine of St. Ambrose the probability of which strikes us at first sight. F. Valverde, who studied the holy fathers deeply, is equally of opinion that the Blessed Virgin did not leave her relations till she had embraced and blessed the precursor of the Messias.

those cool valleys, the oaks of which had afforded shelter to angels;* perchance, like the sea-bird, she had a presentiment of storms.

CHAPTER X.

VIRGINAL PREGNANCY OF MARY.

On her return to Nazareth, Mary returned with ease to the life of the people, and resumed the humble occupations which she must have suspended in the more elevated sphere which she had just quitted. She became again the young housewife, active and diligent, who found time for work, time for prayer, time for reading the sacred books, whose whole conversation was in heaven, and who seemed to have applied to herself those beautiful and sage words of the Psalmist: "All the glory of the king's daughter is within." But meanwhile she advanced in her virginal pregnancy, and Joseph began to be full of anxious thought.

A poignant uncertainty, a painful perplexity, tortured the great and upright soul of the patriarch. At first he did not believe his eyes, and he found it more reasonable to doubt the testimony of his senses, than the purity of a woman who had always appeared to him a prodigy of candour and sanctity. But the condition of Mary became more and more visible; *she was found with child*, says the gospel, which means that all Nazareth was informed of it, and that Joseph's relations, in the innocence of their hearts, offered him painful congratulations, which he was obliged to receive without

* In the vale of Mambre, which is only six furlongs from Hebron, there was still shown in the time of St. Jerom, a tree of enormous growth, beneath which it was said that Abraham had received the visit of the three angels who announced to him the birth of Isaac.

changing countenance, and which struck him at once like a flash of lightning. According to the Proto-Gospel of St. James, in the first transports of his grief, he prostrated himself before God with his face on the ground, and all bathed in tears, crying out, "Who has betrayed me? who has brought evil into my house?" Then, yielding to his tender affection for the young orphan whom he had ever regarded as the pearl and honour of her sex, he bitterly accused himself of not having guarded her with sufficient care. "Alas!" he said to himself, "my history is that of Adam; when he reposed with the greatest confidence in his glory and happiness, behold on a sudden Satan deceived Eve with lying words, and seduced her."* When Joseph was sufficiently calm in mind to reflect, he found himself in great perplexity.

According to the Jewish law, adultery was punished by death. When there were no witnesses,—a single one would suffice,—and the woman denied the crime laid to her charge, she was led, by order of the sanhedrim, to the eastern gate of the temple, and there, in presence of all, after snatching off her veil, placing about her neck a cord brought from Egypt, to put her in mind of the miracles which God had wrought in that land, and covering her shoulders with her dishevelled hair, because it was a disgrace for a Jewish woman to be seen with her hair in that state, a priest, pronouncing a terrible formulary of malediction, to which she had to answer *Amen*, presented her with the famous cup of the *waters of jealousy*, which were also called *bitter waters*, because they had the taste of wormwood.† This cup of malediction infallibly caused the guilty wife to die, unless the husband himself had been guilty of infidelity; for then the miracle did not take place, "because," say the doctors of Israel, "it would not have been just that one of the guilty

* Protevang. Jac., in the apocryph. of Fabric., t. i. p. 97.

† Basn., liv. vii. c. 22.

should be absolved, while God punished the other."* A husband of a violent temper would not have failed to drag Mary before the priests of the Lord, to subject her to the formidable trial of the bitter waters; but Joseph, the most moderate, as well as the most just of men, did not so much as think of taking this extreme course. Not being able to retain Mary under his roof, since both the law of honour and the law of Moses conspired to prevent him from so doing, he wished at least to take all possible precautions to prevent this painful separation from casting any shade upon her virtue,—for *he was a just man, and not willing publicly to expose her.* "I will put her away," said Joseph mournfully to himself, "but before God, and not before the judges, who would condemn her to die, and me to cast the first stone at her;† I will save her from the reproaches of her family and the contempt of the world: but how can I get clear of this labyrinth, where dishonour and death present themselves at every outlet?" And the son of David remained plunged in extreme depression of mind.

The gloomy sadness of the just man, to whom God himself had entrusted her, could not escape Mary, and no doubt it cost her a great deal to conceal from Joseph the glorious embassy of the angel; but how could she unveil an event so unheard of, so miraculous, as that of her divine maternity, with no other proof than her own word? Persuaded with reason that, to be believed, the mystery of the Incarnation must be revealed by supernatural means, and leaving to Him, who had wrought so great things in her, the care of convincing Joseph of her innocence, "the daughter of David," says the great Bishop of Meaux, "at the risk of seeing

* Wagenseil, in Sotah, p. 244.

† The Jewish law required that the accuser should cast the first stone at him whom he had caused to be condemned.—(Voy. Institut. de Moïse, t. ii. p. 65.)

herself not only suspected and forsaken, but even lost and dishonoured, left all to God, and remained in peace."

The Eternal, from the height of his starry throne, looked down with complacency upon the just man, whom he had subjected to this severe trial,* before he raised him to the supreme honour of being his own representative upon earth, and the angels, with their eyes fixed on the holy house of Nazareth, anxiously awaited the result of this close contest, in which humanity, duty, and the noblest sentiments of the soul were engaged. At last, the patriarch ended with an idea so generous and heroic, that it places him almost on a level with the Queen of angels: he resolved to sacrifice his honour, the esteem which he had acquired by a spotless life, the means of existence which gave him his daily bread, and the air of his native land, so good to breathe when one is drawing near to the tomb, in order to save the reputation of a wife, who did not even attempt to justify herself, and who was so cruelly accused by appearances. There was but one way of parting with Mary without ruining her, for her family would have been urgent for explanations which would have terminated fatally: and this was to banish himself, to go and die afar off in the land of exile, and to take upon his own head all the odium of such a desertion. There are resignations as glorious as triumphs, and sufferings patiently supported, which heaven rewards as munificently as martyrdom; the unknown sacrifice of the spouse of the Virgin was of this number. To reconcile together his duty and his humanity, he accepted by anticipation the sad reproaches of being a

* "Doubtless," says Bossuet (Elev. sur les Myst.), "God could have spared Joseph all this pain, by revealing to him earlier the mystery of the pregnancy of Mary: but his virtue would not have been put to the trial which was prepared for him; we should not have witnessed the victory of Joseph over the most untameable of all passions, and the most righteous jealousy that was ever conceived, would not have been laid prostrate at the feet of virtue."

husband without a heart, a father without feeling, a man without conscience and without faith; he accepted the contempt of his relations, the mortal hatred of the relatives of Mary, and resolved to tear off with his own hand the crown of his good name to cast it before the feet of that young woman, whose mysterious and inexplicable position filled his heart with sadness, and his life with bitterness.

St. John Chrysostom is never tired of admiring the fine and noble conduct of St. Joseph. "It was necessary," says this great saint, "that when grace was approaching, there should be many signs of this sublime dispensation. For as the sun, though not yet showing its rays, still at a distance enlightens the greatest part of the earth, so also Christ, when about to issue from that womb, enlightened the whole world before his birth. Therefore, even before his birth, prophets exulted, women prophesied, and John, not yet born, leaped in the womb. Here, also, Joseph exhibited great wisdom."

We have here adopted the opinion of St. John Chrysostom in preference to that of St. Bernard, who supposes that Joseph himself discovered the mystery of the birth of Jesus Christ, and that seeing Mary pregnant, he did not doubt, from the profound veneration which he had for her, that she must be the miraculous Virgin of Isaias. "He believed it," says the apostle of the crusades, "and it was with no other sentiment than one of humility and respect,—like that which made St. Peter afterwards say, 'Depart from me, for I am a sinful man, O Lord,'—that St. Joseph, who was no less humble than St. Peter, also thought of departing from the Virgin, not doubting that she bore in her sacred womb the Saviour of mankind."

This interpretation, doubtless one of great piety, and worthy of one who has been honoured with the title of the *devout chaplain of Mary*, is more in accordance with the ascetic notions of the middle ages than agreeable to the manners of the ancient Hebrews, and must fall to the ground before a careful examination of the text. In fact, the words of the gospel are so clear, that no small ingenuity would be required to obscure them. It is not that instinctive movement of religious awe which makes us keep at a distance from a sacred object, which suggests to Joseph the idea of forsaking Mary; it is a thought of conscience and duty. "He was a just man," says Bossuet, "and his justice did not allow him to remain in company with a wife whom he could not believe innocent; for merely to suspect what had happened by the operation of the Holy Ghost, that was a miracle of which God had hitherto given no example, and which could not come into any human mind." *

The words of the angel would have no sense, and would lead to a false conclusion, in the supposition of St. Bernard. "Fear not," says the ambassador of the Most High, "to take unto thee Mary, thy wife, for that which is conceived in her is of the Holy Ghost." Does Joseph object his unworthiness at the moment when he becomes certain that Mary bears in her womb the Author of nature himself? Does he lay before the angel his scruples, which must be now more urgent than ever? Does he ask that this humble cup, which the celestial envoy presents him, may pass from him to some more worthy mortal? He does nothing of all this; the storms of the soul are appeased, and he falls into the profound calm which follows great moral tempests.

It is objected that the great oracles relating to the Messias were familiar to Joseph as they were to all the Hebrews, that he must have known that the time of the Messias was near at hand, and that he ought to have understood from the very first, considering the holiness of Mary, that she bore in her womb the Saviour of the world. To understand the prophecies which treated of the mystery of redemption was not so

* Bossuet, Elev. sur les Myst., t. ii. p. 135.

easily attained as is here supposed. Whether the allegorical descriptions of the glorious reign of the Emmanuel of Isaias had led the doctors of the synagogue into error, or whether the avaricious thoughts of the Jews could not rise above the earth, and reduced everything to temporal possessions, it is certain that the Hebrew people, "that people of a hard head," had got upon a wrong track, and would not deviate from it. He who was sent from God, the Desired of nations, was to be a lawgiver, a leader of war, a magnificent and formidable monarch, like Solomon. The apostles themselves were long under a mistake as to the humble and peaceful mission of "the poor King who passed noiselessly along;" we see them clinging to golden dreams and kingdoms in prospect, even in sight of the deicide city, which their Master was entering to die. It was not without some difficulty that our Lord brought them back to a spiritual sense,—that he rectified their ideas, always ready to fall into the narrow compass of material and palpable goods, where they were tossed about by the ambitious reveries of traditionary doctors and pharisees.

If then the apostles, those divine men who founded Christianity, had so much difficulty in divesting themselves of the prejudices of their childhood, they who lived in the midst of the miracles of the Messias, and in familiar intercourse with him, how could Joseph do this of himself, and without succour from above? The coarse garment of the artisan but little accorded with the purple of the kings of Juda, and the thing of all least expected was to have a Messias born from the ranks of the common people. Galilee, moreover, was the last place which would have been thought of. "Doth the Christ come out of Galilee?" said the doctors of the law to the disciples of Christ. In fact, the prophets had pointed out Bethlehem of Juda by name, Bethlehem, "the house of bread," as the birthplace of the Messias: and the rabbinical commentators, improving upon the prophets, distinguished even the quarter of the town where he was to be born. Joseph was too humble to suppose that his modest roof could harbour so much greatness, and the silence of Mary left him nothing to conjecture.

As to the project of sending back the Virgin to her family "out of pure respect," as some learned theologians would have it who adhere to the opinion of St. Bernard, it would have been impracticable in a nation so apt to take umbrage at everything that affected the honour of women. Mary was an orphan, and so far dependent upon her kinsfolk, who were not all of a peaceful temper, and some of whom had not approved of the union of their young relative with the obscure Nazarean. It is not likely that they would have accepted the reasons of Joseph, and admitted, without more ample information, that the Virgin bore in her womb the *King Messias.* It is much more to be presumed that they would have denounced the husband before the tribunal of the ancients, to force him to give the reasons which influenced his conduct; for there was no longer any question of a simple divorce, but of the condition of the child of Mary,—a young woman of noble blood and badly married, according to those eleven who had entered themselves on the lists to espouse the young and fair heiress of Joachim.

Thence would have resulted two grave facts: either Joseph would have kept silence, and then he would have been condemned to take back his wife, with the prohibition ever to separate from her,† or he would have declared upon oath that the child which Mary bore was not his; and then the child, disowned, became incapacitated for any employment; his birth, defiled in its source, shut him out from the assem-

* Whence comes he (the Messias)? From the royal city of Bethlehem, of Juda. Where are his parents to be found (those of the Messias)? In the quarter Biral Harba of *Bethlehem Juda.*—(See Talmud of Jerusalem.)

† Inst. de Moïse, t. ii. liv. vii.

blies of the nation, the public schools, entering the temple, and the synagogues; his posterity, paying for his disgrace, would not have been admitted to the privileges of the Hebrews till the tenth generation; he became a *Paria*,—without an asylum, without rights, without country,—and the decree which would have condemned his mother to be stoned would have branded in the forehead, both him and his descendants, with Cain's mark of reprobation. But things would not have come to this pass: rather than submit to this stain upon their royal genealogy, the proud descendants of David would have killed the Virgin with their own hands. Such examples are not rare, and appear again even in our days in Judea, as well as in Arabia.*

Joseph was too wise and too humane to place himself in either alternative; and it happened, as it always does, that

* Niebuhr relates, that "in a coffee-house of Yemen, an Arab having asked one of his fellow-countrymen if he was not the father of a young woman lately married in his tribe, the father, who suspected some intention to ridicule in this question, and thought the honour of his family compromised, coolly rose up, ran to his daughter's house, and without uttering a word plunged his *cangiar* in her heart." F. de Geramb mentions an anecdote of the same kind:—"The widow of a Catholic of Bethlehem," says he, "was the object of a painful suspicion; not knowing how to escape the vengeance of her relations, she took refuge in the convent of the Fathers of the Holy Land, and placed herself under the sacred protection of the altar. Her asylum was discovered, the gates of the monastery were forced, and the young woman dragged, with her hair all dishevelled, into the public market-place, amidst the shouts of the populace and the suppliant voices of the religious, who implored, in the name of a crucified God, forgiveness and mercy for this unhappy creature, who protested with tears that she was innocent. She appealed in despair to her father and her brothers, adjured them in the most moving manner to save her from a cruel death: they came forward sullenly; each held a dagger; the poor creature shuddered; and a moment after, the three daggers were buried in her breast, and the murderers, washing their hands in the blood of their respective daughter and sister, congratulated themselves on having washed away the disgrace of their family."

the more generous course was also the better. He resolved then to leave his city, and the woman who since their chaste hymen had made his life so sweet and happy. As he was preparing for this sad separation, and sleeping with troubled sleep upon his solitary couch, "The angel of the Lord appeared to him in his sleep, saying: Joseph, son of David, fear not to take unto thee Mary thy wife, for that which is conceived in her is of the Holy Ghost. And she shall bring forth a Son; and thou shalt call his name Jesus; for he shall save the people from their sins."

After this dream, and the word of the angel, Joseph found himself changed. The honour which God had done him, in transferring to him his own rights over his only Son, had not in the least affected his humility; but he had become father, he had become spouse, in heart, and his only thought now was, to take care of Mary and her divine Infant.

St. John Chrysostom asked himself why the angel of the Lord appeared in a dream to Joseph, and not manifestly, as he did to the shepherds, to Zachary, and to the Virgin. "He was," said he, answering himself, "a man of wonderful faith, nor did he need such a vision. For the Virgin, to whom so great a thing was announced, and much greater than to Zachary, required a wonderful kind of vision even before the thing itself took place; and the shepherds, as being less refined, had need of a more manifest vision. But this man after the conception, being beset with an evil suspicion of mind, and yet ready to be brought back easily to good hope, if any one should appear to guide him in this matter, receives the revelation. . . . . See then what great things are done; the philosophy of the man is exhibited, and what the angel declares so opportunely serves to confirm his faith, and the word itself remains without suspicion, which shows that he suffered what every man might justly endure."*

* S. Joan. Chrysost., Serm. 4, in S. Matt.

CHAPTER XI.

BIRTH OF THE MESSIAS.

MEANTIME, the *wicked empire** had planted its eagles even to the extremities of the globe; the Romans had taken the oriental world as in a net; the Samaritan trembled before them in the depth of his deserts, and the most remote nation of Asia, the peaceful Chinese, sent a solemn embassy to Cæsar to seek his powerful friendship. Egypt and Syria were already no more than Roman provinces; Judea itself was tributary, and the King of the Jews, purchasing with gold a capricious protection, was but a crowned slave. The time was come; the oracles relating to the Messias were about to be accomplished; the power of Rome was on the decline, as Balaam had foretold, and according to the grand prophecy of Jacob, the sceptre had departed from Juda: for the phantom of royalty which still hovered over the holy city was not even national. It was then that an edict of Augustus Cæsar was published in Judea, for an enrolment to be made of the people subject to his sceptre. This enrolment, much more complete than that which had taken place in the sixth consulship of the nephew of Julius Cæsar,†

* The Jews designated the Roman empire by the name of "the wicked empire."

† Augustus had three general enrolments in every province of the empire: the first, during his sixth consulship with Agrippa, in the year 28 before the Christian era; the second under the consulate of C. Marius Censorinus and C. Asinius Gallus, in the year 8 before the Christian era; and the third and last, under the consulate of Sextus Pompeius Nepos and Sextus Apuleius Nepos, in the year 14 of the Christian era. It is of the second enrolment that St. Luke speaks; the decree which ordered it was made in the eighth year before the Christian era.—(Sueton., in Octav. 27.)

comprised not only persons, but property and the several kinds of land: it was the basis on which it was intended to ground the tax on servitude.*

The Roman governors were ordered to see the imperial edict executed, each in his department.† Sextus Saturninus, governor of Syria, began first with Phœnicia and Cœlo-Syria, rich and populous cantons, which required long and patient labour; that which, in our Europe, William the Conqueror, a thousand years later, caused to be done, in order to draw up that famous register so well known to the English, under the name of "Domesday Book," can alone give an idea of it. After having executed the orders of Cæsar in the Roman province, as well as in the kingdoms and tetrarchies dependent upon it, at the end of three years from the date of the decree,‡ they found themselves arrived at length at Bethlehem, precisely at the memorable epoch of the birth of our Saviour. Cæsar and his agents had no other thought than

* Augustus at that time had a work prepared which contained the description of the Roman empire, and of those countries dependent upon it. Tacitus, Suetonius, and Dion Cassius make mention of this book, and of all the separate descriptions which were drawn up in the provinces. By the way in which they speak of it, it must have been something very complicated.

† Tertullian assures us that it was Sextius Saturninus who had to do it for Syria, he being president thereof.

‡ The three years which were taken up with this enrolment, executed by the Roman prefect, cannot raise any difficulty, for certainly it required no less time to draw up the register of Syria, Cœlo-Syria, Phœnicia, and Judea. Joab had consumed nearly ten months in making the simple list of men capable of bearing arms in the ten tribes; and the census of Augustus, at the birth of Jesus Christ, embraced many other details, as it extended not only to every individual, but to all particulars of their landed possessions. William the Conqueror, who had a work something similarly compiled among the English, employed six whole years about it, although Domesday Book contains neither Scotland, nor Ireland, nor Wales, nor the Channel Islands.

of doing an administrative work, by ascertaining the population and resources of the empire; but God had other designs, which they executed unconsciously by their merely human views. His son was to be born at Bethlehem of Juda, the humble country of King David: he had caused it to be foretold by his prophet, more than seven hundred years before; and now behold the whole world in commotion to accomplish this prophecy.

It appears that faithful to ancient usage, the Jews still had themselves inscribed by families and tribes. David was born at Bethlehem, his descendants regarded that little city as their natal town, and the nursery of their house; there it was, then, that they assembled to give in their names, and the state of their fortunes, in compliance with the edict of Cæsar.

The autumn was coming to an end; the torrents rolled with a loud noise in the depths of the valleys, the north wind blew through the lofty turpentine-trees, and a sky laden with grey clouds announced the approach of snows. One dull and gloomy morning, in the year of Rome 748,* a Nazarene was seen busily occupied with preparations for a journey, which no doubt he was not at liberty to put off; for the time seemed ill-chosen, and the young wife who accompanied him, and whom he seated carefully on the quiet and gentle animal which is still preferred by the women of the East, was far advanced in pregnancy. At the saddle of the fine animal† ridden by the young woman of Galilee, was fastened a basket, made of palm leaves, containing provisions for the journey: dates, figs, and raisins, some thin cakes of

* Never was any date more disputed than that of the birth of Jesus Christ We adopt that of the authors of l'Art de Verifier les Dates, which appears to us the best founded, and which places the birth of our Saviour on the 25th of December, in the year of Rome 748. According to Baronius, the day of our Saviour's birth was a Friday.

† The asses in Palestine are remarkably beautiful.

barley meal, and an earthen vessel from Ramla, to hold water from the spring or the cistern. A goat-skin bottle, of Egyptian make, was hung on the opposite side. The traveller threw over his shoulder a wallet containing a bundle of clothes, girded his loins, wrapped himself up in his cloak of goats' hair, and holding in one hand his hooked stick, held with the other the bridle of the ass which carried the young woman. Thus they quitted their poor dwelling, which was left to itself, and passed down the narrow streets of Nazareth, amidst wishes of a good journey, and safe return to their kindred and neighbours, who exclaimed on all sides, "Go in peace!" These travellers, who set out on a journey in a cloudy morning, were the humble descendants of the great kings of Juda—Joseph and Mary—who were going, by order of a pagan and a stranger, to enrol their obscure names by the side of the most illustrious names of the kingdom.

This journey, undertaken during the rigorous season, and across a country like Palestine, must have been extremely painful to the blessed Virgin, in the situation in which she found herself; yet she made no complaint; this feeble and delicate young woman had a mind firm and courageous,—a great soul, which was not elevated with greatness, knew how to possess itself in joy,—and in silence accepted misfortune. Joseph, who moved along pensive at her side, meditated on the ancient oracles, which promised, four thousand years ago, a deliverer to his people; as he travelled on to Bethlehem, whither he was led by the supreme will of a Roman, he thought of the words of the prophet Micheas: "And thou, Bethlehem Ephrata, art a little one among the thousands of Juda; out of thee shall he come forth unto me that is to be the ruler in Israel."* Then, looking at his poor equipage and his humble companion, whose simple outfit was suitable to her condition, he thought over in his mind the great

* Mich. v. ii.

oracles of Isaias: "And he shall grow up as a tender plant before him, and as a root out of a thirsty ground: . . . . despised, and the most abject of men."* And the patriarch began to understand the designs of God with regard to his Christ.

After a painful journey of five days, the travellers distinguished Bethlehem at a distance, the city of kings, seated on an eminence, amid smiling hills planted with vines, olive-groves, and woods of green oaks. Camels carrying women wrapped in purple cloaks, and with their heads covered with white veils, Arab *nakas*, ridden at full gallop by young horsemen splendidly clad, groups of old men upon beautiful white she-asses, discoursing gravely, like the ancient judges of Israel,† were going up to the city of David, which was already occupied by a multitude of Hebrews who had arrived during the preceding days. Outside, but at a little distance from the city, a building arose of quadrangular form, the white walls of which stood out from the pale green of the olive-trees which covered the hill: one would have said it was a Persian caravansary. Within its open gate, a number of slaves and servants were seen going and coming in its ample court: it was the inn. Joseph, urging on the beast on which the Virgin was mounted, made up to it, in the hope of arriving in time to secure one of those small apartments which belong by right to the first comer, and which were refused to no one;‡ but the

* Is. liii. 2.

† The horse was used, especially among the Jews, by the warrior; it was also taken as the symbol of combats. The judges, on the contrary, rode upon asses of a species perfectly beautiful. Hence those words of the Bible: "Speak: you that ride upon fair asses, and you that sit in judgment."—(Judges v. 10.)

‡ Nothing is found in the cells of the caravansary, or palace of caravans, but the four walls, dust, and sometimes scorpions. The keeper's business is merely to give the key and a mat: the traveller ought to have provided himself with the rest; thus he should take his

caravansary overflowed with merchants and travellers; there was not a place left; at a price of gold one might perhaps have been found, for the hotel-keeper was a Jew, and a Jew of Bethlehem: but Joseph had no gold.

The patriarch returned sorrowful to Mary, who smiled upon him with resignation, and again seizing the bridle of the poor animal, who was ready to drop with fatigue, he began to wander about the places and streets of the little city, hoping, but in vain, that some charitable Bethlehemite would offer them a lodging for the love of God. No one offered them anything. The night wind fell cold and piercing upon the young Virgin, who never uttered a complaint, but who became more and more pale: she could hardly keep life within her. Joseph continued his fruitless efforts in despair; and alas! more than once he saw the door which had been unfeelingly shut against him opened to some more wealthy stranger. Self-interest, that ruling passion of the Jews, must have petrified the soul of every one, for the situation of Mary to excite no compassion. The night came on: the two, seeing themselves rejected by every one, and despairing of obtaining a shelter in the city of their forefathers, went out from Bethlehem without knowing whither to direct their steps, and moved forward at hazard into the country, lighted by the expiring glimmer of the twilight, and echoing with the cry of the jackals who prowled about in search of their prey.

On the south, and at a short distance from the inhospitable city, a dark cave appeared, which was hollowed out of the rock; this cave, the mouth of which looked towards the north, and which became narrower towards the end, served the Bethlehemites as a common stable, and sometimes as a refuge for the shepherds in stormy nights. They both blessed heaven, who had guided them to this rude shelter;

bed, his cooking apparatus, and even his provisions with him.—(Volney, Voyage en Syrie.)

and Mary, leaning on the arm of Joseph, went and sat down upon a bare piece of stone, which formed a kind of narrow and inconvenient seat in a hollow part of the rock.

It was there, "in the fortification of the rock," as the prophet Isaias had foretold,* at the moment when the rising of the mysterious constellation of the Virgin marked the hour of midnight,† that the *alma* ‡ of the grand prophecy of the Messias, in the midst of a solemn pause of nature, concealed by a luminous cloud,§ brought into the world Him to whom God himself had given birth "before the hills,"‖ and "whose generation was from eternity." He appeared all at once, like the sunbeam parting from the cloud, to the eyes of his astonished young mother, and came to take possession of the throne of his poverty, while all the angels of God, bending the knee before him, adored him under his human

* Justin appeals to the prophecy of Isaias for the birth of Jesus in the cave: "He shall dwell on high; the fortifications of rocks shall be his highness."—(Ch. xxxiii. 16.)

† "It is a fact independent of all hypotheses," says Dupuis, "independent of all consequences which I desire to draw from it, that *precisely at the hour of midnight*, on the 25th of December, in those ages when Christianity made its appearance, the heavenly sign which rose in the horizon, and the ascendant of which presided at the opening of the new solar revolution was, the *Virgin of the Constellations.*"

‡ The word *alma*, which Isaias used, signifies in Hebrew a virgin in all her innocence. We have already said, in note *, p. 32 of the first chapter, that this word has given occasion to very great controversies between Jews and Christians.

§ Protevang., S. Jac., c. 17.

‖ According to the opinion of the rabbins, the Messias was in the terrestrial Paradise by the side of our first parents.—(Sohar Chadasch, f. 82, 4.) He existed even before the world.—(Nezach Israel, c. 35.) And before he became man, he was in the state of glory with God.—(Phil. ii. 6.) Thus, immediately before the time of Jesus Christ, the idea of a pre-existence of the Messias existed in the superior theology of the Jews.

form.* This virginal parturition was free from cries and pains; and not a single groan disturbed the sacred silence of that night full of prodigies and mysteries. Miraculously conceived, Jesus is born still more miraculously.

God prepared for the world a grand and novel spectacle, when he caused a poor king to be born. The palace which he destined for him was a deserted stable—a fit shelter for him who as he advanced in years was to say, "The foxes have holes, and the birds of the air nests; but the Son of man hath not where to lay his head." Moses, proscribed from his birth, had at least a cradle of rushes, when his sister, the youthful Mary, exposed him in the midst of the bulrushes and sacred lotus plants which dip their leaves in the Nile at the close of day;† but Jesus, the divine forsaken one, who came among us to suffer and die, had not even so much magnificence as this: he was laid in a manger, upon a handful of damp straw providentially forgotten by some camel-driver of Egypt or Syria, in haste to set out before daybreak. God had provided for the couch of his only Son, even as he provides for the nests of the birds of heaven.

It was necessary to cover this new Adam, whose members would have been starved by the cold air, and whom modesty and necessity alike required to be clothed. Mary made him out of her veil swaddling bands, with which she wrapped him up with her chaste hands; then was the God newly born adored by her and her holy spouse, as Joseph of old, the finest type of Jesus Christ, had been before by his father and mother.

St. Basil, entering into the mysteries of fervour and

* Heb. i. 6; Psalm xlvi. 7.

† The *lotus*, which was consecrated to the sun, is a water-plant, the leaves of which dip into the Nile when the sun sets, and emerge from it when he rises. This plant has the virtue of lulling to sleep. They used to say to those who made long journeys that they had eaten of the *lotus*, that is, they had forgotten their country.—(Basn., liv. ix. c. 15.)

rapture which passed in the soul of the Virgin, exhibits her to us as if divided between the love of the mother and the adoration of the saint. "What should I call thee?" says she, addressing her Infant-God; "what should I call thee? . . . . a mortal? . . . . but I conceived thee by divine operation . . . . A God? . . . . but thou hast a human body. Ought I to come before thee with incense, or to offer thee my breast? Ought I to lavish upon thee all the cares of a tender mother, or to serve thee with my forehead bowed down to the dust? O wonderful contrast! the heavens are thy abode, and I nurse thee on my knees! Thou art upon earth, and yet thou art not separated from the inhabitants of the celestial regions: the heavens are with thee."

Thus were accomplished the grand oracles of Micheas and Isaias:—

"And there were in the same country shepherds watching and keeping the night-watches over their flock. And behold, an angel of the Lord stood by them, and the brightness of God shone round about them, and they feared with a great fear. And the angel said to them: Fear not, for behold I bring you good tidings of great joy, that shall be to all the people; for this day is born to you a Saviour, who is Christ the Lord, in the city of David. And this shall be a sign unto you: you shall find the infant wrapped in swaddling-clothes, and laid in a manger. And suddenly there was with the angel a multitude of the heavenly army, praising God, and saying: GLORY TO GOD IN THE HIGHEST; AND ON EARTH PEACE TO MEN OF GOOD WILL."*

* In a very pleasant plain, situated a quarter of a league to the north of the town of Bethlehem, is found the village of the shepherds, and in the depth of the valley the celebrated field where these shepherds were tending their flocks during the night of the nativity. According to grave authors, both sacred and profane, the appearance of the angels to the shepherds is not the only prodigy which signalised

The marvellous vision had disappeared, the heavenly songs had ceased, and the shepherds, leaning forward upon their knotty staves, were still listening.

the birth of the Infant-God. It is related, that during that sacred night, the vines of Engaddi blossomed, and that at Como the temple of Peace fell down on a sudden, and the oracles of the demons were silent for ever. The very birth of our Lord was a sentence of banishment for those pagan divinities who had been till then permitted to give oracles. Milton, in an admirable poetic vein, thus describes, in one of his earliest pieces of verse, the departure of those pretended divinities on the eve of the nativity:—

"The oracles are dumb.
No voice or hideous hum,
Runs through the arched roof in words deceiving.
Apollo from his shrine
Can no more divine,
With hollow shriek the steep of Delphos leaving.
No nightly trance, or breathed spell,
Inspires the pale-eyed priest from the prophetic cell.

"The lonely mountains o'er,
And the resounding shore,
A voice of weeping heard and loud lament;
From haunted spring and dale,
Edged with poplar pale,
The parting Genius is with sighing sent;
With flower-inwoven tresses torn,
The nymphs in twilight shade of tangled thickets mourn.

"In consecrated earth,
And on the holy hearth,
The Lars and Lemures moan with midnight plaint:
In urns and altars round,
A drear and dying sound
Affrights the flamens at their service quaint;
And the chill marble seems to sweat,
While each peculiar power forgoes his wonted seat.

"Peor and Baalim
Forsake their temples dim,

When the night breezes moaned alone in the valley, and there was only left in the sky a single white and shining spot, which might seem to be an angel, the shepherds consulted together, and "said one to another, Let us go over to Bethlehem, and let us see this word that is come to pass, which the Lord hath showed to us." Then taking in baskets such humble presents as their huts could supply, they made their way, by the bright light of the stars, to the little city of David. At the sight of the stable they felt, like the disciples at Emmaus, that their hearts were burning, and they said one to another, "Perhaps this is the place;" for they knew that the divine Infant who was born unto them had not seen the light beneath a rich roof, and that he was not laid in a sumptuous cradle for a throne; the angel had made no such announcement. They approached then with faith, with hope, with love, towards the place where they well deserved to meet the promised Saviour, since they came to seek him there with upright intentions and pure souls.

Looking into the farthest recess of the cave, to ascertain whether they had really come to the end of their nocturnal pilgrimage, *these men of good-will* discovered Him who came

With that twice battered god of Palestine;
And mooned Ashtaroth,
Heaven's queen and mother both,
Now sits not girt with taper's holy shine;
The Lybec Hammon shrinks his horn,
In vain the Tyrian maids their wounded Thammuz mourn.

"And sullen Moloch fled,
Hath left in shadows dread
His burning idol all of blackest hue;
In vain with cymbal's ring,
They call the grisly king,
In dismal dance about the furnace blue
The brutish gods of Nile as fast,
Isis and Orus, and the dog Anubis, haste."

to preach the gospel to the poor, and to abolish *the malediction of slavery*, under the humble form of a little infant quietly asleep in his manger.

The Virgin, bending over her new-born son, contemplated him with affecting humility and profound tenderness; above them, Joseph bent down his aged head before this adopted son, who was God; a mild ray of the moon shone upon this divine group, enclosed in the red recesses of the rock: without, everything reposed under a fine starlight night.*

"Here must be the place," said the shepherds to each other; and prostrating with respect before the manger of the King of kings, they offered to the poor and new-born God the mite and the homage of the poor.

Then they proceeded to relate the apparition of the angels, their ravishing concerts, their words of hope, peace, and love. Joseph admired and wondered at this divine manifestation, and Mary, who heard in silence this simple narrative, laid up every word of it in her heart. When this duty was performed, and their mission ended, the shepherds retired, glorifying God, and spread abroad in the mountains the wonders of that sacred night. Those who heard them, struck with a long fit of amazement, said one to another, "Is it really possible? Are we then in the time of Abraham, that angels should visit shepherds?"

Perhaps it was these recitals, made in the evenings on the borders of the woods, or in the depths of the ravines, while the camels drank together at the solitary spring, which led a tribe of Arabs to consider Mary and the Infant as divinities. The sweet image of the Virgin holding her Son on her knees, was painted on one of the pillars of the Caaba, and solemnly placed in the number of the three hundred and sixty divinities of the three Arabias. In the time of Maho-

* "The Persians call Christmas night *scheb jaldai*, night bright and luminous, by reason of the descent of the angels."—(D'Herbelot, Bibl. Orientale, t. ii. p. 294.)

met it was still to be seen, as the Arab historians attest.* After the massacre of the Holy Innocents, this brave tribe rose up to a man, uttered a long cry of vengeance, and without being overawed by numbers, attacked Herod's son, though he was a vassal and *protégé* of the Romans.†

This authentic anecdote, so curious and generally unknown, comes to the support of the supernatural fact recorded by St. Luke, a fact which the deriding philosophers of the school of Voltaire, and the adepts of pantheism,—if possible, still more pagan,—have not failed to banish to the rank of fables. The capricious devotion of these Arabs, who blended idolatry with the worship of the true God befóre the preaching of the gospel, can be accounted for only in connection with the knowledge of the miracles of the sacred night of the Nativity.

On the eighth day after his birth, the Son of God was circumcised, and named Jesus, in conformity with the order of his heavenly Father. He must have had a godfather, like all the Israelites, but we are completely ignorant upon whom that honour fell. As to the ceremony of the circumcision, which always took place under the auspices of Elias, who

* "El Azraki adduces the ocular testimony of several respectable persons," says Burckhardt, "to prove a remarkable fact, of which, I believe, no mention has hitherto been made : it is that the figure of the Virgin Mary, with the young Aisa (Jesus) on her knees, was sculptured as a divinity upon one of the pillars nearest to the gate of Caaba."—(Burckhardt, Voyage en Arabie, t. i. p. 221.)

† This particular circumstance, which confirms the account of the Arab historian, is found recorded in the *Toldos*, a Jewish book, very ancient, and written in a tone of furious animosity against Christianity. We see there that Herod the Great and his son had to sustain a war against the tribe of the desert, who adored the *image of Jesus and Mary his mother*. This tribe attempted to form alliances with several cities of Palestine, and particularly with that of Haï. Now, as the Jews themselves place this event in the lifetime of Herod, it must have been prompted by the massacre of the Innocents, as the aged king survived only one year the birth of our Saviour.

never failed, said the Hebrews, to assist at it invisibly,* it took place, according to St. Epiphanius, in the very cave in which Jesus was born, and St. Bernard presumes, with sufficient probability, that St. Joseph was the minister on the occasion

Men of the common people, docile to the summons of the angels, had come to adore the infant God in his poor manger, and share with him their black bread and the milk of their goats. A miracle of a higher character, and of much greater renown, conducted shortly after to the same cradle the first fruits of converted Gentiles: the shepherds of Juda had led the way; it was now the turn of sages and kings.

CHAPTER XII.

ADORATION OF THE MAGI.

In the course of the autumn which preceded the birth of Jesus Christ, certain Chaldean Magi, learned in the study of the courses of the stars, discovered a star of the first magnitude, which they recognised by its extraordinary motion and other no less certain signs, as that star of Jacob, long before predicted by Balaam, which was to arise in their horizon at the time of the parturition of the Virgin. According to the ancient traditions of Iran, collected by Abulfarage, Zoroaster —the restorer of the science of the Magi, a learned man, a great astronomer, and well versed, moreover, in the theology of the Hebrews †—announced under the first successor of

* See Basn., liv. vii. c. 10.

† Some have made Zoroaster a disciple of Jeremias; but their times do not correspond; it is more probable that he was a disciple of Daniel.

Cyrus, and a short time after the rebuilding of the temple, that a divine infant, called to change the face of the world, would be born of a virgin, pure and immaculate, in the most western region of Asia. He added that a star unknown to their heavens would signalise this remarkable event, and that on its appearance the Magi would themselves bring presents to this young king. Faithful and religious executors of the wishes of Zoroaster, three of the most illustrious wise men of Babylon,* had no sooner remarked the star, than they sounded the cymbals of departure. Leaving behind them the city of Seleucidæ, with its elegant edifices of palm-tree wood,† and Babylon, where the wind of the desert, moaning over immense ruins, seemed to tell to these silent wrecks the sinister oracles of the son of Amos, they left the country of date-palms, and took the sandy road of Palestine. Before them, like the pillar of light which guided the fugitive cohorts of Israel to the desert shores of the Red Sea, moved forward the star of the Messias. This new star, free from those unchangeable laws which rule the starry spheres, had no regular motion proper to itself; sometimes it advanced at the head of the caravan, always following a straight line in the direction of the west; sometimes it remained stationary

* Men are not agreed as to the country of the Magi; some make them come from the interior of Arabia Felix, others from India, which is not at all probable. The best authorities give them Persia for their country, and this opinion has seemed to us founded in truth. The name Caspar, Melchior, Balthazar, which are attributed to the Magi, are Babylonian. In fact, Babylon, and after its destruction, Seleucia, situated at a short distance, were the abode of the most celebrated astronomers of antiquity. Finally, these cities are to the east of Jerusalem, and in twenty days' march one may travel from the borders of the Euphrates to Bethlehem. Origen, who was learned and well-informed, assures us that the Magi studied astrology. Drexelius ridicules Origen for this very unreasonably; which proves that he was little versed in the history of the East in olden times, where every astronomer was also an astrologer.

† Strabo, lib. xvii.

above the tents pitched for the night, and seemed gently poised on the bosom of the clouds, like an albatross asleep in fields of air: at daybreak it gave the signal for departure, as it had given the one to halt.*

At length, the lofty towers of Jerusalem appeared in the distance in the midst of the bare and wild summits of her mountains; the camels and the mares were quenching their thirst at a cistern by the way-side, when the Magi uttered a cry of surprise and affright; the star had just hidden itself in the heights of the sky, like an intelligent creature aware of some impending danger.†

As much disconcerted as the navigators of ancient times when a barrier of black clouds concealed from them the polar star, the Magi consulted together for a moment. What was the meaning of the sudden disappearance of their brilliant guide? Were they then at the end of their long journey, and should they set up the tent of abode? That the infant king whom they came to adore from the banks of the Tigris should be found at Jerusalem, was a thing both possible and probable. "The *God of heaven*," they thought, "does not prolong his miracles in vain; they cease when human agency suffices: this is all in right order. What if the star has left us? We can very well, without its aid, find him whom we

* St. Joan. Chrysost., Serm. 6 in S. Matt.—Chalcidius, a pagan philosopher, who lived at the end of the third century, makes mention of this star, and of the sages of the East whom it conducted to the cradle of Jesus Christ. St. Augustin, the doctor of doctors, speaks thus on this subject: "At his birth, he declared a new star, who, when put to death, darkened the old sun. What was that star which never appeared before among the stars, nor remained to be pointed out afterwards? What was it but a magnificent tongue of the heavens—to declare the glory of God, to proclaim with unusual brightness the unheard-of parturition of the Virgin."—(Serm. cci., in Epiph. iii.)

† This cistern, or well, situated on the road to Jerusalem, still bears the name of the *Cistern of the three Kings*, or *of the Star*, in memory of this event.

seek in the capital of his dominions. To discover the cradle of the young King Messias, we have only to enter the first street strewed with green boughs, perfumed with essence of roses, and carpeted with drapery of rich colours embroidered with gold; the sound of the harps of the Hebrews, their dances, and their songs of joy, will sufficiently indicate to us in what direction to proceed." Then urging on their animals, they passed the gate of the enclosure, and entered the ancient Sion between two files of barbarian soldiers.

The aspect of Jerusalem was sad: its population, weakened and silent, had no appearance of joy or festivity; groups only formed here and there, to see the travellers pass by, whom they recognised by their long white robes, fastened by magnificent oriental girdles, and their *bazubends** enriched with precious stones, and, above all, by the manly beauty of their features, as satraps of the great king. As they went along, the oriental cavaliers, leaning down upon the necks of their dromedaries, asked some of the numerous spectators who crowded the way, where was the new-born King of the Jews, whose star they had seen in Babylon. The people of Jerusalem, looking at one another in amazement, knew not what to answer to this inquiry. . . . . A King of the Jews! . . . . What king? They knew none but Herod, whom they abhorred from the bottom of their souls, and who had no infant son. The Magi, astonished on their part that all whom they interrogated should protest their ignorance, and seeing moreover around them no signs of festivity, moved in consternation up the crowded street which led to the ancient palace of David, and pitched their tents in its ruinous and shaded courts.

Nevertheless, the appearance of these grandees of Persia, who

* Bazubends, antique bracelets of diamonds, turquoises, and pearls, which the satraps wore above the elbow: the King of Persia and his sons still wear the bazubends.—(See Morier, Voyage en Perse et en Armenie.)

travelled very rarely at that time in the mountains of Judea, their startling questions, which astonished and intimidated at the same time a people whom the vast system of espionage organised by Herod * held in fear, soon put into commotion the most seditious and restless city of the East. The name of King Messias, pronounced by the Pharisees, ever on the alert to make the aged monarch uneasy about the future fortunes of his house and the duration of his own power, fell among the curious groups like a spark upon thatch. The King Messias? It was emancipation! It was conquest! It was glory! It was the banner of Juda waving like a ruler over the vanquished world! The Persian satraps passed for the first astrologers in the world; † they had, no doubt, read in the stars the birth of the Hebrew *Goel.* ‡ The heir of the kings of Juda was about to reascend the great throne of his ancestors, and drive from it the race of the Herods, those *half-Jews*, who were the slaves of Rome! A low rumour, like that which precedes the tempests of the ocean, soon circulated in the houses, in the streets, on the public places; never had the Jews of Jerusalem felt less disposed to conform to the royal edict, which forbade them *to meddle with any affairs but their own.* § In vain did the fierce soldiers of Herod line the ramparts and platforms of

* See Josephus, Ant. Jud., lib. xv. c. 13.

† The whole of the East at that time believed in astrology; and Philo informs us that the satraps of Persia passed for the first astrologers in the world.

‡ *Goel* (Saviour), one of the names by which the Hebrews designated the Messias.

§ Herod had strictly forbidden the Jews to talk of affairs of state; they could not even meet together in family parties to make great feasts, according to custom. His spies, scattered about Jerusalem, and even over the high roads, immediately arrested those who disobeyed the king's edict; they were placed secretly, and sometimes n open day, in strongholds where they were severely punished.—(Josephus, Antiq. Jud., lib. xv. c. 13.)

the towers; the people were strong; they had no more fear, and they conspired in the street. "All Jerusalem was troubled," says the gospel, and it was soon the tyrant's turn to be troubled also.

Herod at that time was living in his palace at Jerusalem, the gardens of which—full of flowers, stocked with rare birds, and intersected with clear streams, which lost themselves beneath the branches of an actual little forest*—could not avert his mind from the gloomy recollections and sinister anticipations which rendered life an annoyance to him. Informed by the chief of his spies of the arrival of the Magi, and of their strange discourses, his broad forehead, wrinkled with anxious thoughts, darkened like a stormy sky, and his uneasiness was visible to every one.

The trouble of the King of the Jews is easily understood and explained by his position. Herod was neither the anointed of the Lord, nor the choice of the people; a branch of laurel, gathered in the idolatrous precincts of the Capitol, formed his tributary crown,—a crown of vassalage, entwined with thorns, every leaf of which had been paid for with heaps of gold abstracted from the savings of the rich and the indigence of the poor. Hated by the rich, whose heads he cut off at the first suspicion—feared by his relatives, whose tombs he tragically filled up—the horror of the priests, whose privileges he had trampled under foot—detested by the people for his doubtful religion and his foreign extraction—he could only oppose his courtiers, his assassins, his artists, and the opulent but small sect of Herodians, who were fascinated with his magnificence, to the active, ardent, and openly declared hatred of the rest of the nation. Often was the friend of Cæsar insulted to his face by his obstinate subjects: the Pharisees, an artful and powerful sect, had refused with insult and derision to take the oath of fidelity to him; the Essenians, whose courage in battle rendered

* Josephus, de Bello, lib. v. c. 13.

them formidable, had followed the example of the Pharisees; and the young and ebullient disciples of the doctors of the law had recently thrown down in open day, with their vengeful axes, the golden eagle which he had placed above the gate of the temple to please the Romans.

On every side plots, secretly favoured by his nearest and dearest relatives, were contrived in the dark against his life, and he was very near falling, in the crowded theatre, beneath the poignards of certain young high-minded men, who thought to do a deed of virtue and patriotism, by ridding the earth of a prince who reigned like a madman.* Attributing this unusual daring to the contempt inspired by his old age, he exhausted all the secrets of art to appear young again.† He would fain have persuaded himself and others, that he was still that young and brilliant Herod who surpassed the greater part of the Hebrews in gymnastic exercises: Herod, the bold rider, the expert hunter, the handsome and disdainful monarch, who had despised the love of that celebrated Queen of Egypt for whom Anthony had lost the empire of the world. But, alas! the silvery network which began to mix with the black hair of his sons, their impatience to reign, the spirit of revolt and mutiny which crept in among the people, and the insolence of the banditti who re-commenced their depredations in Galilee, made him understand but too well that his reign drew near its end. Tormented with suspicions, and distrustful even of his spies, he wandered about, sometimes at night alone and in disguise, in the streets and public places of his capital;‡ there he

* The people were so far from applauding the discovery of this conspiracy, and rejoicing at the safety of the king, that they seized the informer who had disclosed it, tore him in pieces, and had him eaten up by dogs.—(Josephus, Ant. Jud., lib. xv. c. 11.)

† Herod painted in order to look younger than he was, and had his hair and beard dyed black.—(Ibid., lib. xvi. c. 11.)

‡ He often mixed at night, in disguise, with the populace, says

heard with his own ears the muttered imprecations, the cruel reproaches, the bitter railleries which fell upon "the man without ancestors," the "Ascalonite," the "wild beast," who had killed his innocent wife,—a pearl of beauty, a model of honour,—and who had afterwards had his two sons by her strangled, those two princes so sad, so handsome, so brave, whom the people loved for the sake of the Asmonean heroes, their ancestors, and their unfortunate mother. The day after these nocturnal wanderings was a day of mourning and punishments: none were spared. The executioner, after cutting off the heads of the highest, fell upon the lowest of the rabble. Thus on every side vows were made against the life of the prince; and each time that the report of his death was circulated, whether by chance or design, in the distant provinces, the people, greedily seizing the treacherous bait which flattered their hatred, hastened to light up bonfires in every direction, which Herod extinguished with blood.

Amidst these elements of civil discord,—when a fever of insurrection was sullenly working its way in the army, and revolt, like a ripe fruit, seemed to invite the hand of the seditious,—strangers of high bearing arrive at Jerusalem, who inquire without any mystery or circumlocution, for a new-born King of the Jews, whose star they have seen. Herod is astonished; he anxiously calls up his recollections; the predictions fatal to his dynasty which the Pharisees cause to be circulated—the oracles of the ancient seers—to which he has hitherto lent but a distracted and secondary attention, come to his remembrance. This warrior Messias, this prophet sprung from David, who is to carry his victorious ensigns from west to east, begins to give him vague disquietude; it is not the God who makes the aged king so

Josephus, to know what opinion the people had of him, and he punished without mercy those who did not approve of what he did.—(Josephus, Ant. Jud., lib. xv. c. 13.)

full of thought, it is the prince. The more he thinks upon it, the more this mysterious event seems to him connected with one vast conspiracy tending to raise up a secret and rival power upon the ruins of his own. What then! did he pour out like water the illustrious blood of the Macchabees, without any concern for the beating hearts of his wife and children; did he crush beneath the iron wheels of his despotism all that offered any resistance; lose his soul, his honour, the rest of his nights, in which his bleeding victims troubled his dreams* . . . . and all this to what purpose? —to smoothen the way to the throne for the family of David!† . . . . This sceptre so dearly purchased,—this sceptre, still wet with the blood of his own relatives, will be then no more than a reed, sterile and accursed, which the blast of death shall break over his tomb! . . . . He will have passed, like the meteor of a stormy night, over this land, whose ancient glory will brilliantly revive after him! . . . . And this people, who hated him with a hatred so strong, so deadly, so furious, that even his favours could do nothing towards assuaging it, how will they surround with their love and sympathy the offspring of their ancient kings! And this last thought fell as bitter as wormwood upon the dark and desolate heart of the aged monarch; for in the

* Josephus, Ant. Jud., lib. v. c. 13.

† We wonder at the alarm caused to Herod by an offshoot of the family of David; yet it was not only Herod that persecuted that noble family, out of hatred for its ancient rights and glorious expectations. Eusebius, after Hegesippus, relates that, after the conquest of Jerusalem, Vespasian commanded the posterity of David to be sought out and destroyed. Under Trajan, the persecution still continued. Finally, Domitian had two descendants of that illustrious race brought to Rome, whose grandfather was the apostle St. Jude. The emperor, after interrogating them, learning that they possessed no more than thirty-nine acres of land, which they cultivated with their own hands, sent them back to their own country, being made easy as to their ambition by their poverty.

midst of his acts of violence, he felt the want of being loved, a strange want certainly, but perfectly real in this exceptional being, who seemed made up of contrasts, and who had employed very noble qualities in the service of the most absorbing and most cruel passion which could lay waste the human soul—ambition!

"Be this child prince of the land or prophet of God," said Herod, after a pause, "he must die; . . . . and die he shall, even though I were sure to extinguish with this feeble spark all the glories which our *seers* dream of for future times. Athalia, that clever woman, who knew how to reign, forgot only one infant in his cradle in the massacre of the royal family of Juda. That child deprived her of her throne and her life. I will take care to forget nothing. But where is this *new-born* king of the Jews concealed, who is proclaimed by the stars, and whom these insolent satraps come to seek at the very gates of my palace? Can he be in reality the *Shiloh* foretold by Jacob? These are perhaps mere reveries of the astrologers? No matter, we must make sure." A few hours after, the doctors of the law and the chief priests, assembled in council under the presidency of Herod, heard this question, which appeared to them strange in the mouth of such a prince: "Do you know in what place the Messias should be born?"

The answer, which was not expected, was unanimous: "*In Bethlehem of Juda.*" And the ancients of Israel, delighted to make the friend of the Romans uneasy, did not fail to add that, as the last of the weeks of Daniel was near its end, the time for the Messias was drawing near. These indications, little calculated to give security, were not sufficient for Herod, who wanted to know where to strike the blow: he resolved to interrogate the Magi, and to know, if possible, the precise time of the birth of the child, calculated by that of the appearance of the star. Too clever a politician to grant a public audience to the sages of Iran, which would have given consistency to a rumour which it was his interest to stifle, the king sent for them privately, and pressed them with questions as to the time of the star's appearing to them. "He inquires," says St. John Chrysostom, "not the time of the child, but of the star, lying in wait for his prey with great diligence." Informed of what he wished to know, the man of blood dismissed the strangers in an affable and gracious manner. "Go," said he, "to Bethlehem, and search diligently after the child, and when you have found him, bring me word again, that I also may come and adore him."

Now the Magi, like all superior men, like all the sons of meditation and science, were good, sincere, and little inclined to suspect evil. They understood arbitrary conduct and cruelty in a prince, they did not understand falsehood; for the first thing that the kings of Persia taught their children was to tell the truth. Accordingly they believed the false words of the Idumean, and passing again beneath the elegant porticoes of this palace, which vied in magnificence with those of the great king, but which had not in the midst of its bronzes and arcades the golden bell of the *suppliants*,* they left the Betzetha,† struck their tents, and traversed a second time the holy city, to go to the presumed birthplace of the Messias. As they passed by the walls of the new amphi-

* The kings of Persia administered justice in a manner quite patriarchal. They had above their heads a golden bell, and to this bell was attached a chain, the end of which hung outside of the palace. Every time that the bell rung, the officers of the prince left his apartments, and introduced before the *great king* the petitioners, who demanded justice of the prince himself, and the king rendered it to them on the spot with equity.—(Antar, translated from the Arabic by Terrick Hamilton.)

† The quarter called *Betzetha*, or the new town, which Herod had joined to Jerusalem, was situated to the north of the temple: it included the lower pool, the probatical pool, and the palace of Herod.

theatre, enriched with trophies,—the extraordinary decoration of which was an inexhaustible subject of sarcasms to the Pharisees,—they met King Herod, surrounded by a forest of Thracian and German lances, who was going in the direction of Jericho.*

The Persians left Jerusalem by the gate of Damascus; then taking the left, they entered upon valleys intersected with hills, which they were obliged to climb. They were about an hour's journey from the capital of Judea, and were watering their camels at a cistern, when a brilliant light appeared directly over them, and descended rapidly to them, like a falling star. "The star! our star!" cried out the slaves, transported with joy. "The star!" repeated their masters, with the same rapture; and being certain this time that they had entered on the right way, they resumed their journey with fresh ardour.

They were about to enter the city of David, when the star, lowering itself towards the south, stopped all at once over a cave, which had the appearance of being a rustic stable, and descending as low as possible in the air, rested, as it were, over the head of the infant God. The sight of this motionless star,—the softest rays of which fell in a luminous sheaf upon this cave hollowed out of the rock,—filled the Magi with great faith, and their faith indeed needed to be great to acknowledge the King Messias, in an infant destitute of everything, lodged in a poor place, laid in a manger, and

* We have followed the authors who maintain that Herod departed for Jericho, where he was for some time sick, at the time when the Magi journeyed to Bethlehem; this agrees every way with the account of the gospel; for if Herod had been at Jerusalem at the time when the Persians returned, they would probably have seen him before the admonition of the angel, who did not inform them of the designs of the king till the first night. The sickness of Herod, taking off his attention from the Magi and the infant, left the former at liberty to return peaceably into their country, and the Holy Family time to return by the road to Nazareth.

whose mother, though beautiful and full of every grace, was evidently of a very obscure condition.

God, who would make the Jews ashamed of the hardness of their hearts, by setting before them the religious eagerness and the docile faith of infidels, permitted that the extraordinary humiliation of the Holy Family should not shake the firm belief of the Magi.

The worshippers of the sun, the Gentiles, whom the cross came to save, as well as the children of promise, made their way into the sorry abode of Christ with as much veneration as in their temples built over subterranean fires, where starry spheres revolved.* According to the custom of their people, they put some of the dust of that poor threshold on their foreheads, and after taking off their rich sandals, they adored the new-born Infant, as every son of the East at that time adored his gods and his masters. Then opening caskets of odoriferous wood, which contained the presents intended for the Messias, they took out of them most pure gold, found in the environs of Ninive the Great, and perfumes which were exchanged for fruits and pearls with the Arabs of the Yemen. These mysterious gifts had nothing carnal about them, like the offerings of the Jews. The cradle of HIM who came to abolish the sacrifices of the synagogue was not to be sprinkled with blood; therefore the Magi did not sacrifice to him lambs without spot, nor white heifers; they presented him gold, as to a prince of the earth, myrrh, and frankincense, as to a God; † then, touching the earth with their foreheads

* These spheres, composed of circles of gold, cut out like those of our armillary spheres, revolve brilliantly at the rising of the sun. They are still seen at Oulam, where the Ghebers have a temple.—(Rabbi Benjamin.)

† Those verses of Juvencus, the most ancient of Christian poets whose works have come down to us, on the presents of the kingly Magi, have been justly praised:—

> "Aurum, thus, myrrham, regique, Deoque, hominique
> Dona ferunt. . . ."

before Mary, whom they found fair "as the moon, and humble as the flower of *nenuphar*," they invoked upon her the benedictions of God, and wished that "the hand of woe might never reach her."

This was the last scene of splendour in which the Blessed Virgin bore a part. The first period of her life, like a sweet dream of Ginnistan, had passed beneath roofs of cedar and gold, in the midst of sacred perfumes, melodious chants, the sound of lyres and harps; the second, full of wonders and mysteries, had placed her in correspondence with the inhabitants of heaven and the princes of Asia; the third was about to open under other auspices: it was the turn of persecutions, troubles, and indescribable sorrows.

And now the Magi, whom nothing retained in Judea, prepared to leave Bethlehem. They proposed, according to their promise, to go and find the king in his palace of Jericho, to tell him where the Messias was; but the angel of the Lord admonished them, in a dream, of the dark designs of that perfidious prince, and intimated to them the order to change their route. The children of Ormuzd returned their thanks to the "Master of the sun and of the morning star," gave the honour of this nocturnal revelation to their good genius,* and meriting by their perfect docility the gift of faith which they received later on,† instead of going along the sterile and dangerous borders of the accursed lake which reflects in its

* Of Ormuzd, in Zend, *ahurô-mazdao* (the very learned king), and of Ahriman, in Zend, *ahyro-maingus* (the intelligent merchant), according to the Persian mythology, were born the good and evil genii to whom are attributed different functions in the universe, whether for the diffusion of good or the propagation of evil. One of these good genii, named Serosch, went round the earth every night to watch for the security of the servants of Ormuzd.—(See the Amschaspand-Named, and The Book of Kings of Firdousi.)

† Very ancient authors affirm that the Magi received baptism from St. Thomas; it is thought that they suffered martyrdom in India, where they preached the gospel.

heavy and stagnant waters the shadows of the reprobate cities, they turned the heads of their camels towards the Great Sea, and imagined themselves in the plains planted with date-trees* and covered with roses, bathed by the Euphrates and the Bend-Emyr, while they were traversing the fine regions of Syria.

CHAPTER XIII.

THE PURIFICATION.

FORTY days after the birth of our Saviour, the Virgin considered it her duty to repair to Jerusalem, to obey the precept of Leviticus, which prescribed the purification of mothers, and

* "The palm-trees of Babylonia," says Diodorus Siculus, "bear exquisite dates; they are half a foot long, some yellow, others red, and others of a purple colour, so that they are no less agreeable to the sight than to the taste. The trunk of the tree is of an astonishing height, and everywhere alike straight and smooth; but the head, or tuft, is not of the same form in all. Some palm-trees spread out their branches in a circle, and the fruit of some projects in bunches from the bark, which is open about midway; others bear their branches on one side only, and their weight bending them down towards the ground, gives them the figure of a lamp suspended; others, in fine, divide their branches into two portions, and let them fall to the right and to the left in perfect symmetry." (Diodorus, b. ii.) The following is the description of the banks of the Euphrates, by a poet anterior to Mahomet: "They saw populous towns, plains abounding in flowing streams, date-trees, and warbling birds, and sweet smelling flowers; and the country appeared like a blessing to enliven the sorrowing heart; and the camels were grazing and straying about the land; and they were of various colours, like the flowers of a garden."—(Antar, translated from the Arabic, by Terrick Hamilton.) —For the fields and gardens of roses so common in ancient Persia, see Firdousi, The Book of Kings.

the ransom of the first-born. Doubtless this law did not oblige Mary; for if she had been a mother for our Redeemer, she had remained a virgin for herself, and her conception without stain had been followed by a parturition without defilement: "but she submitted voluntarily, for an example to the world, to a penal law to which she was only so far subject," says Bossuet, "as her virginal maternity was unknown."

Poorly equipped, and lost in the crowd on their first appearance upon the dusty road of Ephrata, Joseph and Mary, who had not attracted any notice, had not either left behind them those long recollections which pass into tradition among nations. It was different on their return to Jerusalem; thanks, no doubt, to the miraculous recitals of the shepherds, and the brilliant visit of the Magi. At some distance from Bethlehem, Mary rested beneath a turpentine-tree to give the breast to her divine Infant, and this tree, according to the common belief, had from that time a hidden virtue which effected, during sixteen centuries, a multitude of wonderful cures. This, at least, is related by the Christians of Asia and the Turks, to whom this tree was still, two centuries ago, an object of veneration and a term of pilgrimage.*

After this halt, the memory of which is preserved, the holy spouses arrived at the tomb of Rachel,† where every Hebrew

* This tree, under which Mary rested to give Jesus the breast, was destroyed during the century before the last, but the memory of the place where it was is still preserved.

† According to the Jewish doctors, Jacob buried his beloved wife on the road to Bethlehem, only because his prophetic knowledge led him to discover that a portion of his descendants would follow this road as captives of the Assyrians, and because he wished that Rachel might intercede for them to Jehovah, as they passed before her tomb. The Protestants have declaimed strongly against the Talmudists on account of this passage, which favours the intercession of the Virgin and of the saints. This tomb of Rachel was in such veneration, that all the Jews who passed by it made it a religious duty to engrave

was bound to pray as he passed. This tumulus of primitive times, which was composed of twelve great stones eaten by moss, upon each of which was read the name of a tribe of Israel, had no epitaph but a white rose of Syria; sweet and frail emblem of the beauty of that young woman, who faded at the moment when she had just blossomed, like the flower spoken of by Job. As they stopped to say the prayer for the dead over the revered dust of one of the saints of their nation, the Virgin and Joseph little thought that the plaintive cries of the dove, which the Scripture attributes to this fair Assyrian, would so soon be applicable; and that the mother of Joseph and Benjamin was the desolate type of mothers who would bewail, some days afterwards, upon the mountains of Judea, their children massacred instead of Jesus Christ.

On leaving the valley of Rephaim, whose old oaks overshadowed the grassy tombs of the giants of the race of Enac, the virgin perceived a tree of forbidding aspect, the sight of which afflicted her heart. It was a barren olive-tree, which spread its pale foliage to the breezes of the night, and the mournful noise of which resembled the moaning of some human being. As she passed under its melancholy branches, which no bird of heaven enlivened with its song, Mary felt that sensation of poisonous cold diffused by the fatal shade of the manchineel-tree. This tree, if the local tradition was not mistaken, was the "infamous" wood on which Christ was nailed.*

their names on one of the stones: these enormous stones were twelve in number.—(Talm. de Jer.) We know that the tears of Rachel, spoken of by Jeremias, were only a figure of the tears shed by the Jewish women after the massacre of the innocents.—(St. Matt. xi. 17, 18.)

* At the distance of half a league from Jerusalem is found the monastery of the Holy Cross. In the church of this monastery is shown the place where stood the barren olive-tree, which the men of Jerusalem used to make the cross of our Lord. The place where the

PRESENTATION IN THE TEMPLE.

At the very moment [illegible]

[illegible] the second [illegible]
the [illegible] and the devo[illegible]
Simeon,* to whom it had been [illegible]
not [illegible] seen Christ [illegible]
by inspiration of the Spirit of God. [illegible]
Family, the eye of the just man [illegible]
the King Messi[illegible] swaddling-clo[illegible]
people [illegible]
[illegible] began to [illegible]
while tears of joy [illegible]
cried out the pi[illegible] old man [illegible]
heaven, "now thou dost dismiss thy s[illegible]
ing to thy word, in peace, because [illegible]
salvation, which thou hast [illegible]
people; a light [illegible] the revelation of the [illegible]
glory of thy people Israel." As he finish[illegible]
Simeon solemnly blessed the [illegible]
himself to Mary, after a moment [illegible]
that this child, [illegible] for the ruin [illegible]
Israel, would [illegible] a sign of contradi[illegible]
sorrow should pierce the soul of he[illegible]
point of a sword.

By this unexpected light, which s[illegible]
the great destiny of [illegible] the ignom[illegible]
agonies of the cross, [illegible] disclosed [illegible]
Virgin. The [illegible]
wind made her bend do[illegible]

[illegible] of [illegible] tree w[illegible]
[illegible] the bottom of a small m[illegible]
temple [illegible]

[illegible] gave Simeon [illegible]
[illegible] witness to the [illegible]
[illegible] son of Jesus [illegible] Mary, [illegible]
[illegible] ive as such [illegible] erb., Bibli[illegible]

PRESENTATION IN THE TEMPLE.

At the very moment when Joseph and Mary made their way into the second inclosure, with the sicles of silver for the ransom and the doves for sacrifice, a holy old man, named Simeon,* to whom it had been divinely revealed that he should not die till he had seen Christ the Lord, came into the portico by inspiration of the Spirit of God. At the sight of the Holy Family, the eye of the just man became inspired; discovering the King Messias beneath the poor swaddling-clothes of the people, he took him from the arms of his mother, lifted him up to his face, and began to contemplate him with emotion, while tears of joy rolled down his venerable cheeks. "Now," cried out the pious old man, raising up his streaming eyes to heaven, "now thou dost dismiss thy servant, O Lord, according to thy word, in peace; because my eyes have seen thy salvation, which thou hast prepared before the face of all people: a light to the revelation of the Gentiles, and the glory of thy people Israel." As he finished these words, Simeon solemnly blessed the holy pair; and then addressing himself to Mary, after a mournful and grave silence, he added that this child, born for the ruin and resurrection of many in Israel, would be a sign of contradiction to men, and that sorrow should pierce the soul of his mother like the sharp point of a sword.

By this unexpected light, which shed a sombre gleam over the great destiny of Christ, the ignominies, the sufferings, and agonies of the cross, were disclosed at once to the Blessed Virgin. The inauspicious words of Simeon, like a stormy wind, made her bend down her head, and her heart was

trunk of the olive-tree was is now occupied by a marble-stone, which is at the bottom of a small niche beneath the high altar, where a lamp burns perpetually.

* The Arabs give Simeon the title of *Siddik* (he who verifies), because he bore witness to the coming of the true Messias, in the person of Jesus, the son of Mary, whom all Mussulmans are obliged to receive as such.—(D'Herb., Biblioth. Orientale, t. iii. p. 266.)

painfully oppressed.* But Mary knew how to accept, without complaint and without murmur, all that came to her from God; her pale lips were placed upon this chalice of wormwood and gall; she drained it even to the dregs, and then said, sweetly, as she dried up her tears, "O Lord, thy will be done!" At that moment the daughter of Abraham was exalted above the head and father of her people; she, too, sacrificed her son upon the altar of the Lord, but she had the sad assurance that the sacrifice would be accepted,—and *she was a mother!*

She was still pondering in her mind these deep thoughts, when a prophetess came in, named Anna, the daughter of Phanuel, of the tribe of Aser, who was far advanced in years. This holy widow departed not from the temple, by fastings and prayers serving God night and day. At the sight of the divine Infant, she began to praise the Lord aloud, and to speak of him to those who looked for the redemption of Israel.

"Not only," says St. Ambrose on this subject, "does the generation of the Lord receive testimony from angels, and prophets, and shepherds, but also from the aged and the just. Every age, and both sexes, and the miracles of events attest it. A Virgin brings forth, one that was barren becomes a mother, the dumb speaks, Elizabeth prophesies, the Magian adores, he who is shut up in the womb leaps for joy, the widow proclaims, the just expects."

As the farthest court of the temple was forbidden to Mary, and as the infant, on account of his sex, was to be offered there to the Lord, Joseph himself carried him into the *court of the first-born*, asking himself at the same time whether the scenes which had taken place at the entrance of Jesus into the holy house would be renewed in the compartment of the

* "Mary, my sovereign," says St. Anselm on this subject, "I cannot believe that you could have lived a moment with such sorrow, had not God strengthened you, who gives life."

Hebrew priests. But nothing discovered the infant God in this privileged part of the temple; everything there remained sad and frozen beneath the rising ray of the young Sun of justice. A priest unknown to Joseph received in a desultory manner from the rough hands of the man of the people, whom he regarded as the "offscouring of the world,"* the timid birds ordained by the law, and did not even deign to honour Christ with a single look. The love of gold—that shameful idolatry, which hides its unacknowledged worship in the shade as long as it retains enough shame to blush—had changed into hard stone the narrow, egotistical, and malignant heart† of the princes of the synagogue. Leaving the monopoly of labour and privations to the simple Levites, whom they reduced to live upon herbs and dried figs,‡ they passed by the poor man stretched upon their marble thresholds, and the traveller wounded in the mountain pathway, turning their heads away with indifference; in reality they loved neither God nor men. And with this does our Lord, who HIMSELF instituted a priesthood exclusively of charity, reproach them, with holy and piercing irony, in the parable of the Samaritan. Therefore, as Malachy had announced, "God cursed their benedictions," and turned away his face from their temple, which he was soon to deliver up to the sword and fire of the Romans.

* Prideaux, History of the Jews.

† The Jewish doctors had then, and still have, a maxim which fills us with horror: they hold that he who does not nourish his hatred, and avenge himself, is unworthy of the name of rabbin. (Basn., liv. vi. c. 17.)

‡ The luxury and avarice of the chief priests of Jerusalem were incredible. The pontiffs sent people into the country to take the tithes in the granaries, and appropriate them to themselves, which left the inferior priests to die of hunger. At the least remonstrance, the miserable Levites were accused of revolt and insubordination, and delivered up to the Romans: the governor Felix alone cast forty of them into prison, out of complaisance to the doctors and princes of the synagogue.—(Josephus, Vita.)

The presence of the Messias, who inflamed the heart of the disciples at Emmaus, even before they had recognised their Master in the breaking of bread, beamed upon the soul of the Aaronites, as the ray of spring glistens on the eternal snows of Ararat. That solemn moment, which suspended the sacred concerts round the throne of God, and fixed the eyes of the heavenly host on a single point of the universe, that moment announced by Aggeus, when the glory of the second temple effaced that of the first, passed unperceived before the darkened eyes of the priests and doctors. None of them recognised "the pure and never sullied oblation" which Malachy had predicted. The desired of nations, HE whose way had been prepared by angels, the great Redeemer so long promised and expected, was there bodily present, in his holy house, and no one thought to welcome him with palms, crying out upon the battlements of the temple and the roofs of Jerusalem, "Hosanna to the Son of David!" They knew well, says the gospel, how to prognosticate the approach of rain by the clouds which gathered in the west; they knew well how to foresee heat when the south wind blew; but these men, so skilful in drawing presages from the different aspects of the sky, did not see "that the fig-tree of Solomon was about to put forth its figs,"* and the child of the people did not lead them to presage the God. O poverty, how excellent a disguise art thou, even for the divine nature! The true CHRIST was in the midst of his own; but he was poor, and his own received him not: therefore have they remained without a Saviour; for no *Melech-Hamaschiak* has come to justify their incredulous contempt for the divine Son of the Virgin, and they are on this account reduced to say, with cold and despairing rage, "Perish those who calculate the time of the Messias!"†

Meanwhile the infant God, who had recognised as he

* St. Luc., c. 12, v. 55 et 56, et c. xxii. v. 29, 30.

† Basn., liv. vi. c. 26. Talmud, 349.

passed through the streets of Jerusalem the sites of our redemption, counted his executioners in silence in this grave and glittering assemblage; among the choirs who sung to the harp hymns of praise to the Eternal, CHRIST distinguished the arrogant and malevolent voices which should cry out later on, "Crucify him! crucify him!"

Race of Aaron, where art thou now? The avenging breath of the Crucified has scattered thee like chaff in every part of the globe; absorbed in those masses which thou despisedst, the companions of thy exile no longer know thee! But at that time, little troubled about that future which was lowering over their heads, the Hebrew priests offered to the God who rejected them the chosen victims of the great and of the common people. One of them took the doves from Joseph, mounted the general ascent of the altar of holocausts, and offered to the Lord this poor and simple sacrifice.

"And after they had performed all things according to the law of the Lord," says St. Luke, "they returned into Galilee to their own city, Nazareth."*

* We have followed the opinion of St. Luke, St. John Chrysostom, and some other authorities, in making the Holy Family leave for Nazareth after the Purification. This is the only way to reconcile St. Matthew—who says nothing of the marvellous events of the Presentation in the temple—with St. Luke, who is silent on the massacre of the Innocents, and the flight into Egypt. "What then shall we say?" says St. John Chrysostom, "that St. Luke calls this the time, describing that which preceded the descent into Egypt. For he did not lead them thither before the Purification, lest the law should be in any way infringed; but he waited till the Purification should be accomplished, and they should have returned to Nazareth, and then they were to go down into Egypt."—(Hom. ix. in St. Matt.)

Where shall they take the frugal repast, to recruit their strength?"

Tradition is silent as to a great part of this affecting and perilous journey. No doubt the holy travellers made long and painful marches across the mountains, taking advantage of the earliest hours of daylight, and often waiting, too, for the rising of the moon to proceed on their way. As long as they were passing through Galilee, the deep caverns which are sunk in it, caverns of unknown windings, where it is easy to hide from all observation, afforded them a place to stop and repose: but these dens with hollow sides had their dangers too; for numerous and predatory bands, who had long defied all the forces of the kingdom, and who were emboldened to reappear by the sickness of Herod,† chose them by preference for their places of security. The fear of penetrating unconsciously into one of these resorts of assassins must have made Joseph hesitate more than once at the sheltering openings of these isolated caverns.

At length, after a thousand inconveniences of every kind, the Holy Family had reached the environs of Jerusalem. Here precautions and uneasiness were multiplied by reason of the imminence of danger; the fugitives no longer dared to come near towns, nor even populous villages, where numbers of spies and informers had their eye upon strangers:‡ they followed the bed of torrents, dived into deserted roads, or the damp shade of woods, not daring to go far out of the way

* S. Bonav., De Vita Christi.

† These large armies, often two or three thousand strong, were commanded by experienced chiefs, who gave Herod and the Romans full occupation. Some had a political aim, and made party war; others were only a mere collection of assassins, who carried long daggers under their cloaks, and killed those whom they wished to get rid of, even in the streets of Jerusalem.—(De Bello, lib. ii. c. 5.)

‡ Herod, who brought espionage to perfection in the East, covered the great roads with spies in every part of Judea.—(Josephus, Ant. Jud., lib. xv. c. 13.)

to renew their exhausted provisions, and suffering at once from fear, cold, and hunger. They had passed by Anathoth, and were moving in the direction of Ramla, to descend into the plains of Syria. Anxious to get out of a dangerous neighbourhood, they had borrowed some hours of the night, when they saw some armed men issue forth from a dark ravine, who stopped their passage. He who appeared to be the chief of this troop of banditti came forward from the hostile group to inspect the travellers. Joseph and Mary had stopped, and looked at each other with alarm: Jesus was asleep. The robber, who had come to take blood and gold, looked with astonishment at this old man, unarmed, just like a patriarch of olden times; at this young woman, covered with a veil, who seemed anxious to hide her child from him in her heart, so closely did she press him painfully to her breast. "They are poor," said the robber to himself, "and travel by night, like fugitives!" He too, perhaps, had a son in the cradle; perhaps the atmosphere of meekness and mercy which surrounded Jesus and Mary acted upon this ferocious soul: he lowered the point of his lance, and holding out a friendly hand to Joseph, he offered him a lodging for the night in his fortress, suspended upon the corner of a rock, like the nests of birds of prey. This offer, honestly made, was accepted with holy confidence, and the roof of the robber afforded hospitality, on this occasion, as well as the tent of the Arab.* The next day, towards noon,

* The site where the local tradition has placed this scene, and where the ruins of the fortress of the banditti are still visible, continues to be very ill-famed. During the crusades, the Franks, to whom this tradition was familiar, had exalted the banditti chief to a feudal lord. "It is rare, however," says F. Nau, with amusing gravity, "that a lord of note becomes a highway robber." The crusaders were better versed in history than F. Nau. To this history, which seems authentic, has been added an embellishment, for which we cannot answer, asserting that the hospitable robber was the good thief in person.

the Holy Family stopped at the extremity of a vast forest of palm-trees, nopals, and wild fig-trees, which extends at a short distance from Ramla;* a carpet of everlasting flowers, narcissuses, and anemones received the Sovereign of heaven and earth; the heats of summer ruled in the plain, and the warbling of birds, the perfume of plants, the tufted shade of fig-trees, and the distant bubbling of a spring, acted as a charm on the sleep of Christ. After a short rest, the moments of which were counted, the travellers proceeded on their journey. Their motive for moving towards Bethlehem is unknown; tradition has preserved the memory of their passing by it, and the Christians have erected an altar in the cave where Mary concealed her infant,† while Joseph went up to the town, either to inquire for the departure of a caravan, or to exchange the slow travelling beast which had carried the Blessed Virgin for a camel. Whatever was the motive which led Joseph and Mary to the crater of a volcano, there is no doubt that they stayed there but a few hours, and that they made haste to reach a maritime town of the Philisthines, to join the first caravan going to Egypt.

If we rely on the learned calculations of chronologists, who allow of no interval in this long journey, the holy pair must have found a caravan on the point of starting, on the coast of Syria. This is the more probable, as the vernal equinox was at hand, and every one would be anxious to anticipate the season when the *simoom* exercises its empire over the desert, and makes its sea of sand as treacherous as the waves themselves.‡ Excepting the mortal apprehension

* The spot fixed by tradition as one of the resting-places of the Holy Family is very charming; the ruins of a monastery are still seen there.—(Itinéraire de Paris à Jerusalem, t. ii.)

† This cave is called *the Grotto of the Virgin's Milk*, because it is supposed that some drops of milk of the Mother of God fell upon the rock, while she suckled the infant Jesus.

‡ "The Arabs call the hot wind of the desert *simoom*, or poison: the impression it makes may be compared to that received from the

of the enraged pursuit of Herod, the second part of the journey of the Holy Family did not yield to the first in fatigue or suffering or even in danger. On quitting Gaza, the ruined towers of which resounded with the dying sound of the waves, the travellers beheld nothing before them but immense solitudes of sand, of a dreary aspect and frightful barrenness, ploughed up by the hot wind of the desert, and oppressed by a fiery sky. No vegetation, except a few thin patches of heath, growing here and there on the lonely plain; no water except the brackish spring where the Virgin and Joseph, who were weary, who were poor, and whom no one cared for, could not quench their thirst till after the rich merchants, their slaves, and camels had exhausted it, and there remained of this poor muddy water barely enough to fill the hollow of one's hand. The farther they went from the frontiers of Syria, the more did they feel thirst, and the springs were more scarce. At times, they discerned at a distance, in the middle of a boundless plain, a large blue clear lake, like the lake of Genesareth; the sky was reflected in its limpid waters, in which a solitary date-palm beheld its own image. A cry of joy hailed this discovery; they urged on the speed of the camels, and Mary raised her drooping head, like a rose of Jericho which foretells rain.* They were close upon this blessed lake, and already slaking their thirst in imagination; but, oh wretched fate! a mocking demon transported the lake some leagues farther on, and left nothing in its place but parched-up sand! †

mouth of a large oven when the bread is drawn. These winds prevail most frequently during the fifty days which comprise the equinoxes." (Volney, Voyage en Syrie.)

* This rose, the cup of which opens and shuts according to the variations of the atmosphere, is consulted as a barometer by the Arabs.—(The Viscount Marcellus, in his Voyage en Orient, t ii.)

† This is the phenomenon known by the name of *mirage*. During the expedition which the French made in Egypt in 1798, the soldiers, traversing the arid deserts of that burning country, parched with

Another optical illusion, which is often repeated in this dry and burning region, made travellers at a distance assume gigantic proportions. Arab horsemen, covered with their flowing cloaks striped brown and white, and armed with the *djombié*—a dagger with a curved blade, which all the dwellers of the desert wear in their girdles—appeared afar off as tall as towers, and seemed to be moving in the air. The Virgin started, and pressed Jesus more closely to her heart; but the placid countenance of Joseph calmed her fears, although she could not understand the phenomenon which gave rise to them.*

At the approach of evening, the song of the camel-drivers ceased,† the leader of the caravan unfurled the flag which gives notice of the halt, and all the travellers assembled round

thirst, were often deceived by this cruel illusion. Every prominent object which offered itself to their eyes in the midst of these seas of sand, appeared to them surrounded with water: thus a hillock, which they perceived at a distance, seemed to them to rise out of the midst of a lake. Dying with want they ran towards it; but, when they arrived at the place itself, they discovered their mistake: the lake had fled, and appeared yet farther off to their eager eyes.—(See de Fellens, du Mirage. Art. 6.)

* "I had occasion," says Niebuhr, "to remark a phenomenon which struck me as very singular; but which, in time, became familiar to me. An Arab mounted on a camel, whom I saw coming from a distance, appeared to me as tall as a tower, and seemed to move in the air; yet he was marching on the sand like ourselves. This optical illusion proceeds from a stronger refraction of the atmosphere, in these arid regions loaded with vapours of a different nature from those which fill the air of temperate countries."—(Voyage en Arabie, t. i. p. 208.)

† It is an almost universal custom in the East to enliven one another on the march, or at work, by singing. A Mussulman pilgrim has given a very picturesque description of the nocturnal march of a caravan of Mecca, by the light of lanterns fixed upon the camels, and to the measured singing of the camel-drivers.—(Voyage d'Abdoul Kerim.) The camel-drivers still sing songs peculiar to themselves in Syria and Egypt.—(Correspondance d'Orient, t. vi.)

this signal of order. An animated scene soon followed this halting-time. They unloaded the camels, who were kneeling at the feet of their masters, their burdens were piled up pyramidally; they set up a row of round stakes, to which the beasts of burden were to be tethered; the rich travellers pitched their tents, and the leader of the caravan placed sentinels to give notice of the approach of the Bedouins, those pirates of the desert, who were, and are still, robbers like Ismael, and hospitable like Abraham. Every merchant, after taking his repast of dates and milk, composed himself to sleep in his tent of mohair till the rising of the moon. The slaves and the poor travellers, in which number were the Son of God, his divine Mother, and Joseph, sat upon a rush mat, spread upon the ground, without any roof but the sky, and felt the icy breeze of the night* upon their limbs, languid with heat, and worn out with fatigue. At times was heard a cry of alarm: it was the Arabs of the desert, prowling about the slumbering caravan; disconcerted by the vigilance of the guards of the camp, they announced their departure by a volley of arrows, accompanied by the groans of the wounded. Then the Virgin, who had made a rampart with her body for her adored Son, raised up to heaven her eyes moist with tears, and her forehead pale with fear; she knew but too well that her Jesus was mortal as well as the least of the children of men!

When the moon diffused her white light over that shadowless and noiseless desert, where the breezes of the solitude found not a blade of grass to raise a sigh, they struck their tents, and the painful march began again, with all the inconveniences, sufferings, and terrors experienced the day before.

At length, they arrived at the extremity of this region of illusions and silence. Egypt, that ancient nursery of every light, and every species of idolatry, presented itself to the tra-

* Although the days are scorching in the desert at this season, the nights are very cold.—(Voln.; Sav.)

vellers, with its obelisks of rose granite, its temples with tops of polished steel,* its colossal pyramids, its villages resembling islands, and its providential river, bordered with reeds, and covered with vessels. This country appeared richer, more populous, and more commercial than Judea; but it was the land of exile! on the other side of the desert was their own country! The hearts of the exiles of Israel had remained there.

After a journey of a hundred and forty leagues,† the fugitives reached Heliopolis, where their nation had founded a colony. In that city arose the temple of Jehovah, which Onias had built upon the plan of the holy house. The ornaments of this Egyptian temple were almost equal to those of the other; only, as a sign of inferiority, a massive lamp of gold, suspended from the ceiling supplied the place of the famous candlestick with seven branches at Jerusalem. At the gate of this city, the population of which was in great measure composed of Egyptians and idolatrous Arabs, was a majestic tree, of the mimosa species, to which the Arabs of the Yemen, established on the banks of the Nile, paid a kind of worship.‡ At the approach of the Holy Family, the *fetiche* tree slowly bent down its shady branches, as if to offer the

* On the dome of the sanctuary of the principal temple of Hiliopolis was observed an immense mirror of polished steel, which reflected the rays of the luminary of heaven. There was a similar one on the top of the lighthouse of Alexandria, and the images of ships were reflected in it long before they appeared in the horizon.—(Correspondance d'Orient, t. v.; Lettres de Savary.)

† See Barad., t. i. c. 8.—The author of the Voyages de Jesus Christ reckons only a hundred leagues, but perhaps he takes no account of the windings of the roads.

‡ The Arabs, who had gradually forgotten the God of Abraham, adored at that time a number of idols, each more monstrous than the other. "The date-tree," says Azraki, "was adored by the tribe of Khozua, and the Beni-Thekif worshipped a rock; a large tree named *sat arouat* was adored by the Koreisch, &c." The Persians scornfully designated the Arabs by the title of "adorers of stones."

salam to the young Master of nature, whom Mary carried in her arms;* and, if we may believe the historian Palladius, at the moment when the divine travellers passed under the granite arches of the gate of Heliopolis, all the idols of a neighbouring temple fell on their faces to the ground.†

Joseph and Mary only passed through the City of the Sun, and repaired to Matarieh, a beautiful village shaded by sycamores, where the only fountain of sweet water in Egypt is found. There, in a dwelling like a bee-hive, where the doves built their nests, the fugitive family reposed in peace, far away from Herod.

This cruel prince, after waiting in vain for the Magi in his palace at Jericho, his favourite residence, learned at length that they had repassed the frontiers of his kingdom, and that, without giving him an account of their mission, they were gone back to the country of the Persians. Pale already from the slow fever which consumed him, the King of the Jews became still paler with wrath. He was deceived at the very moment when he was delighted at the thought of his unequalled cleverness in deceiving others—deceived by these uncircumcised men, who, contrary to all expectation, had found out his tortuous and wily policy! If the Magi

* We are indebted to Sozomen for this event, which it requires some courage to reproduce in this age of mockery, and which, after all, is hardly a miracle. It is certain that there exists in Arabia a tree of the species of the sensitives and mimosas, which bends down its branches at the approach of man. Niebuhr, who is not suspected of credulity, found this tree in the Yemen, and the Arabs, who give it the name of tree of hospitality, hold it in such veneration that it is not lawful to pluck a leaf from it. If this mimosa, by a natural phenomenon, bends down its branches at the approach of man, much more must it have had cause to lower them at the approach of the Son of God.

† Palladius is not the only one who relates this miracle; the martyr Dorotheus, St. Anselm, St. Bonaventure, Lira, Dionysius the Carthusian, Testatus, Ludolphus, Barradius, &c., attest it in like manner.

had not discovered the child to whom the star had conducted them, they would have told him so on their return.—They had then discovered his secret retirement, and this was somewhere in Bethlehem or its environs, since they had not carried their search any farther.—How was this dangerous child now to be distinguished from common children?—There was but one last expedient left, one extreme measure to destroy him: this was to include him in one general massacre.—But the people!—At this thought the aged king mused for a moment; then a wild and scornful smile passed over his lips. The people dare nothing, said Herod to himself, against kings who dare everything!

"And sending, *he* killed all the men-children that were in Bethlehem, and in all the borders thereof, from two years old and under, according to the time which he had diligently inquired of the wise men."*

According to a number of grave authors,† who have tradition and probability on their side, the Holy Family remained seven years in Egypt. There are still found traces of their dwelling there: the spring where Mary used to wash the infant's linen;‡ the hill covered with bushes, where she dried it in the sun; the sycamore, in the shade of which she

* This gospel fact, which the school of Voltaire has called in question, is proved, not only by our sacred books, but also by the testimony of Jews and Pagans.—(Macrobius, lib. xi. c. 4, De Saturnal.; Orig., Contra Celsum, lib. xi. c. 58; Toldos Huldr., pp. 12, 14, 20.)

† See Trombel, in Vit. Deip.; Zachariam, in Diss. ad Hist. Eccl.; Anselm; Cantual; Euseb.; St. Thom.

‡ This fountain is still called *the Fountain of Mary;* an ancient tradition records that the Blessed Virgin bathed the infant Jesus in it. In the earliest times of Christianity, the faithful built a church in this place; later on, the Mussulmans constructed a mosque there, and the disciples of both creeds came to pray at *the Fountain of Mary* for the cure of their maladies; the fountain is still there; the pilgrimages continue, but no vestiges remain either of church or mosque.—(Savary, t. i. p. 122; Corresp. d'Or., t. vi. p. 3.)

loved to sit with her Son upon her knees,* are still there after the lapse of eighteen centuries. The pilgrims of Europe and Asia knew the way to them, and the descendants of the nation of Pharaoh treat them with honour. To every spot some original legend of the olden time is attached, like the moss on the damp wall of a religious ruin.†

At Nazareth, Mary had led an humble and laborious life, but at Heliopolis she beheld misery in all its aspects. It was necessary to find means of support,—a difficult thing out of one's own country, and among a people parcelled out in national and hereditary corporations, who were by no means fond of strangers. As they were poor, observes St. Basil, it

* "Not far from the mountain, I was taken into an enclosure planted with trees; a Mussulman who was our guide stopped us before a sycamore, and said to us, *This is the tree of Jesus and Mary.* Vanslab, rector of Fontainebleau, informs us that the old sycamore fell down from old age in 1058. The cordeliers of Cairo piously preserved in their sacristy the last remains of this tree; there remained in the garden only a stump, whence, no doubt, came the tree which we saw. General Kleber, after the victory of Heliopolis, would visit as a pilgrim the tree of the Holy Family: he had written his name on the bark of one of the branches: this name has since disappeared, effaced either by time or by some envious hand."—(Corresp. d'Or., t. vi. lettre 141.)

† The following is one of those legends brought from the lands beyond the sea by one of our good old French barons, the Seigneur d'Englure: we give it with all the original grace of the good old time—"When our Lady, the Mother of God, had passed over the deserts, and when she came to this said place, she laid our Lord down upon the ground, and went about in search of water, but could find none; so she returned full of sorrow to her dear infant, who lay stretched upon the sand, who had dug into the ground with his heels, so that there sprung up a fountain of very good and sweet water. So our Lady was very glad of this, and thanked our Lord for it, and our Lady laid her dear infant down again, and washed the little clothes of our Lord in the water of this fountain, and then spread them out on the ground to dry; and from the water which ran off these little clothes, as it dried up, there grew from each drop a shrub, which shrubs yield balsam, &c."

is evident that they must have submitted to painful labour to procure the necessaries of life.—Alas! had they always even these? "Oftentimes," says Ludolph of Saxony, "did the child Jesus ask his mother for bread, when she could give him nothing but her tears!"

Meanwhile, Herod had died of a horrible and nameless disease, after seeing himself devoured alive by the worms of the tomb. Dwelling to his last breath upon the joy that the people would feel at the news of his decease, he had with tears requested his sister Salome, a wicked woman, to have the flower of the Jewish nobility shot to death with arrows, whom he had imprisoned with this intention, that people might weep at his funeral whether they would or not.* He was carried to his castle of Herodion in a golden litter, covered with scarlet and precious stones. His sons and his army followed his bier with downcast looks, while the people, having the happiness of deliverance before their eyes, cast upon him as many maledictions as a cloud showers down drops of rain.

Admonished in a dream, by the angel of the Lord, of the death of the tyrant, Joseph returned with Mary and the child into the land of Israel; "but hearing that Archelaus reigned in Judea in the room of Herod, his father, he was afraid to go thither: and being warned in sleep, he turned aside into the quarters of Galilee."

* Josephus, Ant. Jud., lib. xvii. c. 8.—The memory of Herod remained in such execration among the princes of the people and the priests, that they instituted a feast, which was celebrated on the 25th of September, out of joy that he was dead. "There is a feast on the 7th of Chisleu," says the Jewish calendar, "on account of the death of Herod; for he had hated the wise, and we rejoice before the Lord when the wicked depart out of this world."—(Basn., t. i. liv. ii. c. 8.)

CHAPTER XV.

RETURN FROM EGYPT.

How sorrowful is exile! and how sweet to breathe the air of our native land! The bread of the stranger, like that of the wicked, leaves grit in the mouth and bitterness in the heart; his streams tell not of the sports of our childhood; the song of his birds has no melodious notes; his scenes are destitute of that sweet and charming attraction possessed by the scenes of our own country! . . . .

What must have been the joy of the two holy spouses when they beheld again that land of Chanaan, whose grand boundaries, soft outlines, universal harmony, and variety of aspects contrasted so happily and so strikingly with the monotonous splendours of Egypt! Here a population rustic and hardy, with a warlike turn, an open address, a worship grave and pure; there, slaves herded by castes, given to plunder, mingling with their worship infamous practices, and exhausting their resources to erect temples to the ox Apis, the crocodile, and the sea-onion! One must be profoundly religious, as Joseph and Mary were—one must love one's country as the Hebrews loved theirs, to understand the pious and sweet impressions which the two Galilean spouses felt at the sight of the land of Jehovah and their beautiful city of Nazareth.

After so long an absence, the Holy Family returned to their humble hearth, amidst the congratulations, the astonishment, the eager inquiries of their relations, who all vied with each other in entertaining them; but desolation and bitter reverses soon succeeded to all this joy. The deserted dwelling of the poor family was scarcely habitable: the roof, decayed and fallen-in in places, was ornamented here and there with long grass, and had afforded free entrance into the interior to the wintry blast and the beating rains of the equinoxes;* the lower apartment was cold, damp, and green; wild pigeons made their nests in the mysterious and hallowed cell where the WORD was made flesh; brambles shot up their brown thorny garlands in the small court; everything, in fine, in that old dwelling, already gilded by ages, had assumed that ruinous and desolate appearance which fastens upon deserted edifices as the seal of the master's absence. It was necessary to set about these urgent repairs; it was necessary to replace tools and furniture either unfit for use or altogether vanished; perhaps they had to repay a sum borrowed in Egypt to enable them to return. Then it was, no doubt, that they sold the paternal fields till the year of jubilee. Of all that Joseph and Mary possessed before their long journey, they had nothing left but the ruined house of Nazareth, the workshop of Joseph, and their own arms; but Jesus was there. Young as he was, Jesus took up the axe, and followed his aged father into the villages, where work was found for them;† his work, proportioned to his age and strength, was never wanting to aid his mother. Easy circumstances had long disappeared; but by dint of privations, working late and early, and good courage, they provided for absolute necessity. Jesus, Mary, and Joseph gave themselves up to hard labour, and He who could command legions of angels never asked of God, for himself or those belonging to him, anything but daily bread.

The interior life of this happy family, who have been sur-

* The time of rains in Judea, is that of the equinoxes, and especially of the autumnal equinox: it is also the season for storms. which are accompanied with violent showers, or hail.—(Volney, Voyage en Syrie.)

† St. Justin, martyr (Dialog. cum Tryphone), relates that Jesus Christ helped his father to make yokes and ploughs. And Godescard, t. xiv. p. 436, Vie de la Sainte Vierge, says, "A very ancient author assures us, that in his time yokes were shown which our Saviour had made with his own hands."

named the *terrestrial Trinity*, has not come to the knowledge of men: it is the course of water lost among the grass; it is the holy of holies, with its cloud of perfumes and its double veil. Nevertheless, by studying minutely and examining one by one, and in all their aspects, the facts of the gospel, what we know leads us to surmise to a certain extent what we do not know; and the public life of Jesus Christ casts certain brilliant lights upon his hidden life, and that of the Blessed Virgin. We will endeavour to fill up this void with all that reserve, and all that conscientious application, which so grave a subject demands.

Jesus, in whom were hidden all the treasures of wisdom and knowledge,* had no need of being taught by men; therefore every supposition to the contrary is positively rejected by the Church. St. John also, in his gospel, informs us that the Jews in the time of Jesus Christ considered him as a young man without learning,† and the astonishment of the Nazareans to see him so profoundly versed in sacred literature, sufficiently testifies that they had no knowledge of his having been, like St. Paul, educated at "the feet of a master." The Talmudists and the Jewish authors of the Toldos maintain, on the contrary, that a celebrated rabbin initiated Jesus in the mysteries of science and magic; but setting aside the second part of the assertion, which is absurd, and taking the matter only from a mere human point of view, as the rationalists do, this is evidently false, for two reasons. First, Jesus was neither a zealot, nor a man wedded to traditions; and we see, all through the gospel, that he strongly disapproved of the narrow-minded views, captious distinctions, and low subtilties of the doctors of the synagogue. Secondly, the rabbi Josue Perachia, whom they assign him as preceptor, had still to be born, since he flourished a century later.

* S. Paul., Ep. ad Coloss. c. ii. v. 9.

† S. Joan., c. vii. v. 15.

To place Jesus in the midst of the rabbins as a scholar, would be as illogical as to attempt to support an oak by surrounding it with reeds. He did not teach like them, says the evangelist,* and this it is easy to conceive, for he derived his wisdom from himself; and his teaching, still taking it from a natural point of view, seems to flow from a soul most elevated, most pure, and upright, and from a mind so vast and so uniformly sound, that assuredlv it had not been warped in the disputes of the schools.

Strauss admits that all the wisdom and science of the time would not have been able to form a man like Jesus Christ. "If," says he, "Jesus Christ had exhausted all the tuition of his time, it is no less true that none of those elements sufficed, even by a great deal, to cause a revolution in the world; and the leaven indispensable for so great a work, could have been derived only from the depths of his own soul."

His eloquence, like his morality, was his own. It was not the emphatic exaggerations of the rabbins, nor the majestic, striking, and violently contrasted diction of the ancient prophets; it was, as he himself said, a fountain of living water, reflecting in its course the birds of heaven, the harvests and the flowers of the fields. . . . . This eloquence, perfectly simple, penetrated to the bottom of things, and was allied, without effort, to great thoughts. Each word was a precious seed of virtue; every instruction cast into the mysterious spaces of the future a long train of light, which was to grow insensibly, and extend to the perfect day of the regeneration of the world. Even those who have audaciously denied his miracles, have not been able to help acknowledging that his words were those of a God.†

* Matt. vii. 29.

† "I own to you that the majesty of the Scriptures astonishes me," says Rousseau; "the sanctity of the gospel speaks to my heart. Look at the books of the philosophers, with all their pomp, how

Jesus was endowed with a soul profound and meditative, which needed an ample space in which to extend itself. Confined during the day to manual labour, which absorbed all his time, he made up at night for his obscure fatigue, and became again lawgiver and prophet in presence of the starry heaven. Standing upon an elevated platform, whence could be seen the mountains and extensive woods of the land of Chanaan, he poured forth his soul before the Author of nature, of whom he was the envoy, the Son, and the equal. These communings, all alone with God, in the silence of the night, and the desert, and in silent thought, were one of the habits of Jesus Christ; we find many examples of them in the gospel. The model of men, the Word incarnate, would, no doubt, teach his followers to separate the pure gold of prayer from the monstrous alloy of ostentation and hypocrisy which the Pharisees of his time were accustomed to mix up with it.

The Blessed Virgin, who was never importunate or exacting, made no sort of opposition to this retirement; she knew that Jesus then sounded the depths of the immeasurable abyss which opened beneath the feet of the human race, and that the redemption of the world would be the fruit of these silent meditations. Respecting the labours of that mighty mind which redoubled upon itself, and looking to the future glory which every moment brought nearer and nearer, Mary already saw the heavens opened, death vanquished, and the Messias rallying all nations beneath his standard. . . . . But on a sudden the prophecy of the aged man in the

small they are by the side of this! Can it be that a book at once so sublime and simple could be the work of men? Can it be that he whose history it relates could be himself but a man? Is that the tone of an enthusiast, or of an ambitious sectarian? What meekness! what purity in his manners! what affecting gracefulness in his instructions! what sublimity in his maxims! what profound wisdom in his discourses! . . . ."—(Emile, t. iii. p. 365.)

temple presented itself, dark as a funeral bier, at the end of this enchanted perspective; a cold chill ran through the veins of the poor mother, and her heart, in which the love of Jesus had so large a share, melted in infinite agony. A secret voice cried out to her, "There must be an expiation of blood! Christ must die!" Then, humbly laying down the work to which she was condemned by her indigence,* the daughter of David came to look after her Son; she wanted to see him, to make sure, in a maternal embrace, that he was still there,—that he was still alive!

When he saw her, Jesus cast down his pensive eye, which had been fixed upon the stars; his youthful forehead, contracted by a thought as vast as the world, became again the smooth and shining forehead of the child. Then Mary, shutting up in her heart her sinister fears, advised repose after the long watch. It was necessary to recruit his strength for the following day; the walk would be fatiguing and the labour painful . . . . The Son of God followed his mortal mother in silence, for he loved her, and *was subject to her*.

An extraordinary incident, which overpowered the soul of the Blessed Virgin, marked the entrance of Jesus into the state of adolescence. Joseph and Mary, religious observers of the law of their fathers, went up regularly every year to Jerusalem, at the time of the Passover. This journey, which they had performed stealthily, and lost in the crowd, as long as the son of the enemy of God had occupied the throne of the Macchabees, had become easier since the exile of Archelaus, and the occupation of the country by the Romans. When Christ had reached his twelfth year, his parents, freed from apprehension on account of Herod, took him with them to Jerusalem. They departed in a body from Nazareth;

* Tertullian, says, in the third century, that Mary earned her livelihood by working; and Celsus, in the second century, said that Mary was a woman who had lived by the work of her hands.

and then, as they travelled along, the Hebrew pilgrims divided into small companies, according to age, sex, and family relationship or intimacy.

Around the Virgin were Mary of Cleophas, sister-in-law of Joseph; another Mary, designated in the gospel by the name of *altera Maria;* Salome, the wife of Zebedee, who came from Bethsaida with her sons and her husband; Joanna, the wife of Chus, and a number of Nazarenes of her family connexions and neighbourhood. Joseph followed them at some distance, conversing gravely with Zebedee the fisherman, and the ancients of his tribe. Jesus walked amidst some young Galileans, whom the gospel, according to the genius of the Hebrew tongue, has called his brethren, and who were his near relatives.*

Among this group of young men, who went before the rest, were distinguished the sons of Zebedee: James, impetuous as the lake of Tiberias on a stormy day; John, younger even than Jesus, whose sweet countenance, by the side of that of his brother, seemed to personify the lamb of Isaias, living in peace with the lion of Jordan. Next to the fishermen of Bethsaida, whom Jesus named later on *Boanerges* (sons of thunder), were the four sons of Alpheus; James, who was Bishop of Jerusalem, an austere and grave youth, with long flowing hair, a pale face, and a cold and mortified appearance. Proud of being devoted as a Nazarene, he gave himself airs of offensive superiority over him whom he then considered the son of the carpenter. The virtues and imperfections inherent in the soil were seen in his character; an

* St. Epiphanius and St. Bernard inform us that in these journeys, the men went in companies separate from the women, and that St. Joseph and the Blessed Virgin were in different companies, which was the reason why they did not feel uneasy at first at the disappearance of Jesus, and did not perceive it till the evening, when all the travellers assembled together.—(See also Aëlred, abbot of Rieval, Serm. seu Tractatus de Jesu duodeni, Dom intra oct. Epiph.)

unshaken firmness, inclinations upright and religious; but at the same time a strong contempt for all that had not sprung from Abraham, and an excellent opinion of himself. Jude, Simon, and José, the other sons of Alpheus, were youths of rough, simple, and warlike appearance, already arrived at adolescence, and who looked upon the son of the humble Mary as their inferior in every way—a thing which they had a difficulty in shaking off afterwards, as we see in the gospel.* And what of Jesus? Jesus pretended to nothing, neither to devotion, nor austerity, nor wisdom, nor knowledge, because he possessed the plenitude of all these things, and people usually affect what they have not.

To have seen him, simply attired as an Essenian, his long hair, of the colour of antique bronze,† parted over his dark forehead, and gracefully flowing over his shoulders, one would have taken him for David, at the moment when the prophet Samuel saw him come, little, timid, and in the dress of a simple shepherd, to receive the holy unction. There was, however, in the brown, soft eye of Christ,‡ something

* S. Joan Chrysost., Serm. 44.

† The rabbins have taken occasion from the colour of the hair of Jesus, to give way to malicious declamations against him; but what is extraordinary is, that they utter against him precisely the same reproaches as they do against David. "He was red like Esau; he had his blood upon his head; the soul of Esau had passed into him." They have forgotten nothing but the *evil eye* with which they favoured the prophet king.

‡ Niceph., Hist. Eccl., t. i. p. 125. His portrait of our Lord, traced after tradition, is the most authentic which has come down to us. The Rev. Mr. Walsh, the author of quite a recent book, devoted to rare or unpublished monuments of the first age of Christianity, has just called our attention to a very curious medal, known as early as the fifth century. The obverse represents the head of our Lord, seen in profile; the hair is parted after the manner of the Nazarites, smooth as far as the ears, and flowing over the shoulders: the beard thick, not long, but forked; the countenance handsome as well as the bust, over which the tunic falls in graceful folds.

more than in the eye of his great ancestor, full as it was of poetry and inspiration; something penetrating and divine was discovered in it, which laid bare the thought and sounded the depths of the heart; but Jesus veiled at that time the brilliancy of his look, as Moses did his radiant brow when he came forth from the tabernacle. He walked along, conversing sensibly, but suiting his conversation to his age, with his young relatives according to the flesh, whom he intended to make his apostles; he discerned beneath their rude exterior, the weight and value of these rough diamonds, who were one day to shine with so great brilliancy, and he loved them in their future career. His expectations were not disappointed; these men, who, like the rest of their nation, had had their dreams of gold and power in connection with the Messias, at his voice cast off all their prejudices, both national and religious, to adopt a doctrine calumniated, the principles and promises of which, like the maledictions of the old law, spoke of nothing but sufferings to be endured, and persecutions to be undergone. They bound themselves to him by chains so strong, that neither the princes of the earth, nor cold, nor nakedness, nor famine, nor the sword, could separate them from his love; they walked in his footsteps, trampling courageously on the thorns which the world strewed in their path, and suffering themselves to be treated like the refuse of the human race. They were not ashamed, either of the Son of man, or of his gospel, or of *the foolishness of the cross!* Why should they? It is for impostors to blush, and the apostles never preached but from their own intimate conviction. These upright and guileless hearts gave to their testimony all that could render it credible and sacred among men; they abandoned everything, suffered everything, forgave everything, and sealed with their blood the gospel of their divine Master.*

* Pascal has said, "I willingly believe these histories, whose witnesses expose themselves to death."

But at the time of which we are speaking, these heroic virtues were not even yet expanded, and these youthful Galileans little thought that they should one day give their lives in support of the divinity of their travelling companion. At the end of four days' journey, the pilgrims reached the Holy City, whither an immense concourse of foreign Jews flocked together.* The family of Joseph and Mary assembled to eat the paschal lamb, which the priests had the charge of immolating between the two vesper hours,† in the court of the temple; to this they added unleavened bread, wild lettuces, and whatever appertained to this ancient ceremony. The days of the feast being over, the relations of Christ assembled to return to their province. As they returned in the same order in which they had come, the holy couple did not at first perceive that Jesus was missing. Mary thought he was with Joseph, or with the two named James; Joseph, for his part, thought he was with his young relations, or with Mary. In the evening, the several companies assembled together, and the Blessed Virgin sought, but in vain, for Jesus in the crowd of travellers who arrived in succession at the caravansary; no one knew what had become of our Saviour. The grief of the two holy spouses was inexpressible. "The deposit of heaven, the Son of God!" muttered Joseph, sorrowfully. "My son!" said the poor young mother, with a voice drowned with tears. They sought him all night, they sought him all day, calling after

* The feast of the Passover collected together at Jerusalem as many as two million five hundred thousand persons.—(De Bello, lib. vii. c. 17.) Cestus, wanting to persuade Nero that the Jewish nation was not so contemptible as he believed it to be, had the people numbered by priests. At the feast of the Pasch, there were slain two hundred and fifty-six thousand six hundred lambs; there was a lamb for each family.

† That is, from noon or one o'clock till sunset.—(Basn., t. v. liv. vii. c. 2.

him along the road, calling out his name in the woods, looking anxiously down the precipices, sometimes fearing for his life, sometimes for his liberty, and not knowing what they should do if he was lost. They re-entered Jerusalem, ran to all their friends, and weary with going about the quarters of that great city, they at last made their way into the temple. Underneath the portico, where the doctors of the law were, was a child, who delighted the ancients of Israel by the depth of his understanding, and the clearness of his answers to the most difficult questions; they gathered round him, and every one was in admiration at his precocious and miraculous wisdom. "It is either Daniel or an angel," they said, at a little distance from the afflicted Virgin. "It is Jesus!" said the young mother, pressing forward towards the place where the doctors were. Then, coming up to the Messias with the expression of extreme tenderness, which in a manner extinguished the last reflex of sorrow: "My son," she said, sweetly, "why hast thou done so to us? Behold, thy father and I have sought thee sorrowing!"

The child was effaced before the God; the answer was dry and mysterious. "How is it that you sought me? Did you not know that I must be about my Father's business?" The holy couple kept silence; they did not at first understand the meaning of the answer of the Messias.

Jesus rose up and followed them to Nazareth; his perfect submission to their will speedily effaced this slight cloud. "And his mother kept all these words in her heart. And Jesus increased in wisdom and age, and grace with God and man."

CHAPTER XVI.

MARY AT THE PREACHING OF JESUS.

"THERE are two worlds in our history,' as one of the finest geniuses of our age has said, "the one beyond the cross, the other before it." The primitive world, fallen into decrepitude at the time of the regenerating mission of Jesus Christ, presented a strange spectacle, for the burlesque lent a hand there to the horrible. The Arab and the Gaul, after having retained for ages the primitive idea of the unity of God, adored the acacia and the oak; * the Hindoo made a divinity of the Ganges, and sacrificed human victims to Sactis, the goddess of death; † the Egyptian, that wisest of all people, paid devout worship to garlic, to the lotus, and almost every bulbous-rooted plant; ‡ the unknown populations of young America adored the tiger, the vulture, storms, and roaring cataracts; § in fine, the Greeks and Romans, by their own acknowledgment, filled their temples with demons,|| and

* The Pagan Gauls of the sixth and seventh centuries made gods of oak-trees; they burned torches before these trees, and invoked them as if they could hear; the enormous stones which were near these trees participated in the honour which was paid to them.—(Hist. ecclésiastique de Bretagne, t. iv., seventh century; Capitul. Caroli Magni, lib. i. tit. 64.)

† See Picture of India, by Buckingham.

‡ The sarcasm of Juvenal is well known: "O sanctas gentes, quibus hæc nascuntur in hortis Numina."—(Sat. xv. v. 10.)

§ Garcilasso, l. i. c. 2 et 12.

|| Prophyrius, who so well knew the foundations of polytheism, acknowledges that the demons were the objects of worship among the Gentiles. "There are," says he, "spirits impure, deceitful, malevolent, who would pass for gods and get themselves adored by men: they must be appeased, lest they should do us mischief. Some, who are lively and joyous, allow themselves to be propitiated by shows

these nations, so refined, so polished, who abounded in men of superior genius, had deified vice in its most hideous shades, and peopled their Olympus with robbers, adulterers, and murderers. Morals corresponded with creeds; corruption, rushing down like a vast torrent from the heights of the seven imperial hills, inundated all the provinces. Judea, which had not escaped the contagion of vice any more than other countries, grew depraved with frightful rapidity; her religion no longer rested on fundamental dogmas, but on an innumerable multitude of parasitical superfœtations, and the reveries of her rabbins were enthroned on the chair of Moses.*

In the midst of these deplorable abberrations, what became of proud reason, that queen of intelligences, who takes her own narrow horizon for the boundaries of the universe, and places the gods upon the bed of Procrustes? Where did she hold her empire? Where had she planted her standard, while on every side breaches were made in her bulwarks? If she could without foreign aid reconquer the territory which she had lost, why did she not do so? . . . . But she felt that the torrent would overflow her weak embankments, and unable to restrain it, she was content to observe its ravages. Supported by philosophy, she groaned over the inanimate remains of the social body whose fall she

and games; the gloomy temper of others requires the odour of fat, and feeds on bloody sacrifices."

* It is a maxim among the Jews that the covenant was made with them on Mount Sinai, not on the footing of the written law, but on that of the oral law. They annul the former to enthrone the latter, and reduce all religion finally to tradition. This corruption had risen to such a height among the Jews, even in the time of our Lord, that he reproaches them, in St. Mark, with having destroyed the word of God by their traditions. But it is much worse in these days; they compare the sacred text to water, and the *Misnah*, or *Talmud*, to the best wine; moreover, the written law is salt, but the *Talmud* is pepper, cinnamon, &c.

had been unable to prevent: Christianity supervened, who said to the corpse, "Arise, and walk!" . . . . And it was done according to her word.

From that day a new race, healed of all its evils, washed from all its defilements in the sacred piscina, assembled round the cross which the Son of Mary had planted on the regenerated earth, as the trophy of God over hell.

This glorious revolution, which set charity on the throne, and placed all the virtues in her train,—this ever-memorable event, which changed the face of the world, and the echo of which will make itself heard even to the consummation of ages,—had Nazareth for its starting-point; from the hollow of that nameless rock flowed humble Christianity, "an obscure spring, a drop of water unnoticed, where two sparrows could not have slaked their thirst, which one ray of the sun might have dried up, and which at this day, as the great ocean of minds, has filled up every abyss of human wisdom, and bathed with its never-failing waters the past, the present, and the future." *

We know nothing of the means which prepared this great fact, which holds so high dominion over the history of modern times. From the time of his manifestation in the temple, the Son of God led a life hidden and contemplative, between his adoptive father and his mother. This period, lost to the world, was doubtless that in which the Virgin passed her most tranquil days. It is not when human life moves on in commotion, like a wintry torrent, that it is the most happy; it is when it resembles the course of that water which meanders in a silvery thread among the grass of the meadows. Mary, deprived indeed of all the enjoyments of luxury, and all the sweets of ease, but living with her Son, working for him, studying his inclinations, seeing him at all times, offering herself to him as the first fruits of his sacred harvest; making herself the first, the most humble, the most

* M. de Lamartine, Voy. en Orient.

docile of his disciples, and bowing down her matured reason before the superior reason and divinity of her Son, Mary must then have been a happy Mother! If, at those times when Jesus revealed to her the most profound sense of the prophecies, he met with some passage which spoke of sufferings to be undergone, a dark cloud spread over the chaste brow of the Virgin; but soon her sweet and gracious countenance recovered a little serenity. The storm murmured as yet at a distance, and their bark was moored in a tranquil bay. Her Son was there! she hung upon his looks, his words, and his smallest actions. How eager was she to serve him—her Son! how happily did she sit up whole nights to spin and to weave his tunics for labour, his holiday garments, that seamless coat, a masterpiece of ingenuity and patience, which later on! . . . . . but at this time the "Lord had anointed his Christ with an oil of gladness only." A companion of the spouse, the wise Virgin of the gospel "left the morrow to provide for itself," "and the peace of God, which surpasseth all understanding, kept her heart and her mind."

Jesus was perfection itself, the omniscient, thrice holy, surpassing all in power and wisdom; as God, he could be indebted for nothing to creatures, but as man he owed something to Mary. She it was who initiated him, from his earliest infancy, in the humble virtues inherent in humanity, and in her own simple and poetic tastes. That patient and unalterable meekness which he knew how to unite with the firmness of a legislator and a prophet; that merciful compassion which tempered the indignation of an irritated God, and rendered him, HIMSELF, the model man, the accomplished just one, the support of sinful man; that tenderness which was all good, all unaffected towards children, whom he loved to caress and bless during his divine mission; a thousand imperceptible shades, a thousand reflexes, half-absorbed in the large masses of light, which composed the mortal life of Jesus Christ, bear the impress of Mary.—Thus does heaven readily accept the aroma of flowers, though flowers are the daughters of earth.*

It cannot be doubted that Jesus returned the Virgin tenderness for tenderness, and solicitude for solicitude; a woman so noble in blood and heart had certain claims upon all, and above all upon a Son, for the love of whom she had imposed upon herself, in the spring-time of her age, so many privations, labours, and sacrifices. HE, who will take account in heaven of a cup of cold water given in his name, must have affectionately preserved the memory of the obligations he was under to Mary; and if we perceive in the gospel, that he sometimes spoke to his divine Mother less like her son than her Lord, it was because at those times that he divested himself of his earthly appendages, the more to glorify his Father, whose interests always held the foremost place in his view. The Virgin knew too well the sacred mission of her Son, to be uneasy at his words, which were sometimes severe; she waited for the legislator to give place to the young Galilean whom she had fed with her milk, and the transformation was never slow in coming; the human nature soon granted what the divine nature had refused.

At the time when Jesus had attained his twenty-ninth year, the angel of death came to decimate the Holy Family. Joseph, that patriarch of ancient manners, whose submissive faith and simplicity of heart recalled the remembrance of Abraham and the era of his tent,—Joseph, whom the Holy Ghost himself has adorned with the beautiful name of "just," sweetly fell asleep in the bosom of the Lord, between his adopted Son and his chaste spouse. Jesus and Mary wept over him, and made a mournful vigil of the dead over

* Nel vestire il Verbo d'umana carne non gli diede ella (la Vergine) punto, o di potenza, o di santita, o di giustizia che egli (Gesù) gia da se solo non possedesse; ma gli die molto bensi di misericordia.—(P. Paolo Segneri, *Magnificat* spiegato.)

his cold remains; the midnight breeze mingled with the lamentations of the poor family: the Nabals of Galilee died more sumptuously, though, as they lowered their heads to pass under the sunken gate of the tomb, they had not the magnificent hopes of the carpenter of Nazareth.

The funeral of the son of David was humble, like his fortune; but Mary shed abundant tears over his funeral couch, and the Son of God conducted this simple mourning. What emperor ever obtained the like obsequies?

At length, the time for preaching the gospel approached, and HE, whom God destined from all eternity to be its high priest and apostle, left Nazareth, to repair to the banks of the Jordan, where John baptized. There must have been an affecting and solemn scene of adieu between the Virgin and her Son. The public life of Jesus was about to commence. Alone, poor, sprung from the people, without any resource but his courage, his patience, and that gift of miracles which he never used for his own personal benefit, he went forth to confront an order of things, "not strong enough to resist him, but strong enough to cause his death."* The Virgin could not help a feeling of alarm at seeing Jesus embark upon this stormy sea of the Jewish world, where so many prophets, and so illustrious, had been wrecked. She knew the insurmountable pride of the Pharisees, the narrow and malignant fanaticism of the princes of the synagogue, the sanguinary caprice of Herod Antipas; she knew also the oracles relating to the Messias, which spoke of suffering and ignominy! . . . . . The daughter of the kings of Juda, who was not of the race of the feeble, and who knew that her Son was God, had not her soul the less wounded by this first separation, which seemed to her the prelude and image of a separation cruel in a very different way. She let Jesus depart with her heart bursting with agony; and when the sound of his footsteps grew fainter in the distance, when she

* M. de Lamartine, *liv. cité.*

found herself alone—entirely alone—in that house where she had spent so many sweet hours, between her Son and her spouse, she hid her head in her hands, and remained silent and thoughtful, like the statue of grief upon the stone of a mausoleum.

The absence of CHRIST was prolonged; the Virgin learned with profound admiration, but without surprise, the wonders of his baptism, during which the Trinity had, in a manner, become palpable and revealed to men. They told her of the white dove, extending his divine wings over the Saviour, and that, at the same time, a voice from heaven proclaimed the Son of the Most High. This joy, however, gave place to an extreme anxiety, when she knew that Jesus, when scarcely come forth from the waters of the Jordan, had penetrated into the deep and perilous defiles of the high mountain of the *Quarantaine*,* to prepare himself for the work of the salvation of the world, by fasting, meditation, and prayer. How much she must have suffered, when she thought how Jesus was wandering in a labyrinth of bare rocks, where the bird finds not a blade of moss for its nest, or a wild berry to sup-

* The desert where Jesus Christ fasted during forty days, which procured it the name of the Quarantine, is situated in the mountains of Jericho, at about a mile from this town, and towards the east bank of the Jordan. The mountain of the Quarantine is one of the highest on the north side, presenting a deep abyss, hollowed out of the base as if to prevent access to it; from the west to the north it exhibits a succession of steep rocks, which open in several places, and contain caves. The only way to reach the fourth part of the height of the mountain from the foot, is by a slope extremely steep, covered with pebbles, which roll about under one's feet. When you have reached this fourth part, you find a small path, very narrow, which ends in a small flight of steps, surrounded by horrible precipices, to the top of which you must climb, with the greatest danger, by means of a few stones which project a little in certain places, to which you are obliged to cling with feet and hands, and if these supports should fail, you would fall from the height of the rock down a frightful precipice. (Voyages de Jesus Christ, 11me voyage.)

port its little life, where all is stones and heat! What anguish did she feel when the tempest howled out of doors! Where was Jesus? What was he doing, alone and unsheltered, on those high mountains of Jericho, where the steep paths, full of rolling stones, wind among frightful precipices?* No means of saving himself if his foot slipped on the edge of an abyss! No help if during this fast, so complete, so long, so little proportioned to the strength of nature, he fell through weakness on the way. These forty days were to Mary forty ages,—maternal anxiety making of every minute thus passed an eternity; but Jesus returned to Nazareth, with his disciples, and his beloved presence was to Mary like the breath of spring after the cold of winter.

Then it was that the marriage took place at Cana, in Galilee. The married couple, who were related to the Blessed Virgin,† invited Mary, Jesus, and his disciples. All of them accepted this cordial invitation, and the Virgin, ever good and obliging, took the lead in forwarding the preparations for this feast, where the national customs required a certain degree of splendour. The assembled company was numerous, and the family were poor; the bridegroom had not calculated well, and the bottles of wine were almost ex-

* The sacred retreat where the God-man spent forty days is a natural cave, which is reached only after climbing up a path cut in the rock. A recess has been made in one side of it, as if to set up an altar. Some frescoes are to be seen there, almost effaced, which represent angels. A thick wall encloses this sort of chapel, which is lighted by a window, from which you cannot look down without terror.—(Ibid.)

† The oriental tradition, which the Mahometans have received from the Christians, is that St. John the Evangelist was the bridegroom of the marriage feast of Cana, and that, after witnessing the miracle which Jesus Christ performed there, he immediately left his spouse to follow him.—(D'Herbelot, Biblioth. Orientale, t. ii.) Baronius, t. i. p. 106. Mald. (in Joan.) also adopts this opinion, which we do not guarantee.

hausted, when our Lord, who was pleased to elevate marriage to the rank of holy things, by purifying it by his holy presence, entered the banqueting-room, followed by Peter, Andrew, Philip, and Nathanael, four young fishermen, whom he had impressed with confidence in his character. The wine failed entirely in the middle of the repast, and Mary, having been the first to perceive it upon a sign of distress given by the new married couple, turned her head towards Jesus, who was seated near her, and said to him significantly, "They have no wine."

Jesus answered in a low and emphatic voice, "Woman, what is it to me and to thee? My hour is not yet come."*

The Virgin, wishing to spare her relatives a humiliation which would have filled them with confusion, did not consider this a refusal; she judged that, if the hour of manifestation was not come, CHRIST, notwithstanding his austere words, would anticipate it for her sake; and with that faith which would remove mountains, she said softly to the waiters, "Whatsoever he shall say to you, do ye." Now there were set there six water-pots of stone, according to the manner of purifying of the Jews; and by the command of Jesus, they were filled to the brim from a neighbouring spring; and this water was changed into delicious wine.

Thus it was that the Blessed Virgin had the first fruits of the miracles of her divine Son, and that her intercession caused even the will of God to bend in her favour.

The miracle of Cana was soon followed by many others,

* The answer of our Saviour to his Holy Mother must have been, as we should say, *aside;* the gospel narrative gives us so to understand. It was impossible in the outset that Jesus Christ should have made this enigmatical answer aloud to his mother; the guests, who were not in the secret, would have considered it as something very harsh to Mary. It is evident that the waiters, by their listening to what the Blessed Virgin said to them, were ignorant of the apparent refusal of our Saviour.

which marked the high and providential mission of our Saviour with the seal of the Divinity. At his voice the storms were hushed, human infirmities disappeared, the devils sunk back to their gloomy kingdom, dead bodies came forth from the tomb, and, upon that corner of the earth where his blessed feet trod, there was made a great healing of all sufferings of soul and body.* They came to him from Sidon, Tyre, Idumea, and Arabia; and crowds of people, gathering together on his way, kissed the hem of his garments, and humbly begged of him health and life,—things which God alone can give.

Mary, whom our Lord had not yet thought fit to associate with him in his painful and wandering life, heard these extraordinary accounts with a joy mingled with trouble and an uneasy admiration. Her alarm was well founded; for, if the people followed the Messias, loading him with benedictions, the Pharisees, the Scribes, and the princes of the synagogue began to be greatly scandalised—worthy souls!—at the conduct of the Son of God. He forgave sins; blasphemy! He consoled and converted sinners; degradation! He healed the sick on the Sabbath-day; crying and notorious impiety! His doctrine fell from his lips like a beneficent dew, and not

* A Mussulman poet has depicted in graceful verses this command, which Jesus Christ exercised over the maladies of the soul: the following is a translation from the French version of D'Herbelot:—

"The heart of the afflicted draws all its consolation from thy words.
"The soul recovers its life and vigour from only hearing thy name pronounced.
"If the mind of man can ever rise to the contemplation of the mysteries of the Divinity,
"It is from thee that he derives his light to know them, and it is thou who givest him the attraction with which he is penetrated."

A Christian could not have explained himself more energetically, observes the learned orientalist.

like stormy rain; then he was not at all like the ancient prophets! He preached humility, the forgiveness of injuries, voluntary poverty, alms given for God's sake, universal charity.—What novel doctrine was all this! A multitude of enemies arose up against him every time that he preached, whether in the desert or in the cities. He could not attack hypocrisy without coming into collision with the Pharisees, or declaim against avarice without alienating from himself the doctors of the law; the discontented, ever ready to contrive dark plots which broke out into mad and sanguinary revolts, were scandalized at him for not preaching sedition against Cæsar; the Herodians accused him of aspiring to the throne; and the Sadducees could not endure that he should proclaim eternal life. These men, divided in views, creeds, and political interests, made a truce with their absurd antipathies out of hatred for the *Galilean;* they girded themselves with the intention of injuring him, and pressed forward against him to destroy him. Every word was a snare, every smile was a treason. Some treated him unsparingly as an imposter and a *Samaritan*; others gently hinted that he was a madman; the dense mass of the envious, tired of the praises which the people gave to this new prophet, and unable to deny his miracles, disputed his claim to them, to give the honour of them to Satan. "If he casts out devils," said they, "it is by Beelzebub, the prince of devils: *in Beelzebub, principe dæmoniorum, ejicit dæmonia.*"* These vague rumours alarmed Mary, and the

* The *Methnevi-Manevi*, speaking of the impotent and envious hatred of the Jews against Jesus Christ, expresses its opinion in these terms against those attacks which are so common against all that meet with success,—attacks which are, in the end, hurtful to those only who make them. "The moon sheds her light and the dog barks," says the Persian author, "but the barking of the dog does not hinder the moon from shining. Sweepings are cast into the current of a

bad spirit of her own neighbourhood was little calculated to encourage her. Of all the cities of Galilee, Nazareth was the most unbelieving and hardened against the sacred Word; of all the families of Nazareth, the family of Jesus Christ was apparently the least disposed to accept him for the kingly Messias. As the divine parturition of the Virgin had never been revealed to her relations, and as the miracles which had been displayed during the infancy of the Lord had taken place in distant countries, they saw nothing in the supposed son of Joseph but a young Israelite without learning, brought up among themselves, fed like themselves, more poorly lodged, more simply clad, and living from day to day by very hard labour, which connected him only with the lower classes. Christ, who would ennoble poverty by taking it for his own portion, suffered the consequences of the position which he had chosen. "*His brethren,*" says St. John, "did not believe in him." * The fame of the miracles which accompanied the preaching of the gospel astonished these obstinate Nazareans, without the power to convince them. Knowing that Jesus was saluted throughout Galilee by the dangerous title of son of David, and that crowds of two or three thousand persons ran to hear him, they were afraid that these numerous assemblies would give umbrage to Herod Antipas, and that they themselves might be molested on account of the young prophet. With this idea they said publicly that Jesus was insane, and swore that they would take him back to Nazareth well guarded. Concealing this family conspiracy from Mary, they induced her to come

river, and these ordures swim on the surface of the water without stopping or disturbing it. The Messias, on the one hand, raises the dead to life, and you see, on the other, the Jews, gnawed with envy, biting their nails and plucking their beards." — (Hussein-Vaëz. D'Herbelot, Bibl. Orient.)

* St. John, c. vii v. 5.

with them to Capharnaum, that they might approach him under the authority of her name.*

The Messias was teaching in the synagogue, in the midst of a crowd of attentive and silent hearers, when the Nazareans arrived. Displaying ostentatiously an authority which they were not sorry to magnify in the sight of the multitude, as St. John Chrysostom remarks, they deliberately caused our Saviour to be informed that his brethren and his mother were outside inquiring for him; but Jesus reading the secret thoughts of his relations according to the flesh, and laying hold of this circumstance to extend the limits of the old law by adopting solemnly and without respect of persons the whole family of mankind, made this admirable answer to the indiscreet message of his relatives, "Who is my mother, and who are my brethren?" Then casting his eyes over his numerous disciples, "My mother and my brethren," he exclaimed, "are they who hear the word of God, and do it." After this severe reprimand, which the sons of Alpheus may have understood, the Son of God went out immediately, says St. John Chrysostom, "to pay his mother all the honour which propriety required of him."

When he had greeted Mary, and remained some time with her on the sea-shore, our Saviour went up into a ship, whence he began to teach the people. The Virgin, hidden among the crowd, but profoundly attentive, heard in religious silence the parable of the sower. The Nazareans, petrified by the irresistible eloquence and superhuman dignity of Jesus Christ, asked themselves, in surprise, if he really was the son of Mary: they experienced that sort of fascination which charms the serpent of the American savannahs, when he hears in the depths of the woods soft music which attracts him. They had come with the celerity of fear, with the eloquence of egotism, with the

* St. Mark. c. iii. v. 21, 31, 32, 33, 34, and 35.

arrogance of superiority, to turn Christ from his compromising and perilous mission, and they were so far disabled by his very look as to be afraid to open their mouths in his presence. This is clearly indicated by the text of St. Mark, who, after initiating us into their hostile intentions, does not give us anywhere to understand that they even dared to speak to our Lord.

Some time after this, Jesus returned to Nazareth. Great was the joy of the Blessed Virgin. To see her Son seated on the same mat on which he sat in his childhood, eating the bread which he had broken as he blessed it; to take him stealthily to the bedside of some poor sick person, whom he restored to health, enjoining him secresy; to see him powerful in words and works, he who had so long been the man of silence and labour; this was too much happiness in the cup of her existence! Accordingly God, who afflicts those whom he loves, soon mixed with it a drop of gall. On the Sabbath-day, the Son and the Mother went together to the synagogue. A great concourse of people had assembled there to see and hear Jesus; but the eagerness of the Nazareans had not that character of confidence and respectful attention which Christ had so often met with elsewhere. There they were, scandalised already at what the Son of Mary was to say and do, and admirably disposed to stone him if opportunity offered.

There are countries decidedly hostile to all that does them honour, even till the grass grows upon the tomb of what they envy.

One of the ancients, however, handed to the Saviour of men the book of the prophet Isaias; and Jesus, unrolling the parchment, read this passage, with simple gracefulness and marvellous dignity,—"The Spirit of the Lord is upon me: wherefore he hath anointed me to preach the gospel to the poor; he hath sent me to heal the contrite heart; to preach deliverance to the captives, and sight to the blind, to set at liberty them that are bruised, to preach the acceptable year of the Lord, and the day of reward." Having closed the book, he sat down, and speaking with that animated and natural eloquence which made so strong an impression upon his hearers, he applied the oracle relating to the Messias to himself, and taught, not like a disciple of the synagogue, but as the actual master of the synagogue. A low murmur ran through the assembly. Some were in admiration at the power and gracefulness of his words: others, faithful to their system of contemptuous defamation, said aloud, "Is not this the carpenter's son?" And Jesus, penetrating into their thoughts, and reading as in an open book those false and envious hearts, hurled at them those words, so true, which have become proverbial, "A prophet is not without honour, save in his own country, and in his own house." As he knew that they had a mind to ask him for prodigies, like those of which Capharnaum had been the theatre, he told them plainly that their unbelief had made them unworthy of them, and that to obtain miracles, these must be solicited with faith. Thence, in allusion to the propagation of his gospel, and to that wild olive engrafted on the old trunk of the synagogue, which symbolised the vocation of the Gentiles: "In truth I say to you, there were many widows in the days of Elias in Israel, when heaven was shut up three years and six months: when there was a great famine throughout all the land: and to none of them was Elias sent, but to a widow at Sarepta of Sidon. And there were many lepers in Israel in the time of Elias the prophet: and none of them were cleansed but Naaman the Syrian."

These last words were the drop of water which makes the vessel run over. Wounded in their national pride, in their hereditary antipathies, in their traditional expectations, all those of the synagogue were filled with anger which called for blood. "And they rose up and thrust him out of their city: and they brought him to the brow of the hill, whereon their city was built, that they might cast him down headlong."

Seated among the women of the people in a latticed tribune, the Virgin had observed, with anxiety mingled with fear, the increased progress of the storm. Reading the sinister projects of the Nazareans in their haggard eyes and furious gestures, she did not hesitate to brave danger to force a passage to her Son; but her strength deceived her courage. Those Jews ran,—they who had always light feet to shed blood; and Mary, trembling like a leaf, scarcely able to support herself, walked at a distance after them, as if in a dream. She sees Jesus on the top of the steep rock which overhangs a frightful precipice; she hears afar off cries for death; her knees give way under her; a mist spreads over her sight; her voice expires in a sorrowful moaning; she falls, broken down like a blossomed bough which the tempest has torn off in its course, and remains stretched out with her face on the ground upon the hill.*

Meanwhile the wolves, furious in pursuit of the lamb, had been deceived in their expectation; the hour of sacrifice had not yet struck for the Son of Man, and no one could take his life unless he gave it. Striking this murderous crew with blindness,† Jesus passed through the midst of his

* Between the steep mountain from which the Jews had formed the design to cast down Jesus Christ, and the town of Nazareth, "You perceive halfway," says F. de Geramb, "the ruins of a monastery formerly inhabited by religious, and those of a very fine church, built by St. Helen, and dedicated to the Blessed Virgin, under the name of Our Lady del Tremore (of terror). According to some, Mary was already in this place when the Jews were dragging her son towards the top of the mountain to throw him down from it. According to others, at the news of the murderous project of these madmen, she had run thither in great haste, but had arrived too late: seized with terror, 'she could proceed no farther.'"

† The oldest heretics, opening the door to modern rationalism,

enemies without being known by them, and took again the road to Capharnaum, where his mother, Mary of Cleophas, and the sons of Alpheus came to rejoin him.

After having preached the gospel in the environs of the beautiful lake of Tiberias, the waves of which shine like light, and wrought the great miracle of the multiplication of the loaves in the desert of Bethsaida, Jesus reascended the Jordan with his disciples to go to Cæsarea Philippi, the ancient Dan of Nephtali, the name of which Philip, the son of Herod, had lately changed; and he visited as he passed the towns and villages situated on his way.

It was probably at this time—for Euthymius,* who relates this traditionary fact, leaves the date undecided—that the waters of the Jordan, already sanctified, beheld an affecting ceremony. Jesus, the Virgin, and the apostles, directed their steps, one day at sunrise, towards this deeply-enclosed river, which runs through two lakes, says Tacitus, and rushes into the third.† Magnificent vegetation adorned its banks; islets rising here and there from its humid bosom, displayed themselves in the midst of its gilded waves, like graceful baskets of verdure, fruits, and flowers; blue herons hovered over these flowery isles, where ringdoves and white turtle doves still hung their nests of moss upon the branches of the wild pomegranate-trees. The dew sparkled upon the green branches of the willows, like a shower of pale

which decks itself out in the old rags, without acknowledgment, insisted that our Lord had passed through, by means of an illusion produced by a fog, "illudere per caliginem." Tertullian strongly opposes this supposition.—(Adv. Marcion., 4, 8.)

* According to St. Euthymius, our Lord baptized only the Blessed Virgin and St. Peter, who afterwards baptized the other apostles. "Some," says this abbot, who flourished in Palestine in the fourth century, "have written that Jesus Christ himself baptized the Virgin and Peter."

† "Nec Jordanes pelàgo accipitur; sed unum atque alterum lacum integer perfluit; tertio retinetur."—(Taciti, Historiarum, lib. v.)

diamonds; and the rushes of the Jordan, which sometimes conceal tigers, bent softly beneath the light breeze, which moved the tops of the palm-trees, from which hung fine bunches of dates of the colour of coral. In the distance, on the opposite bank, troops of gazelles were seen bounding on the declivities of high mountains, grey and streaked with fire; and in the sandy plain were flying along, on their coursers fleet as the wind, some wild sons of the desert, armed with those long lances of cane from the banks of the Euphrates, which they used from the times near to the deluge, if we believe the legends of Persia.* Clouds of violet of the richest tint, or of delicate rose-colour paler at the edges, floated like flowers in the deep blue of the sky, and the nightingale was singing in the tall sycamores which overshadow the sacred river of Palestine: nature held a festival for the baptism of Mary.

The Virgin was dressed in white, according to the custom of the Hebrews when they individually took part in any religious ceremony, and she stood grave and profoundly recollected by the side of her Son and Saviour: they both went down into the river. Then, lifting up with his divine hand the Oriental veil of his fair and holy Mother, Christ looked upon her with his sweet and penetrating look of infinite tenderness; then he poured upon the Virgin's forehead the sacred water of regeneration, and baptized her in the name of the Trinity,—HE who was himself one of the Three Divine Persons.

It was then that the Blessed Virgin broke through her solitary habits to follow her Son in his journeys. She had served him for thirty years, on a foreign soil and in the land of her fathers; she had worked for him, wept over him,

* Reeds grow on the banks of the Euphrates which are almost equal to the bamboos of the Indies. From the earliest times, the Arabs and Assyrians have made lances of them.—(Firdousi, the Book of Kings.)

suffered for him, and adored him without ever failing, night and morning in his cradle while he still slept there, as Albert the Great informs us. It was natural that following his persecuted fortunes, she should leave the peaceful roof which had witnessed her birth to walk in his blessed footsteps, while he preached the gospel to the Hebrews. Amid the agitations of this life of trouble and alarm, the Virgin was admirable as ever. Loving Jesus more than any mother ever loved her child, and alone able to carry this extreme love without sin to the farthest limits of adoration, she never intruded her presence upon him to divert the short and precious moments of his mission of regeneration in favour of her own maternal tenderness; never did she speak to him of her fatigues, fears, sinister forebodings, or personal wants. Mary was not only a holy dove hiding in the clefts of a rock —a pure virgin called to feed with her milk, and cradle in her arms, a heavenly guest; she was a valiant woman, whom the Lord delighted to place in turn in every situation of life, in order to leave to the daughters of Eve an example to follow, and a model to imitate.

It would not have been proper for the Mother of God to follow Jesus and his apostles alone throughout Judea; therefore Mary of Cleophas, the mother of James, Simon, Joseph, and Jude, commonly called the brothers of the Lord; Salome, mother of the sons of Zebedee, whom the Lord especially loved; Joanna, wife of the steward of the tetrarch, and several rich women of Galilee, who had made themselves poor for Jesus Christ, formed the companions of Mary. One among them, a Jewess, young, rich, of noble birth and remarkable beauty, was most affectionately attentive to the divine Mother of *her Lord*. This woman, whose heart, strong but assaulted by storms, like the waves of the Egean Sea, had burned with a thousand impure flames in the sight of the world, and defied public opinion with mockery and disdain, had come, submissive and penitent, to lay down her proud head at the feet of Christ, and to beg of him whom she confessed to be her God, the cure of the maladies of her soul. And the chaste love of the Lord had absorbed all her insane amours, all the worldly attachments of the young lady of Magdalum. She had trampled under her feet her collars of pearls, her chains of gold and precious stones; sold her country house, situated among the rose-laurels which fringe the beautiful Sea of Galilee, and now, with no other ornament than a dress of coarse cloth, and her fine black hair, with which she had wiped the Lord's feet, the young patrician, rich in her alms-deeds, adorned with new virtues, shed her penitent tears on the pure and compassionate bosom of Mary. The immaculate Virgin had received in her arms and pressed to her heart the grievous sinner, and cultivated in this soil, fertile but long left waste, those flowers which expand for heaven.

After many sufferings, many terrors too long to relate, the Virgin entered Jerusalem, the fatal city, in company with Jesus Christ, to celebrate the last Passover which the Lord kept with his disciples. She saw the inhabitants of the city of kings come in crowds to meet the son of David, who came to them full of meekness, riding as the young princes of his race formerly did, and receiving with benignity the simple honours which this multitude, eager to behold their prophet, spontaneously offered him; for Jesus Christ never rejected the humble testimonies of gratitude and love which were offered to him by his creatures. However small were these pledges of affection and gratitude, they were received with a divine goodness the moment that they proceeded from the heart.

Magdalen, examining by turns *her Lord* and that multitude of people who made the air resound with their *hosannas*, wept silently beneath her veil. Mary, too, had her eyes moist with tears; but her look was turned to the north-west, in the direction of Calvary.

CHAPTER XVII.

MARY ON CALVARY.

The palms which the children of the Hebrews had cast beneath the feet of Christ still strewed with their green tufts the rugged road of Bethania; the echo of the valley of cedars * still muttered the dying sounds of those cries of triumph and joy, with which the daughters of Sion had saluted the *King* who came to them *poor*, when Jerusalem was deeply moved by a new event of great and sad importance.

The princes of the priests, the senators, and Pharisees sought to get possession, even at the price of gold, and without shrinking from domestic treason, of a *great criminal*, who, as they said, placed both religion and the state in danger. This man must indeed have been very dangerous, since these *honourable* personages had bound themselves to an extraordinary fast to lay hold of him,† and had indeed distributed on this occasion some alms throughout the city with sound of trumpet. The Pharisees, those *conscientious* Jews, who plundered none but the uncircumcised, and who would have left their neighbour at the bottom of a pit on the sabbath-day, though they would have speedily drawn out their ox or their ass, had undertaken to spread among the people—whom it is so easy to make impression upon, and to deceive—frightful reports and vague rumours, which had thrown them into a kind of feverish anxiety, from which they could not free themselves but by a fit of ferocity. Things being thus prepared, a well-armed troop were seen, one evening, coming

* *Valley of Cedars*, the ancient name of the valley of Josaphat.

† This anecdote is found in the Toldos, published by Huldric, p. 56 and 60.

down from Mount Moria, in which were some senators, and which was commanded by the captain of the guards of the temple;* the troop of servants of the princes of the priests came after, and at the head of this battalion, which marched on with a measured step by the light of those large lanterns which the Asiatics fix upon long poles, to raise them up high, and of some resinous torches, was a man with a low forehead, an irresolute look, and an abject countenance, whose girdle was swelled out with gold robbed from the poor,† to which he already added in imagination the thirty pieces of silver which he was to earn, by delivering up to the princes of the synagogue—too Jewish to pay for his treason beforehand—his master, his friend, his God! For it was the son of David, the triumpher but a few days before, Jesus of Nazareth, the great prophet of Galilee, at whose voice greedy death gave up his prey, and whose commands the winds and the waves respected, whom the ruffians of the chief priests and the Pharisees were going in search of upon the Mount of Olives, whither he retired at night after teaching in the temple, as St. Luke relates. They had not dared to arrest him in open daylight, because they feared some resistance on the part of that multitude of disciples who came

* This office is known by the gospel, which often speaks of these captains of the temple, who must be distinguished from the Roman commandant, who kept guard with his cohort round this great edifice to prevent crowds, and those disorderly acts to which the multitude might give occasion. These captains of the temple necessarily were Jews, and were taken from the priestly families; to them were confided the care and the keys of the temple, to provide for the safety of the treasury and the sacred vessels: by right of his birth this officer had the liberty to enter into all the counsels of the priests.—(Basn., liv. i. c. 4.)

† "Then one of his disciples, Judas Iscariot, he that was about to betray him, said, Why was not this ointment sold for three hundred pence, and given to the poor? Now he said this, not because he cared for the poor, but because he was a thief, and having the purse, carried what was put therein."—(St. John xii. v. 4, 5, 6.)

to hear him early in the morning beneath the porch of Solomon.

The armed troop, headed by the Iscariot, crossed th ravine where flows the Cedron, that torrent of dark waters, which witnessed the passage of King David, when he fle with a handful of faithful servants from the rebels in the pa of his son Absalom. While the soldiers of the temple fol lowed, silent and savage, along the banks of the torrent i which their torches were reflected, in order to reach th heights of Gethsemane, and while the night wind shook th dishevelled tops of the willows, which were soon to se Judas hanging upon one of their branches,—a punishmen too light for such a traitor, but which is continually increase by the undying contempt of successive generations upon th globe,—a sad and solemn scene was passing in that garden of olives where the worthless apostle went in search of his master on purpose to destroy him.

After praying a long time, on his face on the ground, and undergoing that frightful agony which covered his divine forehead with a sweat of blood, CHRIST had risen up with submissive resignation to the awful will of his Father, and quite prepared to drink the chalice of bitterness to the dregs. He raised up his large, soft, and piercing eyes to the starry heavens, the stars of which told that it was midnight, and high in which shone the moon, that fair lamp of the firmament, whose useful light is blessed by the children of Abraham in their prayers;† she was then at the full, and cast a

* The *Cedron* is a torrent which runs down the valley of Josaphat, between Jerusalem and the Mount of Olives. It was called *Cedron*, because it has its course in deep and dark places; its Hebrew name signifies *tenebrosus fuit*.

† The day of the new moon is a festival day for the Hebrews; the women abstain from work, and the devout fast the preceding day. After reciting a number of prayers in the synagogue, they take a repast, at which they are very merry. Three days after, the Jews assemble on a platform, where they look steadfastly at the moon, and

sheet of resplendent light upon that austere passage, where the dark mountains stood out from the limpid blue of heaven. Jerusalem, half-drowned in shade, and splendidly lighted up in places, sent forth afar the aromatic perfume of the rare plants of her gardens, and waved in the breath of the breeze her clusters of palm-trees, out of which arose white towers of marble. The silence was profound on the side of the mountains, but a slight murmur arose from the bottom of the valley:—Jesus suddenly started. There they are, he thought, and he slowly moved towards the place where he had left three of his apostles, whom he had chosen from all the rest to share his solitary night-watch. Alas! fatigue, or the lulling breath of the wind which made the grey foliage of the olive-trees rustle, had gradually made these negligent sentinels fall asleep. Jesus beheld them asleep for a moment with a holy feeling of grief; he had announced to them that his death was near, that the hour of peril was come, and they were asleep—they, his kinsmen, his friends, his chosen disciples, to all appearance indifferent about his danger or his death! . . . . . . O the vanity of benefits of ties of blood and friendship! . . . . . . They were awake enough on Thabor at the hour of the glorious transfiguration, but they slept in the hour of trial and distress!

A confused noise was heard in the hollow path which led up to the little village of Gethsemane; and soon the glare of torches shone upon the trees. Then Jesus, leaning over his apostles, who were still asleep, said to them in a low but

bless God by a long prayer for having created it, and for renewing it, to teach the Israelites that they ought to become new creatures: "O moon! blessed be thy Creator, blessed be He who made thee!" and then they jump three times, as high as they can, and say to the moon, "As we leap towards thee, without being able to touch thee, may our enemies rise up against us without reaching us! . . . ."—(Basn., liv. vii. c. 16.)

deep voice, "Arise, let us go! Behold, he that betrayeth me is at hand!" He had hardly pronounced these words, when Judas and his band arrived. Coming up to Jesus, with boldness in his eyes, and the smile of hypocrisy on his lips, he pointed him out to the hostile troop who were in search of him, by giving him that sacrilegious kiss which has taken his name. It was the signal agreed upon. Jesus Christ received the traitor with kindness, and said to him with meekness which pierced to the quick, "Friend, whereto art thou come?"

Whereto was he come? . . . . He was come to earn the thirty sicles of silver of the synagogue. Avarice, which is a cold and calculating passion, commits ten times more crimes than violence, and much blacker crimes.

Judas had not time to answer this embarrassing question, for all the rest advancing, fell upon Jesus and laid hold on him. Then anger arose in the heart of Ben-Cephas,* the prince of the apostles; he drew his sword, and struck with it one of the servants of the high priest; but Jesus, restraining that arm which was the only one raised in his defence, commanded that the sword should be returned to its scabbard. "How then shall the scriptures be fulfilled, that so it must be done?" The Lamb of God desired to be immolated for the sins of the world.

Then was heard in this enclosed spot mingled sounds of hurried footsteps, broken boughs, and cries of alarm; and a number of men were seen leaping over the low wall, scarcely three feet high,† which surrounded the garden: they were the disciples flying away! . . . .

* *Peter Ben-Cephas* (Peter, son of Peter); it is by this name that the prince of the apostles is known in the East.

† The garden of Gethsemane or of Olives, at the foot of the mountain of that name, is surrounded by a wall three feet high; its length is two hundred paces, by a hundred and forty broad. There is a rock in it, forming a reddish-coloured cave, where it is said the three apostles fell asleep.—(Voyage de Jesus Christ, 44 voyage.) Its

The hostile troop, after binding Jesus like a criminal, returned by the road to the Holy City, and went in the direction of the stone bridge which the Asmonean princes had thrown over the Cedron; but the people of Jerusalem, who had come out in crowds, already occupied it, and tradition relates that Jesus was dragged through this channel of water; which accomplished to the letter the prophecy, "He shall drink of the torrent in the way." The sacred footsteps of our Saviour, and the impression of one of his knees, are marked in the bed and on the stone margin of Cedron; at least this is asserted by the Christians of Jerusalem, who still show them. After ascending the hill of Sion, they entered Jerusalem by the Sterquilinian Gate, and repaired to Caiphas, the high priest, where the scribes and ancients were assembled. The chief priests and scribes then asked Jesus if he was the Christ. "If I shall tell you," our Saviour meekly answered, "you will not believe me." "Art thou the Son of God?" asked Caiphas. "I am," replied Jesus. "He hath blasphemed!" cried the high priest, rending his garments. "He is guilty of death!" said the scribes and Pharisees.

"Then did they spit in his face," and they struck him with their fists, and gave him blows, while they cried out to him, in derision, "Prophesy, CHRIST, who is it that struck thee?"

During this time Peter, who had sworn to die rather than abandon him, denied him thrice in the court of the high priest.

The next day, the chief priests and Pharisees dragged Jesus before Pontius Pilate, who was supremely odious to them since the affair of the imperial standards, which he had introduced by night into Jerusalem;* but as they hated the

name of Gethsemane is derived from the goodness of the soil; in Hebrew Gethsemane signifies "fertile valley."

* Josephus, Ant. Jud., liv. xviii. c. 4.

Son of God much more, and as the Romans alone could condemn him to death,* they were resigned to appear at the pretorium of this idolater, after taking the most minute precautions to avoid exposing themselves to any unclean contact with his garments, his standards, and even his tribunal, which would have rendered them impure for the whole day. After doing everything, therefore, to avoid so serious an inconvenience, these *scrupulous* men accused Jesus of having perverted the people by his doctrine, of having opposed their paying tribute to Cæsar, and, finally, of having taken the seditious title of the King of the Jews.—As many falsehoods as words.

Jesus met these false accusations only with silence. Pilate, convinced of the profound wickedness of the accusers, and the perfect innocence of the accused, would have saved Jesus: he did not succeed. The Pharisees, skilful in raising popular tumults, worked up the people, who seditiously demanded the death of the descendant of their ancient kings; and the governor, who knew well how to appease the clamours of the Jews, in a way perfectly oriental, when he chose to do so, was content tamely to defend against the madmen who wanted to force from him an unjust judgment, the innocent man whom he ought to have protected with firmness. Wearied with their clamours, overcome by

* Before Judea had become subject to the Romans, the sanhedrim possessed the right of life and death; but those conquerors deprived them of that privilege. It was the custom of the Romans to leave the conquered nations their temples and their gods; but in civil matters they were obliged to follow the laws and orders of the republic. At the time when Jesus Christ was condemned, the Romans were absolutely masters of temporal jurisdiction, and the authority of the Jewish senate was limited to affairs purely ecclesiastical. The Talmudists recognised it, for they acknowledged that the power of judging was taken away from the senate forty years before the destruction of Jerusalem, that is, three years before the death of Jesus Christ.—(Basn., liv. vii. c. 4.)

their persistence, the Roman washed his hands of the sentence which he pronounced.* After which,—no doubt with a view to excuse himself for his show of clemency towards Jesus Christ, and to win back the hearts of the populace of Jerusalem, whom he had recently had beaten by his lictors in a commotion,† on occasion of the sacred treasure, which he wanted to grasp largely, under pretence of building an aqueduct which they did not want,—he had the Son of David

* The decree pronounced by Pilate against our Lord is preserved at Jerusalem. We give it here, not as an authentic document, but as a local tradition:—Jesum Nazarenum, subversorem gentis, contemptorem Cæsaris, it falsum Messiam, ut majorum suæ gentis testimonio probatum est, ducite ad communis supplicii locum, et cum ludibrio regiæ magistatis in medio duorum latronum affigite. I, lictor, expedi cruces. "Jesus of Nazareth, the subverter of the people, the despiser of Cæsar, and the false Messias, as it has been proved by the testimony of the ancients of this nation, take ye to the common place of punishment, and crucify him in derision of his royal majesty between two thieves. Go, lictor, prepare the crosses."—(Adricom., In descript. Jesu.)

† Pilate undertook to build an aqueduct with the money of the sacred treasure, to bring water to Jerusalem from a distance of two hundred furlongs. The people, violently irritated against the Roman governor, whose intentions they discovered, assembled in large bodies of several thousand men in the streets and the public squares of Jerusalem, which they made ring with vociferations against Pilate, and there were some even, says Josephus, who exasperated the governor by gross insults; as it always happens with people in commotion. Pilate, who was not alarmed at a little, made his own people take great bludgeons under their garments, and surround the populace; when the seditious, after taking breath, recommenced their clamours and insults, Pilate gave the signal to his men to lay on them, and they began to strike more than they were ordered to do, and without any distinction gave great blows with their cudgels as well to those who were silent as to those who made a noise. These poor people, who were unarmed. were thus inhumanly treated, adds Josephus, with compassionate sympathy for the Jewish outbreak; some were killed, others wounded, and by this means was the tumult appeased.—(Joseph. Ant. Jud., lib. xviii. c. 4.)

and Solomon scourged with rods, while the deicidal people applauded, who had dared to take upon their own heads, and those of their children, the terrible responsibility of his death. This done, he delivered him up, at the same time admiring and lamenting over him,* to the insults of a soldiery whom the princes of the synagogue, who had a positive horror of them, had condescended to corrupt, that their own hatred might be the better served;† for they knew how to hate strongly, these *zealots* for the law of Moses, who would kill and divide CHRIST "for the love of God!"

When Jesus had arrived at the court of the pretorium, they made him sit down on a broken column,‡ and the whole cohort did their utmost to disport themselves with him in the most atrocious and insolent manner. It was the season when the dangerous rhamnus§—which long before had

* Tiberias, in consequence of the accounts which came to him from Pontius Pilate, proposed to the senate to grant divine honours to Jesus Christ; Tertullian relates it as a well-known fact in his Apology, which he presented to the senate in the name of the Church, and he would not have been willing to weaken a cause so good as his by things where it would have been so easy to confound him.—(Tertull. Apolog. 5; Euseb., Hist. Eccl. ii. 2.)

† M. Salvador would fain exculpate his co-religionists, by imputing to the Roman soldiers the unheard-of outrages which Jesus received in the pretorium; but it is clear that the Romans acted only by the instigation of the enemies of Jesus Christ. The following is the opinion of St John Chrysostom on this subject:—"It is the Jews themselves who condemn Jesus to death, although they shelter themselves under the name of Pilate. 'They desire that his blood should fall upon themselves and upon their children.' It is they alone who direct all these insults against him, who bind him, who lead him away to Pilate, and who cause him to be dragged along so cruelly by the soldiers. Pilate had not ordered any of these things."—(Serm. 77, in Matt.)

‡ This pillar, of grey marble, being only two feet high, is at Rome, in the church of St. Praxedes.

§ Some separate thorns of this crown, in the possession of individuals, are now recognised as the *rhamnus spina Christi* of Linnæus.

entangled in its thorny thickets the symbolical lamb for the sacrifice of Abraham*—was in full flower; one of the soldiers ran to gather a branch of it, and made a mock crown, the flowers of which were soon tinged with his blood, and every thorn gave him a deep and insupportable wound. After stripping him like a slave, they threw over his shoulders a purple rag, they put a reed in his hand for a sceptre, and they saluted, with bitter sarcasms and derisive genuflexions, that mockery of royalty. His whole body was but one wound, for the scourges with sharp points had made red pieces of his flesh fly off a long way in the hall of executions; spittle disfigured his face, where clots of dark blood settled down here and there from his wounded forehead, which his fettered hands could not reach! The chief priests, the doctors, and Pharisees, looked upon this scene with secret satisfaction; these *honourable* men regarded compassion as baseness of soul! †

When the Pharisees thought that the idolatrous soldiers had degraded Jesus in the eyes of the people enough to destroy the idea of his divinity, the approach of the Sabbath obliging them to hurry, they took their victim, whom the Roman governor gave up to them with reluctance, and, after loading his bleeding and mangled shoulders with the enormous weight of the cross, they urged on, with the staves of

* St. Jerom (in Philem.) says that the ram which Abraham saw in the thorn-bush was the figure of Jesus Christ crowned with thorns.

† Basn., liv. vi. c. 17. The punishment of the whip was of very ancient usage among the Jews, and was not considered disgraceful. According to the Talmud, kings themselves were subjected to it on certain occasions. "Tradition informs us," says Maimonides, "that the king may not have more than eighteen wives; if he marries one above that number, let him be whipped. If he has more horses than he has need of for the service of his chariot, let him be whipped. If he amasses more gold and silver than he wants for the payment of his ministers, let him be whipped."—(Maimonid., Halach., Malach., c. 3.)

their lances, his painful and slow march toward Calvary, where they were going to crucify him.

Crowds of spectators lined the streets and stopped up the ways: some openly showed a savage joy, and cried anathema upon the son of David; others pitied the fate of that youthful prophet, who had done nothing but good to men, and whom men had forsaken and betrayed. But these signs of barren sympathy made hardly any impression; the good wept in silence; all those whom he had fed with five loaves in the desert, those whom he had healed, those whom he had loved were there, lost in the crowd, and no voice protested against his punishment;* that one among the apostles who loved him most had cowardly denied him! the rest, with only one exception, had fled away and left him!

As he painfully passed down the long street which leads to the Judiciary Gate, a woman made her way through the crowd: this woman, remarkably beautiful, and bearing in her mild and sweet countenance the image of virtue, seemed wholly absorbed in unutterable grief; she suffered so much; she was so pale; her eyes, which had shed all their tears, cast a look so dead—a look of sorrow so holy upon the frightful wounds of our Saviour—that, when they beheld her, the daughters of Jerusalem muttered with compassion, "Poor Mother!" She glided through the people, who made

* We read in the Misnah that, in the time when the Jews were governed by their own laws, when a condemned person was conducted to the place of punishment, a herald of arms went before him, on horseback, making this proclamation,—"Such a one is condemned for such a crime; if any one can bring forward anything in his defence let him speak." If any one came forward, the criminal was taken back, and two judges, who walked one on each side of him, examined the validity of the reasons which it was attempted to substantiate; the prisoner might be led back in this manner as far as five times.—(Misnah, Tract. de Syned., c. vi. p. 233.) Jesus Christ being condemned by the Romans, could not avail himself of this national custom.

room for her by an instinctive feeling of pity and sympathy. Some of the Pharisees with hardened hearts called Jesus, bathed as he was in perspiration, and ready to die with fatigue beneath the cross, by insulting names; she did not hear them: the foreign soldiers who surrounded her Son made threatening signs to her; she did not see them: but when a number of lances, with their points directed to her breast, were thrust between her and Jesus, there came from her fixed and piercing eyes a lightning flash which revealed the blood of David, and her fine and inspired head assumed such an expression of sorrowful grandeur, and cool contempt of death, that the soldiers, overcome, slowly lowered their arms before the heroic and saintly woman. Savage as the life of the camp had made them, they remembered their own mothers.

Mary turned her trembling steps towards our Saviour; she fixed eyes full of anguish on that humiliated form, dragging himself along, bleeding and half clothed, beneath a heavy burthen; on that imposing, merciful, and mild countenance, which she would have feared to ruffle by the slight contact of her chaste lips, and which, now swollen, blue, covered with filth and blood, scarcely retained any longer the image of the Creator. She passed her hand in sorrow across his forehead, as if to make sure that she was not the sport of some horrible hallucination. Not a groan relieved her oppressed heart, no gesture of despair initiated the spectators in the mysteries of her agony; they only thought she was going to die: and indeed she would have died a thousand times during that solemn and heartrending pause, if He who tempers the wind to the shorn lamb had not divinely supported her. Jesus soon perceived that motionless and mute figure, a few paces from him; bending down before her, his forehead bowed beneath the burthen of the cross, he pronounced the name of "Mother!" At that word, which sounded like a funeral knell in the ears of the holy Virgin, a sharp pain pierced through her heart; she was seen to stagger and turn pale; then, sinking down, she fell at full length on those rough and reddened stones where Jesus had left traces of blood as he passed! * . . . .

A young Galilean with a dark and dejected countenance, and a young woman drowned in tears, made themselves a passage to Mary; thanks to their attentions, the Virgin of sorrows recovered the use of her senses and the consciousness of that physical and moral martyrdom which no martyr, according to the Fathers, ever equalled. Doubtless John and Magdalen did everything to remove her from the scene of blood and death which was preparing on Golgotha; but their entreaties were useless; and rising with difficulty, Mary began to climb, beneath a burning sun, the steepest side of Calvary: it was the shortest way, and that which they had made Jesus follow.†

They had reached the fatal and hallowed place where the Lamb of God was about to satisfy the justice of incensed

* Tradition, fortified by the authority of St. Boniface and St. Anselm, relates that Jesus Christ saluted his mother with these words, "*Salve, Mater!*" As we find the Blessed Virgin again at the foot of the cross, this tradition of the Fathers is very probable. "Faith is not opposed to these traditions," says M. de Chateaubriand; "they show how deeply the marvellous and sublime history of the passion is graven in the memory of men. Eighteen centuries have rolled away; persecutions without end, revolutions without number, have been unable to efface or conceal the trace of a mother coming to weep over her son." There was built, in memory of the Blessed Virgin's swooning away, a church which was consecrated under the name of Our Lady of Spasm. "It was there," says F. de Geramb, "that Mary, repulsed by the soldiers, met her Son painfully dragging along the ignominious wood on which he was about to die."

† This way, which formerly led to Calvary, and by which our Saviour passed, no longer exists: it is covered with houses, in the midst of which is found a large pillar which marks the ninth station. The fanaticism of the Turks has delighted in making the approach to it disagreeable by heaps of filth, in order to keep the Christians away. —(F. de Geramb, t. i. p. 363.)

Heaven, by substituting himself for all other victims and loading himself with all our miseries. There was it that the great sacrifice was about to be offered, the efficacy of which goes back on the one hand to the original transgression, and reaches on the other in the night of future things, even to the consummation of ages. This small rocky declivity was the new altar, whence the blood of CHRIST was to flow in streams to wash away the sins of the world, and annul for ever the compact of perdition, which delivered us over at our birth to the angels of the abyss. But what had become of the sacred victim? Where did his executioners conceal him from the desolate eyes of his mother? Mary cast her anxious looks all over the bare mountain: the people she saw in expectation; the crosses laid down upon the ground, and workmen digging with perfect indifference the deep holes which were to receive the three instruments of punishment. . . . . And Jesus, where was he then?

He appeared, but in what a condition!—stripped of the last of his garments, without a shred to cover his discoloured flesh and bleeding wounds,—he who was so chaste and pure! His executioners, dragging him ignominiously along, exposed him thus some time to the derision of the people; then the Just One laid himself down upon the cross,—that bed of honour offered to him by the gratitude of men as the price of his immense love! It was a spectacle too frightful to behold for those who loved him: they dragged Mary some paces off, into a sort of natural grotto, where she remained standing, white and cold as marble.* There came from without a confused noise, like that of the bees of Engaddi, when the Israelite shepherd drives them out of the hollow of their

* Near the place where our Saviour was fastened to the cross by the hands of the executioners, is seen a chapel dedicated to Our Lady of Dolours. It was into this place that the Blessed Virgin retired during the cruel preparations for the death of her Son.—(F. de Geramb, t. i. p. 151.)

oak-trees. From time to time, in the midst of this gloomy recitative there arose all at once a tempest of shouts, cries of derision and frightful bursts of laughter: the populace of all nations has ever had ferocious instincts, but that of the Hebrews surpassed itself on this occasion.

In an interval of profound silence, employed, no doubt, in some new barbarity which captivated the attention of the multitude, a stroke of the hammer was heard,—a dull stroke, falling upon the wood and the bruised flesh. Magdalen, shuddering, pressed close to Mary, and the beloved disciple leaned instinctively against the side of the grotto. A second blow, duller, more stifled, and more ill-omened, was again heard; it was followed by two or three others, falling at regular intervals, and then all was told. "See, they are nailing him to the cross," coolly observed a Roman soldier. John and Magdalen exchanged looks of desolation; they were under a sentiment like that which is felt in the midst of a nocturnal tempest, when the cries of the shipwrecked, whom it is impossible to succour, are borne on the waves, and are extinguished, one after another, at the bottom of the waters. But Mary! . . . . . a cold perspiration spread over her frame, a convulsive trembling shook her limbs; she too, poor feeble woman, had just been crucified; for never did confessor, stretched upon the rack,—never did martyr in the midst of flames,—undergo in soul and body tortures so dreadful.

They soon distinguished the sharp friction of the cords on the pullies; the cross was slowly raised up in the air, and the Son of Man, with his face turned towards those western lands which had so long waited for the light, was planted like a standard in the sight of unbelieving nations: so it was written. Then the reprobate people gave a hoarse and prolonged roar of joy: "Hail, King of the Jews! If God loves him, let him deliver him! If thou art the Son of God, O Nazarean, come down!" And the thief crucified on his left

hand cursed him also, amid the chokings of his agony; the wretch did his utmost to be a Jew to the end. Jesus, maintaining with calm and sublime dignity his great character as prophet and God Saviour, sealed in silence with his blood the exalted doctrines of the new law. No complaint, no reproach escaped him amid the infamous punishment which he underwent in the sight of a whole city; he looked down with mercy upon this people so far gone astray; and, wishing to appease the divine justice in favour of those who crucified him, "*Father*," he said with his dying voice, "*Father, forgive them, for they know not what they do.*"

"And yet for eighteen centuries the Father has not forgiven them, and they drag their punishment with them all over the earth, and all over the earth the slave is obliged to stoop down to look them in the face."*

The Virgin had left the temporary asylum where she had taken refuge, and walked with her head cast down towards the place of execution. At a little distance from the tree of infamy, rough soldiers were casting lots for the seamless robe which she had wrought with her hands,† and were making a noisy partition of those sacred garments which had wrought so many miracles.‡ A slight shudder passed over the features of Mary; she thought of the time when, rich in nothing but the love of Jesus, but free from immediate cares, she used to work in the evenings at the texture of this holiday tunic, and this thought gave her a desolating sorrow, for the lightning flash which showed her in the past the sight of her days of happiness did but deepen the darkness of her misery. She lifted up her eyes to heaven, to

* M. l'Abbé de la Mennais.

† It is an ancient tradition that the Blessed Virgin had herself woven the tunic of her son.

‡ The cathedral of Trêves possesses one of these sacred garments, and on its being exhibited in the year 1845, the returns of the police certified the presence in the city of twenty-five thousand pilgrims.

seek thence, as she ever did, strength to suffer, and her look met that of the crucified God. At that dreadful spectacle her languid feet were fast fixed to the ground, and she remained petrified with so great horror, with so frightful a shock, that what she had felt up to that time appeared to her no more than a sorrowful dream—a frightful, but almost effaced vision; all was absorbed in the cross.*

Jesus, casting on the Blessed Virgin a sweet and mysterious look, seemed to say to her, as on the previous evening to his apostles, "Mother, the hour is come!"

But what hour?

The hour most memorable and fruitful in extraordinary events, of which the sun's shadow had marked the passage since man had parcelled out the duration of time to keep account of its passage; the hour when the Son of God was about to triumph over the world, over death and hell, and even the divine justice itself; the hour of the accomplishment of the oracles, the abolition of the sacrifices, the reinstatement of woman, the freedom of the slave, and our eternal redemption. And the Virgin thought she saw passing before her eyes the patriarchs, the righteous kings, the prophets inspired of God, who bowed down before CHRIST, like the sheaves of the sons of Jacob before the mysterious sheaf of Joseph. And she thought she saw Moses and Aaron laying at the foot of the new tree of life the ark of the covenant, the ephod, the rational, the plate of gold, and the almond rod, the symbol of the Hebrew priesthood, the mission of which was about to terminate; then David, placing there his prophetic harp by the side of the sword of Phinees, the

* The fathers and the doctors of the church place the sufferings of the Blessed Virgin on Calvary above those of all the martyrs. "Virgo universos martyres tantum excedit quantum sol ad reliqua astra," says St. Basil; and St. Anselm adds, "Quidquid crudelitatis inflictum est corporibus martyrum, leve fuit aut potius nihil comparatione tuæ passionis."—(De Ex. Virg., c. 5.)

sacred knife of Abraham, and the brazen serpent. The priests and the victims, the rites and ordinances, the types and symbols, gathered about the cross, there awaited their consummation; and the book with the seven seals of brass was laid open at the feet of the Great High Priest according to the Order of Melchisedech, who took place of the Aaronites. The old world, receding like the waves, which slowly recoil upon themselves, gave place to other images. Mary then thought she saw all the nations of the earth waiting at the foot of the cross, there to receive the gospel. Ethiopia and the islands stretched out their hands towards the Messias; the desert, which began to rejoice, *flourished like the rose*; the knowledge of God filled the earth, as the great waters cover the sandy bed of the oceans; and a thousand voices seemed to repeat in a thousand barbarous idioms, "Christ has overcome, blessed be his name!"

The noble and generous woman forgot for a short time the poignant sufferings which tortured her, and united herself in sympathy with the triumph of the law of grace, and the great social regeneration; but the vision of glory was not long before it vanished, and sorrow re-entered at every pore; like Rachel, Mary wept over her firstborn, and would not be comforted!

Meanwhile, all nature seemed to participate in the suffering of her God; the daylight gradually became obscured, and the decreasing light gave a mournful tint to that vast and sterile region, so well suited for the crime of which it was the theatre. Every moment the darkness thickened; the dew fell by the sudden interruption of the heat; the eagles shrieked as they resumed their nocturnal shelter; the jackals howled on the banks of the Cedron; and Calvary, in itself so melancholy, took the appearance of a huge catafalque of black marble. The people, strongly impressed by this unusual event, began to keep the silence of fear; and some few voices, insulated and disdainful, the voices of the Pharisees and chiefs of the synagogue, alone continued to utter maledictions against CHRIST.

The stars soon appeared through the dark crape which veiled the face of the firmament, like funeral torches burning round a coffin, and cast a fearful greenish light upon the theatre of the deicide, which gave the masses of spectators standing in groups on the sides of Gihon the air of an assembly of demons and spectres. They looked at each other and turned pale. In vain did the scribes and Pharisees—too far plunged in the waters of crime to attempt to regain the bank—strive to attribute this prodigy to natural causes; the more the absence of light was prolonged, the less did their reasons appear conclusive. The old men, shaking their grey heads, declared that they had never seen such an eclipse; and the learned men versed in the science of the Chaldeans maintained, on the other hand, that no eclipse was either foreseen or possible in the actual position of the moon.*

This eclipse, of three hours' duration, was one of the prodigies connected with the Messias, which were intended to mark the anger of Heaven when CHRIST should be put to death. The prophet Amos had said, "And it shall come to pass in that day, saith the Lord God, that the sun shall go down at mid-day, and I will make the earth dark in the day of light." This darkness extended to Egypt, where at that time was St. Dionysius the Areopagite, who was studying philosophy at Hermopolis. Struck with terror, the young Greek cried out, addressing himself to his preceptor

* Phlegon relates that in the 202nd Olympiad, corresponding with the year 33 of our era, there was the greatest eclipse of the sun ever seen, and that at the hour of noon the stars appeared in the heavens; but astronomy demonstrating that there was no eclipse in that year, obliges us to acknowledge that the cause of that darkness was wholly supernatural. "We observed," says St. Dionysius the Areopagite—who was at that time at Heliopolis—"that the moon came unexpectedly to interpose between the sun and the earth, although it was

Apollophanes, "*Either the world is coming to an end, or the God of nature suffers.*"*

Amidst the general consternation, Jesus was occupied with his faithful friends, who had rallied round his cross in the hour of his ignominy. Touched with the courage of John, and the profound sorrow which this young and ardent disciple did not attempt to conceal, he would leave him a pledge of his divine affection. He could not bequeath to him a part of his earthly goods, he who had not a stone whereon to lay his head, and who was about to owe to the charity of a disciple even the loan of a tomb; he had nothing left in the world but his mother!—his mother, who had never left him, and who was dying at his death. He solemnly bequeathed her to his favourite disciple, as a pledge of those heavenly goods which he reserved for him in the kingdom of his Father. Knowing how much he was loved by these two holy souls, he foresaw, with his adorable goodness, the dreadful isolation in which his death was about to leave them, and would strengthen these two plants, devoid of support, by intertwining their separated branches.

By this arrangement, which added a new and cherished interest to her life, the Virgin must have understood that it was not granted her to follow her Son to the tomb, and that she had not arrived at the termination of her pilgrimage on earth. She resigned herself to the divine decrees out of love for us, whom she adopted in the person of the holy apostle. The sacrifice of Mary almost equalled then, humanly speaking, that of Jesus Christ. He willingly consented to die; and she to live! . . . They were two mighty hearts, inflamed with love for men, and which alone fully under-

not the time for such a conjunction in the natural order of those laws to which the heavenly bodies are subject, &c."—(Seventh Epistle to Polycarp.)

* St. Dionysius, Seventh Epistle to Polycarp.

piercing his side with a lance, and the divine blood which was to wash away the crimes of the world ran down in great drops upon the earth. At some distance, two women covered with veils, one of whom leaned upon the other in an attitude which betrayed the most heartrending grief, timidly beheld the proceedings of the Roman soldiers: they were Mary and Magdalen, for Magdalen too was there; and in the distance were perceived the other women from Galilee, who had left all to devote themselves to Jesus, and who had not forsaken him in the hour of punishment and ignominy. "Honour to them!" says Abeilard, "for when the disciples and apostles fled like cowards to the mountains, these weak but courageous creatures accompanied Christ even to the foot of the cross, and did not leave him till he was laid in the sepulchre!"

Then Joseph of Arimathea came up, a rich senator, who had obtained of Pontius Pilate the body of Jesus, of whom he was a disciple in secret, to pay him the honours of sepulture. He took him down from the cross, and prepared to wrap him up in a winding-sheet of fine linen from Egypt, which he had purchased at Jerusalem, when he beheld at his feet a woman pale as death, who stretched out her arms with the most affecting and sublime sorrow, to receive the crucified God. This woman, whose whole body trembled

says, that when the judgment trumpet shall sound, Aïsa (Jesus Christ) will descend from heaven to the earth, and will announce to all its inhabitants the great day of the last judgment: then he will die, and be buried at the side of Mahomet: when the dead shall come forth from their graves, both shall arise together, and ascend into heaven. Burckhardt, who visited the great mosque of Medina, where are the tombs of Mahomet, Aboubekir, and Omar, three tombs of black stone, covered with precious stuffs and surrounded with magnificent *ex voto's*, says that a vacant place has been left by the side of Mahomet's tomb for the reception of Jesus after his death. Above this place and the tomb of Mahomet, was hung a magnificent brocade cloth enriched with diamonds, which was stolen by Sioud when he took Medina.

and was convulsed with shudderings of agony, had no voice left to articulate the request which seemed to move upon her lips, but there was not, upon her face bathed in tears, a muscle which did not petition. The senator, who recognised Mary, made a sign of sympathetic compassion, and laid upon her trembling knees the divine burden with which he had respectfully laden his shoulders. Then the Blessed Virgin could give herself up to the bitter joy of pressing to her suffering and bleeding heart the disfigured body of her Son, and of applying her colourless lips to the wounds which had been made by the nails of the cross. Magdalen on her knees, bathed with her warm tears the bleeding feet of her Lord, and moaned like a wounded dove. In the background of this picture of desolation were the women of Galilee, weeping.* During this time, some of Joseph's servants prepared the perfumes on the stone *of unction*,† and others opened the sepulchre hewn out of the rock, which was to receive the mortal remains of the Son of God.

CHAPTER XVIII.

DEATH OF MARY.

TRANQUILLITY began to return, and the signs of the wrath of heaven had ceased to alarm the Jews, who had just shed

* There are some authors who hold that these holy women picked up some of the earth quite saturated with the precious blood of Jesus Christ, and that it was by this means that some of it has been in the possession of certain churches in France, as St. Denis, and the Sainte-Chapelle, of Paris.

† The stone of the anointing is at present in the chapel of Calvary; it has been necessary, for its preservation, to cover it with white marble and surround it with an iron balustrade.

the blood of our Saviour. Like al! wild anmials, the executioners of Christ had for a moment lost their savage instincts in the hour of peril. Terrified at first at what they had done, they had feared that the tottering rocks of Calvary would crush them in their fall, and that the earth would make them go down alive into the dark depths of *scheol*; but this remorse disappeared with their terrors, and they gradually returned to their spiteful and malicious nature, as they saw the heavens become again serene.

Unable to deny the prodigies which an immense number of people had seen with their eyes, and which were attested by the rent sides of the mountains, the tombs scarcely covered over again, and the veil of the temple in tatters, they attributed them to magic, and maintained that this Jesus, so powerful in word and work, was only a son of Belial, who had fascinated the people, and commanded the elements by means of the ineffable name of the God of Israel, which he had stolen by surprise from the Holy of Holies.* And the people suffered themselves to be led away by this ridiculous falsehood which their leaders cast before them; for there is no calumnious absurdity which does not find credulous ears to welcome it, and nimble tongues to spread it abroad. Meantime a vigilant guard, chosen from the satellites of the high priest, watched in arms around the tomb; for Jesus had announced that he would rise again on the third day, and the princes of the synagogue pretended to fear that his disciples would take him away during the night.

The third day began to appear, and the east was scarcely tinged with colour, when several women from Galilee, bringing perfumes and aromatic plants, to embalm Jesus after the manner of the kings of Juda,† appeared upon the

* See Basn., liv. vi. pp. 27 and 28.

† It is clear that they were going to embalm Jesus in a new way; Nicodemus had already wrapped it up in bandages of myrrh.

mountain of punishment, pensively making their way towards the garden where the tomb of Christ was. According to tradition, Mary was with these holy women.* Her dejected countenance resembled a marble laid prostrate by the stormy wind of adversity; but her look did not express merely sorrow—it depicted expectation. The deicidal city was slumbering, enveloped in the transparent vapours of the morning; the flowers had half opened their cups laden with dew, the birds were singing in the humid branches of the wild fig-trees, and one would have said that the sun scattered rubies over the blue vault of the firmament; nature seemed to have put on again, with unusual joy, her brilliant robe of light, and that scenery so grand, and yet so dark and sad, which surrounded Jerusalem, assumed a sweet and cheerful expression which it had never had till then, and which seemed to announce a glorious mystery which it would keep secret.

On a sudden, in the midst of this smiling scene, a shock is felt; the stone which closes the sepulchre rolls over as if moved by some mighty arm; the guards fall down half dead on their faces on the ground; and the women, who did not desert Jesus upon the cross, turn pale themselves, and fall back, fearful of seeing those frightful prodigies renewed, which accompanied the death of the Son of Man.

But an angel, whose garments equalled in whiteness the mountain snow, and whose gracious countenance shone like lightning, seats himself upon the stone of the sepulchre, and encourages the servants of Jesus Christ. "Fear not you," says a sweet voice, "for I know that ye seek Jesus of

* This is the only passage of the author on which the TRANSLATOR feels called upon to insert a note. It is contrary to all probability, as well as to the general opinion of spiritual writers, to suppose that the Blessed Mother, who so well knew the approaching resurrection of her divine Son, would have accompanied, and so far encouraged, those who came to embalm him without hope

Nazareth, who was crucified; he is not here, for he is risen as he said. Come and see the place were the Lord was laid." While the pious Galilean women entered with fear into the tomb, and were astonished at the sight of the winding-sheet and bands perfumed with myrrh, which were left at the entrance, the Virgin, whose face shone with accumulated joy, was leaning against an aged olive-tree at some distance. A young man, dressed in the ordinary costume of the people, was conversing with her in a low voice. This young man was the "first born from among the dead," the glorious conqueror of hell, Jesus Christ.* No one ever knew what passed at this solemn interview; but we may believe that Mary, whose valiant soul had undergone the greatest possible paroxysm of grief, experienced at that time a degree of joy which we could not feel without dying.

Our Lord, during the forty days which followed his resurrection, frequently appeared to the apostles, and conversed with them of the things concerning the kingdom of God, and the regeneration which would be wrought in men by baptism. Pious authors have supposed that the Virgin was the most favoured in these consoling apparitions, and that in them she experienced a foretaste of the happiness of the elect. The bitter waters of her affliction were changed into fountains of grace, and our Saviour "fed her with the hidden manna which he reserves for those who keep patience according to his word."

At length the hour arrived when the divine decrees re-

* St. Ambrose, who lived in the fourth century, says that the Virgin was the first who had the happiness to see Jesus risen; and the poet Sedulius, who flourished shortly after St. Ambrose, records this tradition in his verses. They both speak of it as of generally received belief among Christians. The Arab historians have preserved this tradition: Ismaë, the son of Ali, relates that Jesus descended from heaven to console Mary his mother, who wept for him. An altar has been erected on the spot where this affecting interview took place.

called Christ to heaven; his mission of redemption was fulfilled, and the apostles, whom his resurrection had fully convinced of his divinity, had received from him the necessary instructions for converting the nations to his admirable gospel.

In the middle of the fortieth day, he went out of Jerusalem with them, and proceeded towards the heights of Bethania. This direction was not taken accidentally: there was that mountain crowned with olive-trees, where our Saviour, withdrawing from the crowd, had often prayed to his father at the hour when the silent moon shone with its opal light upon the leaden waters of the Dead Sea, the green valley of the Jordan, and the giant palm-trees of the plain of Jericho,—distant sites, which seemed to display themselves at her feet. There also was that celebrated garden where Jesus had painfully experienced the first attacks of agony. It was just that his glory should commence in the same places where his generous sufferings had begun, and that those fields, those woods, those shady solitudes, which had so often been witnesses of his meditations and his prayers, should receive the impress of the last steps he took before he reascended to heaven.

Arrived at the summit of that high mountain, whence he could discern a great part of Judea, and salute with a farewell sign the spots which he had made celebrated by his miracles and his death, our Savour stopped in an open space at a short distance from a wood of olive-trees, which spread out their pale foliage to the burning noonday sun. There, after lifting up his hands, still pierced by the nails of the cross, to his heavenly Father, as if to recommend to him his infant Church, he lowered them upon his mother and his disciples, as Jacob had done to the sons of Joseph; then he arose by his own power, and ascended slowly to heaven. This last act of our Saviour put a worthy seal upon his divine mission. During his life, "he went about doing good;" upon Calvary he prayed for his executioners, and he ascended into heaven blessing the humble friends whom he was leaving behind him upon earth. While he had his hands still stretched out over his prostrate disciples, they saw him enter a white cloud, which took him out of their sight.

The Ascension of our Lord had not that dark and terrifying character which chilled the people with fear in the days of old. The law of Moses had been proclaimed with the sound of trumpets, the noise of thunder, and ominous flashes of lightning; Elias had been carried up to heaven in a fiery chariot; but the Saviour of the world was gently borne upon a light cloud, with that serene and calm majesty which becomes the genius of the gospel and the touching character of its Author.

The angels, those benevolent spirits who rejoice in the happiness of men, figured also in that scene which unravelled the grand drama of Redemption. Their divine canticles had announced to the shepherds the birth of the kingly Messias; their voice had proclaimed his resurrection from the dead; it was fitting that their words should come to confirm his glorious ascension.

As the desciples were steadfastly looking at Jesus ascending into heaven, two men, clothed in white, suddenly appeared, and said to them, "Ye men of Galilee, why stand you looking up to heaven? This Jesus, who is taken up from you into heaven, shall so come as you have seen him going into heaven."

The apostles and disciples cast down their eyes, dazzled at the voice of the angels; but did the Virgin cast down hers? Was it denied to her to see her divine Son majestically take his place at the right hand of Jehovah in the inaccessible light of the saints? Was she really less favoured than St. Stephen and the beloved disciple? That is hardly to be presumed. She who had been morally crucified with

Jesus upon Calvary deserved to be glorified with him; it was her right: she had dearly paid for it! Yes, Mary was entitled to look with her mortal eyes into that peaceful and blessed region, the entrance of which Jesus had just opened for us by his blood, and where he himself wipes away the tears of the just; * then the pearl gates of the heavenly Jerusalem † slowly closed upon the victorious God, and the Virgin, separated for a short time from Him whom she loved, found herself alone upon the earth, like a climbing plant uprooted.

Ten days afterwards, we find her again in prayer in the upper room, where she received the Holy Ghost with the apostles.

Mary was the pillar of light which guided the first steps of the infant Church. To her the apostles attributed the numerous ears of corn which they plucked from the rebellious field of the synagogue, to lay them up in the granaries of the Householder. She accepted this tribute in the name of her Son with graceful humility, and she was seen constantly surrounded by the poor, the afflicted, and sinners; for she always loved with a love of predilection those to whom she could do good. The evangelists came to her to seek light; the apostles, unction, courage, constancy; and the afflicted, spiritual consolations; all left her with benedictions: *the Sun of Justice* had set on the blood-stained horizon of Golgotha; but *the Star of the Sea* still reflected its softest rays on the renovated world, and poured benign influence upon the cradle of Christianity.

The Virgin remained at Jerusalem till the terrible persecution, which broke out against the Christians in the year 44 of our Lord, obliged her to depart from it with the apostles. Her adopted son then took her to Ephesus, whither Magdalen would follow her.

* Apocal., cap. xxi. v. 4.

† Ibid. v.21.

Nothing has come down to us of the abode of Mary at Ephesus; but this void is easily explained by the incessant occupations of that period. After the resurrection of our Saviour, the apostles, occupied exclusively with the propagation of the faith, considered as secondary matter all that was not directly and prominently connected with that absorbing subject. Full of their high mission, entirely devoted to the salvation of souls, they so completely forgot themselves as to have hardly left us a small number of incomplete documents on the evangelical labours which changed the face of the globe; so that their history is more like some epitaph, sublime, but almost effaced, which has neither beginning nor end. That the Mother of Jesus shared the lot of the apostles is readily conceived; the latter years of her life were spent far away from Jerusalem, in a foreign country, where her abode was not marked by any striking fact, offering only a blank surface, which has left no lasting impression on the fugitive memory of men. Nevertheless, the flourishing state of the Church of Ephesus, its tender devotion to Mary, and the praises which St. Paul gives to its piety, sufficiently indicate the fruitful care of the Virgin, and the divine benedictions which followed her wherever she was. The Rose of Jesse left some little of its perfume in the air, and this vestige, slight as it was, is a precious revelation of its passage.

The coasts of Asia Minor, studded with opulent cities, rich in wonderful vegetation, and bathed by a sea ploughed in every sense by a multitude of vessels, would have appeared to ordinary exiles a splendid compensation for the lofty and barren mountains of Palestine. It is doubtful if the Virgin of Nazareth judged thus: the footsteps of the Man-God had not sanctified this enchanted ground, and the tombs of her forefathers were not there! . . . . How often, seated beneath a plane tree, on the shore of that beautiful Icarian Sea, the waves of which expire at the feet of myrtles upon a narrow belt of sand, did Mary and Magdalen call up recollections of their native country, as they followed with their eyes some Greek galley whose prow was turned towards Syria! The spotless snows of Libanus, the blue tops of Carmel, the waters of the Lake of Tiberias, then revived in their conversations; the sites of the absent country, embellished by distance, passed by turns before them, and seemed to them a thousand times preferable to that soft and smiling Ionia, which was in fact to the land of Jehovah what the lyre of Anacreon is to the harp of David.

It was during her abode at Ephesus, that the Virgin lost the faithful companion who, in imitation of Ruth, had left her country and her people to follow her beyond the seas: Magdalen died, and Mary wept for her, as Jesus had wept for Lazarus.*

Of all her ties of affection and relationship, there remained to the Virgin none but St. John, the good and amiable disciple to whom her dying Son had bequeathed her; she followed him, as it is believed, in his journeys; and it was, no doubt, in his conversations with the Queen of prophets that St. John completed the wonderful knowledge which he displays in his gospel. Assisted by the lights of Her whom the Fathers have compared to the golden candlestick with seven branches, the young fisherman of Bethsaida pene-

* We read, in some Greek authors of the seventh and following centuries, that after the ascension of Jesus Christ, St. Mary Magdalen accompanied the Virgin and St. John to Ephesus; that she died in that city, and was buried there. This also is the opinion of Modestus, Patriarch of Jerusalem, who flourished in 920; of St. Gregory of Tours and St. Guillebaud. This last, in the account of his journey to Jerusalem, says that he saw at Ephesus the tomb of St. Magdalen. The Emperor Leo, the philosopher, had the saint's relics translated from Ephesus to Constantinople, and deposited them in the Church of St. Lazarus, about the year 899. Another tradition supported by esteemed men of learning, would have it that St. Mary Magdalen ended her days in Provence; we have adopted the contrary opinion, because it appeared to us the more probable, without, however, deciding the question.

trated farther than any one into the incomprehensible mystery of the increated essence of the Word, and his thought soared up with a flight so bold into the mystic heights of heaven, that in comparison with him the other evangelists seem only to graze the earth.*

Meanwhile the sowers of CHRIST had scattered the good seed of the sacred word over all points of the Roman world; the gospel harvest was green, and the workmen of the Householder laboured earnestly in the holy field. Mary judged that her mission upon earth was accomplished, and that the Church could henceforth support itself by its own strength. Then, like a wearied labourer in the harvest, who seeks shade and repose in the middle of the day, she began to sigh for the fair shade of the tree of life, which grows near the throne of the Lord, and for the living and sanctifying streams which water it.† He who sounds the depths of the soul met this desire in the heart of his Mother, and the angel who stands at his right hand came to announce to the future Queen of Heaven that her Son had graciously heard her.‡

At this divine revelation, which was accompanied, according to Nicephorus, with that of the day and hour of her decease, the daughter of Abraham felt the love of her absent country powerfully revive in her heart; she wished to behold again the lofty mountains of Judea,—where the recollec-

* The Abbot Rupert (in Cant.) assures us that the Blessed Virgin supplied, by the light she possessed, what the Holy Spirit, who was given by measure to the disciples, had not been pleased to reveal to them; and the holy Fathers all agree that it was from the Blessed Virgin that St. Luke received divers marvellous and particular circumstances of the infancy of Jesus Christ.

† Apocal., c. xxii. v. 1, 2.

‡ Tradition relates that the Blessed Virgin received the announcement of her approaching death by the ministry of an angel, who informed her of the day and hour.—(Descout., p. 235; F. Croiset, t. xviii. p. 158.)

tions of redemption were still lively,—and to die in sight of Calvary, where Jesus had died. St. John, to whom her slightest desires had ever been commands, immediaetly prepared to depart and return to Palestine.

The Hebrew travellers probably embarked at Miletus, the famous port of which was the resort of the galleys of Europe and Asia, which navigated those seas. During their voyage on the Grecian seas, the Virgin and the Evangelist recognised as they passed, the island of Chios, the people of which, who long possessed the empire of the sea, were the first to introduce the odious custom of purchasing slaves, a custom which the gospel was gradually to abolish; then Lesbos, the country of the lyric poets, where the hymn to the Virgin most pure was to succeed the burning odes of Sappho, and the more manly songs of Alceus. On seeing the top of the temple of Esculapius rounding in the clouds, which attracted an immense concourse of strangers to the island of Cos, the Mother of the Saviour of men was reminded of her divine Son, who, during his sojourning upon earth, had employed his divine power in curing the sick on the spot, and raising the dead to life.* Delos, the cradle of Apollo, Rhodes, the birthplace of Jupiter, arose in turn from the midst of the waters, with their verdant mountains and their antique temples, quite peopled with gods, soon to be banished to the infernal regions by the God crucified on Golgotha. At some distance from Cyprus, a black peak was distinguishable in the clouds, traced upon the velvet blue of heaven; it was the môuntain where the prophet Elias had erected, in ancient days, an altar to the future Mother of our Saviour, and where his disciples were on the point of placing themselves

* The followers of Mahomet have preserved the memory of the miracles of Jesus Christ. They maintain that the breath of our Lord, which they call "bad Messih" (the breath of the Messias), not only raised the dead, but could even give life to inanimate things.—(D'Herb., Bibl. Or., t. i. p. 365.)

under her helping protection. The next day, the galley entered with oars a port of Syria, perhaps Sidon, which had frequent commercial intercourse with Palestine, as the sacred books inform us.

They returned into Israel, after an absence of several years. Mary retired to Mount Sion, at a short distance from the ruined and deserted palace of the ancient princes of her race, and into the house which had been sanctified by the descent of the Holy Ghost. St. John on his part went in search of St. James, who was related to the Blessed Virgin, and Bishop of Jerusalem, to inform him, as well as the faithful who composed his already numerous Church, that the Mother of Jesus was come among them to die.

The day and the hour were come: the saints of Jerusalem beheld again the daughter of David, still poor, still humble, still beautiful; for one would have said that this admirable and holy creature escaped the destructive agency of time, and that, predestined from her birth to a complete and glorious immortality, nothing in her was to decay.* Serious, but not ill, she received the apostles and disciples, seated on a small bed of poor appearance, suitable to her costume as a woman of the common sort of people, which she had never discontinued. There was something so solemn and affecting in her air, full of dignity and grandeur, that the whole assembly melted into tears. Mary alone remained calm in that ample and lofty chamber, where a crowd of old disciples and new Christians flocked in, alike eager to hear her and contemplate her.

The night had come on, and lamps with many branches seemed to cast, with their white light, something mysterious and solemn upon this sad and silent assembly. The apostles, deeply moved, stood round about the funeral couch. St. Peter,

* St. Denis, an eye-witness of the death of the Blessed Virgin, affirms that at that advanced period of her life she was still wonderfully beautiful.

who had so loved the Son of God during his life, contemplated the Virgin with a feeling of sorrow, and his speaking look seemed to say to the Bishop of Jerusalem, "How much she is like Jesus Christ!" Indeed the likeness was striking;* and the stooping posture of Mary, which brought to mind that of our Saviour during the Last Supper, completed it. St. James, who had received from the Jews themselves the surname of "Just," and who knew how to control his emotions, suppressed his tears; the prince of the apostles, a man of openness and first impulse, was deeply affected, and showed it; St. John had hid his head in one of the folds of his Grecian mantle, but his sobs betrayed him. There was not in the whole assembly a heart which was not broken, or an eye which was not moist. Mary, sharing in the general emotion, and forgetting the splendours which awaited her on high, in order to wipe away the tears which were shed on earth, began to speak, with a view to strengthen the faith of her children, to revive their sacred hopes, and inflame their charity; she spoke to them, with unrivalled eloquence, those strong and sublime things which we listen to breathless, which exalt man above himself, and enable him to undertake everything. Her speech, so sweet that the Scripture has poetically compared it to a honeycomb, became gradually powerful; the daughter of David and Solomon, the inspired prophetess who had pronounced, without premeditation, the triumphant hymn of the "Magnificat," rose to consideration so sublime, that every one forgot, in his delight, that death was at the end of this song of the swan. But the fatal hour drew near. Mary stretched out her protecting hands over the poor orphans whom she was about to leave, and raising up her fine countenance to the stars which shone outside with serene majesty, she beheld the heavens opened and

* Jesus Christ stooped a little, and this made him appear something shorter; his countenance was very much like that of his mother, particularly in the lower part of it.—(Nic., Hist. Eccl., t. i. p. 125.)

the Son of Man stretching out his arms to her from the bosom of a bright cloud.* At this prospect, a rosy tint diffused itself over her countenance, her eyes expressed all that maternal love mingled with divine joy carried to its completion, and adoration arrived at the state of ecstasy can express, and her soul, leaving without the least effort her fair and virginal mortal enevelope, softly sunk into the bosom of God.†

Mary was no more,—but her face, which had taken the expression of a tranquil sleep, was so sweet to behold, that one would have said that death hesitated to plant his banner on that trophy which he was to hold but for one day.

The lamp of the dead was lighted; all the windows were opened, and the summer breezes made their way into the apartment with the pale rays of the stars. It is said that a miraculous light filled the mortuary chamber at the moment when Mary had just drawn her last breath; it was

* St. John Damascen.

† Some of the ancient fathers, and among others St. Epiphanius, seem to doubt whether the Mother of God really died, or whether she has remained immortal, having been taken up body and soul into heaven; but the sentiment of the Church is that she really died according to the condition of the body, and the Church plainly declares this in the prayer of the mass on the day of the Assumption.—The Blessed Virgin died in the night before the 15th of August. The year of her death is very uncertain. Eusebius fixes it in the year 48 of our era; thus, according to him, Mary would have.lived sixty-eight years; but Nicephorus (lib. xi. c. 21) formally says that she ended her days in the year 5 of the reign of Claudius, that is, in the year 798 of Rome, or 45 of the common era. Then, supposing that the Blessed Virgin was sixteen years old when our Saviour came into the world, she would have lived sixty-one years. Hippolytus of Thebes assures us in his chronicle that the Blessed Virgin gave birth to our Saviour at the age of sixteen, and died eleven years after Jesus Christ. According to the authors of the Art de verifier les Dates, the Virgin died at the age of sixty-six.

ıerhaps the glory of God surrounding the spotless soul of he predestined Virgin. When the death of Mary was no onger doubtful, nothing was heard at first but weeping and leep groaning; then, funereal canticles arose amid the silence ıf night; the angels accompanied them on their golden harps,* ınd the echoes of the mouldering palace of David sorrowfully 'epeated them to the tombs of the kings of Juda.

The next day, the faithful brought, with holy profusion, he most precious perfumes and the finest stuffs for the ɪurial of the Queen of Virgins. She was embalmed, according to the custom of her people, but her blessed remains ıxhaled an odour sweeter than the perfumed bandages in vhich they enveloped her. The funeral preparations being inished, they placed the Mother of God upon a portable itter full of aromatic ingredients: † they covered her with ı sumptuous veil, and the apostles bore her upon their houlders into the valley of Josaphat.‡ The Christians of Ferusalem, carrying lighted torches, and singing hymns ınd psalms, followed the funeral of Mary with sad and lowncast looks.

Arrived at the place of sepulture, the mournful procession stopped. By the care of the holy women of Jerusalem, the omb was deprived of its unpleasant aspect, and the sepul-

* "All the heavenly host," says St. Jerom, "came to meet the Mother of God with praises and canticles, and surrounded her with a ight of intense brilliancy, and conducted her to the throne. 'Militiam coelorum, cum suis agminibus, festive obviam venisse Genitrici Dei ɪum laudibus et canticis, eamque ingenti lumine circumfulsisse et ısque ad tronum perduxisse.'"

† The coffins among the Jews in the time of Mary, were a sort of itter, made so that the body could be easily carried; this litter was illed with aromatical herbs. Josephus, describing the interment of Herod the Great, says that his litter was ornamented with precious stones, that his body reposed upon purple, that he had the diadem on ɪis head, and that all his household followed his litter.

‡ Metaphrastes affirms that the apostles bore the Virgin to the omb on their shoulders.

chral cave appeared only like a cradle of flowers.* There the apostles gently laid Mary, and as they laid her down, they wept. Of all the panegyrics pronounced on this circumstance, that of Hierothus was the most remarkable. St. Dionysius the Areopagite, who describes this scene as an eye-witness, relates that in praising the Virgin, the orator was almost out of himself.†

For three days the apostles and the faithful watched and prayed near the tomb, where sacred concerts of angels seemed to enchant the last sleep of Mary.‡

An apostle, returned from a far distant country, and who had not been present at the death of the Virgin, arrived in the meantime: it was Thomas, he who had put his hand to the wounds of his Master risen from the dead. He hastened to take a last look, and to water with his tears the cold remains of the privileged woman who had borne in her chaste womb the sovereign Master of nature. Overcome by his entreaties and his tears, the apostles removed that piece of stone which closed the entrance of the sepulchre; but they found nothing but the flowers, scarcely faded, upon which the corpse of Mary had rested, and her white winding-sheet of fine linen from Egypt, which diffused a celestial odour. The most pure body of the immaculate Virgin was not the destined prey of the worms of the coffin: during her life,

* Greg. Tur., lib. i. de Gl., c. 4.

† Books of the Divine Names. c. iii. These books of St. Dionysius, the Areopagite, have been rejected by Protestants; but they are no less authorised by an infinity of testimonies of the most ancient Fathers and Doctors of the Church, by the third ecumenical council of Constantinople, and also by others.

‡ Juvenal, Patriarch of Jerusalem, who lived in the fifth century, writing to the Emperor Marcian and the Empress Pulcheria, says that the apostles, relieving one another, spent the day and night with the faithful at the tomb, mingling their canticles with those of the angels, who, for three days, ceased not to make the most heavenly harmony heard by them.

earth and heaven equally had part in that admirable creature; after her death, heaven had taken all, and glorified all.*

* A very judicious remark of Godescard comes in support of the Assumption: it is that "neither the Latins, nor even the Greeks, so greedy after novelties, and so easily persuaded in the matter of relics, histories, and legends—no people, in a word, no city, no church, has ever boasted of possessing the mortal remains of the Blessed Virgin, nor any portion of her body. Thus, without prescribing the belief of the corporal assumption of Mary into heaven, the church sufficiently gives us to understand the opinion to which she inclines."—(Godescard, t. xiv. p. 449.)

Dei · Genitrix · sine · labe · originali ·

Concepta · a · Pio · IX · definitur ·

Deo · gratias · et · Mariae ·

Hodie · VIII · Decembris · MDCCCLIV

THE Eighth of December, MDCCCLIV: Some Account of the Definition of the Immaculate Conception of the Most Blessed Mother of God, with the Dogmatic Bull of His Holiness, and a Preface by a Priest of the Diocese of Westminster.

✠ Tota pulchra es, amica mea, et macula non est in te.—Antiph. Eccles.

To the Most Eminent Prince,

Nicholas Cardinal Wiseman,

Archbishop of Westminster

and Metropolitan,

the following pages are

(by permission)

most humbly

and most respectfully

inscribed.

Westminster,
Feast of the Purification
of the B. V. Mary, 1855.

PREFATORY.

The Eighth of December, 1854, was, perhaps, to the Christian world, the most important day that has dawned since the Council of Trent. For, whether we consider it in its mere outward and historical aspect, or in its deeper and far more important relation to the divine economy of man's redemption, the Catholic Christian cannot fail to be intimately penetrated with the feeling, that he has been peculiarly blessed. If the saints and prophets of old looked longingly for days and events which were but the harbingers of blessings to descend, not upon themselves, but upon those who should come long after they had slept with their fathers, it is surely no small grace to have lived in a day when promises long fulfilled, and ever since abounding in grace and benediction, seem to give earnest of yet more graces than ever, and when truths, long ago revealed, instead of growing, after many ages, old and tarnished, shine forth with new glory.

We know that many, long since gathered to the eternal abodes of heavenly glory, longed to see this day. They were men who walked in holiness before God; they were, moreover, gifted with extraordinary graces; but this one they did not possess; it has been reserved for those who are, perhaps, far less worthy in the sight of Heaven. They saw, and bore witness to this truth; but it was as the traveller who sees the sun sinking through the morning mist. The orient has now risen in full splendour, and no longer can its beams seem in any way less bright than they are. We have seen the day when so much has been fulfilled, that the venerable Pontiff has been moved to say, that he has done so much for the glory of the Mother of God, that he sees not well how more could be done; thus "honouring in her more and more, her only begotten Son, Jesus Christ our Lord, since the honour and praise that are offered to the Mother redound to the glory of the Son."

Thus, the last and the brightest jewel has been added to the crown of Mary; and surely, to those who love her as their Mother, the day of so great a triumph must be a day of joy, ever memorable and dearly to be cherished.

Besides, what consolation to the Catholic heart to see, even in this his day, things that are to its peace; that Peter still speaks and confirms his brethren; that his Church is the living stream, ever flowing from the mount of God. "I saw upon a mountain a Lamb standing, from beneath whose feet there flows a living stream. The stream of the river maketh joyful the city of God."* And if such an allusion be not, perhaps, intrusive on the present occasion, to the convert, this event should, indeed, be one of gladness and consolation. It might, perchance remind him of an anxious day, when he too looked for a decision from what then seemed to him the voice that should pronounce its definitive sentence upon what was in dispute; and how, when that voice fell coldly upon his ear, to tell him, not that a Truth intimately regarding man's salvation must be fearlessly asserted, but that it was an open question—or, in other words, might be, at the same time, truth and error;—how, at that moment, he clearly saw the negative, and, therefore, destructive character of that which professed to plant and to build up; and showed him that the Catholic Church alone is a living body,

* Office of St. Clement.

full of energy and life, to strengthen the weakly, and to preserve those that are strong.

For these, and other reasons, it has been thought that Catholics would gladly possess, in a permanent and convenient form (though small may be its pretensions), a complete and connected narrative of so important an event as that of December 8th, 1854, together with the Dogmatic Bull ot the Holy Father, proclaiming Mary's glory. The account contained in the following pages has been derived principally from foreign papers, and the correspondence of our own Catholic journals; the whole having been carefully revised, and several additions made from private sources of information.

J. V.

WESTMINSTER,
Feast of the Espousals of the
B. V. Mary, 1855.

the faithful on earth; the holy souls in the state of temporary suffering; and all who appreciate in any degree the sublime dignity of God's Mother, and her office in the blessed economy of Redemption, derive joy and consolation from the event that we have just celebrated.

The late decision has not been arrived at without the assistance and concurrence of the heads of the Church throughout the world; so that on Gallican or even Anglican principles, it is binding on the acceptance of Christians. When it is considered that the Bishops of the Catholic Church, united in faith and communion, and in obedience to a common head—being also recognised as true Bishops even by those who are without the fold—amount to many hundreds, and that the thirty or forty Prelates of the Anglo-Irish Episcopate are divided amongst themselves, even as to the most elementary truths of Christianity, whilst their episcopal character is denied all the world over, and by every ancient Church—it seems wonderful that any persons professing "Church principles" should prefer the authority of the latter to that of the former. But the truth is, that they do not submit to either, any farther than their views accord with their own preconceived notions; private judgment, in some form or other (either their own, or that of some other equally fallible individual), being of necessity the only real religious authority in the case of those who are without the Church. Such a spectacle, however, as that which we have *now* witnessed in the Holy City—hundreds of Bishops meeting together from all parts, to proclaim, as at Ephesus, without contest or question, the glories of the great Mother of God—is surely calculated to arrest their attention, and to suggest a comparison with their own divided Episcopate in this corner of the world, deriving its jurisdiction from the state, and with no pretensions to communion with the rest of Christendom.

The subject of the Immaculate Conception has been

strangely misrepresented by the Protestant press, whose writers are unable to appreciate the unearthly aims and objects of the Vicar of Christ. Nearly all of them regard the recent definition as the putting forth of a *new* doctrine, and making an addition to the Faith, supposing also that the heads of the Church have been occupied in the consideration of its *truth;* And yet the fact of its public celebration in our churches, and the authorised invocations of Our Lady under that title, ought to have prevented such a mistake, and have shown them that the Church was very far from regarding the Immaculate Conception as a doubtful doctrine. And it will be recollected that we have many Churches, not of very recent erection, dedicated to the Blessed Virgin, under the title of her Immaculate Conception. As to its being an addition to the Faith, it is obvious that the same might be said with equal truth of the definitions of Nicæa with regard to the Trinity and Incarnation; for the Church still possesses the powers she then exercised. Even their own mutilated calendar still retains the "Conception of the Blessed Virgin Mary;" but if it were not sinless, how could it be an object of celebration? Those who, while professing to honour the Blessed Virgin (which some Anglicans do), refuse to admit the privilege of her sinless Conception, place her in a position *inferior to that of Eve* (who was certainly created without contact with sin), whose evil she came to repair, crushing the serpent's head, and bringing life into the world, as our first mother brought death. But the Protestant mind cannot divest itself of the impression that the doctrine of the Immaculate Conception is some invention of Pius IX., or of Cardinal Wiseman, and so open to the charge of novelty; whilst Anglicans of respectable name and position have not hesitated to brand it as "heretical" (which, indeed, it would be if really novel), and inconsistent with a due appreciation of the mystery of the Incarnation. Could they, however, be induced to reflect a little more deeply upon that mystery, and what it involves (as set forth in Mr. R. Wilberforce's recent learned work), it would be found that the belief is in itself most reasonable and congruous; and that, so far from being in the least degree inconsistent with the Incarnation, it gives a new grace and beauty to that and all other mysteries, and a fuller and deeper meaning to the types and prophecies by which it was prefigured and foretold. But there are some Anglicans who do not hesitate to admit this in private, and we have heard of one who is even zealous in defence of the doctrine. The Protestant author of *Justorum Semita*, in his notice of this festival of the Anglican calendar, thus defends "the higher mystery which the day commemorates":— "Churchmen (he says) who may feel it strange to hear so much made of the Blessed Mary and her history, would do well to remember, that if a mysterious virtue could go out of the very hem of the Lord's robe, and so purifying as to heal the infirmity of her who drew near to Him in faith, how much more mysterious an influence may have passed upon her of whose substance He condescended to be made man, inasmuch as she was permitted to approach nearer to His Divinity than any other creature. . . . If she was preserved from all stain of sin, it was no less by an act of His grace than if she had been cleansed from it as Christians ordinarily are. . . . . And is it unreasonable to believe that she was indeed so miraculously kept from the stain of sin, when we reflect how carefully, if we may say so, God provided for the building of His temple at Jerusalem—how jealous he was lest anything impure should come near it? . . . But if we may reverently compare with that temple of stone the more precious temple of the Lord's Body, where his Divinity is eternally enshrined, how much greater purity may He have required in her who was admitted to be the only fellow-worker with Himself, and not finding that purity in her naturally, may He not have bestowed it on her by doing that for her which He does not for any other, because none other has been admitted to the same nearness to himself?" * And he quotes the words of the Protestant Bishop Hall, who certainly never betrayed any "leaning to Popery," but who in a moment of devotion spoke as follows in praise of the Blessed Virgin:—"How worthily is she honoured of men whom the Angel proclaimed beloved of God! O! Blessed Mary, he cannot bless thee, *he cannot honour thee too much, that deifies thee not* [thus expressing exactly, though unconsciously, both the doctrine and practice of the Catholic Church]. That which the Angel said of thee thou hast prophesied of thyself. We believe the Angel and thee. All generations shall call thee Blessed, by the Fruit of whose womb all generations are blessed."

So far from this doctrine being open to the charge of novelty, it can be traced to very early ages, especially in the Eastern Church, with which some Protestants profess much sympathy, and in which the feast appears to have been first observed. A Bishop of Nicomedia, writing more than a thousand years ago, mentions it as of *ancient date;* but its observance was not rendered obligatory until the middle of the twelfth century. It is supposed to have been introduced into England by St. Anselm, Archbishop of Canterbury, about the year 1150; and it was observed in ancient times with great devotion. Its place in the Protestant calendar is a proof that it must have retained a strong hold on the affections of the English; for among the many festivals which were abolished at the Reformation, neither the Feast of her Holy Conception, nor of the Nativity of the Blessed Virgin, was included, though the Assumption, and Corpus Christi, and many other important festivals, were altogether expunged. St. Augustine, the great Doctor of the Church, writing fourteen centuries ago, emphatically declares (*De*

* See also Wordsworth Eccl. Sonnets, part ii. 21. But another Wordsworth has been declaiming against the Immaculate Conception lately, within the sacred walls of the Catholic Abbey of Westminster.

Nat. et Grat.) that he will not so much as have the Blessed Virgin mentioned when there is any question of sin. Assemani demonstrates from the marble calendar of Naples, engraved in the ninth age, that this festival was then kept in that city, and that that Church was the first in the West that adopted it from the Greek Church. The question of the Immaculate Conception was warmly argued in the University of Paris; and in 1387, both the University and the Archbishop condemned certain propositions in which this privilege was denied. The Council of Basil, in 1439, declared the belief to be conformable to the doctrine of the Church, and to be held by all Catholics; and in 1497 the University of Paris decreed that no one should be admitted to the degree of Doctor of Divinity who did not bind himself by oath to defend the doctrine. Pope Sixtus IV., in 1483, commanded the feast to be kept as a holiday, and granted certain indulgences to those who assisted at the Mass and Office. The Council of Trent declared that in its decree concerning original sin it was not its intention to include "the Immaculate Virgin." Sixtus IV. and other Pontiffs forbade any one to censure the observance of the festival, or to condemn the doctrine of the Immaculate Conception; and Alexander VII., in 1671, commended this devotion as pious, and tending to the glory of God and His Blessed Mother. Benedict XIII. granted to the empire of Austria a weekly office, in honour of the Immaculate Conception. We have said enough to show that this doctrine—that in the case of the Blessed Virgin, the *labes*, or spot of original sin, was, at the moment of conception, by grace prevented (as in the case of St. John the Baptist it was healed after conception, but before birth)—is at least no new opinion in the Church, and no invention of living Pontiffs; while the extracts we have made will tend to show that it is neither unreasonable nor incongruous; and certainly not derogatory to the honour of Our Lord, as some have supposed; but, on the contrary, is suggested by a consideration of what is due to it—not to say a necessary consequence of its due appreciation.

It is impossible to realise sufficiently the greatness of the event which has just taken place within the sacred walls of the Basilica of St. Peter. The doctrine of Our Blessed Lady's sinless Conception has been declared an article of the Catholic faith; and henceforth no one can deny it without rejecting the authority of the Church herself, the "pillar and ground of the truth," whose Prelates and Pastors we are commanded to hear and obey. Not, indeed, that the Catholic reader needs to be reminded of this fact; for the doctrine has long been universally believed in the Church, even when not explicitly declared to be included in the tradition of the faith, as the unanimity of our Bishops, assembled from all parts of the world, testifies. When the fundamental dogmas of the Trinity and Incarnation were defined at Nicæa, and other early councils, the decisions of the Church were caused by, and directed against, certain forms of error, which had, more or less, imperilled the faith of Catholics, and had thus rendered necessary an exact definition of her belief. But in the present case no such necessity existed; nor was there any difference of opinion amongst Catholics as to the truth of the doctrine about to be defined. And we are now precluded from entertaining such a feeling, even though previously disposed to do so, by the unanimous voice of our chief Pastors on the subject, and the infallible decree of the Vicar of Christ. But as a fact every devout Catholic is full of joy on this occasion; and we cannot but thank God that we have been permitted to see what so many Saints and holy persons have for ages desired to witness, but have died without the sight. They will now, however, join the Church Militant in her devout thanksgivings; and even the suffering souls in Purgatory have rejoiced in the triumph and glory of the Empress of that holy land of sinless suffering, in which they are compelled to sojourn for a time. The late decision has the concurrence, probably, of a thousand Bishops, for even the Greek Church, though in schism, adds her testimony to the truth of the doctrine, being contained in her authorised services.* The only dissentients are a handful of prelates in these kingdoms and the British colonies, whose claims are admitted by none but themselves, their jurisdiction derived from the state, and their orders from Matthew Parker; their claim to be considered a *teaching* body being, moreover, sadly contradicted by their want of unity amongst themselves—in itself most conclusive evidence against them. But even Anglicanism is not without its witness on this occasion; some of its best and most devotional writers having (as we have shown) admitted and defended this doctrine, the antiquity of which is proved by the very service-books in their churches, as any one who will open them may see. And thus even error and heresy are, in this case at least, compelled to pay, in spite of themselves, involuntary homage to the truth; in the same manner that the evil spirits confessed

* "God," says the Greek Church, "by a singular providence, caused the Most Blessed Virgin to be as perfectly pure, *from the very first moment of her existence*, as it was fitting that she should be who was to be the most pure Mother of Christ." (*In mem. die XXV. Martii.*) The Greek Clergy, so far from finding any fault with the recent decision of the Church, only complain that it was not put forth long ago, adding that in the East it has been believed as a true doctrine, and included in the deposit of the faith, *ab antiquo*. (Vide *Cath. Standard*, Jan 27, p. 6.) Our own St. Anselm, the thirty-fourth Prelate who has occupied the Chair of Augustine, writing nearly 800 years ago, says, "Was the wisdom of God unable to form a pure dwelling for His Son, by preserving it from the common contagion? He could preserve Angels in Heaven spotless in the midst of the surrounding devastation, and was He then unable to preserve the Mother of His Son, and the Queen of Angels, from the common fall of men?" (*De Concept. B. M. V.*) And to come to more modern times, the great St. Alphonsus observes, that as "God could grant to *Eve* the grace to come immaculate into the world, He would surely grant the favour to Mary also." (*Glories of Mary*, Clapham ed. p. 249.)

Our Lord, and whom Scripture tells us really "believe" as well as Christians.

If we carry back our thoughts to the ages of eternity, before the work of creation had commenced, and when the Most Holy Trinity existed alone, Themselves the object of their ineffable complacency and delight—even then, before sun or moon was created, Mary was predestined to be the Mother of the Eternal Son, and at that early period God determined to fill her with all those gifts and graces which were required to make her a fitting habitation of so great a guest. "From the beginning and before the world" was her predestination, and before men or angels were created, the election of Mary took place in the Divine mind of the Eternal God. And how did not the fathers and saints of the Old Law anticipate, and long for the advent of Messiah's Mother! Scripture is full of allusions to her, no less than to her Divine Son. Thus the Psalmist celebrates the glories of the "King's daughter"—the sun and centre of that goodly company of holy virgins who were to be brought to the King—as well as those of His Son; and St. John, in the Apocalypse, beheld her in the heavens—the "Woman who brought forth the Man-child"—clothed with the sun, the moon beneath her feet, and her head encircled with a diadem of stars. She, indeed was the harbinger and precursor of the Sun of Justice, and the mystery of her Immaculate Conception was the *first dawn* of Redemption. All other mysteries, whether of Jesus or of Mary, arise out of and flow from this, as the river from its source. "Her coming into the world resembled the approach of the radiant morn, and being enveloped in the resplendency of the true sun, her very Conception was Immaculate. The Sun of Justice sent his early coruscations before Him to beautify her rising, transfusing into her the abundance of His own light, whereby were put to flight those powers of darkness to which Eve had given entrance."*

* St. Thomas of Valentia, in the new Office of the Immaculate Conception.

What he was by nature, she too was by grace; and there is, so to speak, a community of treasures between them. Their likeness and similitude are the very basis and groundwork of our devotion to Mary; and were it not that their interests are common and indivisible, we could never venture to apply to her those passages of Scripture which are found in the offices of the Church, and the approved writings of her Saints, and which in their primary and highest sense are applicable to the Eternal Wisdom alone. But it is this identity of feeling and interests between them, as well as her real participation in the very highest gifts and graces which it was in the power of God to bestow, that is at once the justification and explanation of our use of the passages to which we allude.

She possessed nothing in herself—nothing but what she received from God; and it is therefore plain, that in praising her, we ultimately, and chiefly, give glory to Him who *made her* what she is, and to whose grace and mercy alone, (purchased by the Incarnation and Death of her Divine son,) she owes, not merely the privilege of her Immaculate Conception, but all the glories which are exhibited in her life and character, from her first existence in the womb until her Assumption into Heaven and her triumphant Coronation.* The mystery of the Incarnation is the source and foundation of all others; and even those which preceded it in the order of time, as the Immaculate Conception of the Blessed Virgin, were but the preparation for its accomplishment. We have lately celebrated the Festivals of Christmas, which commemorate, till time shall be no more, that wondrous fact which has created, and on which depends, the entire Sacramental system of the Church; to which every minutest ceremony of

* It is not unworthy of remark that these latter mysteries, though universally believed and celebrated in the East and in the West, have never yet been declared *de fide*. The Assumption occurs even in the Oxford and other Anglican Almanacks.

her ritual, and every devotional practice of her children, has reference, and owes its existence. The Holy Eucharist itself is but the extension, so to speak, of the mystery of the Incarnation; and those who have in any degree realised the words *Verbum caro factum est*, find little difficulty in believing that He who became man for our sakes is also offered in sacrifice for, and given to us, under the appearance of bread; and that in the Most Holy Sacrament He resides perpetually amongst us:—

> Verbum caro panem verum
> Verbo carnem efficit.

And why is it that the Church so highly honours the Blessed Virgin, except as the favoured instrument of the Incarnation, and the channel of God's graces to men; *Dei Genitrix* being her first and most glorious title, and the foundation of all others? Christmas speaks of God Incarnate; God Incarnate supposes all matter to be in a manner hallowed, and made capable of blessing, with the hallowing of human flesh; and this is at once the origin and the explanation of every rite and ceremony of the Catholic ritual. And throughout the entire year the great mystery of the Incarnation is honoured and commemorated by the Church and her faithful children. The daily *Angelus*, thrice repeated, and the devout adorations in the Creed and last Gospel of every Mass, are instances of this. We do not kneel at the *Crucifixus*, but at the *Incarnatus est*, and at the *Verbum caro* in the Gospel of Christmas, which is repeated at the end of Mass throughout the year; and on Christmas Day alone is the Holy Sacrifice thrice offered by the same Priest. But if the Incarnation is thus continually honoured by the Church, it is not less true that it is the object of the incessant attacks of heresy (insidious or open); and from Arius to Luther, as predicted by St. John, the mark of Antichrist has ever been the denying or impairing of the doctrine that God has "come in the flesh," and taken our nature upon Him, of the substance of the Blessed Virgin. In the Church there is not a doctrine, a discipline, or a practice, which has not for its end and object, direct or indirect, the preservation or application of the wondrous fact which we commemorate at Christmas — God-man. But all forms of error, from that of the Galatians to those of Luther, Calvin, and Cranmer, and all other subsequent sects to which these have given birth,—all attempts of the secular power against the Church, from the Roman emperors to Elizabeth and Victoria, are only devices of the serpent to reverse the prophecy, that in this mystery "the Woman" should "crush his head." Here in England it has only just been made lawful for our Clergy to administer even the Sacraments of the Church, and thus apply to individuals the benefits of the Incarnation; and we know that in the lifetime of some amongst us a Catholic Bishop has been prosecuted for saying Mass and giving Confirmation. Protestantism is the last, the subtlest, and perhaps the most pernicious form of error that has appeared; and the doctrines of the Anglo-Irish Establishment are all the more pernicious, in consequence of the disguise which it has assumed; for, having borrowed certain forms and ceremonies, words and formulas, from the Church, it is capable of much greater success in its deception than other forms of Protestantism. "It has been for her," says a recent writer, "to pretend to an Apostolical succession of 'Bishops,' to steal large fragments of old Catholic prayers, to chant old Catholic hymns, to repeat old Catholic creeds, and to ape the very exclusiveness of the Church. She commands the proudest of all races to admit with one breath the Athanasian Creed and the Royal Supremacy, and bribes her victims to assent with a revenue of £3,000,000 sterling." But the nominal retention of the creeds of Athanasius and Nicæa has not secured the acceptance of the doctrine of the Incarnation by her members, who are for the most part simply ignorant of the belief that the Divine and human natures are indissolubly united in one Person; and that of this Divine Person the Blessed Virgin is the real and true Mother.* It was this mystery which was the cause of the fall of Lucifer; and it will ever be the great object of his attacks. Arius openly denied the Divinity of Our Lord; Protestantism, subtle and cunning, concealing its end and object, and pretending zeal for the honour of Our Lord, has attacked the Incarnation more insidiously and effectually by reducing his Blessed Mother to the level of a "mere [ordinary] woman" (as some of its writers do not hesitate to call her), and denying all those doctrines and rites which were the result or growth of this mystery. But at Trent as at Nicæa, and now at Rome, the Church has defended by her definitions and her anathemas the true doctrine; and, as at Ephesus, fourteen centuries ago, she condemned the errors of Nestorius, and by proclaiming the Divine Maternity of Mary, effectually guarded the true doctrine of her Son's Incarnation; so now, in this age of unbelief and irreverence, when so many Christians refuse to honour the Mother of God, has she declared that other great mystery —the first in order of time, and the preparation for the former, being required for the honour of Our Lord himself—

* We have known a respectable High Church Anglican express horror and astonishment at the statement, that Our Lord's Sacred Humanity was now in heaven; and others have been equally surprised at hearing it said that His dead Body upon the cross, or a single drop of His Blood at its foot, were objects of divine worship and adoration. We have even heard a Puseyite divine reply to an ultra-Protestant interrogator, who was arguing against the Real Presence, that "of course," our Lord's Body in the Sepulchre was no object of adoration; and probably many of them would be perplexed at the question, where was the *Divinity* when His Body and Soul were thus separated? But the most ordinarily instructed Catholic child would reply without hesitation, that *neither* was separated (or separable) from the Divinity; and that both the one and the other wherever *really* present (whether in Heaven or on our altars), where objects of Divinest worship and adoration.

of her Immaculate Conception. The glories of Mary (to quote the title of one of Dr. Newman's discourses) are "for the sake of her Son," and they are never entirely separated in the commemorations of the Church. The first verse of the beautiful hymn, *Memento rerum Conditor*, which so many Catholics recite daily in the Office of the Blessed Virgin, occurs also in the Vesper Hymn of Christmas:—

Remember, O Creator, Lord,
  That in the Virgin's sacred womb
Thou wast conceived, and of her flesh
  Didst our mortality assume.

And on all Festivals of Mary the hymns of the Church conclude with an ascription of praise to her Divine Son:—

Jesus, tibi sit gloria,
Qui natus es de Virgine.

As Dr. Faber observed in one of his recent sermons, the honour or dishonour of Mother and Son invariably go together; and we know from the history of the Reformation in this and other countries, that the destruction of the images and altars of Mary quickly followed the profanation of the Blessed Sacrament; while, on the other hand, those who cherish devotion to Our Lord in the Holy Eucharist are also devout in proportion to His Blessed Mother. And when He is exposed on the altar to the adoration of the Faithful, it is His Holy Mother whom we invite to present our prayers to Him, addressing her by all the titles with which the Church has taught us to invoke her assistance, concluding with that of her Immaculate Conception.

For many ages it had been the most earnest desire of the devout servants of Mary that the mystery of her Immaculate Conception should be dogmatically defined by the Holy See; and during the late pontificate of Gregory XVI. petitions were presented from all parts of the Church to hasten the dogmatical decision. Our present Holy Father, during his residence at Gaeta, nearly six years ago, issued an Encyclical Letter, desiring to be informed of the sentiments of the Catholic Episcopate; and he also appointed a council of twenty theologians to examine and report upon the subject, with which was connected a particular council, composed of twenty-two eminent Cardinals. On his return to Rome, the Holy Father appointed another board of theologians, selected from the members of the first, under the presidency of the late Cardinal Fornari, whose report, which was in favour of the definition, was approved by the particular congregation of Cardinals. The replies to the Pope's Encyclical from the Bishops of the Catholic world were also, with *four* exceptions, in favour of the definition, and not a single Bishop expressed an opinion opposed to the *doctrine* in question.

The Holy Father having determined that the time was now come for pronouncing a dogmatical decision on the subject, invited to Rome a number of Prelates from each country, to represent its Hierarchy. England was represented by His Eminence Cardinal Wiseman, Archbishop of Westminster; the Right Rev. Dr. Briggs, Bishop of Beverley; Dr. Wareing, of Northampton; Dr. Brown, of Newport and Menevia; Dr. Grant, of Southwark; Dr. Roskell, Bishop of Nottingham; and the Right Rev. Dr. Goss, Coadjutor of Liverpool. As the great day approached, the attention of Catholics became more and more absorbed with the subject of the anticipated definition, all eyes being fixed on Rome—the Jerusalem of Catholics—with a new and peculiar interest. She had just convoked a senate of Pontiffs, in comparison with which the confused and agitated assemblies which men have convened are poor indeed. Bishops arrived from all countries; and His Holiness received them with a truly sovereign magnificence; entertaining them either in his own palace, or in the several establishments in which suitable residences had been prepared for them. Thus apartments had been provided in the Quirinal, in the Palace of the Consulta (where Cardinal Wiseman resided for several months), and in the Canonica of St. Peter's, the edifice appropriated to the Canons of that Basilica. So early as the 7th of November all the work was prepared. Never had a doctrinal thesis been more thoroughly examined, or treated more maturely. In the early part of November were placed in the hands of the Bishops the collection of letters written by the Prelates of every nation to express their votes and attest the tradition of their Churches.

On four different days the Prelates met in the chamber of the Vatican, under the presidency of Cardinals Brunelli, Caterini, and Santucci. The eminent Cardinals met, after the discussions of the Bishops, in Secret Consistories, under the presidency of the Pope himself. Already were preparations made in Rome to celebrate worthily the great event. The Novena had commenced in almost all the churches with redoubled fervour. In the Church of *Santi Apostoli*, where the Holy Father himself was to celebrate the Novena, the decorations were of a most costly nature. In the Church of *Ara Cœli*, where the pious association of prayers for the dogmatic definition of the Immaculate Conception was established, the songs of joy and triumph were reserved for a *Triduo*. In the Basilica of St. Paul-without-the-Walls men were at work day and night preparing it for consecration. Each Prelate was accompanied by one or two Priests, and, besides these, a great number of the Clergy, both Secular and Regular, were led by their devotion to the Eternal City on this occasion. The number of foreign Priests thus collected was probably from five to six hundred.

The Bishops held their last conference on the 24th. It concluded by the most affecting and most glorious manifestaion of attachment to the Holy See. When the Bull had been read in its integrity, and when it was possible thus to comprehend its entire spirit by the explanations and elucidations of the delegated Cardinals and Theologians, it was found that there was in the assembly but one opinion—but one simple, identical feeling. The thought of the Holy Father was the thought of all the Episcopate; and one unanimous acclamation welcomed the decree, prepared by the Vicar of Jesus Christ, to manifest to the world the most glorious privilege of the Queen of Virgins, and to establish upon a dogmatical foundation the universal belief in her Immaculate Conception. A holy joy filled all hearts; tears of devotion and tenderness flowed from all eyes; and the assembly separated most deeply impressed with the sweetest emotion.

If such was the result of the *réunion* of the Bishops, we can well conjecture what were the *réunions* which the Sacred College held. The same deep love for Mary again burst forth—the same attachment to her glorious privilege—the same acclamation hailed the decree of her Immaculate Conception. The unanimity and fervour of the Pastors of the Church on this occasion can only be attributed to an extraordinary impulse of the Holy Spirit, whose assistance had been so solemnly and specially invoked. It was the last session. The midday bell was heard; and the august assembly knelt to recite the *Angelus.* The illustrious Prelates had no sooner resumed their places when a shout of adhesion to the Holy Apostolic See burst from every mouth —*Petre, doce nos; confirma fratres tuos*, (O Peter, teach us; confirm thy brethren.)—"Fine, indeed," said a distinguished Italian Prelate, "is the assemblage of Bishops in this city. The circumstance of it *could not* be more solemn or more sublime. . . . Much do we hope from the protection of the Blessed Virgin, now so soon to receive so beautiful a wreath of glory. Let us all invoke her with the greatest faith and love."

The great event was accomplished on the morning of the 8th of December, 1854, in the Basilica of the Vatican. The Sovereign Pontiff, Pius IX., defined as a dogma of faith, that which has been for ages the universal belief relative to the Immaculate Conception of the Most Holy Mary. The dawn of that day, although on the previous evening rain fell in abundance, broke pure and serene as a beautiful morning in spring. And Rome, that, in consequence of her unbounded devotion to Mary, awaited with more of anxiety than any other city the oracle of the Vatican, was in motion from the first streaks of day, and manifested so early her joyfulness. The citizens of all classes, joined by an immense concourse of strangers who had hastened to Rome from all parts, proceeded towards the Vatican. All wished to be present at the solemn function, and to hear the definition of this great and glorious mystery.*

* The Festival was likewise observed with the greatest solemnity and devotion in our own diocese, and no doubt throughout the entire province of Westminster. Notwithstanding the absence of our venerated Metropolitan and the Bishop of Southwark, even this benighted city, which honours not because it knows not Mary, was not without a Pontifical celebration on this most joyful occasion; the celebrant and preacher at the Oratory being the Right Rev. Dr. Morris, Bishop of Troy, who eloquently defended the doctrine, at that moment being defined, from the attacks of our antagonists. Everywhere the greatest zeal was manifested; and different schools (so to speak) of taste and feeling amongst us, vied with each other, though in no spirit of jealousy, to do honour to the occasion, and to promote and secure a fitting celebration of so great an event. There was High Mass, Vespers, and Benediction, in nearly all our Churches and Chapels; in some the First Vespers was also sung: and in many of them there was Benediction daily during the Octave, the Octave-day being observed with solemnity, and devout Novenas or *Triduums* performed, or Retreats given, in preparation for the Feast. The Cardinal Archbishop granted a plenary indulgence, on the usual conditions, on the Festival and on the Sunday within the Octave; and desired that at Benediction of the Blessed Sacrament an antiphon might be sung allusive to the Immaculate Conception. His eminence's Pastoral Letter announcing the dogmatic definition has been published by Messrs. Jones and Co.

At St. James's Church, the sermon at the High Mass was preached

Towards half-past eight o'clock all the Cardinals, Archbishops, and Bishops, arrayed in their Pontificals, assembled,

by the Rev. Dr. Manning, who took for his text the words (Gen. iii.)—"She shall crush thy head, and thou shalt lie in wait for her heel." The Reverend Preacher glanced at the principal festivals of the Christian year, comparing those of our Lord to the bright and burning glories of an eastern sun, and those of the Blessed Virgin to the pure and silvery light of an unclouded moon, calm and loving, drawing forth the fragrance of the sweet night flowers, and awakening gentle and holy thoughts. He said that at that very moment one-sixth of the Prelates of the Church were assisting at the offering of the unbloody Sacrifice by Christ's own Vicar, and that, after the gospel had been read, a decree would go forth from the lips of the Sovereign Pontiff by which the final seal would be put to a belief that, from the first descent of the Holy Ghost, more than 1800 years ago, had been cherished by Catholics, not as the weak point of their doctrine, but as one inseparably connected with the mysteries of our Redemption.

The following "Little Rosary of Mary Immaculate" is recited in some of our Churches:—

V. Incline unto my aid, O God.

R. O Lord! make haste to help me.

Glory be to the Father. As it was.

After this an Our Father *is recited, in honour of the Eternal Father, and in thanksgiving for all the graces bestowed on Mary; and is followed by four* Hail Maries. *The same is repeated in honour of the Son, and again in honour of the Holy Ghost. After each* Hail Mary *are added these words:*—May the Immaculate Conception of Mary be ever praised. *After each fourth* Hail Mary, the *following* verse is sung or recited:—

As 'mid the thorns the lily fair,
Art thou, Virgin, Immaculate;
From Sin preserved by Him whose care
Did thee His Mother blest create.

V. In thy Conception, O Virgin Mary, thou wert Immaculate.

R. Pray for us to the Father, to whose Son thou didst give birth.

Let us pray.

"O God, who by the Immaculate Conception of the Virgin, didst prepare a worthy habitation for thy son, grant us by her intercession, faithfully to preserve our hearts and bodies immaculate for thee, who didst preserve her from every stain. Through the same," &c.

with the several colleges of the Prelacy, at the Sixtine Chapel. And we saw in that assembly not only the Cardinals and Prelates, whose residence is at Rome, but Archbishops and Bishops from all parts of the world, from the several states of Italy, from the Austrian states, from France, Belgium, England, Spain, and Portugal; the Archbishops and Bishops of Holland, Greece, Bavaria, Prussia, and other Germanic countries, and of others also who had crossed the ocean, who came from China, from America, and even from the most remote parts of Oceanica, all hastening to the centre of Catholic unity, to hear the voice of the successor of Peter.

When the Sovereign Pontiff, having entered the chapel,

To excite all Christians to a great devotion to the Immaculate Conception, Pius VI., at the petition of the Religious of St. Francis, by a Rescript dated the 21st November, 1793, granted an indulgence of one hundred days to the faithful, each time they devoutly recite, with contrite heart, either of the following aspirations:—

"Blessed be the Holy and Immaculate Conception of the Most Blessed Virgin Mary" (*Benedicta sit Sancta et Immaculata Conceptio B. Mariæ Virginis*), or

"In thy Conception, O Virgin Mary, thou wast Immaculate. Pray for us to the Father, whose Son Jesus, conceived of the Holy Ghost, thou didst bring forth."

There are also great indulgences for observing the Novena before the feast of the Immaculate Conception, and the other principal Festivals of the Blessed Virgin. Let us hope that the former will soon be made a day of obligation, like the Assumption.

Some Catholics have commenced the pious practice of adding an invocation having reference to the Immaculate Conception, to the Hail Mary,—*S. Maria, sine labe concepta, ora pro nobis*; or the well-known aspiration on the medal of the Immaculate Conception: "O Mary, conceived without sin, pray for us, who have recourse to thee." And in many Churches of this and other dioceses, the devout practice has been introduced, of having Benediction of the Blessed Sacrament (as at St. Mary's, Chelsea, and the Oratory), or the Litany of Loretto, on Saturdays, in honour of Mary. At Southwark Cathedral the Litany is sung in procession, and there is a discourse at Clapham Church, where the above short Litany is also recited.

had been invested with his Pontifical robes, the procession set out to descend by the royal staircase into the Basilica of the Vatican. In the first rank walked the Apostolic Preacher and the Confessor of the Pontifical household, followed by the Purveyors-General of the Religious Orders, by the Papal Messengers, the Chaplains in Ordinary, the Pontifical Couriers, and Assistant Chamberlains. Next came the Private Clerks, and the Honorary Private Chaplains, the Consistorial Advocates, the State Chamberlains, and the Pontifical Precentors. After them the Abbreviators of the Briefs, the Votants of the Signature, the Clerks of the Chamber, the Auditors of Rota, and the Master of the Holy Hospital. Then followed the Cross, born by an Auditor of Rota, in the midst of seven Prelates, bearing candlesticks with lighted wax tapers; following the Cross walked the Latin Sub-Deacon, the Greek Deacon and Sub-Deacon, the Penitentiaries of St. Peter's, the Bishops, Archbishops, and Cardinals. Lastly, under the canopy came the Sovereign Pontiff, immediately following whom, before the Roman Magistracy, were the Vice-Camerlengo of the Holy Church, the two Assistant Cardinal Deacons, and the Cardinal Deacon whose duty it was to assist the Pontiff in the celebration of the Solemn Mass. Then followed the Dean of the Rota, the Auditor of the Chamber, the Major Domo, the Master of the Chamber, the Regent of the Chancellery, and the Apostolical Purveyors.

During the procession, the Litany of the Saints was chanted, which was concluded at the moment when the Pontiff entered the Basilica. After the recital of the prescribed prayers, the Holy Father went to adore the Most Holy Sacrament; from thence he proceeded, still accompanied by the procession, to the Papal altar, and from his throne, placed at the Epistle side, he received the homage of the Cardinals, Archbishops, Bishops, and Penitentiaries. All the Archbishops present at the ceremony, and who were not yet assistants at the throne, were declared such by the express will of the Sovereign Pontiff, and from that time the twelve Senior Archbishops placed themselves around the throne during all the time that the ceremony lasted. After the Office of Tierce had been intoned and finished, the Holy Father was arrayed in his vestments for the Pontifical Mass, having for Assistant-Bishop His Eminence Cardinal Mattei, Sub-Dean of the Sacred College; for Deacon, serving at the Mass, His Eminence Cardinal Antonelli, Secretary of State; and for Sub-Deacon, Mgr. Serafini, Auditor of Rota.

After the Gospel, chanted successively in Latin and in Greek, His Eminence Cardinal Macchi, in his capacity of Dean of the Sacred College, accompanied by the Deans, Archbishops, and Bishops present at the august ceremony, and also by the Archbishop of the Greek rite and the Archbishop of the Armenian rite, presented himself at the foot of the throne and addressed (in Latin) these words to the Sovereign Pontiff:—

"That which the Catholic Church, Most Holy Father, ardently desires and calls for with all her heart, for a long time past is, that your supreme and infallible judgment should pronounce on the Immaculate Conception of the Most Holy Virgin Mary, Mother of God, a decision which may be for her an increase of praise, of glory, and veneration. In the name of the Sacred College of Cardinals, of the Bishops of the Catholic world, and of all the Faithful, we demand humbly and urgently that the universal wishes of the Church may be accomplished in this solemnity of the Conception of the Blessed Virgin.

"At the time, then, when the august Sacrifice of the Altar shall be offered in this temple consecrated to the Prince of the Apostles, and in the midst of this solemn assembly of the Sacred College, the Bishops and the people, deign, Most Holy Father, to raise your Apostolical Voice, and to pronounce that dogmatic decree of the Immaculate Conception of Mary, which will be a subject of joy for Heaven, and of the most lively gladness for the earth."

The Pontiff replied to these words that he received willingly the prayer of the Sacred College, of the Episcopacy, and of the Faithful, but that in order to grant it, it was necessary to invoke first the assistance of the Holy Ghost. Immediately the *Veni Creator* was intoned, and the improvised chant of that hymn was executed not only by the singers of the Papal Chapel, but by all the people assembled.* Animated with the most ardent faith and love towards her whom all nations call blessed, each invoked the light of Heaven upon the Sovereign Pontiff, ready to give from the Chair of Peter a decision which would spread throughout the whole earth, notwithstanding all diversities of language, legislation, manners, and climates.

After the singing of the hymn, His Holiness, in the midst of a profound silence, read the decree in a loud voice, and with such deep emotion that the reading of it was frequently suspended by his tears. Every one who assisted at this great act shared the emotion of the Pontiff.

In this Decree the Sovereign Pontiff has solemnly defined: "THAT IT IS A DOGMA OF FAITH, THAT THE MOST BLESSED VIRGIN MARY, FROM THE FIRST INSTANT OF HER CONCEPTION, BY A SINGULAR PRIVILEGE AND GRACE OF GOD, IN VIRTUE OF THE MERITS OF JESUS CHRIST THE SAVIOUR OF MANKIND, WAS PRESERVED PERECTLY FREE FROM ALL STAIN OF ORIGINAL SIN." †

Such is the solemn dogmatical definition for which the Holy Apostolic See had received so many prayers, and consulted the entire Catholic Episcopate; the definition which

* See the Cardinal Primate's recent Pastoral Letter (Jones & Co.)

† Essere domma di fede, che la Beatissima Vergine Maria nel primo istante della sua Concezione, per singolare privilegio e grazia di Dio, in vertu dei meriti di Gesu Cristo, Salvatore dell' uman genere, fu preservata immune da ogni macchia della colpa originale."

so many Bishops hastened to hear with joy, and have announced to the Faithful on returning to their respective dioceses.

After the reading of the Decree, the Cardinal Dean returned to the foot of the Throne, and returned thanks to the Holy Father for having, by his Apostolical authority, defined the dogma of the Immaculate Conception, praying him to be pleased to publish the Bull relative to that dogmatic definition. The Apostolical Prothonotaries then presented themselves, and the Promoter of the Faith, Mgr. Frattini, in his capacity of Consistorial advocate, made entreaty that they should proceed to the drawing up of the deeds of the process verbal of that solemn act. His Holiness gave his consent, and the Dean of the Apostolical Prothonotaries said that it should be thus done.

Meanwhile the cannon of the Castle of S. Angelo announced to the whole city the promulgation of the Decree, and its multiplied salvos seemed to wish to make the ditings of this great event reach the most distant countries. All the bells of the towers and steeples of Rome rung a full peal, and the inhabitants, to manifest their joy, adorned their windows and their balconies with tapestry and hangings.

After the Pontifical Mass, at which her Royal Highness the Princess of Saxe Coburg, the diplomatic body, and the officers of the French army were present; the Secretary and the Special Councillors of the Extraordinary Congregation of the Immaculate Conception, and such a multitude as had never before been seen in the vastest temple of the world, sung the *Te Deum* in thanksgiving for the definition. The Sovereign Pontiff, who accompanied the voices of the Cardinals, Archbishops, and Bishops, chanted a verse, to which the people replied by the following verse. The emotion was universal and most intense.

The Holy Father, carried upon the *Sedia gestatoria*, then proceeded processionally to the Chapel of Sixtus IV., commonly called the Chapel of the Choir of the Most Reverent Chapter of the Vatican, and caused to be solemnly crowned the image of Our Lady of the Immaculate Conception; the crown being of gold enriched with precious stones. His Holiness then passed into the chapal called *Della Pieta* to divest himself of his Pontifical vestments; and the Holy Father received there the thanks of the Very Rev. Father General of the Order of Friars Minors of the Observance and of the Friars Minors Reformed, for having defined, in reference to the Immaculate Conception of the Virgin, that which the Franciscan Fathers have always taught. His Holiness afterwards returned to his apartments.

On the evening of that glorious solemnity Rome presented a magnificent spectacle. All the houses, from the palace of the nobleman to the garret of the poor man, were resplendent with lights. The municipality had caused to be illuminated the dome of St. Peter's and the Palace of the Capitol, where two orchestras performed until a very advanced hour of the night some choice pieces of music, which were much applauded by the crowd. The magistrates took care to prepare in their hall, in honour of the Immaculate Conception, an academic *réunion*, at which His Eminence Cardinal Wiseman pronounced an eloquent discourse in the presence of a numerous concourse of Cardinals, Bishops, Prelates, and other illustrious personages.

Rome, upon this solemn day, manifested in the most striking manner what is her devotion to the Most Holy Virgin; and the Bishops, on returning to their dioceses, and in announcing to their people what they have heard from the Vicar of Christ, could also tell them what honours people render to the Blessed Virgin in the capital of the Catholic world, and if Rome on this occasion was beneath Ephesus, when, fourteen centuries ago, her great Council defended and proclaimed the Divine Maternity of Mary.

Pius IX. presented to each of his brethern of the Sacred

College and the Catholic Episcopate, in memory of the definition of the dogma of the Immaculate Conception, a blessed medal, composed of the gold which Australia had sent as a tribute to the Queen of Angels, and an engraving to commemorate the proclamation of the decree of the 8th December. The medal bears the words *Honorificentia populi tui*, on one side; and on the other the following inscription: *Deiparæ Virgini, sine labe conceptæ*, PIUS *IX., Pont. Max., ex auri Australii primitiis sibi oblatis cudi jussit, VI. Id. Dec., MDCCCLIV.* The engraving for each of the Cardinals, Archbishops, and Bishops, is thus entitled :—

Cardinales S. R. E.,
Patriarchæ, Archiepiscopi, et Episcopi,
In Basilicâ Vaticanâ
Adstantes
PIO IX , Pont. Max.,
Dogmaticam Definitionem
De Conceptione Immaculatâ
Deiparæ Virginis Mariæ
Pronunciati
Inter Missarum Solemnia,
Die VIII. Decembris, 1854.

One of the princes of the Church, Cardinal Bonald, had been chosen to be the mouthpiece of the Sacred College and of the Episcopate of the Catholic world, and to offer to the common Father of Christendom the expression of the gratitude, respect, and love of the whole Church ; to declare their inviolable attachment to the Chair of Peter, and the docility with which they listen to its infallible decrees ; and to assure the Holy Father that all the Bishops would endeavour, with the grace of God, to correspond to his pious and holy decrees, and to follow faithfully the advice which he had been inspired to give them through his care for the Holy Church.

Happy those to whom it was granted to hear the reply of

the Pope to this address; who beheld Pius IX. once more pour forth his soul to his brethren, and manifest again and again his joy that he was chosen to acquire for Mary this completion of her greatness, and to express his hope that the Holy Mother of God would be pleased to reward so much love with a more abundant effusion of graces and blessings; adding, with truly filial simplicity,—"We have done much for Mary, we have prayed much, dealt and laboured much to increase her glory; we have done so much (though we should not, perhaps, say this), that we cannot see how more can be done on earth to enhance the glory of our tender Mother—this glorious and powerful Queen." These words will never be forgotten by the Bishops who had the happiness of hearing the tones of faith and love with which they were pronounced.

The Church of the Apostles was the privileged place chosen for the promulgation of the decree with which the angels saluted Heaven, and which the faithful proclaimed upon earth; and it was just that the Church of the Apostle of the Gentiles should be, in some degree, associated in this honour, and that its unfinished aisles should witness a holy ceremony which would for ever engrave on the memory the triumph of Mary. Thirty years ago, under another Pius, who had, like ours of to-day, suffered exile and persecution, the Church of St. Paul was destroyed by an incendiary. The flames shed a melancholy light upon the death-bed of Pius VII., that pious and learned monk, whom the cloisters of this illustrious church had so long sheltered. The Sovereign Pontiffs who succeeded him—Leo XII., Pius VIII., and Gregory XVI.—all laboured towards the rebuilding of St. Paul's; and the latter Pope, like Pius VII.—a son of the Benedictine Order—consecrated the altar of confession on the 5th of October, 1840, the anniversary of the Coronation of Leo XII., who first projected the rebuilding. More happy still, Pius XI. has been enabled to consecrate the entire Church, and his Pontificate will, no doubt, witness the conclusion of this gigantic labour; and under what blessed circumstances has he been permitted to do this! The morrow of the grandest day of his reign—a day which will live in the history of the Church amongst its most glorious, most happy days! Happy Church! future generations will learn that its dedication marked the final triumph of the Queen of Heaven, and that hundreds of Bishops from all corners of the earth, and from all nations, assembled round his Holiness on this grand solemnity.*

It is needless to repeat the description already given of a function which will be remembered till the day of doom; but we must speak of one or two incidents which greatly affected those who witnessed them. At half-past eight in the morning, a sedan chair might be seen borne by the Papal servants towards the Confession of St. Peter. They are reverently conducting to the festival a learned Bishop, who, when hastening to obey the summons of the Holy Father, was attacked by illness, yet resolutely braved the fatigues of a long journey, and the dangers of a stormy sea, fearing neither tempest nor death itself, on his way to place a jewel in the crown of the Queen of Heaven, and to hear that dogma proclaimed which had been the object of his fervent aspirations and prayers. He hears the desired oracle from the infallible mouth of Peter, speaking through Pius IX., and he retires happy and contented, ready for death, for he has witnessed the triumph of his beloved Mother on earth. He too has gained his victory. On leaving the Church, he was accosted by one of his subjects, who expressed his pleasure at meeting him. "I too, am happy," replied the holy prelate, "I have seen what I so long desired, *and I have come here to die!*" "Oh no, my lord," replied the other,

* It may be interesting to mention, that our own Cardinal Archbishop was one of the active assistants at the Consecration of this Basilica.

"The Blessed Virgin will cure you!" "If Mary Immaculate will cure me I shall return to my diocese to proclaim her power and goodness; but I can well die here, it would be well for me to die here." This Bishop was a French prelate, Mgr. Bouvier, Bishop of Mans, who exposed himself to the danger of dying at sea, or on the road through Italy, rather than be wanting to the summons of the Sovereign Pontiff, and of the Blessed Virgin herself; and he died a few days after the dogmatic decision, his last hours being consoled by the presence of the Sovereign Pontiff. Having sung his *Nunc dimittis* with joy, he went to offer his congratulations to Mary at the foot of her Mediatorial Throne, and to sing the Divine praises for a long eternity.

And who is that other venerable prelate, clothed in white, who advances, leaning on the arms of two other persons, and takes his seat in the midst of the assembled Cardinals? He is a Prince of the Church, beloved by the poor, to whom, though himself poor, he is a protecting father; the friend of Gregory XVI., whose virtues are the ornament of the whole Sacred College. It is Cardinal Bianchi, who has come to the festival to hear the reading of the decree which will crown his wishes to assist at the triumph of the Queen of Heaven. And when the Vicar of Christ has proclaimed the dogma so dear to his heart as a Religious and a Cardinal, he withdraws, supported by his two attendants, also repeating, doubtless, in his heart, the canticle of holy Simeon.

The late illustrious Cardinal Fornari, who presided over the commission appointed to investigate the subject of the Immaculate Conception, and who manifested so much zeal in the cause, was not permitted to hear the dogmatic definition, but was called away like Moses, just within sight, so to speak, of the accomplishment of his pious wishes. And the same may be said of several other Princes of the Church. "It is unnecessary to express," says the late Cardinal Lambruschini, in concluding his

Dissertation on the Immaculate Conception (which has just appeared in an English dress), "what are the ardent wishes of our heart. If, during the short space of time which yet remains for us to live, the Holy Roman Apostolic See, always guided by the light of the Holy Ghost, should judge fit to define the important question of the Immaculate Conception of Mary, how joyfully then should we close our eyes in peace." But his devout wishes were not to be gratified. Whilst writing we have received information of the deaths of three other aged Princes of the Church,—Cardinals Simonetti, Pecci, and Romo, whose lives seem to have been prolonged in order that they might hear the proclamation of Mary's glory. Our own eminent Cardinal Primate has been permitted this consolation; and we cannot doubt that it *has* been a consolation to him, amidst the trials and anxieties which are inseparable from his exalted office, and the malignancy of the enemies of the Church. In his Pastoral Letter on this subject nearly six years ago, quoting the Encyclical of the Holy Father addressed to the entire Catholic Hierarchy, His Eminence says:—"To no part of the Catholic Church can this announcement and this call to prayer be more welcome than to us, whose fathers so particularly held and promoted belief in this mystery of Mary's Immaculate Conception, and gave to the Church the Feast in which it is commemorated. Who then shall feel more anxious than we to learn the decision of so great a point, the sure holding of which by the affections, as well as by the constant belief of the faithful, has been already a source of so many blessings to the Church? Who shall pray more fervently than we that the Spirit of God may guide the counsels of the Holy Father to the right definition of so important a doctrine, which interests the dearest feelings of the breast alive to the prerogatives of Mary? It is in truth a solemn and most moving occurrence, when the Church of God, not aroused from without by the assaults of heresy, not alarmed within by the creeping spread of baneful error, but moved and almost uplifted by the heaving and swelling piety of her own best children, rises up to declare a dogma of faith, which needs not to be hedged with anathemas to guard it, but lodges safely in the glad embrace of every Catholic heart; which bears not with it one drop of bitter condemnation, but sheds forth on every side a new fragrance and a new sweetness, over the surface and within the soul of the entire Catholic world."* Whilst those who are without are striving about the very Sacraments themselves (which are openly denied amongst them, and with the sanction of authority), and contending for the most elementary truths of religion—the children of Peter's blessed fold are united in heart and doctrine, in mind and in judgment, in all that affects the unity of the faith; and it is at such a

* In a publication put forth nearly seven years ago, His Eminence says:—"From early youth I have grown up under the very shadow of the Apostolic Chair; week after week I have knelt at the shrine of Peter and there sworn him fealty; I have served, as good masters, successive Pontiffs, in their very households, and have been admitted to confidence, and if I dare say it, friendship by them. The *second* altar at which I knelt, in the holy city, was that which marks the spot whereon St. Peter cemented the foundations of his unfailing throne with his blood. The *first* was that of our own glorious S Thomas. There I returned thanks for the great blessing of being admitted among his children. For two and twenty years I daily knelt before the lively representation of his martyrdom; at that altar I partook ever of the bread of life; there for the first time I celebrated the Divine Mysteries; at it I received the episcopal consecration. He was my patron, he my father, he my model. Daily have I prayed and do pray to him to give me his spirit of fortitude, to fight the battles of the Church, if necessary unto the shedding of blood. And when withdrawn from the symbols of his patronage, by the supreme will of the late Pontiff, I sought the treasury of his relics at Sens, and obtained the mitre which had crowned his martyred head." These words have acquired a fresh interest since the writer's elevation to the Cardinalate, and to the first place in our new Hierarchy, which has obtained for him the pallium of St. Augustine and St. Thomas.

time that the Church adds a fresh defence to its outworks by the definition of last Advent.

"O thou lamp most bright," exclaims St. Thomas of Valentia, whose words occur in the new Office of the Immaculate Conception—"to how many didst thou bring joy when, glowing with the light of Deity, thou wast conceived Immaculate in thy mother's womb. Thy Conception, O Virgin Mother of God, was the herald of joy to the universal world. With reason did the chief minstrel of the Divine nuptials, gazing from afar upon thy rising, exclaim, 'Who is this that cometh forth as the aurora, fair as the moon, elect as the sun, terrible as an army in array?' Well did thy coming into the world, O Mary, resemble the approach of radiant morn, for being enveloped in the resplendency of the true Sun, thou wast Immaculate in thy Conception. . . . . Thou art called 'fair as the moon,' and with good reason, for of all luminaries the moon most resembles the sun; and thou, like her, lovely in thy brightness, and glowing amid the thousand stars that encircle the throne of God, outshinest them all in the glorious and manifold purity of thy rays. Fair thou art as the moon, yea, and much more fair, because thou art all fair, because thou art free from the faintest shadow of either actual or original sin. Thou art 'elect as the Sun.' The Sun, that is to say, Christ, the Creator of the natural sun, is elect among the thousands of mankind—thou among the thousands of womankind. Thou art 'terrible as an army in battle array.' For how must the princes of darkness have trembled when they saw a Woman advancing against them, conceived beyond all precedent immaculately, and invested with powers never yet given to mortals!"

A colossal statue, representing the Immaculate Virgin, and in commemoration of the great event of last December, will be erected on the Piazza di Spagna, in front of the Palace of the Propaganda, to be cast in bronze in the capital of Bavaria, so renowned for works of art. It will be placed on a magnificent antique column, which, to the great joy of the city, has already been removed to the place where it is to be erected. The entire monument, including the pedestal, will be about eighty feet in height, and will overlook the Piazza di Spagna.

✠ Laus Deo.

SANCTISSIMI DOMINI NOSTRI PII DIVINA PROVIDENTIA PAPÆ IX. LITTERÆ APOSTOLICÆ DE DOGMATICA DEFINITIONE IMMACULATÆ CONCEPTIONIS VIRGINIS DEIPARÆ.

Pius Episcopus, Servus servorum Dei.

Ad Perpetuam rei Memoriam.

INEFFABILIS Deus, cujus viae misericordia et veritas, cujus voluntas omnipotentia, et cujus sapientia attingit a fine usque ad finem fortiter et disponit omnia suaviter, cum ab omni aeternitate praeviderit luctuosissimam totius humani generis ruinam ex Adami transgressione derivandam, atque in mysterio a saeculis abscondito primum suae bonitatis opus decreverit per Verbi incarnationem sacramento occultiore complere, ut contra misericors suum propositum homo diabolicae iniquitatis versutia actus in culpam non periret, et quod in primo Adamo casurum erat, in secundo felicius erigeretur, ab initio et ante saecula Unigenito Filio suo matrem, ex qua caro factus in beata temporum plenitudine nasceretur, elegit atque ordinavit, tantoque prae creaturis universis est prosequutus amore, ut in illa una sibi propensissima voluntate complacuerit. Quapropter illam longe ante omnes Angelicos Spiritus, cunctosque Sanctos caelestium omnium charismatum copia de thesauro divinitatis deprompta ita mirifice cumulavit, ut Ipsa ab omni prorsus peccati labe semper libera, ac tota pulchra et perfecta eam innocentiae et sanctitatis plenitudinem prae se ferret, qua major sub Deo

LETTERS APOSTOLIC OF OUR MOST HOLY LORD PIUS IX., BY DIVINE PROVIDENCE POPE, CONCERNING THE DOGMATIC DEFINITION OF THE IMMACULATE CONCEPTION OF THE VIRGIN MOTHER OF GOD.

Pius, Bishop, Servant of the servants of God.

For a perpetual remembrance.

THE Ineffable God, whose ways are mercy and truth, whose will is omnipotence, and whose wisdom reaches powerfully from end to end, and sweetly disposes all things, when He foresaw from all eternity the most sorrowful ruin of the entire human race to follow from the transgression of Adam, and in a mystery hidden from ages determined to complete, through the Incarnation of the Word, in a more hidden sacrament, the first work of His goodness; so that man, led into sin by the craft of diabolical iniquity, should not perish contrary to His merciful design; and that what was about to befall in the first Adam should be restored more happily in the Second;—from the beginning and before ages chose and ordained a Mother for His only-begotten Son, of whom made flesh, He should be born in the blessed plenitude of time, and He loved Her above all other creatures, and in Her alone He pleased Himself with a most benign complacency. Wherefore, far before all the Angelic Spirits and all the Saints, He so wonderfully endowed Her with the abundance of all the heavenly gifts drawn from the treasure of divinity, that She might be ever free from every stain of sin, and all fair and

nullatenus intelligitur, et quam praeter Deum nemo assequi cogitando potest. Et quidem decebat omnino, ut perfectissimae sanctitatis splendoribus semper ornata fulgeret, ac vel ab ipsa originalis culpae labe plane immunis amplissimum de antiquo serpente triumphum referret tam venerabilis mater, cui Deus Pater unicum Filium suum, quem de corde suo aequalem sibi genitum tam quam seipsum diligit, ita dare disposuit, ut naturaliter esset unus idemque communis Dei Patris, et Virginis Filius, et quam ipse Filius substantialiter facere sibi matrem elegit, et de qua Spiritus Sanctus voluit, et operatus est, ut conciperetur et nasceretur ille, de quo ipse procedit.

Quam originalem augustae Virginis innocentiam cum admirabili ejusdem sanctitate, praecelsaque Dei Matris dignitate omnino cohaerentem catholica Ecclesia, quae a Sancto semper edocta Spiritu columna est ac firmamentum veritatis, tamquam doctrinam possidens divinitus acceptam, et caelestis revelationis deposito comprehensam multiplici continenter ratione, splendidisque factis magis in dies explicare, proponere, ac fovere nunquam destitit. Hanc enim doctrinam ab antiquissimis temporibus vigentem, ac fidelium animis penitus insitam, et Sacrorum Antistitum curis studiisque per catholicum orbem mirifice propagatam ipsa Ecclesia luculentissime significavit, cum ejusdem Virginis Conceptionem publico fidelium cultui ac venerationi proponere non dubitavit. Quo illustri quidem facto ipsius Virginis Conceptionem veluti singularem, miram, et a reliquorum hominum primordiis longissime secretam, et omnino sanctam colendam exhibuit, cum Ecclesia nonnisi de Sanctis dies festos concelebret. Atque idcirco vel ipsissima verba, quibus divinae Scripturae de increata Sapientia loquuntur, ejusque sempiternas origines repraesentant, consuevit tum in ecclesiasticis

perfect, and might possess that plenitude of innocence and holiness than which, under God, none is greater, and which, except God, no one can reach even in thought. And indeed it was most becoming that She should be always adorned with the splendour of the most perfect holiness, and free even from the very stain of original sin, should gain a most complete triumph over the ancient serpent,—the Mother so venerable, to whom God the Father gave His only Son, whom begotten and equal to Himself He loved as Himself, in such a manner that He would be by nature One and the Same common Son of God the Father, and of the Virgin, and whom the Son himself chose to make substantially His Mother, and from whom the Holy Ghost willed and operated that He would be conceived and born from whom He himself proceeds.

Which original innocence of the august Virgin agreeing completely with her admirable holiness, and with the most excellent dignity of the Mother of God, the Catholic Church, which, ever taught by the Holy Spirit, is the pillar and ground of Truth, as possessing a doctrine divinely received, and comprehended in the deposit of heavenly revelation, has never ceased to lay down, to cherish, and to illustrate continually by numerous proofs, and daily more and more by splendid facts. For this doctrine, flourishing from the most ancient times, and implanted in the minds of the Faithful, and by the care and zeal of the holy Pontiffs wonderfully propagated, the Church herself has most clearly pointed out when she did not hesitate to propose the Conception of the same Virgin for the public devotion and veneration of the Faithful. By which illustrious act she pointed out the Conception of the Virgin as singular, wonderful, and very far removed from the origin of the rest of mankind, and to be venerated as entirely holy, since the Church celebrates festival days only of what is holy. And, therefore, the very words in which the Sacred Scriptures speak of the Uncreated

officiis, tum in sacrosancta Liturgia adhibere, et ad illius Virginis primordia transferre, quae uno eodemque decreto cum Divinae Sapientiae incarnatione fuerant praestituta.

Quamvis autem haec omnia penes fideles ubique prope recepta ostendant, quo studio ejusmodi de Immaculata Virginis Conceptione doctrinam ipsa quoque Romana Ecclesia omnium Ecclesiarum mater et magistra fuerit prosequuta, tamen illustria hujus Ecclesiae facta digna plane sunt, quae nominatim recenseantur, cum tanta sit ejusdem Ecclesiae dignitas, atque auctoritas, quanta illi omnino debetur, quae est Catholicae veritatis et unitatis centrum, in qua solum inviolabiliter fuit custodita religio, et ex qua traducem fidei reliquae omnes Ecclesiae mutuentur oportet. Itaque eadem Romana Ecclesia nihil potius habuit, quam eloquentissimis quibusque modis Immaculatam Virginis Conceptionem, ejusque cultum et doctrinam asserere, tueri, promovere et vindicare. Quod apertissime planissimeque testantur et declarant tot insignia sane acta Romanorum Pontificum Decessorum Nostrorum, quibus in persona Apostolorum Principis ab ipso Christo Domino divinitus fuit commissa suprema cura atque potestas pascendi agnos et oves, confirmandi fratres, et universam regendi et gubernandi Ecclesiam.

Enimvero Praedecessores Nostri vehementer gloriati sunt Apostolica sua auctoritate festum Conceptionis in Romana Ecclessia instituere, ac proprio officio, propriaque missa, quibus praerogativa immunitatis ab hereditaria labe manifestissime asserebatur, augere, honestare, et cultum jam institutum omni ope promovere, amplificare sive erogatis indulgentiis, sive facultate tributa civitatibus, provinciis, regnisque, ut Deiparam sub titulo Immaculatae Conceptionis patronam sibi deligerent, sive comprobatis Sodalitatibus, Congrega-

Wisdom and represent His eternal origin, she has been accustomed to use not only in the offices of the Church, but also in the holy Liturgy, and to apply to the origin of that Virgin, who was preordained by one and the same decree with the incarnation of the Divine Wisdom.

But though all these things everywhere justly received amongst the Faithful show with what zeal the Roman Church, the Mother and Mistress of all Churches, has supported the doctrine of the Immaculate Conception of the Virgin, yet the illustrious acts of this Church are evidently worthy that they should be reviewed by name; since, so great is the dignity and authority of the same Church, and so much due to her who is the centre of Catholic Truth and Unity, in whom alone religion has been inviolably guarded, and from whom it is right that all the Churches should receive the tradition of Faith. Thus the same Roman Church had nothing more at heart than to assert, to protect, to promote, and to vindicate in the most eloquent manner the Immaculate Conception of the Virgin, its devotion, and doctrine, which fact so many illustrious acts of the Roman Pontiffs, Our predecessors, most evidently and fully testify and declare, to whom in the person of the Prince of the Apostles was divinely committed by Christ our Lord the supreme care and power of feeding the lambs and sheep, of confirming the brethren, and of ruling and governing the universal Church.

Indeed, Our predecessors vehemently gloried to institute in the Roman Church by their own Apostolic authority the Feast of the Conception, and to augment, ennoble, and promote with all their power the devotion thus instituted, by a proper Office and Mass, by which the prerogative of immunity from hereditary stain was most manifestly asserted; and to increase it either by indulgences granted, or by leave given to states, provinces, and kingdoms, that they might choose as their Patroness the Mother of God, under the title

tionibus, Religiosisque Familiis ad Immaculatae Conceptionis honorem institutis, sive laudibus eorum pietati delatis, qui monasteria xenodochia, altaria, templa sub Immaculati Conceptus titulo erexerint, aut sacramenti religione interposita Immaculatam Deiparae Conceptionem strenue propugnare spoponderint. Insuper summopere laetati sunt decernere Conceptionis festum ab omni Ecclesia esse habendum eodem censu ac numero, quo festum Nativitatis, idemque Conceptionis festum cum octava ab universa Ecclesia celebrandum, et ab omnibus inter ea, quae praecepta sunt, sancte colendum, ac Pontificiam Cappellam in Patriarchali Nostra Liberiana Basilica die Virginis Conceptioni sacro quotannis esse peragendam. Atque exoptantes in fidelium animis quotidie magis fovere hanc de Immaculata Deiparae Conceptione doctrinam, eorumque pietatem excitare ad ipsam Virginem sine labe originali conceptam colendam, et venerandam, gavisi sunt quam libentissime facultatem tribuere, ut in Lauretanis Litaniis, et in ipsa Missae praefatione Immaculatus ejusdem Virginis proclamaretur Conceptus, atque adeo lex credendi ipsa supplicandi lege statueretur. Nos porro tantorum Praedecessorum vestigiis inhaerentes non solum quae ab ipsis pientissime sapientissimeque fuerant constituta probavimus, et recepimus, verum etiam memores institutionis Sixti IV., proprium de Immaculata Conceptione officium auctoritate Nostra munivimus, illusque usum universae Ecclesiae laetissimo prorsus animo concessimus

Quoniam vero quae ad cultum pertinent, intimo plane vinculo cum ejusdem objecto conserta sunt, neque rata et fixa manere possunt, si illud anceps sit, et in ambiguo versetur, idcirco Decessores Nostri Romani Pontifices omni cura Conceptionis cultum amplificantes, illius etiam objec-

of Her Immaculate Conception; or by approved sodalities, congregations, and religious societies, instituted in honour of the Immaculate Conception; or by praises given to the piety of those who have erected monasteries, hospitals, or churches, under the title of the Immaculate Conception, or who have bound themselves by a religious vow to defend strenuously the Immaculate Conception of the Mother of God. Above all, they were happy to ordain that the Feast of the Conception should be celebrated through the whole Church as that of the Nativity; and, in fine, that it should be celebrated with an Octave in the universal Church, and be placed in the rank of the festivals which are commanded to be kept holy by all; also that a Pontifical function should be celebrated yearly in Our Patriarchal Liberian Basilica on the day sacred to the Conception of the Virgin; desiring to cherish daily more and more in the minds of the Faithful this doctrine of the Immaculate Conception of the Mother of God, and to excite their piety to the worship and veneration of the Virgin conceived without original sin, they have gladly given leave that in the Litany of Loretto and in the Preface of the Mass itself should be proclaimed the Immaculate Conception of the same Virgin, and that thus the law of faith should be established by the law of prayer. We ourselves, treading in the footsteps of so many Predecessors, have not only received and approved what had been most wisely and piously established and appointed by them, but also, mindful of the institution of Sixtus IV., We have appointed by Our authority a proper Office of the Immaculate Conception, and with a most joyful mind have granted the use of it to the universal Church.

But since those things which pertain to worship are evidently bound by an intimate chord to its object, and cannot remain fixed and determined, if that be doubtful, and remain in uncertainty, Our predecessors the Roman Pontiffs, increasing with all their care the devotion of the Conception,

tum ac doctrinam declarare, et inculcare, impensissime studuerunt. Etenim clare aperteque docuere, festum agi de Virginis Conceptione, atque uti falsam, et ab Ecclesiae mente alienissimam proscripserunt illorum opinionem, qui non Conceptionem ipsam, sed sanctificationem ab Ecclesia coli arbitrarentur et affirmarent. Neque mitius cum iis agendum esse existimarunt, qui ad labefactandam de Immaculata Virginis Conceptione, doctrinam excogitato inter primum atque alterum Conceptionis instans et momentum discrimine, asserebant, celebrari quidem Conceptionem, sed non pro primo instanti atque momento. Ipsi namque Praedecessores Nostri suarum partium esse duxerunt, et beatissimae Virginis Conceptionis festum, et Conceptionem pro primo instanti tanquam verum cultus objectum omni studio tueri ac propugnare. Hinc decretoria plane verba quibus Alexander VII. Decessor Noster sinceram Ecclesiae mentem declaravit, inquiens:—"Sane vetus est Christifidelium erga ejus beatissimam Matrem Virginem Mariam pietas sentientium, ejus animam in primo instanti creationis, atque infusionis in corpus fuisse speciali Dei gratia et privilegio, intuitu meritorum Jesu Christi ejus Filii humani generis Redemptoris, a macula peccati originalis, praeservatam immunem, atque in hoc sensu ejus Conceptionis festivitatem solemni ritu colentium, et celebrantium." *

Atque illud in primis solemne quoque fuit iisdem Decessoribus Nostris Doctrinam de Immaculata Dei matris Conceptione sartam tectamque omni cura, studio et contentione tueri. Etenim non solum nullatenus passi sunt, ipsam doctrinam quovis modo a quopiam notari, atque traduci, verum etiam longe ulterius progressi perspicuis declarationibus, iteratisque vicibus edixerunt, doctrinam, qua Immaculatam Virginis Conceptionem profitemur, esse, suoque merito haberi cum ecclesiastico cultu plane consonam, eamque vete-

* Alexander VII. Const. Sollicitudo omnium Ecclesiarum VIII. Decembris, 1661.

studied most especially to declare and inculcate its object and doctrine; for they taught clearly and openly that the festival was celebrated for the Conception of the Virgin, and they condemned as false and most foreign to the intention of the Church the opinion of those who considered and affirmed that it was not the Conception itself but the sanctification, to which devotion was paid by the Church. Nor did they think of treating more leniently those who, in order to weaken the doctrine of the Immaculate Conception, drawing a distinction between the first and second instant of the Conception, asserted that the Conception was, indeed, celebrated, but not its first moment; for Our predecessors themselves thought it their duty to protect and defend with all zeal both the Feast of the Conception of the Most Blessed Virgin, and the Conception at the first instant as the true object of the *cultus*. Hence the words in which Alexander VII. declared the intention of the Church, saying, "Certainly, it is the ancient piety of the Faithful of Christ towards His Most Blessed Mother the Virgin Mary, believing that her soul, in the first instant of its creation and infusion into the body was by a special grace and privilege of God, in virtue of the merits of Jesus Christ her Son the Redeemer of mankind, preserved free from the stain of original sin, and in this sense they keep and celebrate with solemn rite the Festival of Her Conception."

Our predecessors thought it their duty to preserve from contention the doctrine of the Immaculate Conception of the Mother of God; and guarded and protected it with all care and zeal. For not only have they never suffered that this doctrine should be censured or traduced in any way, but they have gone much farther, and in clear declarations on repeated occasions they have proclaimed that the doctrine in which we confess the Immaculate Conception of the Virgin is, of its own merit, to be held in veneration, that it is of ancient and nearly universal belief, which the Roman

rem, ac prope universalem et ejusmodi, quam Romana Ecclesia sibi fovemdam, tuendamque susceperit, atque omnino dignam, quae in sacra ipsa Liturgia, solemnibusque precibus usurparetur. Neque his contenti, ut ipsa de Immaculata Virginis Conceptu doctrina inviolata persisterit, opinionem huic doctrinae adversam sive publice, sive privatim defendi posse severissime prohibuere, eamque multiplici veluti vulnere confectam esse voluerunt. Quibus repetitis luculentissimisque declarationibus, ne inanes viderentur adjecere sanctionem: quae omnia laudatus Praedecessor Noster Alexander VII. his verbis est complexus:—

"Nos considerantes, quod Sancta Romana Ecclesia de Intemeratae semper Virginis Mariae Conceptione festum solemniter celebrat, et speciale ac proprium super hoc officium olim ordinavit juxta piam, devotam, et laudabilem institutionem, quae a Sixto IV. Praedescessore Nostro tunc emanavit; volentesque laudabili huic pietati, devotioni, et festo, ac cultui secundum illam exhibito, in Ecclesia Romana post ipsius cultus institutionem nunquam immutato; Romanorum Pontificum Pradecessorum Nostrorum exemplo, favere nec non tueri pietatem, et devotionem hanc colendi, et celebrandi beatissimam Virginem, praeveniente scilicet Spiritus Sancti gratia, a peccato originali praeservatam, cupientesque in Christi grege unitatem spiritus in vinculo pacis, sedatis, offensionibus, et jurgiis amotisque scandalis conservare: ad praefatorum Episcoporum cum Ecclesiarum suarum Capitulis, ac Philippi Regis, ejusque Regnorum oblatam Noblis instantiam, ac preces; Constitutiones, et Decreta, a Romanis Pontificibus Praedecessoribus Nostris, et praecipue a Sixto IV., Paulo V., et Gregorio XV. edita in favorem sententiae asserentis, Animam beatae Mariae Virginis in sui creatione, et in corpus infusione, Spiritus Sancti gratia donatam, et a peccato originali praeservatam fuisse, nec non et in favorem festi, et cultus Conceptionis ejusdem Virginis Deiparae secundum piam istam sententiam, ut praefertur, exhibiti, innovamus, et

Church has undertaken to cherish and protect, and, above all, worthy to be placed in its sacred liturgy and its solemn prayers. Not content with this, in order that the doctrine of the Immaculate Conception of the Virgin should remain inviolate, they have most severely prohibited the opinion adverse to this doctrine to be defended either in public or in private, and they have wished to destroy it, as it were, by repeated wounds. To which reiterated and most clear declarations, lest they might appear empty, they added a sanction; all which things Our illustrious predecessor, Alexander I., embraced in these words:—

"Considering that the Holy Roman Church solemnly celebrates the Festival of the Conception of the Immaculate and Ever-Blessed Virgin, and has appointed for this a special and proper office according to the pious, devout, and laudable institution which emanated from Our predecessor, Sixtus IV., and wishing after the example of the Roman Pontiffs, Our Predecessors, to favour this laudable piety and devotion, and the reverence shown towards it, in the Roman Church, invariably since the institution of the worship itself; in order also to protect this devout practice of venerating and celebrating the Most Blessed Virgin, preserved from original sin by the preventing grace of the Holy Ghost, and desiring to preserve in the flock of Christ unity of spirit in the bond of peace, removing offences and scandals; at the instance and prayers of the said Bishops, with the Chapters of their Churches, and of King Philip and his kingdom—We renew the constitutions and decrees issued by the Roman Pontiffs, Our predecessors, and especially by Sixtus IV., Paul V., and Gregory XV., in favour of the opinion that the Soul of the Blessed Virgin, in its creation and infusion into the body, was endowed with the grace of the Holy Ghost, and preserved from original sin; likewise, also, in favour of the Festival of the same Virgin Mother of God, celebrated according to that pious belief which is recited above; and

sub censuris, et poenis in eisdem Constitutionibus contentis, observari, mandamus.

"Et insuper omnes et singulos, qui praefatas Constitutiones, seu Decreta ita pergent interpretari, ut favorem per illas dictae sententiae, et festo seu cultui secundum illam exhibito, frustrentur, vel qui hanc eandem sententiam, festum seu cultum in disputationem revocare, aut contra ea quoquo modo directe, vel indirecte aut quovis praetextu, etiam definibilitatis ejus examinandae, sive Sacram Scripturam, aut Sanctos Patres, sive Doctores glossandi vel interpretandi, denique alio quovis praetextu seu occasione, scripto seu voce loqui, concionari, tractare, disputare, contra ea quidquam determinando, aut asserendo, vel argumenta contra ea afferendo, et insoluta relinquendo, aut alio quovis inexcogitabili modo disserendo ausi fuerint; praeter poenas et censuras in Constitutionibus Sixti IV. contentas, quibus illos subjacere volumus, et per praesentes subjicimus, etiam concionandi, publice legendi, seu docendi, et interpretandi facultate, ac voce activa, et passiva in quibuscumque electionibus, eo ipso absque alia declaratione privatos esse volumus; nec non ad concionandum, publice legendum, docendum, et interpretandum perpetuae inhabilitatis poenas ipso facto incurrere absque alia declaratione; a quibus pœnis nonnisi a Nobis ipsis, vel a Successoribus Nostris Romanis Pontificibus absolvi, aut super iis dispensari possint: nec non eosdem aliis poenis, nostro, et eorundem Romanorum Pontificum Successorum Nostrorum arbitrio infligendis, pariter subjacere volumus, prout subjicimus per praesentes, innovantes Pauli V. et Gregorii XV. superius memoratas Constitutiones sive Decreta.

"Ac libros, in quibus praefata sententia, festum, seu cultus secundum illam in dubium revocatur, aut contra ea quomodocumque, ut supra, aliquid scribitur aut legitur, seu locutiones, conciones, tractatus, et disputationes contra eadem continentur; post Pauli V. supra laudatum Decretum edita,

We command that it shall be observed under the censures and penalties contained in the same constitutions.

"And against all and each of those who try to interpret the aforesaid constitutions or decrees, so that they may frustrate the favour shown through these to the said belief, and to the festival or *cultus* celebrated according to it, or who tried to recall into dispute the same belief, festival, or *cultus*, or against these in any manner, either directly or indirectly, and on any pretext, even that of examining the grounds of defining it, or of explaining or interpreting the sacred Scriptures, or the Holy Fathers or Doctors; in fine, who should dare, under any pretext or on any occasion whatsoever, to say either in writing, or by word of mouth to preach, to treat, to dispute, by determining or asserting anything against these, or by bringing arguments against them, and leaving these arguments unanswered, or by expressing dissent in any other possible manner; besides the punishments and censures contained in the constitutions of Sixtus IV., we desire to add, and by these presents do add, that they should be deprived, *ipso facto*, and without other declaration, of the faculty of preaching, of reading in public, or of teaching and interpreting, and also of their voice, whether active or passive, in elections; from which censures they cannot be absolved, nor obtain dispensation, unless from Us or Our successors, the Roman Pontiffs; likewise We wish to subject, and We hereby do subject, the same persons to other penalties to be inflicted at Our will, and at that of the same Roman Pontiffs, Our Successors, renewing the constitutions or decrees of Paul V. and Gregory XV., above mentioned.

"And We prohibit, under the penalties and censures contained in the Index of Prohibited Books, and We will and declare to be esteemed prohibited *ipso facto*, and without other declaration, books in which the aforesaid belief and the festival or devotion celebrated according to it is recalled into

aut in posterum quomodolibet edenda, prohibemus sub poenis et censuris in Indice librorum prohibitorum contentis, et ipso facto absque alia declaratione pro expresse prohibitis haberi volumus et mandamus."

Omnes autem norunt quanto studio haec de Immaculata Deiparae Virginis Conceptione doctrina a spectatissimis Religiosis Familiis, et celebrioribus Theologicis Academiis ac praestantissimis rerum divinarum scientia Doctoribus fuerit tradita, asserta ac propugnata. Omnes pariter norunt quantopere solliciti fuerint Sacrorum Antistites vel in ipsis ecclesiasticis conventibus palam publiceque profiteri, sanctissimam Dei Genitricem Virginem Mariam ob praevisa Christi Domini Redemptoris merita nunquam originali subjacuisse peccato, sed praeservatam omnino fuisse ab originis labe, et idcirco sublimiori modo redemptam. Quibus illud profecto gravissimum, et omnino maximum accedit, ipsam quoque Tridentinam Synodum, cum dogmaticum de peccato originali ederet decretum, quo juxta sacrarum Scripturarum, sanctorumque Patrum, ac probatissimorum Conciliorum testimonia statuit, ac definivit, omnes homines nasci originali culpa infectos, tamen solemniter declarasse, non esse suae intentionis in decreto ipso, tantaque definitionis amplitudine comprehendere beatam, et immaculatam Virginem Dei Genitricem Mariam. Hac enim declaratione Tridentini Patres, ipsam beatissimam Virginem ab originali labe solutam pro rerum temporumque adjunctis satis innuerunt, atque adeo perspicue significarunt, nihil ex divinis litteris, nihil ex traditione, Patrumque auctoritate rite afferri posse, quod tantae Virginis praerogativae quovis modo refragetur.

Et re quidem vera hanc de Immaculata beatissimae Virginis Conceptione doctrinam quotidie magis gravissimo Ecclesiae sensu, magisterio, studio, scientia, ac sapientia tam

dispute, or in which anything whatever is written or read against these, or lectures, sermons, treatises, and disputations against the same, published after the decree above eulogised of Paul V., or to be published at any future time."

All are aware with how much zeal this doctrine of the Immaculate Conception of the Mother of God has been handed down, asserted, and propagated by the most distinguished Religious Orders, the most celebrated theological academies and the most eminent Doctors of the science of Divinity. All know likewise how anxious have been the Bishops openly and publicly to profess, even in the Ecclesiastical assemblies themselves, that the Most Holy Mother of God the Virgin Mary, by virtue of the merits of Christ our Lord, the Saviour of mankind, never lay under original sin, but was preserved free from the stain of guilt, and was thus redeemed in a more sublime manner. To which, lastly, is added this fact, most grave and, in an especial manner, most important of all, that the Council of Trent itself, when it promulgated the dogmatic decree concerning original sin, in which, according to the testimonies of the Sacred Scriptures, of the Holy Fathers, and of the most approved councils, it determined and defined that all mankind are born under original sin; solemnly declared, however, that it was not its intention to include in the decree itself, and in the amplitude of its definition, the Blessed and Immaculate Virgin Mary, Mother of God. Indeed, by this declaration, the Tridentine Fathers have asserted, according to the times and the circumstances of affairs, that the Blessed Virgin Mary was free from the original stain, and thus clearly signified that nothing could be justly adduced from the sacred writings, nor from the authority of the Fathers, which would in any way gainsay so great a prerogative of the Virgin.

And, in truth, illustrious monuments of a venerated antiquity of the Eastern and of the Western Church most powerfully testify that this doctrine of the Immaculate Conception

splendide explicatam, declaratam, confirmatam, et apud omnes catholici orbis populos, ac nationes mirandum in modum propagatam, in ipsa Ecclesia semper extitisse veluti a majoribus acceptam, ac revelatae doctrinae charactere insignitam illustria venerandae antiquitatis Ecclesiae orientalis et occidentalis monumenta validissime testantur. Christi enim Ecclesia sedula depositorum apud se dogmatum custos, et vindex nihil in his unquam permutat, nihil minuit, nihil addit, sed omni industria vetera fideliter, sapienterque tractando si qua antiquitus informata sunt, et Patrum fides sevit, ita limare, expolire studet, ut prisca illa caelestis doctrinae dogmata accipiant evidentiam, lucem, distinctionem, sed retineant plenitudinem, integritatem, proprietatem, ac in suo tantum genere crescant, in eodem scilicet dogmate, eodem sensu, eademque sententia.

Equidem Patres, Ecclesiaeque Scriptores caelestibus edocti eloquiis nihil antiquius habuere, quam in libris ad explicandas Scripturas, vindicanda dogmata, erudiendosque fideles elucubratis summam Virginis sanctitatem, dignitatem, atque ab omni peccati labe integritatem, ejusque praeclaram de teterrimo humani generis hoste victoriam multis mirisque modis certatim praedicare atque efferre. Quapropter enarrantes verba, quibus Deus praeparata renovandis mortalibus suae pietatis remedia inter ipsa mundi primordia praenuntians et deceptoris serpentis retudit audaciam, et nostri generis spem mirifice erexit inquiens "Inimicitias ponam inter te et mulierem, semen tuum et semen illius" docuere, divino hoc oraculo clare aperteque praemonstratum fuisse misericordem humani generis Redemptorem, scilicet Unigenitum Dei Filium Christum Jesum, ac designatam beatissimam Ejus Matrem Virginem Mariam, ac simul ipsissimas utriusque contra diabolum inimicitias insigniter expressas. Quocirca sicut Christus Dei hominumque mediator humana assumpta natura delens quod adversus nos erat chirographum decreti, illud cruci triumphator affixit, sic sanctissima Virgo arctis-

of the Most Blessed Virgin, every day more and more so splendidly explained and confirmed by the highest authority, teaching, zeal, science, and wisdom of the Church, and so wonderfully propagated amongst all the nations and peoples of the Catholic world, always existed in the Church as received from Our ancestors, and stamped with the character of a Divine revelation. For the Church of Christ, careful guardian and defender of the dogmas deposited with her, changes nothing in them, diminishes nothing, adds nothing, but with all industry, by faithfully and wisely treating ancient things, so studies to limit and perfect their expression, that these ancient dogmas of heavenly faith may receive evidence, light, distinction, but may still retain their fulness, integrity, and propriety, and may increase only in their own kind, that is, in the same sense, and the same belief.

The Fathers and writers of the Church, taught by the heavenly writings, had nothing more at heart, in the books written to explain the Scriptures, to vindicate the dogmas, and to instruct the Faithful, than emulously to declare and exhibit in many and wonderful ways the Virgin's most high sanctity, dignity, and freedom from all stain of original sin, and Her renowned victory over the most foul enemy of the human race. Wherefore, repeating the words in which, at the beginning of the world, the Almighty, announcing the remedies of His mercy, prepared for regenerating mankind, crushed the audacity of the lying serpent, and wonderfully raised up the hope of our race, saying—"I will place enmity between thee and the Woman, thy seed and hers," they taught that in this Divine oracle was clearly and openly pointed out the merciful Redeemer of the human race—the only-begotten Son of God, Christ Jesus, and that his Most Blessed Mother, the Virgin Mary, was designated, and at the same time that the enmity of both against the serpent was signally expressed. Wherefore, as Christ, the Mediator of God and men, having assumed human nature, blotting out

simo, et indissolubile vinculo cum Eo conjuncta una cum Illo, et per Illum sempiternas contra venenosum serpentem inimicitias exercens, ac de ipso plenissime triumphans illius caput immaculato pede contrivit.

Hunc eximium, singularemque Virginis triumphum, excellentissimamque innocentiam, puritatem, sanctitatem ejusque ab omni peccati labe integritatem, atque ineffabilem caelestium omnium gratiarum, virtutum, ac privilegiorum copiam, et magnitudinem iidem Patres viderunt tum in arca illa Noe, quae divinitus constituta a communi totius mundi naufragio plane salva et incolumis evasit; tum in scala illa, quam de terra ad coelum usque pertingere vidit Jacob, cujus gradibus Angeli Dei ascendebant, et descendebant, cujusque vertici ipse innitebatur Dominus; tum in rubo illo, quem in loco sancto Moyses undique ardere, ac inter crepitantes ignis flammas non jam comburi aut jacturam vel minimam pati, sed pulchre virescere ac florescere conspexit; tum in illa inexpugnabili turri a facie inimici, ex qua mille clypei pendent, omnisque armatura fortium; tum in horto illo concluso, qui nescit violari, neque corrumpi ullis insidiarum fraudibus; tum in corusca illa Dei civitate, cujus fundamenta in montibus sanctis; tum in augustissimo illo Dei templo, quod divinis refulgens splendoribus plenum est gloria Domini; tum in ais ejusdem generis omnino plurimis, quibus excelsam Deiparae dignitatem, ejusque illibatam innocentiam, et nulli unquam naevo obnoxiam sanctitatem insigniter praenunciatam fuisse Patres tradiderunt.

Ad hanc eandem divinorum munerum veluti summam, originalemque Virginis, de qua natus est Jesus, integritatem describendam iidem Prophetarum adhibentes eloquia non aliter ipsam augustam Virginem concelebrarunt, ac uti columbam mundam, et sanctam Jerusalem, et excelsum Dei thronum, et arcam sanctificationis et domum, quam sibi

the handwriting of the decree which stood against us, fastened it triumphantly to the Cross, so the Most Holy Virgin bound by a most close and indissoluble chain to Him, exercising with Him and through Him eternal enmity against the malignant serpent, and triumphing most amply over the same, has crushed his head with Her immaculate foot.

This illustrious and singular triumph of the Virgin, and Her most exalted innocence, purity, and holiness, Her freedom from all stain of sin, and ineffable abundance of all heavenly graces, virtues, and privileges, the same Fathers beheld in that ark of Noah which, divinely appointed, escaped safe and sound from the common shipwreck of the whole world; also in that ladder which Jacob beheld reaching from earth to Heaven, by whose steps the Angels of God ascended and descended, on whose top leaned God himself; also in that bush which, in the holy place, Moses beheld blaze on every side, and amidst the crackling flames, neither consumed nor suffering the least injury; also in that tower unassailable in the face of an enemy, from which depend a thousand bucklers and all the armour of the brave; also in that garden fenced round about, which cannot be violated nor corrupted by any schemes of fraud; also in that brilliant city of God, whose foundations are in the holy mounts; also in that most august temple of God, which, shining with divine splendour, is filled with the glory of God; likewise in many other things in which the Fathers have handed down, that the exalted dignity of the Mother of God, and her spotless innocence and holiness, obnoxious to blemish, have been signally preannounced.

To describe the same totality, as it were, of Divine gifts, and the original integrity of the Virgin of whom Jesus was born, the same Fathers, using the eloquence of the Prophets, celebrate the august Virgin as the spotless dove, the holy Jerusalem, the exalted throne of God, the ark and house of sanctification, which Eternal Wisdom built for itself; and

aeterna aedificavit Sapientia, et Reginam illam, quae deliciis affluens, et innixa super Dilectum suum ex ore Altissimi prodivit omnino perfecta, speciosa ac penitus cara Deo, et nullo unquam labis naevo maculata. Cum vero ipsi Patres, Ecclesiaeque Scriptores animo menteque reputarent, beatissimam Virginem ab Angelo Gabriele sublimissimam Dei Matris Dignitatem ei nuntiante, ipsius Dei nomine et jussu gratia plenam fuisse nuncupatam docuerunt hac singulari solemnique salutatione nunquam alias audita ostendi, Deiparam fuisse omnium divinarum gratiarum sedem, omnibusque divini Spiritus chatismatibus exornatam, immo eorumdem charismatum infinitum prope thesaurum, abyssumque inexhaustam, adeo ut nunquam maledicto obnoxia, et una cum Filio perpetuae benedictionis particeps ab Elisabeth divino acta Spiritu audire meruerit *benedicta Tu inter mulieres, et benedictus fructus ventris tui.*

Hinc non luculenta minus, quam concors eorundem sententia, gloriosissimam Virginem, cui fecit magna, qui Potens est, ea caelestium, omnium donorum vi, ea gratiae plenitudine, eaque innocentia emicuisse, qua veluti ineffabile Dei miraculum, immo omnium miraculorum apex, ac digna Dei mater extiterit, et ad Deum ipsum pro ratione creatae naturae, quam proxime accedens omnibus, qua humanis, qua angelicis praeconiis celsior evaserit. Atque idcirco ad originalem Dei Genitricis innocentiam, justitiamque vindicandam, non Eam modo cum Heva adhuc virgine, adhuc innocente, adhuc incorrupta, et nondum mortiferis fraudulentissimi serpentis insidiis decepta saepissime contulerunt, verum etiam mira quadam verborum, sententiarumque varietate praetulerunt. Heva enim serpenti misere obsequuta et ab originali excidit innocentia, et illius mancipium evasit, sed beatissima Virgo originale donum jugiter augens, quin serpenti aures unquam praebuerit, illius vim potestatemque virtute divinitus accepta funditus labefactavit.

as that Queen who, abounding in delights and leaning on her beloved, came forth entirely perfect from the mouth of the Most High, fair and most dear to God, and never stained with the least spot. But when the same Fathers and the writers of the Church revolved in their hearts and minds that the Most Blessed Virgin, in the name and by the order of God himself, was proclaimed full of grace by the Angel Gabriel, when announcing Her most sublime dignity of the Mother of God, they taught that, by this singular and solemn salutation, never heard on any other occasion, is shown that the Mother of God is the seat of all Divine graces, and adorned with all the gifts of the Holy Ghost—yea, the infinite storehouse and inexhaustible abyss of the same gifts; so that, never obnoxious to an evil word, and alone with her Son partaker of perpetual benediction, She deserved to hear from Elizabeth, inspired by the Holy Ghost, "Blessed art thou amongst women, and blessed is the Fruit of thy womb."

Hence it is the clear and unanimous opinion of the same that the Most Glorious Virgin, for whom He who is powerful has done great things, has shone with such a brilliancy of all heavenly gifts, such fulness of grace and such innocence, that She has been an ineffable miracle of the Almighty, yea, the crown of all miracles, and worthy Mother of God; that She approaches as nearly to God as created nature can do, and is exalted above all human and angelic eulogies.

And therefore, to vindicate the original innocence and justice of the Mother of God, they not only compared Her to Eve as yet virgin, as yet innocent, as yet incorrupt, and not yet deceived by the deadly snares of the most treacherous serpent, but they have extolled Her with a wonderful variety of thought and expression. For Eve, miserably obeying the serpent, fell from original innocence, and became his slave, but the Most Blessed Virgin, continually increasing Her original gift, not only never lent an ear to the serpent, but by a virtue divinely received utterly broke his power.

Quapropter nunquam cessarunt Deiparam appellare vel lilium inter spinas, vel terram omnino intactam, virgineam, illibatam, immaculatam, semper benedictam, et ab omni peccati contagione liberam, ex qua novus formatus est Adam, vel irreprehensibilem, lucidissimum amoenissimumque innocentiae immortalitatis, ac deliciarum paradisum a Deo ipso consitum et ab omnibus venenosi serpentis insidiis defensum, vel lignum immarcescibile, quod peccati vermis nunquam corruperit, vel fontem semper illimem, et Spiritus Sancti virtute signatum, vel divinissimum templum, vel immortalitatis thesaurum, vel unam et solam non mortis sed vitae filiam, non irae sed gratiae germen, quod semper virens ex corrupta infectaque radice singulari Dei providentia praeter statas communesque leges efloruerit. Sed quasi haec, licet splendidissima, satis non forent, propriis definitisque sententiis edixerunt nullam prorsus, cum de peccatis agitur, habendam esse quaestionem de sancta Virgine Maria, cui plus gratiae collatum fuit ad vincendum omni ex parte peccatum; tum professi sunt, gloriossimam Virginem fuisse parentum reparatricem, posterorum vivificatricem a saeculo electam, ab Altissimo sibi praeparatam, a Deo, quando ad serpentem ait, inimicitias ponam inter te et mulierem, praedictam, quae procul dubio venenatum ejusdem serpentis caput contrivit; ac propterea affirmarunt, eandem beatissimam Virginem fuisse per gratiam ab omni peccati labe integram, ac liberam ab omni contagione et corporis, et animae, et intellectus, ac semper cum Deo conversatam, et sempiterno foedere cum Illo conjunctam, nunquam fuisse in tenebris, sed semper in luce et idcirco idoneum plane extitisse Christo habitaculum non pro habitu corporis, sed pro gratia originali.

Accedunt nobilissima effata, quibus de Virginis Conceptione loquentes testati sunt, naturam gratiae cessisse ac stetisse tremulam pergere non sustinentem; nam futurum erat, ut

Wherefore, they have never ceased to call the Mother of God the Lily amongst the thorns, ground entirely unbroken, Virgin undefiled, immaculate, ever blessed, and free from all contagion of sin, from whom was formed the new Adam, a reproachless, most sweet paradise of innocence, immortality, and delights planted by God Himself, and fenced from all snares of the malignant serpent, incorruptible Branch that the worm of sin hath never injured; Fountain ever clear, and sealed by the virtue of the Holy Ghost, a most Divine Temple, or Treasure of immortality, or the sole and only Daughter not of Death but of Life, the Seed not of enmity but of grace, which, by the singular providence of God, has always flourished, budding from a corrupt and infected root, contrary to the settled and common laws. But as if these encomiums, though most splendid, were not sufficient, they proclaimed in proper and defined opinions that when sin should be treated of, no question should be entertained concerning the Holy Virgin Mary, to whom an abundance of grace was given to conquer sin completely. They also declared that the Most Glorious Virgin was the reparatrix of Her parents, the vivifier of posterity, chosen from the ages, prepared for Himself by the Most High, predicted by God when He said to the serpent, "I will place enmity between thee and the Woman," who undoubtedly has crushed the poisonous head of the same serpent; and therefore they affirm that the same Blessed Virgin was through grace perfectly free from every stain of sin, and from all contagion of body, and soul, and mind, and, always conversant with God and united with Him in an eternal covenant, was never in darkness but always in light, and therefore was plainly a fit habitation for Christ, not on account of Her bodily estate, but on account of original grace.

To these things are added the noble words, in which, speaking of the Conception of the Virgin, they have testified that Nature yielded to Grace and stood trembling, not being

Dei Genetrix Virgo non antea ex Anna conciperetur, quam gratia fructum ederet: concipi siquidem primogenitam oportebat, ex qua concipiendus esset omnis creaturae primogenitus. Testati sunt carnem Virginis ex Adam sumptam maculas Adae non admisisse, ac propterea beatissiman Virginem tabernaculum esse ab ipso Deo creatum, Spiritu Sancto formatum, et purpurae revera operae, quod novus ille Beseleel auro intextum variumque effinxit, eandemque esse meritoque celebrari et illam, quae proprium Dei opus primum extiterit, ignitis maligni telis latuerit, et pulchra natura, ac labis prorsus omnis nescia, tamquam aurora undequaque rutilans in mundum prodiverit in sua Conceptione Immaculata. Non enim decebat, ut illud vas electionis communibus lacesseretur injuriis, quoniam plurimum a ceteris differens, natura communicavit non culpa, immo prorsus decebat ut sicut Unigenitus in coelis patrem habuit, quem Seraphim ter sanctum extollunt, ita matrem haberet in terris, quae nitore sanctitatis nunquam caruerit. Atque haec quidem doctrina adeo majorum mentes, animosque occupavit, ut singularis et omnino mirus penes illos invaluerit loquendi usus, quo Deiparam saepissime compellarunt immaculatam, omnique ex parte immaculatam, innocentem et innocentissimam, illibatam et undequaque illibatam, sanctam et ab omni peccati sorde alienissimam, totam puram, totam intemeratam, ac ipsam prope puritatis et innocentia, formam, pulchritudine pulchriorem, venustate venustiorem, sanctiorem sanctitate, solamque sanctam, purissimamque anima et corpore, que supergressa est omnem integritatem et virginitatem, ac sola tota facta domicilium universarum gratiarum Sanctissimi Spiritus, et quae solo Deo excepto, extitit cunctis superior, et ipsis Cherubim et Seraphim, et omni exercitu Angelorum *natura pulchrior, formosior et sanctior*, cui praedicandae caelestes et terrenae linguae minime sufficiunt. Quem usum ad sanctissimae quoque Liturgiae monumenta atque Ecclesiastica officia sua veluti sponte fuisse traductum, et in illis passim

able to proceed further; for it was to be that the Virgin Mother of God should not be conceived by Anna before grace should bear fruit. For She ought thus to be conceived as the first-born, from whom should be conceived the First-Born of every creature. They have testified that the flesh of the Virgin, taken from Adam, did not admit the stains of Adam, and on this account that the Most Blessed Virgin was the Tabernacle created by God himself, formed by the Holy Spirit, truly enriched with purple which that new Beseleel made, adorned and woven with gold; and that this same Virgin is, and is deservedly, celebrated, as She who was the first and peculiar work of God, concealed from the fiery weapons of evil, fair by nature, and entirely free from all stain, came into the world all shining like the morn in her Immaculate Conception; nor, truly, was it right that this Vessel of Election should be assailed by common injuries, since, differing much from others, she had community with them only in their nature, not in their fault.

Far more, it was right that, as the Only Begotten had a Father in Heaven whom the Seraphim extol as thrice holy, so He should have a Mother on the earth, who never should want the splendour of holiness. And this doctrine, indeed, so filled the minds and souls of our forefathers, that a marvellous and singular form of speech prevailed with them, in which they very frequently called the Mother of God immaculate and entirely immaculate, innocent and most innocent, spotless, holy, and most distant from every stain of sin, all pure, all perfect, the Type and Model of purity and innocence, more beautiful than beauty, more gracious than grace, more holy than holiness, alone holy and most pure in soul and body, who has surpassed all perfectitude and all virginity, and has become the dwelling-place of all the graces of the Most Holy Spirit, and who, God alone excepted, is superior to all, and by nature fairer, more beautiful, and more holy than the Cherubim and Seraphim; She, whom all

recurrere, ampliterque dominari nemo ignorat, cum in illis Deipara invocetur et praedicetur veluti una incorrupta pulchritudinis columba veluti rosa semper vigens, et undequaque purissima, et semper immaculata semperque beata ac celebretur uti innocentia, quae nunquam fuit laesa, et altera Heva quae Emmanuelem peperit.

Nil igitur mirum si de Immaculata Deiparae Virginis Conceptione doctrinam judicio Patrum divinis litteris consignatam, tot gravissimis eorundem testimoniis traditam, tot illustribus venerandae antiquitatis monumentis expressam et celebratam, ac maximo gravissimoque Ecclesiae judicio propositam et confirmatam tanta pietate, religione et amore ipsius Ecclesiae Pastores, populique fideles quotidie magis profiteri sint gloriati, ut nihil iisdem dulcius, nihil carius, quam ferventissimo affectu Deiparam Virginem absque labe originali conceptam ubique colere, venerari, invocare, et praedicare. Quamobrem ab antiquis temporibus Sacrorum Antistites, Ecclesiastici viri regulares Ordines, ac vel ipsi Imperatores et Reges ab hac Apostolica Sede enixe efflagitarunt, ut Immaculata sanctissimae Dei Genetricis Conceptio veluti catholicae fidei dogma definiretur. Quae postulationes hac nostra quoque aetate iteratae fuerunt ac potissimum felicis recordationis Gregorio XVI. Praedecessori Nostro, ac Nobis ipsis oblatae sunt, tum ab Episcopis, tum a Clero saeculari, tum a Religiosis, Familiis, ac summis Principibus et fidelibus populis.

Nos itaque singulari animi Nostri gaudio haec omnia probe noscentes, ac serio considerantes, vix dum licet immeriti arcano divinae Providentiae consilio ad hanc sublimem Petri Cathedram evecti totius Ecclesiae gubernacula tractanda

the tongues of Heaven and earth do not suffice to extol. No one is ignorant that these forms of speech have passed, as it were, spontaneously into the monuments of the most holy Liturgy, and the Offices of the Church, and that they occur often in them; since the Mother of God is invoked and named in them as a spotless Dove of beauty, as a Rose ever blooming and perfectly pure, ever spotless and ever blessed, and is celebrated as Innocence which was never wounded, and a second Eve who brought forth Emmanuel.

It is no wonder, then, if the Pastors of the Church and the faithful people have daily more and more gloried to profess with so much piety and fervour this doctrine of the Immaculate Conception of the Virgin Mother of God, pointed out in the Sacred Scriptures, according to the judgment of the Fathers, handed down in so many mighty testimonies of the same, expressed and celebrated in so many illustrious monuments of revered antiquity, and proposed, and with great piety confirmed by the greatest and highest judgment of the Church; so that nothing would be more dear or more pleasing to the same than everywhere to venerate, invoke, and proclaim the Virgin Mother of God conceived without original stain. Wherefore from the ancient times the Princes of the Church, Ecclesiastics, and even emperors and kings themselves, have earnestly entreated of this Apostolic See that the Immaculate Conception of the Most Holy Mother of God should be defined as a dogma of Catholic faith. Which entreaties were renewed also in these Our times, and especially were addressed to Gregory XVI., Our predecessor of happy memory, and to Ourselves, not only by Bishops, but by the Secular Clergy, Religious Orders, and the greatest princes and faithful peoples.

Therefore with singular joy of mind, well knowing all these things, and seriously considering them, scarcely had We, though unworthy, been raised by a mysterious dispensation of Divine Providence to the exalted Chair of Peter,

suscepimus, nihil certe antiquius habuimus, quam pro summa Nostra vel a teneris annis erga sanctissimam Dei Genetricem Virginem Mariam veneratione, pietate et affectu ea omnia peragere, quae adhuc in Ecclesiae votis esse poterant, ut beatissimae Virginis honor augeretur, ejusque praerogativae uberiori luce niterent. Omnem autem maturitatem adhibere volentes constituimus peculiarem VV. FF. NN. S. R. E. Cardinalium religione, consilio, ac divinarum rerum scientia illustrium Congregationem, et viros ex clero tum saeculari, tum regulari, theologicis disciplinis apprime excultos selegimus, ut ea omnia, quae Immaculatam Virginis Conceptionem respiciunt, accuratissime perpenderent, propriamque sententiam ad Nos deferrent. Quamvis autem Nobis ex receptis postulationibus de definienda tandem aliquando Immaculata Virginis Conceptione perspectus esset plurimorum Sacrorum Antistitum sensus, tamen Encyclicas Litteras die 2 Februarii anno 1849 Cajetae datas ad omnes Venerabiles Fratres totius catholici orbis Sacrorum Antistites misimus, ut, adhibitis ad Deum precibus, Nobis scripto etiam significarent, quae esset suorum fidelium erga Immaculatam Deiparae Conceptionem pietas, ac devotio, et quid ipse praesertim Antistites de hac ipsa definitione ferenda sentirent, quidve exoptarent, ut, quo fieri solemnius posset, supremum Nostrum judicium proferremus.

Non mediocri certe solatio affecti fuimus ubi eorundem Venerabilium Fratrum ad Nos responsa venerunt. Nam iidem incredibili quadam jucunditate, laetitia, ac studio Nobis rescribentes non solum singlarem suam, et proprii cujusque cleri, populique fidelis erga Immaculatum beatissimae Virginis Conceptum pietatem, mentemque denuo confirmarunt, verum etiam communi vel uti voto a Nobis expostularunt, ut

and undertaken the government of the whole Church, than, following the veneration, the piety, and love We had entertained for the Blessed Virgin from Our tender years, We had nothing at heart more than to accomplish all these things which as yet were amongst the ardent wishes of the Church, that the honour of the Most Blessed Virgin should be increased, and her prerogatives should shine with a fuller light. But wishing to bring to this full maturity We appointed a special congregation of our Venerable Brethren the Cardinals of the Holy Roman Church, illustrious by their piety, their wisdom, and their knowledge of the sacred sciences, and we also selected Ecclesiastics, both Secular and Regular, well trained in theological studies, most carefully to weigh all those things which relate to the Immaculate Conception of the Virgin, and report to us their opinion. And, although from the entreaties lately received by us for at length defining the Immaculate Conception of the Virgin, the opinions of most of the Bishops of the Church were understood; yet We sent Encyclical Letters, dated at Gaeta, the 2nd day of February, in the year 1849, to all our Venerable Brethren the Bishops of the Catholic world, in order that having offered prayers to God they might signify to Us, in writing, what was the piety and devotion of their flocks towards the Immaculate Conception of the Mother of God, and especially what the Bishops themselves thought about promulgating the Definition, or what they desired, in order that We might pronounce Our supreme judgment as solemnly as possible.

Certainly we were filled with no slight consolation when the replies of our Venerable Brethren came to Us. For, with an incredible joyfulness, gladness, and zeal, they not only confirmed their own singular piety, and that of their Clergy and faithful people, towards the Immaculate Conception of the Most Blessed Virgin, but they even entreated of Us with a common voice that the Immaculate Conception of

Immaculata ipsius Virginis Conceptio supremo Nostro judicio et auctoritate definiretur. Nec minori certe interim gaudio perfusi, sumus, cum VV. FF. NN. S. R. E. Cardinales commemoratae peculiaris Congregationis, et praedicti Theologi Consultores a Nobis electi pari alacritate et studio post examen diligenter adhibitum hanc de Immaculata Deiparae Conceptione definitionem a Nobis efflagitaverint.

Post haec illustribus Praedecessorum Nostrorum vestigiis inhaerentes, ac rite recteque precedere optantes, indiximus et habuimus Consistorium, in quo Venerabiles Fratres Nostros Sanctae Romanae Ecclesiae Cardinales alloquuti sumus, eosque summa animi Nostri consolatione audivimus a Nobis exposcere, ut dogmaticam de Immaculata Deiparae Virginis Conceptione definitionem emittere vellemus.

Itaque plurimum in Domino confisi advenisse temporum opportunitatem pro Immaculata sanctissimae Dei Genetricis Virginis Mariae Conceptione definienda, quam divina eloquia, veneranda traditio, perpetuus Ecclesiae sensus, singularis catholicorum Antistitum, ac fidelium conspiratio et insignia Praedecessorum Nostrorum acta, constitutiones mirifice illustrant atque declarant; rebus omnibus diligentissime perpensis et assiduis, fervidisque ad Deum precibus effusis minime cunctandum Nobis esse censuimus supremo Nostro judicio Immaculatam ipsius Virginis Conceptionem sancire, definire, atque ita pientissimis catholici orbis desideriis, Nostraeque in ipsam sanctissimam Virginem pietati satisfacere, ac simul in Ipsa Unigenitum Filium suum Dominum Nostrum Jesum Christum magis atque magis honorificare, cum in Filium redundet quidquid honoris et laudis in Matrem impenditur.

Quare postquam nunquam intermisimus in humilitate et jejunio privatas Nostras et publicas Ecclesiae preces Deo Patri per Filium Ejus offerre, ut Spiritus Sancti virtute mentem Nostram dirigere, et confirmare dignaretur, im-

the Virgin should be defined by Our supreme judgment and authority. Nor, indeed, were We filled with less joy when our Venerable Brethren of Our Holy Roman Church, the Cardinals of the Special Congregation aforesaid, and the consulting Theologians chosen by Us, after a diligent examination demanded of Us with equal alacrity and zeal this definition of the Immaculate Conception of the Mother of God.

Afterwards treading in the illustrious footsteps of Our Predecessors, and desiring to proceed duly and properly, We proclaimed and held a Consistory, in which We addressed Our Brethren, the Cardinals of the Holy Roman Church, and with the greatest consolation of mind We heard them entreat of Us that We should promulgate the dogmatic definition of the Immaculate Conception of the Virgin Mother of God.

Therefore, having full trust in the Lord that the fitting time had now come for defining the Immaculate Conception of the Virgin Mary, Mother of God, which the Divine words, venerable tradition, the perpetual opinion of the Church, the singular agreement of Catholic Prelates and Faithful, and the signal acts and constitutions of Our predecessors wonderfully illustrate and proclaim; having most diligently weighed all things, and poured forth to God assiduous and fervent prayers, We resolved that we would no longer delay to sanction and define, by Our supreme authority, the Immaculate Conception of the Virgin, and thus to satisfy the most pious desires of the Catholic world and Our own piety towards the Most Holy Virgin, and, at the same time, to honour more and more the Only-Begotten Son, Jesus Christ Our Lord, since whatever honour and praise is given to the Mother redounds to the Son.

Wherefore, after We had unceasingly, in humility and fasting, offered Our own prayers and the public prayers of the Church to God the Father, through His Son, that He would deign to direct and confirm Our mind by the power of

plorato universae caelestis Curiae praesidio, et advocato cum gemitibus Paraclito Spiritu, eoque sic adspirante, ad honorem Sanctae et Individuae Trinitatis, ad decus et ornamentum Virginis Deiparae, ad exaltationem Fidei catholicae, et Christianae Religionis augmentum, auctoritate Domini Nostri Jesu Christi, beatorum Apostolorum Petri, et Pauli ac Nostri declaramus, pronunciamus et definimus, doctrinam, quae tenet, beatissimam Virginem Mariam in primo instanti suae Conceptionis fuisse singulari omnipotentis Dei gratia et privilegio, intuitu meritorum Christi Jesu Salvatoris humani generis, ab omni originalis culpae labe praeservatam immunem, esse a Deo revelatam, atque idcirco ab omnibus fidelibus firmiter constanterque credendam. Quapropter si qui secus ac a Nobis definitum est, quod Deus avertat, praesumpserint corde sentire, ii noverint, ac porro sciant, se proprio judicio condemnatos, naufragium circa fidem passos esse, et ab unitate Ecclesiae defecisse, ac praeterea facto ipso suo semet poenis a jure statutis subjicere si quod corde sentiunt, verbo aut scripto, vel alio quovis externo modo significare ausi fuerint.

Repletum quidem est gaudio os Nostrum et lingua Nostra exultatione, atque humillimas maximasque Christo Jesu Domino Nostro agimus et semper agemus gratias, quod singulari suo beneficio nobis licet immerentibus concesserit hunc honorem atque hanc gloriam et laudem sanctissimae suae Matri offerre et decernere. Certissima vero spe et omni prorsus fiducia nitimur fore, ut ipsa beatissima Virgo, quae tota pulchra et Immaculata venenosum crudelissimi serpentis caput contrivit, et salutem attulit mundo, quaeque Prophetarum, Apostolorumque praeconium, et honor Martyrum, omniumque Sanctorum laetitia et corona, quaeque tutissimum cunctorum periclitantium perfugium, et fidissima auxiliatrix, ac totius terrarum orbis potentissima apud Uni-

the Holy Ghost, and having implored the aid of the entire Heavenly Host, and invoked the Paraclete with sighs, and He thus inspiring, to the honour of the Holy and undivided Trinity, to the glory and adornment of the Virgin Mother of God, to the exaltation of the Catholic Faith and the increase of the Catholic religion, by the authority of Jesus Christ Our Lord, of the Blessed Apostles, Peter and Paul, We declare, pronounce, and define that the doctrine which holds that the Blessed Virgin Mary, at the first instant of her Conception, by a singular privilege and grace of the Omnipotent God, in virtue of the merits of Jesus Christ, the Saviour of mankind, was preserved immaculate from all stain of Original Sin, has been revealed by God, and therefore should firmly and constantly be believed by all the Faithful. Wherefore if any shall dare—which God avert—to think otherwise than as it has been defined by Us, let them know and understand that they are condemned by their own judgment, that they have suffered shipwreck of the faith, and have revolted from the unity of the Church; and besides, by their own act they subject themselves to the penalties justly established if what they think they should dare to signify by word, writing, or any other outward means.

Our mouth is filled with joy and Our tongue with exultation, and We return, and shall ever return, the most humble and the greatest thanks to Jesus Christ Our Lord, because through His singular beneficence He has granted to Us, though unworthy, to offer and decree this honour, glory, and praise to His Most Holy Mother. We rely, moreover, with most certain hope and confidence that this Most Blessed Virgin, who, all fair and immaculate, has bruised the poisonous head of the most malignant serpent, and brought salvation to the world, who is the praise of the Prophets and the Apostles, the honour of the Martyrs, and the crown and joy of all the Saints—who is the safest Refuge and most faithful Helper of all who are in danger, and the most powerful

genitum Filium suum mediatrix, et conciliatrix, ac praeclarissimum Ecclesiae sanctae decus et ornamentum, firmissimumque praesidium cunctas semper interemit haereses, et fideles populos, gentesque a maximis omnis generis calamitatibus eripuit, ac Nos ipsos a tot ingruentibus periculis liberavit; velit validissimo suo patrocinio efficere, ut sancta Mater Catholica Ecclesia cunctis amotis difficultatibus, cunctisque profligatis erroribus, ubicumque gentium, ubicumque locorum quotidie magis vigeat, floreat, ac regnet a mari usque ad mare et a flumine usque ad terminos orbis terrarum, omnique pace, tranquillitate, ac libertate fruatur, ut rei veniam, aegri medelam, pusilli corde robur, afflicti consolationem, periclitantes adjutorium obtineant, et omnes errantes discussa mentis caligine ad veritatis ac justitiae semitam redeant, ac fiat unum ovile, et unus pastor.

Audiant haec Nostra verba omnes Nobis carissimi Catholicae Ecclesiae filii, et ardentiori usque pietatis, religionis, et amoris studio pergant colere, invocare, exorare, beatissimam Dei Genetricem Virginem Mariam sine labe originali conceptam, atque ad hanc dulcissiman misericordiae et gratiae Matrem in omnibus periculis, angustiis, necessitatibus, rebusque dubiis ac trepidis cum omni fiducia confugiant. Nihil enim timendum, nihilque desperandum Ipsa duce, Ipsa auspice, Ipsa propitia, Ipsa protegente, quae maternum sane in nos gerens animum, nostraeque salutis negotia tractans de universo humano genere est sollicita, et coeli, terraeque Regina a Domino constituta, ac super omnes Angelorum choros Sanctorumque ordines exaltata adstans a dextris Unigeniti Filii Sui Domini Nostri Jesu Christi maternis suis precibus validissime impetrat, et quod quaerit invenit, ac frustrari non potest.

Denique ut ad universalis Ecclesiae notitiam haec Nostra de Immaculata Conceptione beatissimae Virginis Mariae definitio deducatur, has Apostolicas, Nostras Litteras, ad per-

Mediatrix and Conciliatrix in the whole world, with Her Only-Begotten Son, and the most illustrious Glory, Ornament, and most firm Defence of the Holy Church, who has destroyed all heresies, and snatched from the greatest calamities of all kinds the faithful peoples and nations, and delivered Us from so many threatening dangers; will effect, by Her most powerful patronage that, all difficulties being removed, and all errors dissipated, Our Holy Mother the Catholic Church may flourish daily more and more throughout all nations and countries, and may reign from sea to sea and to the ends of the earth, and may enjoy all peace, tranquillity, and liberty; that the sinful may obtain pardon, the sick healing, the weak strength of heart, the afflicted consolation, and that all who are in error, their spiritual blindness being dissipated, may return to the path of truth and justice, and there may be One Flock and One Shepherd.

Let all the children of the Catholic Church most dear to Us hear these Our words, and, with a more ardent zeal of piety, religion, and love, proceed to worship, invoke, and pray to the Most Blessed Virgin Mary, Mother of God, conceived without original sin; and let them flee with entire confidence to this most sweet Mother of Mercy and Grace in all dangers, difficulties, doubts, and fears. For nothing is to be feared, and nothing is to be despaired of under Her guidance, under Her auspices, under Her favour, under Her protection, who, bearing towards us a Mother's love, and negotiating the work of our salvation, is solicitous for the whole human race, and appointed by God, Queen of Heaven and Earth, and exalted above all the choirs of Angels, and orders of Saints, standing at the Right Hand of the Only-Begotten Son, Jesus Christ Our Lord, intercedes most powerfully, and obtains what She asks, and cannot fail.

Finally, in order that this Our definition of the Immaculate Conception of the Most Blessed Virgin Mary may be brought to the knowledge of the universal Church, We will

petuam rei memoriam extare voluimus ; mandantes ut harum transumptis seu exemplis etiam impressis, manu alicujus Notarii publici subscriptis, et sigillo, personae in Ecclesiastica dignitate constitutae munitis eadem prorsus fides ab omnibus adhibeatur, quae ipsis praesentibus adhiberetur si forent exhibitae, vel ostensae.

Nulli ergo hominum liceat paginam hanc Nostrae declarationis, pronunciationis, ac definitionis infringere, vel ei ausu temerario adversari et contraire. Si quis autem hoc attentare praesumpserit, indignationem, omnipotentis Dei ac beatorum Petri et Pauli Apostolorum ejus se noverit incursurum.

Datum Romae apud Sanctum Petrum Anno Incarnationis Dominicae Milesimo octingentesimo quinquagesimo quarto VI. Idus Decembris Anno MDCCCLIV. Pontificatus Nostri Anno Nono.

PIUS PP. IX.

that these Letters Apostolic do stand for a perpetual remembrance of the same, commanding that to transcripts or printed copies, subscribed by the hand of some notary-public, and authenticated by the seal of a person of Ecclesiastical rank, appointed for the purpose, the same trust shall be given which would be given to these presents if they were exhibited or shown.

Let no man presume to infringe this Our declaration, pronunciation, and definition, or to oppose and contradict with presumptuous rashness. If any should presume to assail it, let him know that he will incur the indignation of the Omnipotent God, and of His blessed Apostles Peter and Paul.

Given at Rome, at St. Peter's, in the year of the Incarnation of Our Lord, MDCCCLIV. the sixth of the Ides of December, and the ninth year of Our Pontificate.

PIUS PP. IX.

Sermon of St. Bernard

On the Twelve Prerogatives of the Blessed Virgin Mary.

[The following short Sermon by the last of the Fathers, on the description of the Blessed Virgin in the Apocalypse, and which occurs in the New Office of the Immaculate Conception, will be read with much interest and edification.]

MULIER, inquit, amicta sole; plane amicta lumine tanquam vestimento. Non percipit forte carnalis: nimirum spirituale est: stultitia illi videtur. Non sic videbatur Apostolo, qui dicebat: Induimini Dominum Jesum Christum. Quam familiaris ei facta es Domina! Quam proxima, immo quam intima fieri meruisti, quantam invenisti gratiam apud eum! In te manet, et tu in eo: et vestis eum, et vestiris ab eo. Vestis eum substantia carnis, et vestit ille te gloria suæ majestatis. Vestis solem nube, sole ipsa vestiris. Novum enim fecit Dominus super terram, ut mulier circumdaret virum, nec alium quam Christum, de quo dicitur: Ecce vir, Oriens nomen ejus. Novum quoque fecit in cœlo, ut mulier sole appareret amicta. Denique et coronavit eum, et vicissim ab eo meruit coronari.

In capite, inquit, ejus corona stellarum duodecim. Dignum plane stellis coronari caput, quod et ipsis longe clarius micans, ornet eas potius quam ornetur ab eis. Quidni coronent sidera quam sol vestit? Sicut dies verni, ait, circumdabant eam flores rosarum, et lilia convallium. Nimirum læva sponsi sub capite ejus, et jam dextera illius amplexatur eam. Quis illas æstimet gemmas, quis stellas nominet, quibus Mariæ regium diadema compactum est? Supra hominem est coronæ hujus rationem exponere, indicare compositionem. Mihi sane singularis rutilat fulgor, primo quidem in Mariæ generatione, secundo in Angelica salutatione, tertio in Spiritus superventione, quarto in filii Dei inenarrabili conceptione.

Quid ergo sidereum micat in generatione Mariæ? Plane quod ex regibus orta; quod ex semine Abrahæ; quod generosa ex stirpe David. Si id parum videtur, adde quod generationi illi ob singulare privilegium sanctitatis, divinitus noscitur esse concessa; quod longe ante eisdem Patribus cœlitus repromissa; quod mysticis præsignata miraculis; quod oraculis prænuntiata propheticis. Hanc enim sacerdotalis virga, dum sine radice floruit; hanc Gedeonis vellus, dum in medio siccæ areæ maduit; hanc in Ezechielis visione orientalis porta, quæ nulli unquam patuit, præsignabat. Hanc denique præ cæteris Isaias nunc virgam de radice Jesse orituram prænunciabat; nunc evidentius virginem parituram. Merito signum hoc magnum in cœlo apparuisse scribitur, quod tanto ante de cœlo noscitur fuisse promissum.

✠ Benedicta sit sancta et immaculata Conceptio B. Mariæ Virginis.

[*Translation.*]

A woman, he says, *clothed with the sun;* arrayed with light, that is to say, as with a raiment. Doubtless the carnal man does not understand this expression. It is, indeed, spiritual, and, as such, must appear to him foolishness; but not so did a similar expression appear to the Apostle, who says, "Put ye on the Lord Jesus Christ." Ah, how close a familiarity was thine with Christ, O Lady! how near to Him, how intimate with Him didst thou merit to become! What an abundance of grace dost thou enjoy in Him! He abides in thee, and thou in Him. Thou clothest Him, and art clothed by Him. Thou clothest Him with the substance of human flesh, and He, in turn, clothes thee with the glory of His own majesty. Thou clothest the sun with a cloud, and art thyself clothed with the sun. For "the Lord hath brought to pass a new thing upon the earth, that a woman should compass a man,"—no other than the man Christ, of whom it is written, "Behold a man whose name is the Orient." And the same Lord hath also brought to pass a new thing in heaven, namely, that "a woman should appear clothed with the sun." To conclude, the Virgin hath crowned the Lord, and hath merited, in turn, to be crowned by Him.

On her head, he says, *a crown of twelve stars.* And well worthy of a starry crown was this sacred head, which in itself far surpasses all the stars in brilliancy; and, in being crowned with them, rather confers than receives an ornament. Well, indeed, may she whom the sun clothes be crowned with stars. "As the days of spring," says the prophet, "so did the flowers of roses encompass her, and the lilies of the valleys." Assuredly "the left hand of her spouse is under her head, and his right hand now embraceth her." Who can estimate the jewels, who can count the stars, which go to form the regal diadem of Mary? It is beyond the capacity of man to expound the nature of this crown, or to explain its component parts. For my own part I am dazzled with excess of brightness, whenever I contemplate either first, the generation of Mary, or secondly, the angelical salutation, or thirdly, the overshadowing of the Holy Ghost, or fourthly, her ineffable conception of the Son of God.

What, then, in particular, is there of a starry character in the generation of Mary? Evidently her royal descent,—the fact that she sprang from the seed of Abraham, from the noble root of David. Or if this seem insufficient, consider further that Mary, as we know, was divinely vouchsafed to that line, on account of its peculiar prerogative of sanctity,—

that she had been, moreover, promised from heaven to the same line of Patriarchs many ages before she appeared,—that she had been typified in mystic miracles, and foretold in the oracles of the prophets. For instance, the rod of Aaron the high priest, blossoming without a root, was a figure of Mary; so, too, was the fleece of Gedeon drenched with moisture, while the earth all round it was dry; so, too, was the eastern gate in the vision of Ezechiel, that gate open to no man. Lastly, and above the rest, Isaias in one place prophesies of her that a rod shall come forth from the stem of Jesse; and in another place foretells still more clearly that a virgin shall bring forth. With reason then is it written, that a great sign appeared in heaven, for as we see, it was from heaven that this sign had been originally promised many ages before.

PRINTED BY VIRTUE AND CO., CITY ROAD, LONDON.

CPSIA information can be obtained
at www.ICGtesting.com
Printed in the USA
LVHW030121210323
742063LV00002B/467

9 783382 128203